LOLA'S SECRET

ALICE VL

2

Lola's Secret

Alice VL

Lola's Secret

Copyright 2016 by Alice VL

First Printing: 2016

SECOND EDITION

Alice VL

4

Lola's Secret

Alice VL

CONTENTS

Lola's Secret

DEDICATION

My beloved Grandma Lulu,

You gave me a glimpse into a world where characters live and stories come alive. It was an opening into another world I have been unable to leave since.

Sometimes, I find you there. Sometimes, I find him there. I miss you when I leave, I miss my characters, and I miss their world. Most of all, I miss you.

Alice VL

Lola's Secret

SUTHERLAND

Opening the window blinds just as much as was necessary, she peered hesitantly through her bedroom window, almost afraid that someone might see her, but delighted that she was in time to watch the sun rise over Madison, Sutherland. Lola never grew tired of the vision that embraced her morning after morning, winter or summer, spring or autumn. She would wake up merely moments before sunrise, not wanting to miss out on any one of them. She would sit by her bedroom window, her hair unkempt, and her pajamas rumpled before gazing out below at the town awakening. Cars gradually making their way through the paved streets of Madison, where people were rushing to get to work, barely aware of the beauty that surrounded them.

It saddened Lola to realize that folks were excessively hurried and greatly absorbed in their daily routines, instead of being aware of one of God's most beautiful creations, the sun as it starts to rise. Lola thought of the rising sun as God's alarm clock. But for Lola, it was the break of the day that bewitched her, and sunrises as those only happened in Madison, a city she had chosen, a city that promised to take her far away from her haunting past. A city where not a soul would ever know who she was, where she came from, or the secrets that her life had held until then. It was a city that would never know her face, would never recognize her voice, and would certainly not even know her name.

It was a city she had chosen, that would never know of the cruel twists she had endured in her short, and intricate life. It was a new beginning that Lola hoped, would give her a new-fangled life, filled with its spectacular mountains, evergreen trees, and stormy ocean. It was a place that she felt connected to, a city she often dreamed of as a child, but one that she knew she could call home from the moment she arrived in Madison. She had never been to Madison before, but she fell in love with the town, the instant she read of it, in the pages of a magazine she would often sneak away from her mother's collection. She would page through each page, dreaming of a new tomorrow, one she could design and tailor-make only for herself, just as soon as she grew up. A tomorrow that would treat her kinder, than the life she had known until then.

She dreamed of a tomorrow where her future was her own. She dreamed of new memories, and she aspired to a new life, enthusiastic that this one might treat her fairly. Lola never missed a single sunrise, and anxiously slid out from her bed to watch the sun greet her, which in turn, gave her a sense of affirmation that she had chosen the city that would finally raise her. Glancing over at her alarm clock, one that had become a permanent fixture on the pedestal next to her bed, almost hiding behind her lamp, Lola knew that the sun would make its appearance at any moment. She smiled when she felt the warmth embrace her face. She closed her eyes, and for just an instant, she was sure that she could feel the sun wrapping its arms around her, and shower her with warmth all over her body.

It was a sensation Lola adored, and to her, it was a promise of new beginnings, a second chance at a life she was never really fond of, and one more chance at belonging, even if it was only to a town. Above the reverberation of cars mowing down the streets, and the voices of people hanging in the air, Lola could hear the birds chant from a distance. She smiled while embracing the serenity and tranquility they offered her. The freedom and calmness she ran to as fast as she could get there, without pausing for even a moment to look back on what she had contentedly left behind. She could hear the waves crashing on the shore, and at night, she could barely fall asleep without it. She would lay awake at night listening to tug boats entering and leaving the harbor, keenly aware of a ship that was inward bound from somewhere far away, or perhaps, one that was setting off to some place even further away. Lola often hankered after the freedom of these ships and the unknown they would sail to.

Some nights, she would sit quietly and gaze at the reflections of the stars on the ocean. It would swear to Lola that there was something out there for her. Something incredible that would bestow importance on her life, assuring her that her existence was of significance to somebody. She was confident that something extraordinary was just around the corner for her, and Lola was determined to find it. She could almost hear the promise the ocean made only to her with each crashing wave, and for the first time in her life, Lola dreamed of all the miraculous days that were patiently waiting for her. Between the stars and the ocean somewhere, there was a certain enchantment for her, and she waited patiently for it to somehow, someday, seek her out, and find her. "Happy birthday, Lola!" Lola was startled to find Lauren standing in the doorway of her bedroom, carrying in a homemade cup cake with a single burning candle on top. She grinned from ear to ear when she suddenly remembered that it was her birthday, and that August had showed up far too quickly.

"Thank you, sissy." Lola carefully took the cup cake from her seventeen-year-old sister Lauren, who was still clad in her pajamas, her hair still not quite awake, but who was eagerly waiting for her to blow out her only birthday candle. "Nineteen candles wouldn't fit ..." Lauren giggled before planting a nippy kiss on her cheek. "Don't forget to make a wish, and make it mean something this time." Lauren clapped her hands in anticipation, the excitement evident on her face. Lola in turn, beamed affectionately when she realized again that her sister still believed in fairytales and miracles, and she silently wished that Lauren would never, ever mislay that dreamy fraction of herself.

Closing her eyes tautly, Lola considered all there was to wish for, but she reminded herself that she dares not. She was convinced that she was praying and wishing for much too much, and the only wish she had for that birthday, was to soldier on through her final year of high school, and have Lauren safely tucked away with her. The thought of them being separated all over again, terrified, and scared Lola almost to death. It was a thought she could not even begin to imagine. It was the only thing in her world that frightened her. There was nothing that could scare her as much as the very notion of losing Lauren. Lola cautiously blew out the candle, hoping and praying with all her might that her one wish was the only wish she could rely on to come true. "So, what did you wish for?" Lauren placed her arms around her sister's neck. "I wished for a tall, dark and handsome stranger to knock me off my feet, and carry me off to a wonderland where we'll all live happily ever after in! And then, I wished that he had a really cute brother for you!" Lola burst out laughing, tickling a giggling Lauren. "Yeah right! Whatever!" Lauren jumped up in delight, and hastily made her way back to her own bedroom. "No man would ever be able knock you off those dainty feet! Anyways, it's late and we've got to get ready for school!" Lauren hurriedly disappeared down the passage.

While getting up from the seat at the window, Lola glanced around their apartment. It was tiny, but it was home, and to Lauren and Lola, it was a safe place. It was their own. They were each comfortable in their own bedrooms, a cozy living area and for the most part, gloriously magnificent views. At the front of the apartment, they were met by outstanding and breathtakingly beautiful views of the city and the mountains, but from the rear of their apartment, it was the ocean that made its presence known from every single window. Lola never could quite decide which her favorite was, but she was content that they were sanctified with a little bit of both.

Lola moved into the apartment shortly after her sixteenth birthday almost three years before, and without delay following her legal emancipation from her parents, after an extensive and drawn out court battle. It was exhausting for Lola. The continuous hostility and her on-going efforts to persuade the legal system that she could successfully function in the world on her own, even at such a young age. Fortunately, she had chosen a brilliant legal representative who diligently and assiduously assisted her throughout each proceeding and each investigation, as they gradually moved along. An unidentified aunt, whom she had only met once, had left her a little of her wealth after her demise, and which paid for the apartment in Madison, Sutherland. Following Lola's legal battle, Lauren too was liberated shortly after her sixteenth birthday. Lola was overjoyed at the thought of having her sister under the same roof as her, enabling the sisters to successfully bury their haunting past, and begin a brand-new life together.

They vowed that they would under no circumstances ever, make contact with either of their parents again, or a remaining brother and sister. The apartment was a shelter for them. Lola swore to herself that she would do whatever was necessary to care for Lauren, see her through school, and ultimately send her off to college. She often grew chilly when she considered the years with the Storey family, and shuddered at the thought of ever having to see them again. She thought of her mother Sally, and desperately tried to understand how she was able to lack love or concern in her heart for Lola and Lauren. Her razor-sharp tongue had them both in tears on more occasions than she would want to admit to, and the brutality of her words often slit deep into Lola's soul. She never felt safe, protected or loved around Sally, and feared her more than she dreaded death. Her mind drifted off to Peter Storey, a triumphant and highly regarded man amongst all that knew him professionally and personally.

Lola felt terror grip at her core, by the very thought of him. Her heart constantly broke out into a gallop when her mind wandered to him. She often felt as though she could scarcely breathe at the mere mention of his name. Not one significant person was truly acquainted with the Peter Storey she knew. It was a man she wished dead more often than not, but never had the nerve to say it out loud. Lola recalled the nights that he was running late coming home from the office, and how she silently prayed that he was involved in a fatal car crash on his way home. At first, Lola felt colossal remorse for her thoughts, but after a while, she ferociously begged for it to happen. At the same time, she would be aware of the fact that exhilaration welled up inside of her, at the sheer thought that tonight might be the night that he would not make it back home.

It never happened that way on any of those nights, it simply meant that the delay only ever meant he was coming home inebriated, geared up to take his resentment and aggravation out on her, as he did so many nights before. She repeatedly turned to her mother for help, but Sally Storey chose to look the other way. She remained ignorant of what was happening around her. She was unwilling to admit the imperfection of their world, or the inappropriate behavior of her faultless husband. Sally ostensibly exhibited the ideal life, home and marriage, and hid behind the large stainless steel gates of their seven-bedroomed, three-story mansion. Behind closed doors, life for Lola was horrifying, but in public, she would graciously unite with the rest of the Storeys as was demanded and expected from her, while convincing outsiders that they were the blissful, and impeccable family she so often wished for.

When Lola once challenged her, Sally glared at her with paramount revulsion, and accused Lola of trying to fracture the family. She yelled and screamed at her that Peter Storey was a first-class man, and if he in any way harmed her, it was purely based on his love for her. She continued to rationalize the fact that Lola appeared to be the prime hitch in their home, and that Peter would never allow her to run around untamed. She informed Lola that as parents, they were responsible and solely accountable for raising her in an orderly manner, even if it meant that she needed a beating every so often. While she grudgingly listened to her mother's relentless justification of Peter Storey's conduct, Lola came to the agonizing conclusion that she could never tell her about any of the other desecrations that were taking place right under her nose. It left her feeling dejected, desolate and utterly alone. Lola was painfully aware that Sally Storey would simply not believe her.

Lola worried that revealing the true cruelty would engulf her father with even more rage, unleashing him on Lauren in order to teach Lola a lesson. She refused to place any of sisters at risk, and reluctantly accepted that her silence and compliance was the only way to keep the rest of them out of harm's way. She maintained a close eye on Melanie and Lauren, and even though he never harmed her two sisters, she was distraught each time he forced Lauren to witness him beat Lola. Lauren and Lola were born eighteen months apart, and grew extremely close to one another from an incredibly young age.

They had developed an indestructible bond early on, and cherished one another dearly. Lauren regularly tried to shield Lola from their father, even though she was painfully aware that there was nothing she could do to safeguard her from him. Lauren would silently sit beside Lola after a brutal thrashing, and brush her hair, squeezing her hand often. Lola recognized and appreciated the reassurance her sister was attempting to offer her, while neither of them knew what to say to the other one, and elected to remain silent. Quietly, they both were entirely aware of what the other one was enduring, and the security they felt in each other's consoling arms was at all times, enough to repel their crippling fear.

After one particularly rigorous whipping, Lola tearfully vowed to Lauren that someday they would run away together, and leave all the beatings and exploitation behind them. "I promise you Lols, one day it will be only you and I, and we're going to have our own place, and we're going to be happy, I swear it." She held Lauren protectively against her while stroking her beautiful curls, "Just you and me. I promise you sis, they won't find us. We will be free someday. I will never let dad hurt you Lauren, I promise."

Lola would often reassure Lauren when the fear and terror became apparent in her sister's eyes. With tears flooding her face, Lola swore to Lauren that they would disappear, and make their own plans. She would take Lauren away from it all, and place as much distance between them and the Storeys as she possibly could. From the time she was merely a little girl, Lola fantasized about turning her back on the family, and under no circumstances, ever return to them. She promised Lauren that she would dedicate her life to making them untraceable, so that the Storeys would never be able to find them. Melanie was Sally's darling, the apple of her mother's eye. Lola knew she would be alright. But, Melanie had a mean streak, and would often blame her own mistakes on Lola. Ford on the other hand, was ignorant to it all, and carried on as though nothing was off-beam. He was three years older than Lola, but he not once defended or guarded her. Lola looked up to her older brother, but she rarely depended on him. Lola relied only on herself to alter their fate. Although Peter had repeatedly hammered into her that she was unwanted and unloved, Lola felt into her soul that her life and the life of her sister meant something more, something wonderful. She had no clue as to what it was, but she was continuously nudged from the innermost part of her, to find it, for her, and for Lauren.

There was something superior out there for her.

Something that was mercilessly wrenching and tugging at her, but for the moment, she intended only to get through each day, and keep Lauren out of harm's way. Lola was ardently aware of a blazing fire inside her that was growing stronger and more powerful each day. She was relieved that the anxiety and throbbing in her heart had started to grow fainter with each new day. She had an incredible amount of living left inside of her, and even though her flame should have died a long time ago, she felt into her core that there was more out there for her, just waiting for her to grab a hold of it.

She could not shake the feeling that they were strangers in a life they once struggled to fit into, and that they never belonged with the Storeys in the first place. Lola was unreservedly convinced that somehow, they would fit in, in another place, and Lola survived each day to find that sense of belonging for both of them. She stared at herself in the bathroom mirror, her exhausted reflection gaping back at her. She was extremely drained, and undoubtedly, another year older. Lola was instantly reminded of a dream she had the night before, and grimaced, as she frequently would after a dream, and especially, when she realized she was dreaming almost the same thing, again and again. They began when she was only a little girl, and would become more frequent, and would unexpectedly intensify when Peter Storey beat her. Lola was certain that her dreams were removing her from her reality, and soothingly placed her into a world of amity and calm.

A make-believe life where no one at all could ever hurt her. Still glaring at her reflection in the mirror, she tried to evoke what it was that the faceless vision was saying to her. Lola unsuccessfully attempted with each dream to catch a glimpse of what she looked like, but she was sure, by the calmness of her presence, that this was by no means someone out to harm her. By her silhouette, Lola knew that she was a woman, leaving her enthusiastically aware that there was something beautiful about her. She was staggered by how often she would look forward to dreaming of her, night after night. "My girl, open your heart. Don't live so sheltered. Get out of your cage, there is more. You have to find it. You have to find it." Lola vaguely recalled her whispering, but could hardly identify with what she was exasperatingly trying to tell her, or what she even intended for her to absorb. "How? I don't know how? I don't know what you're saying. I don't understand you!" Lola would implore her for answers and explanations, but they never came.

Lola never believed in the significance of dreams, and persistently tried to convince herself that it was a defense mechanism she had created to survive the Storeys, and to endure a life she found insufferable. Even as the dreams persisted long after Lola escaped the Storeys, and as though on schedule, Lola still thought there wouldn't be any significant importance to any of her dreams. Shrugging the dream off as she was yanked back to reality, Lola's thoughts returned to the trust fund that was running out bit by bit. She had to find a half day job to financially see them through to the end of the year when Lola would be able to start working full time. The savings fund had only enough left to pay for Lauren's first car on her eighteenth birthday the following February.

It was a promise Lola made to Lauren after she had bought her own little car, a promise she had no intention of breaking. "Oh, this hair." She mumbled softly to herself while combing through the long blonde tresses that rested neatly down her back. "I should definitely cut this shorter." She unwittingly let out a despondent and weary sigh. "Oh no, Lola, you can't. Your hair is so beautiful!" Lauren was horrified, before she unexpectedly manifested in the reflection of the mirror. "Thanks sis, but it's just pointless having all this hair. I just don't have the time for it." Lola looked back once again at her own reflection in misery. "You are an elfin sis, beautiful hair and brightest eyes, don't do it please! And what if you meet your tall dark and handsome stranger?" Lola burst out laughing while glaring at her sister who humbly possessed her own gorgeous green eyes and blonde mane, only her locks were shorter. She was blessed with stunning natural curls resting in the small of her back.

Lola turned around and walked up to her, and even though Lauren was a great deal taller than she was, she presented her with the most heartfelt embrace her heart could offer her. "I love you, sis, but no stranger for me. Besides, I've got you, and you're more than a handful." Lola gently stroked her flushed cheek. "I got you too Lola, and now, we got to get to school!" They both rushed downstairs before they hurriedly made their way to Lola's car dubbed Bonnie. Lauren constantly found it manically entertaining that she had named their little blue car, but Lola couldn't care less when Lauren made fun of her.

Bonnie was a used little run-around that she was able to buy through an acquaintance when she turned eighteen, and although they've had their nerve-racking moments with her, Bonnie served her purpose well. Other than having to replace a filter here and there, or a spark plug every so often, Bonnie safely transported them from pillar to post without leaving them in the lurch, or disappointing them. "Good morning, Bonnie, are we about to have any trouble this morning?" Lola questioned her little car as she did most mornings, profusely aware of the battery that was on its last legs. Lauren sniggered and so did Lola, but she started up with no problem. They drove in silence, Lauren attentively listening and singing along to her iPod, while Lola glanced around, and welcomed the surroundings on their way to school.

She was utterly content that she had chosen Sutherland, and even though it was classified a city, it was the smallest city in the world, and the most beautiful metropolis she had ever seen. She had regularly heard her parents' converse about Sutherland, but Sally would repeatedly criticize and grumble about the town, reminding Peter that it was too monotonous and tedious for her. Peter on one occasion told her brother Ford, that they had regularly gone there for weekends to visit with friends, but it all came to an abrupt end when they passed away some fifteen years before. Lola was confident that Sutherland was the one city where she would never scamper into them, certain by how they loathed the town.

While driving into the school parking area, Lauren suddenly turned to Lola, "I almost forgot Lola, Tanita asked that we meet up at Joe's this evening for your birthday, and I really want to go. Please just come. I know you hate those places, but we never go anywhere or do anything, plus it is your birthday? Please can we just do something and make something of this day. Please Lola, please-please?" Lauren frantically began pleading with Lola. She flinched at the thought, the intermingling, drinking and gathering of strange people was not something Lola desired or in any way, was enthusiastic to involve herself with just yet. Tanita tirelessly and continuously tried to hook her up with a friend, or a friend of a boyfriend or a brother, and even though

Lola was adamant that she placed little to no importance on having a boyfriend, it was not the response Tanita ever accepted.

"Come on, Lola, please. It's for your birthday, and besides, she has a hot new boyfriend, really cute! Just this once, please!" Lola found it outright despicable when Lauren begged, particularly since she had difficulty in saying no to her. "So actually, Tanita just wants to show him off? And you my darling sis, you just want me to hook up with someone?" Lauren sighed, "Is that so bad, Lola?" Lola snapped in a petulant tone, mindful of the fact that in the innermost part of Lauren, would like nothing more than for Lola to meet someone, her 'go-to' person as she would repeatedly say. Having to find a half day job would only create hurdles for Lola. She was certain that there was currently no breathing space in her life for a boyfriend. "Oh, come on Lola, all she does is talk about him! But, I suppose she does want to show him off too, you know Tanita? Come on sis, I'm only asking because it's your birthday."

They climbed out of the car simultaneously when Lola simply shook her head and smirked, "She shows off all her boyfriends, but yes fine, Lauren. Just for a bit, we still have the ironing to get through, and I haven't rinsed your soccer outfit yet. You know those places aren't for me. I hate parties and I hate drunken people, and I really hate hook-ups." She anxiously wanted Lauren to meet new friends and construct a solid and secure life for herself in Sutherland. Lola felt accountable for holding Lauren back and yet, she was hardly comfortable allowing Lauren to go out on her own. Lauren was Lola's first, and utmost priority at that point in her life, and if it meant she had to spend an hour or so at Joe's, then Lola decided it wouldn't be too much of a sacrifice.

Lauren formed friendships much easier and more fluently than Lola did, making Tanita Lola's only friend. Lola met Tanita while waiting for the Headmaster when Lola enrolled herself at Sutherland High School roughly three years before. Tanita took pity on Lola, who was seated in silence in the waiting area, impatiently waiting for what felt like forever to her. "Hey, are you new here?" Tanita made her way over to an empty seat, and sat down beside Lola. Lola glanced over at Tanita, and smiled nervously, "Yes." "I could show you around if you like? Are your parents in with Mr. Duncan?" Tanita was at once aware of Lola's reluctance to engage with her. "No, I, I'm waiting to enroll myself, and possibly my sister next year." Lola explained hastily without wanting to expose too much about herself. Tanita grimaced, and instantly wondered whether Lola's parents had passed on. "I'd love to show you around, and maybe take you round to get uniforms?" She took immediate pity on Lola. "Thanks, that would be great, thank you." Tanita smiled at her new friend, and extended her hand out to Lola, "Tanita, Tanita Jane Marsh."

With a firm grip, she shook Lola's hand. "Lola, uhm Storey." "Do you live around here?" Tanita smiled and frowned all at the same time. "I'm, I'm looking at places this afternoon." Lola smiled hesitantly and looked down almost immediately. "Oh, you are so screwed. I'm going to take you to see an apartment this afternoon. It's my dad's place. He bought it as an investment a few years ago, but is desperate for new buyers. Tenants have been screwing him over for years. I'm sure I can get him to come down on the price." By the expression on Lola's face, Tanita was sure that Lola was in dire need of a friend. "Oh no, you don't have to, we'll be fine." Lola objected straight away. "I insist. Meet you after school, outside the library." Tanita bolted from the chair, and made her way to Ms. Sheldon who was waiting to hand her, her new roster. Lola smiled when she thought about Tanita's kindness. It instantly confirmed once again that Sutherland was an unsullied, and brand new start for her, and for Lauren. Before going their separate ways strolling to their respective classes, Lola protectively embraced Lauren while recognizing how far they had come. She smiled when she thought of all they had left behind, and she found relief make its way into her heart when she realized once again that they were going about life on their terms, in their own way.

On the direct opposite end of town in a suburb known as Panorama, and the only commercial area in Sutherland, Daniel and Dean Salvatore unlocked the large glass doors to their workshop as they had been doing for the past four years. The Salvatore brothers opened the workshop in the hopes of fulfilling their childhood dreams of creating an empire of repairing and re-building classic cars, while at the same time, carving out a livelihood for themselves. Although Dean was still a student when the doors to Salvatore opened for the very first time, he depleted his afternoons working with Daniel in the shop, often finalizing his assignments or projects in Daniel's office. The two brothers had done exceedingly well in a very short period of time in their first year, which led them to focus on modifying all car brands.

Salvatore was the business they had built up with a loan Daniel received from their father John Salvatore, which they were able to repay after the first year. Daniel was older than Dean, who had just turned nineteen and Bo, who was only fourteen, was still living at home with their parents in Hodgkin's Valley, an hour's drive from Sutherland. When Dean was old enough, he moved in with Daniel in an apartment not too far from the workshop. Even though they worked rigidly, Daniel and Dean still found time to have fun, and more often than not, ended up having a night out on the town together. "Hey bro," Daniel turned to Dean just as they were changing into their overalls, "Tanita asked us to meet up at Joe's tonight, a friend's birthday or something like that. I don't know the details, but, do you want to come?" He hesitantly mentioned it to Dean, before hanging his leather jacket in his locker. Dean had barely any tolerance for Tanita, and often questioned Daniel as to why he was continuously around her. "Sure, as long as I'm not the third wheel on the wagon." Daniel instantly sensed his dissatisfaction. "Come on bro, you know it's not going anywhere. We might as well just have a good time, and who knows? You might just hit it off with her friend." "I doubt that. No school girls for me thanks, but I just don't get why you hang around with her? She's still at school, and what about that Samantha girl? The one you went out with a couple of times?" "Samantha is way too needy and wants too much, you know that. On our third date, she wanted to move in. I realize what you're saying about Tanita, but she's fun to be around. Besides, still waiting for the one, if she's out there."

Daniel knew without hesitation that he was not in love with Tanita, and subsequent to dating a string of women, he persistently questioned whether he had the distinct ability fall in love. Each relationship started off without a hitch until he became uninterested, or until they become challenging. Daniel was convinced that he would grow old a bachelor, but he was not prepared to hang up his hat solely for the sake of settling. He dreamed of the girl that would smack him off his feet, the woman that would be responsible for the hammering and pounding of his heart. Daniel fantasized about finding the perfect one that would fit flawlessly in his arms. He desired what he saw so often with his parents, and prayed that somehow, the right girl would find her way to him. Daniel sought after that special somebody that he could love so utterly profoundly, that he would lay down his own life for. He has as yet, been unable to find that in any of his girlfriends of the past, but he was certain that she was out there, simply waiting for him to pitch up. Dean fell in love time and again, but Daniel couldn't recall any one moment that he had lost his heart to another.

Daniel was a hauntingly attractive man. His dark hair folded neatly around his ears, and his striking blue eyes whispered a million tales. He was blissfully ignorant of the impact he was responsible for on women, and found himself become fractious by the awareness they lavished on him. He was by no means a womanizer, and it troubled him that women would crouch down, and hurl themselves at him. Both Daniel and Dean were first-class men, raised by an amorous and affluent family. John Salvatore insisted early on that his sons would appreciate and respect the value of possessions, and unwaveringly forced them to earn their keep. He taught them reverence and impeccable behavior, and he was steadfast in setting a reputable example for his boys. He continuously addressed Sarah with esteem and equal admiration, whether they were in the presence of company, or when they were alone. John constantly reminded them that admiration is commanded and certainly not demanded. He was proud of Daniel and Dean, and he had utmost certainty that his boys turned into the men he strived them to be. "Do you think we'll ever find the right ones?" Daniel chuckled when he placed his hand on Dean's shoulder, "You know what Mom always says, every pot comes with a lid." He considered her words for a moment. Dean was aware of the sudden somber look on Daniel's face, "I feel she's out there, Dean, you know? The supposed one?' I've just got to find her, or she find me, or however it works. And maybe, just maybe, she might have a cute sister for you."

As Lola entered her first class of the morning, Tanita unexpectedly grabbed a hold of her arm. "Happy birthday, Lola! Come celebrate with us at Joe's tonignt? Please, please, please!" She pleaded with Lola while tugging at her arm.

Tanita was born into a well-heeled family and as a rule, almost constantly had her way, yet she was a great friend to Lauren and Lola when they first arrived in Sutherland. Tanita made it easy for her to find their apartment, and took them on a tour of the city shortly after she moved in. "Sure, Tanita, but only for a bit." "Oh, cool! I would so love you to meet Daniel, my new boyfriend! And, he has a super cute brother." Tanita sniggered breathlessly. "Sure." Lola sighed, aware once again that Tanita's girlish crush was the last thing on her mind. Lola felt as though she didn't at all, belong with other girls her age. She constantly became irritable when they began gushing over this boy or over that boy.

For Lola, there were too many more significant things in life, but moreover, she admitted to the fact that they were only acting their age, and that they were behaving exactly as they were expected to. Yet, it was a life that Lola could barely envision and was not at all familiar with. She was too accustomed to being mom and older sister to Lauren. She cherished their new life in

Sutherland, and was satisfied to fade into the background, while all the golden girls shimmered. "See you there at seven!" Tanita waved dynamically before making her way back to her seat. Life was incessantly and habitually the exact same for Lola. She would get up in the mornings, make Lauren's breakfast, make the beds, wash the dishes, go to school, go home, clean the apartment, wash and iron and finally, attempt her school work before bed.

It was thorny at times, but it was a resolution that Lola had committed to, and it was the only way she knew to break away from the nightmare of their childhood. Even though Lauren's maltreatment was spared, it was complex for her to witness the cruelty and beatings their father had lavished on Lola. Lauren could never understand why their mother never stepped up to protect them, but Lola knew that it was her total disassociation from them, her lack of motherly instincts, and her inability to bond with Lola and Lauren that caused her to thoroughly worship the man she had married. She purposely looked the other way, and when she was present, she effortlessly justified and warranted his behavior.

A CHANCE ENCOUNTER

Lola and Lauren strolled into Joe's just after seven that evening, regardless of the fact that Lola frenziedly made an attempt to pull out of the get-together at the very last minute. Lola at once appreciated the ambience of Joe's pub, and that it was located on the beach. There was a small dancing area under the pub's roof, with more than enough seating for dinners or lunches. What pleased Lola most about Joe's, was that she simply had to turn around to be right on the shore.

Before they left for Joe's that evening, Lola felt severely rushed after quickly loading a bundle of laundry into the washer, while at the same time, completing her history project. She found herself feeling overwhelmed as she struggled to get through all her chores, and instantly made her feel smothered and overwrought. "Lols, I have so much to do, let me drop you off so that you can spend the evening with Tanita. I'll pick you up later. I have to get through this project, and it feels like I'm just not coping tonight." "No Lola, it's your birthday. If you don't go, I'm not going. Besides, you already told Tanita we're going. Can't we just go out just for tonight? You don't have to feel like everything needs to get done today, and I've told you, I don't mind helping you. It's your birthday Lola, it's one day, one night?"

Lola knew Lauren wouldn't go out without her, especially on her birthday. She felt tremendous guilt for having no desire at all to celebrate, or even spend one night out with her sister. She reluctantly surrendered, and agreed to celebrate her birthday at Joe's, and in the process, crafting the finest attempt at enjoying the evening with her. While making their way to the pub, Lola was horrified to realize that she hadn't brushed her hair, and was immediately mortified by her appearance. Lola turned to look at Lauren, and was once again, astounded by how beautiful her sister was. Her curls were flowing gently around her perfectly made up face, and she was elegantly clad in a striking green dress that faultlessly harmonized her perfect emerald eyes.

When she unenthusiastically glanced at herself in a mirror just off the entrance, Lola was once again aware of how plain and simple she was. Her hair was tied back in a simple pigtail, she was dressed in washed out jeans wearing nothing more than a plain white vest. She callously shrugged her shoulders. Lola didn't truly care to impress anyone. There was no one person that she had a need to make an impact on.

When they reached the bar, she spotted Tanita amused and sniggering, entwined in a tête-à-tête with a man who had his back turned to them. When Tanita noticed the sisters walk in, she at once signaled for Lola and Lauren to join them. "Hey, birthday girl!" Tanita got up from her seat to introduce Lola and Lauren to the man she was conversing with. "Daniel, this is my friend Lola and her sister Lauren. It's Lola's birthday today, remember? I told you that I invited her?" As soon as Lola caught a glimpse of him, she was entirely and unexpectedly unprepared for his masculine features and arctic blue eyes. She was met with the darkest brown hair she had ever seen before, not black, yet darker than brown.

He adorned flawless facial characteristics, and possessed

the most enigmatic smile Lola had ever been aware of in a man. His appearance had a surprisingly powerful effect on her, when she wondered for an instant how it was possible for a man to be so breathtakingly beautiful. Without being able to turn away from him, she noticed his endless eyelashes and his full and commanding mouth, unable to do much more than stare intently at him. When she reached for his extended hand, she was sure that there was something proverbial about him, and yet at the same time, she felt extraordinarily diminutive in his presence. It compelled her to hesitate for a second. "Pleased to meet you, Lola. I've have heard so much about you, and I believe a happy birthday is in order. Is Lola short for something?" He smiled with a certain kindness that reflected in his eyes which in turn, compelled Lola to involuntarily smile back at him.

Daniel too, was ill-equipped and caught entirely off-guard when he was at once intensely aware of Lola's powerful beauty. He had never before seen a woman with longer hair than hers, and yet, she was the tiniest little person he had ever laid eyes on. He could barely envisage her petite frame carrying all that hair when he noticed it surging down her back. For an abrupt moment, he questioned how it was possible for a grown woman to be as minute as Lola was. "No, it's just Lola." She responded bashfully, her eyes expressed a definite kind of sorrow, and yet to Daniel, he had never before, seen greener eyes than hers. He shamelessly stared at her, all the while aware of the prodding sensation that somewhere their worlds had collided once before, but incapable of placing her, and not entirely convinced they had in fact, met in the past. "Have we met before? I feel like I've met you before?" Daniel was convinced that he somehow knew her, but at the same time, he was certain that he would never have discarded meeting someone like her. Lola let out an awkward chuckle, "No, no. I don't think so. I would've remembered. I've just got that kind of a face." Daniel grimaced when he heard her tell him that she was often confused with someone else, all the while undeniably sure that he had never seen a face like hers before that night. He wondered again how it was possible that they had never met before, and sure that he would in no way ever, disregard her eyes. "Tanita was impatient and excited to introduce you to us." "Can I get you something to drink?" Daniel was committed to acting normal, desperate to hide his confusion from both Tanita and Lola. "Just a coke, thanks." She had to force herself to turn back to Tanita. Daniel touched her shoulder, instantly alarming Lola. "It's your birthday, you are eighteen, right?" "Nineteen, actually ..." Daniel smirked again when he realized she barely looked a day older than fifteen. "How about some champagne? We should celebrate." Lola had little to no desire to celebrate, and for the first time since meeting him, she glared directly into his eyes. "No thanks, just a coke please. I don't drink."

She was careful not to appear impolite, and she hoped that he wouldn't notice how incredibly uncomfortable his presence was making her. "You look great Tan and thank you for inviting me, us, Lauren and I. I almost backed out earlier." Lola stumbled on her words before she turned to find Lauren who had since disappeared into the crowd. "You're welcome, my friend. You have to come out more." Tanita wanted to dance, and swiftly turned to Daniel, "Come on Daniel, let's dance!" She grabbed Daniel's arm after he handed Lola her coke, and dragged him onto the dance floor. Lola was sure that she saw Daniel hesitate, but he followed Tanita onto the dance floor. Her eyes trailed over to them when they began to dance. She was once again wholly sensitive to Daniel's masculine beauty. He soared above Lola. He was physically perfect, and breathtakingly handsome. His jeans clung snugly to his body whereas his black leather jacket gave the undeniable impression that he had a certain confidence and refinement about him. To take her attention away from Daniel, she found an empty seat right beside Tanita's, and leisurely sipped on her coke. At that very instant, she regretted her decision to celebrate her birthday at Joe's when she realized that she was feeling abandoned, and completely alone.

She reviled places like Joe's and once again, she felt entirely out of place. She would have been much more contented and blissfully comfortable reading a good book at home than lynching out in a nightclub, surveying the night owls caught up in laughter and dance. There were people that seemed careless and carefree as they painted the town red. She spotted Lauren on the dance floor and smiled sadly. She couldn't help staring stared at her, "At least Lauren is having a good time."

"Hey pretty girl ..." Lola was startled when she heard an unfamiliar voice whisper into her ear, but instantly bothered by the stench of alcohol on his breathe. Lola could hardly settle on whether it was garlic, or whether it was beer, or perhaps, a combination of both, but it made her tummy twirl. She turned around to identify where the voice was coming from, when she saw a man in his early twenties looking straight at her. She recognized him as the owner of the only publishing firm in Sutherland. Gregory Pastor had inherited 'Pastor Publishers' from his father when he retired earlier on in the year. Lola had researched publishing firms when she began writing her first novel, but she didn't have a great deal of confidence in her work.

He was an overpowering, yet attractive man with short, ash blonde hair and hazel eyes. Most women would find him eye-catching, but Lola thought him to be arrogant and entirely self-aware. "Hey ..." Lola hesitated, not wanting to appear rude, but eager for him to leave. "You want to dance?" He instinctively took her by her arm. "No thanks." She gradually retracted her arm. "Come on!" He insisted, before grabbing her arm again. "I don't want to dance. I can't ... really dance ..." She was anxious to win back her arm. Lola hated physical contact, especially with strangers. "Come on! I'll teach you!" Lola began to panic and desperately tried to retrieve her arm, but he held on forcefully. When she looked at him again, she was frighteningly aware of an uncultivated look in his eyes that filled her with revulsion and extreme apprehension. She reluctantly and grudgingly followed him onto the dance floor, aware that if she wavered, he would cause an unreceptive and unnecessary scene. He seized her into his arms, and pressed himself securely against her. Again, Lola was anxious and unnerved by the abrupt proximity of a total stranger.

Daniel was taken aback when he noticed Lola and Gregory together on the dance floor. He was determined to keep an eye on them from where he and Tanita were dancing. While scrutinizing them closely, Daniel was once again acquainted with the fact that they had indeed met before, but he was instantly jolted back to reality when he noticed Lola challenging to free her arm from Gregory's ever-tightening grip. Daniel was immediately alerted to the fact that Lola had no interest in Gregory Pastor when he recognized the abrupt terror on her face. He stopped dancing, and continued to glare over at her and Gregory, all the while allowing Gregory an opportunity to walk away from Lola, eerily perceptive to the fact that she was not the kind of girl to be in a situation as that. He noticed that Lola was persistently shunning physical contact with Gregory, and each time he would try to place his hands on Lola, she would subtly move further away from him. At one stage, he noticed Gregory clutching firmly at Lola's arm as she scuffled to free herself from him.

When Daniel unequivocally understood that Gregory had no intention of departing from Lola, he frantically turned to Tanita, "Gregory is up to his old tricks again, this time with your friend." "Gregory? Oh no, she'll be fine. You know Greg, he's harmless. Besides, Lola could do with a hook-up." "Tanita, Gregory Pastor is not harmless. She doesn't stand a chance against him." Daniel abruptly took her by her hand, and marched over to where they were dancing, aware once again that she didn't belong in the clutches of Gregory Pastor. "Gregory Pastor, my, my. Preying on your next victim, I see?" Daniel was glowering when he glared directly at Gregory who had still not released his grip on Lola's arm. Lola was startled to find Tanita and Daniel behind her, and felt an almost immediate sense of relief and saw it as an opportunity to free her arm from him one more time. Gregory mumbled incomprehensibly under his breath, and in a moment of commotion, Daniel grabbed him and held him in a firm grip. "Let go of her arm!" He commanded irately before Gregory unwillingly let go of Lola's arm. Gregory, looking defeated, turned to walk away from them, but peered back at her every so often. "I'm so sorry, I didn't want to make trouble."

Lola was humiliated and turned bright red when she realized that the attention had begun to focus primarily on her. "I'm going to go and get some fresh air." Daniel sensed her mortification, and felt awful on Lola's behalf when she bowed her head, and hurriedly walked away from them. "Tan, I'm going to go see if she's all right ..." "I'll go with you!" Tanita grabbed a hold of Daniel's arm. "Go order us something from the bar, I won't be long." Tanita half-heartedly turned back to the bar when Daniel followed Lola out onto the beach.

Lola had no sooner stepped out onto the shore when she spotted an unrecognizable silhouette next to her. "You okay? You seem so out of place here?" She was instantly relieved to find Daniel standing next to her, "Yeah, I know. I am, but I'm fine, thank you." Lola impatiently pulled to free a band that held her long hair together when she noticed it was caught in a twisted knot. As her hair fell loosely down her back, she gazed out over the ocean, and could hardly refrain from questioning just how she managed to place herself in that position, and how she got herself there. Of all the places in the world, why it was Sutherland that made her feel safe. Daniel stood next to her in silence, and while he too glared out over the ocean, he wondered only about what was going on in her mind. He stood calmly beside her, feeling as though he was expected to say something to her, but unable to find the words. He couldn't comprehend why Lola seemed so entirely distressed, yet, she was one of the most beautiful girls he had ever seen. He was convinced that there was a story to her, and he was certain that there was more about her he was eager to learn. While glancing over at her, Daniel was unexpectedly defeated by her virtuousness and beauty, and once again tried to fathom how she contained her beautiful long hair.

His heart thumped when he recognized sorrow in her eyes. He questioned whether it was ruthlessly placed there by another man. The mere consideration of a broken heart that was unmistakably apparent in a Lola's eyes, a stranger he had never met before, was something Daniel imagined with intricacy. For some reason, the innermost part of him cringed at the thought of her anguish. For an instant, he was reluctantly and cautiously aware of his own unrecognizable emotions that made way for an overwhelming urge to protectively embrace and guard her, even though they had met just moments earlier. There was something indisputably familiar about Lola that made him question all he ever thought he knew about himself. He knew with certainty that he had never had an encounter with her before, yet she irrefutably beleaguered him. Daniel unwittingly and unintentionally became putty around girls like Lola. His mother often tantalized him about it, but at the same time, expressing her gratitude that he never had any sisters. She often laughed and in jester, mocked that he would lock them up in a show case, and never let them out again.

Daniel unnervingly glanced out over at the ocean once again, and wondered whether Lola was one of those girls that needed saving. "What a birthday, huh?" He nervously, but frantically attempted to break the silence between them. Lola reluctantly nodded and smiled. "I've never seen you around before, how long have you been in Sutherland?" Daniel just had to know more about her. "About three years. I, these places aren't really for me." "Lauren, your sister, she's in grade?" Lola hesitated at first, "Eleven, she's in grade eleven." Lola turned back to face him, "Thanks, for back there, and so sorry. I am so embarrassed by what happened." "Oh, don't worry about that. That's just Greg's way. Can't blame him for trying." Lola smiled bashfully, "So how long have you been in Sutherland?" "Twenty-four years, born and bred." Lola was instantly surprised. "Wow!" "My parents live over in Hodgkin's Valley with my youngest brother, Bo. Dean, my middle brother and I live over here in Madison but, we were born there, and spent our childhood in Hodgkin's." He paused for a moment, still sure that he had met Lola before, "Have you ever been there? It's about an hour or so from Sutherland? Very quiet and a very quaint little village." "Hodgkin's Valley? I've heard the name before. Probably just read about it in a magazine somewhere, but no, I've never been there." Daniel was confused but didn't want to press her for more details about her. "You must get this a lot, guys falling over their feet to get your attention?"

Lola turned away at once, "Oh no, I, no. Not at all. It's actually never, ever happened before." She broke out into a nervous laughter. "I really never go anywhere. I'm just here, my sister wanting to go out, and Tanita wanting to celebrate my birthday. Although, I'm pretty sure she just wanted to show you off. I'm actually just a boring bookworm. I honestly don't know why I agreed to come." She at once became anxious, "You and Tanita, how long have you been dating?" Lola was frantic to turn the attention away from her. "Oh no, Tanita and I aren't really dating seriously. We've gone out a few times, but no, not dating like that. I'm glad you came. It's always nice to meet new people."

"There you are! Let's go get our drink, please?" They were suddenly both aware of Tanita's presence. Daniel glanced enquiringly over at Lola and smiled tensely. She was once more conscious of how uncomfortable and out of place she felt just by looking at him, and how enormous his charisma was. "Lola has had enough partying for one night, Tan." Daniel turned to Tanita, abundantly aware of the fact that Lola felt wholly inappropriate at Joe's. "I just told her we'd drive her home. I'll get Dean to drive

Lauren home, if that's alright with Lola?" He turned to Lola, "Do you want to go home Lola?" She was instantly relieved. She had no desire at all to return indoors, or to face Gregory Pastor again. "Thank you, I would like to go actually, but, who is Dean again?" Daniel smiled, "Dean is my brother." He pointed out over to the crowd on the dance floor. "The guy dancing with Lauren, and don't worry, he will take good care of her. He's one of the good guys."

Lola smiled when she spotted Lauren on the dance floor, and hurriedly made her way over to her sister. When she reached Lauren, she gently patted her on her arm, and whispered softly in her ear, "Sissy, Tan and her boyfriend are taking me home. If you want, Dean can bring you home in Bonnie. Do you want to stay a little longer?" "Can I? I'll be home by midnight?" Lauren was having a marvelous time on the dance floor. It was clear to Lola that she was thoroughly enjoying herself with Dean. She agreed to let Lauren stay behind, blindly trusting that she was in good hands, but despondently aware of the fact that she could not force Lauren to return home with her. "Do you rather want me to stay here with you?" "No, that's okay. I'll be fine. I'll call you if anything's wrong, I promise." Dean turned to Lola, and placed his hand on her shoulder, "She'll be fine. I'll have her home by midnight, I promise." Lola smiled uneasily, and half-heartedly handed him the keys to Bonnie while silently hoping that she was doing the right thing. When Tanita and Lola reached the car park, Daniel pulled up in front of them. He climbed out and opened the door for Tanita, while Lola climbed into the back seat.

"I am so in love with this guy Lola! I think he might just be the one, you know?" Tanita gushed as they fastened their seatbelts, waiting for Daniel to make his way into the driver's seat. When they drove out of Joe's, Tanita engaged in chatter with Daniel while directing him to Lola's apartment. Lola giggled softly time and again.

Tanita was blubbering to Daniel about Mr. Fiches, their science teacher who was caught making out with Mrs. Marley at the back of the stage. She told him about Derek Tyler who kept asking her out on a date, and she gossiped to him about Tony Mueller, the new guy in school. When Lola glanced at the rear-view mirror, she often caught a glimpse of Daniel's arctic blue eyes, but she was careful that he never saw her glaring. She could distinguish by the expression on Daniel's face that none of what Tanita was muttering about, fascinated him in the least. He regularly nodded in acknowledgment, but had an incredibly modest response. Lola unintentionally questioned why a man like Daniel would bother himself with a young student, but when she glanced over at Tanita, it was easy to understand. Though still dreadfully young, Tanita was beautiful. She possessed dark, but compelling brown eyes with corresponding dark hair that effortlessly flowed down her back. Tanita was tall and slender, and might be just an inch shorter than Daniel. She was breathtakingly beautiful. Lola instantly understood what attracted her to him.

Daniel was agonizingly aware that Tanita was chattering away without pausing to take a breath, but he was barely paying attention to a single word she was saying. He involuntarily glimpsed at Lola time and again through the rear-view mirror, and found himself inexplicably drawn to her purity and exquisiteness. She was unlike any other girl he had met before, and he could hardly avoid questioning once more, what precisely her story was.

Daniel was wholly familiar with women flinging themselves at him, only to discover that Lola had no detectable awareness of him, which was a breath of fresh air. He scrutinized her smile while she listened to Tanita. He was certain that at times, the sadness in her eyes were agonizingly visible.

While driving through the streets of Madison, Daniel wondered yet again how he had never seen or met Lola before, and he could, without a doubt, sense a world of secrets hiding behind her captivating green eyes. "Thank you for driving me home, Daniel. Tanita, see you tomorrow?" Lola was the first to speak when they pulled up to the apartment building. "We can wait with you until your sister gets home?" Daniel switched off his car, reluctant to leave Lola just yet. "Oh, that's okay. I'll be fine, but thank you. Enjoy the rest of your evening." Lola closed the door and quickly waved them goodbye. Daniel turned and waved, but Tanita instead, presented her with a broad smile. After initially hesitating, Daniel started up the car again, and pulled away from her at a snail's pace. It was at that moment that Lola noticed Daniel's car, big, black and very expensive. "Just the right kind of guy for Tan." Lola whispered before she made her way upstairs, and into her apartment.

When Daniel and Tanita pulled away after dropping Lola off, she promptly placed her hand on Daniel's leg. "So, back to Joe's?" "Yeah, I promised your friend that Dean would bring her car back, and Dean would need a ride home." Tanita sighed, "We can stop off at your place for five minutes?" Daniel frowned, but stared straight ahead, "Rain check?" Tanita was disenchanted at once. While driving back to Joe's, Daniel's attention turned back to Lola, "So, what's the story with your friend, Lola?" Daniel was anxious to know more about her. Tanita let out an enormous sigh, "No story really. She's just a loner. One of those quiet girls. She and Lauren haven't been here long, but I know they have no family, or anything like that. They bought one of my dad's apartments when Lola just got here." "They live alone?" Daniel frowned again. "Yep. Lola is more like Lauren's mom. I know that Lauren's a lot more open and out-going than Lola is. Lola is painfully shy, definitely not a party girl." "So, her parents are dead?" Tanita shrugged, "I don't know? She doesn't talk about it. She's painfully shy Daniel, and doesn't talk about anything, but I've often said to my mom that something really bad must have happened to her." Daniel was intrigued, "Something bad? Like what?"

"I don't know, she doesn't talk much, but whatever it is, it must've been huge. I mean, she doesn't make friends. She never goes anywhere. She just keeps to herself. It's like she's hiding or something. Always running from someone or something. I don't know? She just doesn't behave like someone her age should. I don't even think she knows how to have fun. When I used to ask her about her parents, all she always said was that they're just not around, so, I don't ask anymore." Daniel was once again mystified by Lola, and became conscious of the fact that he was in every respect, drawn to her and the ambiguity that surrounded her.

When they returned to Joe's, Daniel glanced around swiftly before he found Lauren and Dean at a table, caught up in conversation. He smiled looking over at them, and was pleased that for once, Dean was having a good time. He glanced at his wristwatch and noticed that it was later than he thought it was, time to call it a night, and head home. When Daniel ambled up to Dean, he noticed that his brother was grinning from ear to ear, "I've got to drop Tanita off, we should leave so that I can follow you back to Lauren's place." Lauren was dissatisfied that her evening was about to end, but Dean was indisputably certain that he would be seeing Lauren Storey again soon.

Lola had just folded the laundry and packed the dishes away when she heard Lauren unlocking the front door. "Thanks Dean, I had a great time! Thanks for driving me home!" She chuckled nervously when saying goodbye to Dean. "Wait!" Lola, who was dressed in her pajamas, shouted out while sprinting to the front door. "Do you have a ride home, Dean?" She immediately recalled that he had returned her car, and probably had no way of getting home. "His ride is here ..." She was stunned to find Daniel standing in her doorway next to Dean. She was instantly mortified by her appearance. Lola smiled bashfully with a tinge of apprehension before she turned away from them. Not wanting to come across impolite, she turned back for a second, "Thanks again, Daniel, and thank you too, Dean. I didn't mean for us to be any trouble tonight, but thank you, again." Daniel smiled benevolently at her, and was instantly aware of her vulnerable appearance while standing in front of him in her night clothes. Lola smiled back at him, before she turned away from them, leaving Lauren to say a final goodnight to Dean. She was convinced that Lauren was wholly taken in by Dean. Lola was delighted that she had met someone who made her enormous, beautiful smile even greater.

Lola thought he seemed like a decent man, as did Daniel, and she harbored no feeling of discomfort while she watched Lauren with him. She had just swabbed down the last of the countertops when she was startled to find Lauren standing behind her. "So, sis, can I, I've invited them in for a quick coffee, is that okay?" "Sure ..." Lola wavered for a moment. Again, utterly discomfited by the way she looked. Lauren took coffee into the living room, while Lola folded the last of the laundry. She could hear Lauren giggle often. It made her happy to hear the elation in her sister's voice. When Lola made her way into the living room, she noticed that Dean and Lauren were caught up in conversation while Daniel sat on his own, tolerantly waiting for Dean to drink his coffee. "Hey guys, I, I'm going to get into bed. Daniel, thanks again for everything tonight, and again, so sorry." Daniel smiled, "You're welcome, have a good night." Lola turned away from them, ardently perceptive to the fact that joining them would be considered inappropriate.

Lola had scarcely brushed her teeth and climbed into bed, when Lauren tapped softly on her bedroom door. "Can I come in?" Lauren was almost whispering, "Sure ..." Lola opened up the other side of her bed for Lauren to slide into. "Dean is so handsome, Lola, what do you think of him?" "He is, and very charming too but, you've only just met him ..." Lola took her sister's hand, "Are you going to see him again?" "Yes, tomorrow after school. We just clicked!" The excitement was palpable in Lauren's voice, "I'm happy for you, sissy, but just remember, you have to finish school, or they will come and take you away from me." "I know, I know. I promise I won't do anything to spoil this." She leaped out of the bed before she turned back to Lola, "So Lola, I saw you and Daniel on the beach tonight. I remember something about a birthday wish? A tall, dark and handsome stranger?" "Funny girl! That was just because of that thing with Gregory Pastor. I'm not his type, and plus, he's with Tanita."

Lauren frowned slightly, "You're everyone's type, Lola. I wish you could see yourself through my eyes. Anyhooo, I'm off to bed. Goodnight sis, I love you! I had so much fun tonight!" "Love you too ..."

When Daniel and Dean reached their apartment, Daniel sensed that Lauren was still actively present in Dean's mind, "She's a nice girl, that Lauren." He was sure that his brother was instantaneously smitten. "Yeah, really pretty too, and yes, I know she's still in school. I take back everything I said earlier." Dean instantly regretted what he said to Daniel at the workshop earlier in the day, "What did you think of her sister, Lola?" "She's nice, quiet, but nice. Hard to figure out though, but very, very pretty." Dean frowned slightly, "And very out of place too. What happened back there with Greg?" Daniel lowered his head, "Oh, you know Greg. I just didn't want Lola in that position. She doesn't seem like that kind of girl. She seems very sweet and innocent." Dean thought about it for a moment, "Yeah, they're decent girls. So, bro, what was it you said about having a cute sister earlier on?" Daniel erupted into laughter when he recalled their earlier conversation, "You got the sister!" "So, you going over to Tanita's tonight?" "Not tonight, we have a long day tomorrow, plus we need to find a Receptionist. I placed the ad today, so I'm hoping for some responses tomorrow." Dean nodded, "Yeah anyway, I'm off to bed. See you in the morning."

Daniel was once again reminded of Tanita's lack of knowing much about Lola's past, "Just a question, what is the story with Lola and Lauren? Do you know? Did Lauren say anything to you?" Dean shrugged his shoulders, "I didn't ask. I just met her bro, but their setup does seem a bit strange, now that I think of it."

Lola's Secret

Alice VL

SALVATORE

The following morning, Lola awoke to the sound of rain crashing violently against her bedroom window. She sleepily climbed out of bed, and quickly threw a nightgown over her shoulders, before she fuzzily made her way to her bedroom window. She groggily peered out, and realized that the sun was in no way about to rise anytime soon, but she was pleased that it had at long last begun to rain. She sat in silence for a moment before she finally got up, and dressed herself for school. Lola clutched the morning paper, and tiredly sat down at the dining room table with a cup of coffee in hand, waiting for Lauren to wind up in the bathroom.

Without delay, she paged through to the job seekers section and quickly glanced through all the positions available. Lola was tensely aware that finding a half day job would be almost impossible, especially since she still attended classes in the mornings. As she was about to shut the paper, her eye caught a small classified advertisement on the bottom right hand corner of the page. "Receptionist, mornings/afternoons only. Apply at 14 Grover Street, Panorama, Sutherland" She quickly grabbed a pair of scissors, and cut out the advert before she shoved it into her school bag. "What's that?" Lauren had walked in while tossing her school bag over her shoulder, "It's about a job in Panorama, not too far from here." Lola quickly explained, "I want to stop there after school." "But, I've got soccer practice? Oh, never mind, I'll ask Dean to drive me home. I have his number ..."

Lauren's response was almost too swift for Lola's liking, "Oh alright, if you're sure? You've only just met him once Lauren, are you sure?" Lauren simply smiled and turned away before she bashfully whispered, "Yes".

When the last school bell of the day rang, Lola pulled out the advert, and rushed to her car. "Hey Lola, why in such a rush?" Tanita followed closely behind her. "I, I have to find out about a job, and it's on the other side of town, Tan. I really can't stay, see you later?" "All right then, but remember, we have to decide on our dresses for prom!" She shouted out as Lola pulled away. Lola smiled and drove on, entirely uninterested or eager to attend her high school prom. To Lola, it was a squander of funds and a waste of time. She could hardly imagine spending hours fitting on dresses, and then, spending way too much money paying for the supposed perfect dress. Lola decided long ago that prom would be for Lauren, not for her.

Salvatore was written in big bold silver letters on a midnight black board against an innovative and contemporary building. 'This must be 14 Grover Street?'" Lola thought when she parked her car right in front of the gigantic glass doors that were mirrored on the outside. She hurriedly made her way to the reception counter, and noticed that there wasn't anybody around to see her come in. Lola was unexpectedly unnerved at once. "Hello!" She bellowed down the passageway, before pausing for a response. "Just a minute, I'll be right there!" Relieved, she turned to look around, and across from the reception counter, she noticed an empty desk with a nameplate bearing the words 'Design.' Lola gazed at the walls that adorned photographs of cars that were uniquely revamped and supped up, the before and after pictures that were proudly exhibited all around the welcoming area. Lola was stunned at how utterly dissimilar the cars were, and she soon realized that Salvatore was extraordinary. "Hey!" Lola's heart began to hammer and for a second, she was forced to catch her breath. When she turned around, Lola realized that the voice she had imagined she had recognized, was undoubtedly, Daniel's voice. Daniel in turn, was staggered to find Lola standing there, but secretly and unpredictably, pleased to see her again. She looked poles apart in her school uniform from the woman he had met the night before, but he was surprisingly immobile by her incredible splendor. "Hey, Daniel?" She was at once conscious of the blood rushing to her face. "Wow, small world. Shit." "Lola, nice to see you again! What are you doing here?" Lola peeked down at the advert in her hand, and instantly crumpled it while silently hoping Daniel wouldn't know what she was holding. "I'm not sure, do you work here?" "Yeah, is that the ad for the reception job?" Lola began fumbling nervously when, without a doubt, he recognized the advert. "I, I didn't know that this was where you ... I mean ... your ..." "My place of work?" Daniel interrupted her when he realized she was mortified. "Wow, I had no idea. I'm sorry. If I knew, I wouldn't have come here. Of all the places ... I feel so stupid now. I honestly didn't know." "Well, you're here now. Shall we have a chat? You were going to apply, weren't you?" He turned to lead the way. Daniel showed her to an empty seat directly across from his desk. He could at once sense that she was anxious. "Daniel, I can only work afternoons. As you know, I am still at school. I think, I think this was a bad idea. You probably would prefer someone for the mornings, right?" He smiled, desperate to set her mind at ease. "I would prefer afternoons, actually. I work in the back over there, and mornings are okay to handle, but afternoons are tough. Dean is here mornings only."

He paused for just a moment to consider her schedule, "I am fully aware that you are still at school. Grade 12 with Tanita, right?" He smiled again. "Yes." Lola at once felt small. "How do your parents feel about this?" Lola bowed her head and began fidgeting, "Oh no, it's only ... it's only Lauren and I, which is why I need ... I need to find a job." Lola was uneasily sensitive to the suspicion in his eyes, and prayed that he would not further explore the matter. She was not geared up for an interrogation into her past.

She barely made sense of it herself. Daniel was once again astonished to hear that it was just the two of them. They were young, and yet, very well cared for. "Alright then, it can't be too hard to teach you. I'll show you around. It's really not so hard. It's just getting the paperwork up to date and handling the job cards and invoicing. Oh, and from time to time, booking in the cars that come in. Also, it's handling the switchboard, but it's not like we are flooded with calls. Can you start immediately?" Daniel was intrigued by the mystery that surrounded Lola. "Yes, no problem. Thank you so much." She was instantly relieved that he had offered the job to her, but tense and apprehensive about having to work for Daniel. "You're welcome, Lola. So, if you could be here more or less at half past two every day. We normally close up shop at six in the evenings. Is that okay? Do you have sports or extra-curricular activities, anything like that you have to attend at school?" "No, nothing like that, I'll be on time." Daniel immediately thought of her school work, "And your homework? Studying for tests or exams?" "I'll get it done in the evenings, it's no problem. I can do this, Daniel. My school work won't interfere or affect my work, I promise." "We're not that busy Lola, you're more than welcome to do it here. I don't mind, and I am a whiz at mathematics, so anytime you need help, just ask." Daniel wasn't sure why, but felt sorry for her. "Thank you." Lola had hardly expected his reaction to her school work, and was pleased that he was willing to compromise with her schedule.

Daniel showed her back to the reception counter, and promptly explained the order of business. The job cards here, the delivery notes there, the invoicing in that tray, the phones and relevant extension numbers, and all else Lola needed to know about her new job. "So, I'll be in the back if you need me, alright?" "Lola?" She was unprepared for Dean's voice behind her. "Hey Dean ..." "Are you our new receptionist?" "Yeah, it looks that way. Your brother just hired me." "Cool. So, listen, like, I can get Lauren home in the afternoons if you want? I'm just about to pick her up now." "Oh, thanks Dean, but won't it be too much out of your way?" Dean smiled, eager for the chance to spend more time with Lauren. "Oh no, we live just two blocks from you, besides, I go past your apartment every day." Lola began fumbling nervously again, "Oh, alright. Thanks Dean, that would be great if Lauren's okay with it." Lola smiled timidly before she made her way around the counter. On her desk, she found a stack of business cards, and snatched one from the pile. 'Salvatore.' She read out silently, 'Such a strong name.' When she turned the card over, she was taken aback to find his familiar name 'Daniel Salvatore.'

After about an hour of capturing job cards, answering telephones and filing, Lola heard the shop door open. "Lola? Wow! This is a surprise. What are you doing here? Why are you here?" Lola became increasingly panicky when she heard Tanita's voice, and subsequent questions, "Hey Tan. This is the job I was telling you about?" It was clear to Lola that Tanita was gob smacked. "Here? At Salvatore?" Lola was unsure of how to respond, while perceptive to the certainty that flukes like those were intermittent. "I didn't know. I honestly didn't know that Daniel, that he worked here. I saw the ad in the paper this morning. I mean, I didn't even know his surname, until just now." Lola was instantly relieved to hear Daniel's voice behind her. "Hey Tan." When she glanced over at him, Lola realized that there was very little that could make Daniel more attractive and engaging, than the way he looked at that very moment. His overall was covered in oil and grease which had smeared onto his face. It made his blue eyes frostier, and his dark hair was instantly disheveled. "Let me just wash my hands ..." Tanita followed brusquely behind him, and aggressively closed his office door behind her. Lola was certain that Tanita thought she had deceived her, but she tried to convince herself that she had no grounds whatsoever to be concerned by her presence.

In Daniel's office, Tanita was noticeably upset and distraught to find Lola at Salvatore. "Why didn't you tell me you were looking for someone? I would've helped out ..." Daniel sniggered at the notion, entirely aware that a girl like Tanita Marsh would never be found dead behind a reception desk. "What's so funny? And how did Lola end up here?" Daniel sighed, hardly having the patience to deal with her. "She saw the ad in the paper. She knew nothing about me or this place, Tan, come on! She needs this job, and you on the other hand, don't. Besides, she's your friend, and this way, we're helping her." He gradually moved towards her. Tanita folded her arms, anticipating a more suitable and valid clarification from Daniel. He took her hands into his, instantly aware of the fact that she was irate, but not too troubled by her demeanor. "Tanita, we need someone here in the afternoons, and Lola was here at the right time. It could have been anybody. That's all. Nothing more than a coincidence, okay? It just seems that they really need the money. Are you jealous?" Tanita flung her arms around him, "A little …" He gently kissed her while shrewdly convinced that there would never be anything more than what they were engaged in at that very moment in time. "You don't have to be …" Daniel was aggravated by her covetousness, and once again realized how self-indulgent Tanita was.

When Tanita and Daniel emerged from his office, Lola lowered her head in and attempt to distract herself with invoices that were to be filed, while sincerely optimistic that Tanita was no longer incensed. "I didn't mean to make you feel uncomfortable earlier, Lola. See you tomorrow, and enjoy the new job. Daniel and Dean are great guys." She smiled courteously before she strolled out of Salvatore. Lola glanced enquiringly at Daniel before she instantly questioned her attendance at Salvatore, "Daniel, I'm so sorry …" "For what? Don't worry about Tanita. It's just a job, she gets it." He smiled and quickly returned to his office. It was less than five minutes later when her internal telephone rang. "Salvatore, hello?" "Come to my office, please." She bolted from her seat and nervously made her way to his office. "What do you prefer? Anchovies or olives?" He hastily glanced through a menu on his desk. He gazed up at her, and smiled when he noticed the confusion in her eyes, "Lunch, pizza, one of your perks working here at Salvatore, anchovies or olives?" "Olives?" She replied with utmost uncertainty. "Good choice. Is Dean still here?" "No, he left just before Tanita did."

When their order of pizza arrived almost thirty minutes later, Lola found herself settling down and was more at ease in

Daniel's company. He had only moments earlier called her into his office where they both sat around the boardroom table, enjoying lunch. Lola found it simple and uncomplicated to converse with him, and even though they by no means dwelled on any private matters, they were able to chat about the cars he was utterly and irrefutably fanatical about. Lola was bemused by Daniel's many aptitudes which included, but were not limited to, taking in any car and transforming it into a gorgeous, custom-made and one of its kind, brand-new car. He made it look effortless, but glancing over at the drawings spread out on his boardroom table, Lola knew that it took someone extraordinary to dream up conversions such as those. She realized that Daniel was the kind of man who was undoubtedly acquainted with what he sought after, and under no circumstances, lessened his principles solely for the sake of wealth. Lola knew that he was doing well for himself, and was convinced that someday, she too would accomplish something remarkable.

During lunch, Daniel was tempted to question her about her parents, but decided it was too delicate as they had only just met. It was just after six that evening when Daniel strolled into the reception area, wearing his familiar black leather jacket, and holding his car keys in his hand. "Time to go, see you tomorrow? Do you need a ride?" "No, I came with my car, and yes, I'll be here tomorrow. I'll just bring a change of clothes. This school uniform thing isn't doing it for me." She replied in jester while she picked up her bag. "I think it looks cute." Lola felt herself go red in the face once again, and nervously turned away from him. "Lola, I know you're worried about what Tanita might think. Don't worry too much about her. We've gone out a few times, but nothing serious at the moment. She's just a little threatened by ..." Lola interrupted him before he could say anything more, "Oh no, please, she has no reason to be threatened. I just don't want to cause trouble." In that split second, Daniel was sure that he could in no way at all, feel about Tanita the way she felt about him. After he locked up the big glass doors to Salvatore, he patiently waited for Lola to climb into her car, before pulling his own car out. Lola silently prayed that Bonnie would start without any hiccups, and heaved a sigh of relief when she started up the first time. She waved at Daniel before she made her way home.

After that, Lola arrived at Salvatore promptly after school each day and without fail. Daniel was either hectic with paperwork in his office, or laying underneath a car in the workshop. She punctually and habitually greeted him before she busied herself with the administrative duties he would leave for her on her desk. At three o'clock each day, she ordered pizza or Chinese, Italian pasta or burgers, dependent on the menu Daniel had left on her desk for her.

They ate lunch together almost daily while enthusiastically discussing the cars that were coming in or going out. Dean began attending Lauren's afternoon soccer rehearsals, and insisted on supporting her when they were playing matches against other schools. Lola would unite with Dean, and watch once in a while, and there were days that Daniel joined them in support of Lauren.

Daniel treasured the fact that Lola would become tremendously excited during a competition, and she would repeatedly find herself virtually on the playing field. The very first time he witnessed her do that, he laughed hysterically at her when she realized how carried away she became. Daniel often speculated as to why she barely took part in extracurricular activities as Lauren did, and at one particular match, he questioned her about it, "Lola, so, why don't you play soccer?" Lola sighed despondently when she thought about it, and identified that she barely had any time for herself, let alone any outside activities. "I'm not really athletic, besides, I don't have the time. I prefer writing actually. I like doing things on my own." She was hesitant to reveal anything too personal about herself. "Writing?" Lola nodded bashfully. "What do you write about? Stories, like a novel?" "Well, yes. I know it sounds stupid, but I'm dreaming of publishing a novel one day, fiction of course." "Is it any good?" Lola frowned, "Probably not." She burst out laughing when she realized how pathetic she might seem to Daniel. "You should go see Gregory Pastor at Pastor Publishers." Daniel instantly regretted mentioning Gregory Pastor to her, but Lola smiled affectionately at him.

After Lauren's games, they typically went out for pizza or burgers together. Both Lola and Daniel noticed that Dean and Lauren were growing closer to one another, but neither objected to the union. Tanita joined them once or twice, but often left before the games were over.

Daniel and Lola would argue most of the time about whose fault a missed goal was, or who missed a kick, but enjoyed participating in Lauren's activities. Lola missed Daniel when he was unable to attend, while Daniel was vigorous in trying to be present.

JUST FOR ONE NIGHT

Prom night arrived far too abruptly for Lola, and although she made a courageous effort to dodge it, Tanita and Lauren hounded her profusely. Ultimately, Lola agreed to attend on the stipulation that she refused to attend any dress fittings, or splash out on a new dress. Tanita stopped by their apartment a few days before the prom, and dropped off a mountain of dresses for Lola to try on. She wasn't too bothered about choosing a dress, but Lauren demanded a fashion parade.

After settling on an emerald green evening gown, Lola was relieved that the performance was at long last over. "Oh no, Lola!" Lauren was horrified on the morning of the prom. "You don't have a date for the prom!" Lola snorted at the idea of having a date, and realized that it certainly meant the end of the world for Lauren. "I don't need a date, sis. If I did, I would've asked Greg. Besides, I won't be staying long. I am just going to show my face, and leave straight afterwards." "You can't do that. Dean! You can go with Dean. Daniel's going with Tanita, so you have to go with Dean. You must!" Lauren impatiently insisted that Lola had a date. "Lauren, I really don't need a date. I don't have to go with anyone." Lauren's expression was priceless. She could never accept that Lola attend an important function such as her prom, on her own. "Yes, you do Lola, you cannot go alone!" She was utterly appalled at the notion of Lola alone at the prom, and hurriedly speed-dialed Dean from her mobile phone. Lola protested unsuccessfully, and just a moment later, it was arranged and settled that Dean would be Lola's date for the evening. "Well, what about you Lauren? What will you be doing all night long?" "I have a science project to finish, and I wasn't going to see Dean tonight anyway." Lola knew without a doubt that Lauren was being blatantly untruthful. "You are such a liar, Lols!"

Lauren spent the remainder of the afternoon fussing over Lola. She curled her hair loosely down her back, and applied a small amount of makeup to Lola, before she rounded off her look with nail polish. Lola loathed wearing any form of cosmetics, but left Lauren to do what she best accomplished.

When it was more or less time for Dean to turn up, Lauren stood back, and once again admired her sister's beauty, "Wow Lola, you are going to be the prettiest girl at prom tonight. You are beautiful, Lola." She breathlessly flung her arms around her older sister. "Thank you, Lols. And its thanks to you that I look like this. Maybe it's not so bad to be Cinderella for one night."

Dean picked Lola up just before seven on the night of the prom, and for the first time since meeting him, she was aware of how tremendously attractive he was. Outwardly, he bore an uncanny resemblance to Daniel, yet their traits differed like night and day. Dean was light-hearted and good-humored, affectionate and generous whereas Daniel was stern, yet good-natured and passionate. Dean opened the passenger door for Lola, before she slid in while grinning from ear to ear and waving at Lauren. During their drive to school, Lola noticed almost at once that Dean was tensed, "I'm so sorry that Lauren got you into this, Dean. I wouldn't have minded going alone and actually, I didn't even want to go at all." "Oh no, don't be sorry, it's going to be fun. I don't mind this. You look nice, you should do this, and you shouldn't go alone." "Thank you, Dean. She just has a mind of her own that one." Dean grinned shyly, "She's a great girl, Lola. I really like her ... a lot ..." Lola smiled, completely aware of the fact that Lauren had fallen in love with Dean from the moment she met him. "She really likes you too, Dean, a lot."

They continued to drive in silence for the remainder of the way, when Lola unexpectedly became gloomy. She wondered if she would ever meet her special someone who could possibly fall in love with her the way Dean had fallen in love with Lauren. She considered the proposal of lingering through life on her own, and she began to panic when she predicted the probability of growing old entirely alone. "We're here!" Dean announced out of the blue, instantly drawing Lola back to reality. When they climbed out of the car, she hooked her arm into his, and they dreamily, yet timidly walked down the red carpet together. They had only just entered the prom hall when Tanita and Daniel met up with them. "Hey bro ..." Lola heard Daniel's familiar and soothing voice. Daniel found himself inadvertently glaring at her. She once again felt powerless and anxious in his presence. "Lola, wow! Look at you! Wow!" At that very moment, Lola was the most beautiful girl he had ever seen. Her emerald green dress brought out her striking and entrancing green eyes, and her hair was layered in loose curls, all the way down her back.

Daniel unexpectedly and abruptly felt enormous restlessness around her. He was certain that if he stared at her for only a moment longer, he would not at all, have the ability to turn away from her. Daniel was overwhelmed by the hammering of his heart, and hastily glanced over at Tanita. "You ladies look beautiful." With shuddering hands, he took Tanita's into his. Lola was secretly delighted that Daniel had noticed her. It was the first time in her entire life that Lola wanted to look pretty, but at the same time, she was confused by her admission of desiring to be noticed. Lola strived to measure up to Tanita for only one night, but when she glanced over at her, she was devastatingly attentive to the fact that there was no similarity at all. She reminded herself of how much she had accomplished in her own life. She was satisfied with her life and who she was, proud of herself for reasons that belonged only to her. There was nothing at all that could alter what had happened to her, but Lola was determined that there would be no scars or reminders that lingered in her new world.

Surprisingly, Lola had a wonderful evening at the prom with Dean as her date. In between dancing, they would be seated at their table and engage in effortless conversation. Lola appreciated and valued her discussions with him, even though they had spent almost the entire evening chatting about Lauren. Lola was comfortable with him, and again she was truly pleased that a man like Dean had entered her sister's life. Every now and again, she would steal a glimpse of Tanita and Daniel She was unpredictably aware of her heart trouncing each time she glanced at him. Lola stared at Tanita frequently, and again, appreciated her flawless beauty. She was dressed in a flowing red evening gown that embraced her perfect body. Again, Lola felt enormously simple next to her. She could finally understand what it was that magnetized Daniel to her, and for just a moment, Lola secretly coveted and begrudged Tanita. Tanita was closer to Daniel's league than she could ever be. She knew it even though she had trouble admitting it. Tanita had the correct kind of family, and the acceptable kind of upbringing.

Lola's Secret

Daniel observed with pride just how elegant and dazzling Tanita appeared as in her striking red dress, except that it was Lola that trapped his attention. He hopelessly scrutinized her for the most part of the night. He stared at her in admiration and noticed again how incontestably beautiful she was. Daniel was plagued by how alive he felt when she giggled, and was at once dreadfully thankful that Dean was her date, sensitive to the fact that he would by no means, be comfortable with seeing her on the arms of another man. Daniel was utterly bemused by his sudden feelings for Lola. He had no clue what to make of his unexpected infatuation with her. He would repeatedly find himself gazing at her at Salvatore when he thought she couldn't see him. Daniel had an undeniably and powerful urge to shield Lola, and yet, he could barely identify with the emotions that she had stirred up inside of him. He had never before experienced sensations as he was at that very moment, and he had no way of knowing precisely how to handle his abrupt change in sentiment. By the time the evening had come to an end, he grew further perplexed each time he noticed her.

Daniel and Tanita joined Dean and Lola for a short while earlier, and as rigidly as Lola tried, she found it unattainable to turn away from him. When their eyes met, Lola was stunned to find her heart batter as ferociously as it did, and she dreaded the effect Daniel was having on her. Daniel would clear his throat over and over again, harshly alert that Lola had awakened emotions in him he had no way of understanding. "So, listen bro, I'm driving Lola home and might spend an hour or so with Lauren. Don't wait up for me." "Sure, I'll see you later then." He almost immediately turned to face Lola, "See you tomorrow, Lola?" Daniel cautiously and hesitantly embraced Lola. Her tummy twirled when she felt him so close to her. She was undoubtedly certain that it was the strangest and oddest feeling that she had ever experienced, at the very moment he placed his arms around her. She smiled warily at him, powerless to respond appropriately. Daniel gazed at her for a second after that, attentive of how idyllic she felt in his arms.

He was glaringly aware of Tanita gawking at them, but at that single moment, all he concentrated on was how familiar and proverbial Lola felt against him, and how the smell of her skin made his heart hammer more rapidly.

Lauren was impatiently and anxiously waiting for Dean to return home with Lola, eager to pepper Lola with questions about her prom night. Lola excitedly informed Lauren how she enjoyed the prom, and what a superb time she spent with Dean before excusing herself shortly afterwards, leaving the two of them to catch up on what was left of the evening. Lola lay drenched in the bath tub, unable to eject Daniel from her mind. The expression on his face played out over and over in her mind. She realized with abrupt disbelief, that she had never before looked at Daniel in the way she looked at him at the prom. She could smell his scent around her. She closed her eyes in an attempt to revive the way his arms felt around her. Lola felt colossal culpability make its way into her heart, when her mind drifted off to Tanita. She convinced herself that she was surreptitiously betraying her only friend. "The prom was great Daniel, and you, you looked smoking hot. I could see all the girls drool over you. Thank you for taking me and for being my date. It was the best night ever. Even Lola stared at you a few times and she doesn't stare at anybody, ever." Tanita flung her arms around Daniel when they reached her house. He was wholly distracted, but attempted a smile for her. He again realized how much growing up Tanita still had to do. "You want to come in? My parents are out of town." Daniel smiled benevolently, but kindly declined her offer while agonizingly aware that Lola was all he could think of. "I can't, Tan. I really have to be up early tomorrow morning. Sleep tight, and I'll see you tomorrow. I had a good time tonight too, you looked pretty."

Daniel drove away, painfully aware that Tanita was not the girl he desired, instead a brand-new craving had crept up on him, and Lola was all that was on his mind. He was undecided when he dialed her number after pulling up in front of her apartment, unsure of what precisely he had hoped to accomplish by being there. When she answered his call, he realized how vastly defenseless and bewildered he was feeling, fanatically conscious of how entirely alone he felt at that precise moment. "Hey Lola, its Daniel …" Lola was at once caught off-guard by Daniel's voice, "Daniel, is everything okay?" "Yeah, great, I'm fine. I just wanted to say goodnight, and tell you that you looked beautiful tonight. Knowing my brother, he only has eyes for Lauren, and I just thought it'd be a shame if nobody told you." He realized at once that he was faltering over his own words, and that he sounded incredibly dim-witted. "Oh? Thank you, I think? You sure everything is alright? Did you and Tanita argue?" "No, and yes. Everything is fine. I just wanted you to know. Can I come up? I'm downstairs …" "Downstairs here? Sure, of course!" Lola grinned when she ended her call to Daniel, delighted that his voice would be the last thing she would hear on that magical night. It would be a perfect ending to a wonderful evening. She was certain that in the innermost part of her, Daniel thought she looked beautiful, and that he was there only to see her.

When Daniel pitched up at her front door, Lola was anxiously waiting for him. She smiled bashfully when she invited him in, aware that Dean and Lauren were snuggled up in front of the television. "Do you want to sit out on the balcony?" "That'll be fine, thanks …" When they strolled out onto the balcony, Daniel realized for the first time how close the apartment was to the shore. "Why don't we take a walk on the beach?" He gently took Lola's hand into his. "Sure …"

When they touched the shore, Daniel stood quietly while gazing out over the ocean. Lola was enthralled by the reflection of the stars on the water, while they both stood staring ahead of them in silence. The wind was blowing a little stronger than they had anticipated, and without hesitation, Daniel placed his jacket around her shoulders. Lola smiled nervously at him, "Thank you. I just had a bath and didn't realize it was so cold." She was particularly vulnerable all of a sudden. Daniel and Lola sat down on the beach in silence, still gazing out over the ocean.

After what felt like forever to Lola, he unexpectedly turned to her, "I love it here, it always helps me think. You know, about life, tomorrow, the future, things like that. It's just so peaceful." "Yeah, I love it too." Daniel became serious all of a sudden, "Has your life turned out the way you thought it would, Lola?" Lola paused for a moment, convinced that nothing at all had turned out the way she dreamed it would. "Not really. Actually, not at all like I thought, but, it's not over yet, hopefully!" Daniel wanted to know more, but wasn't ready to push her. "Yeah, mine has you know. I have everything I ever wanted, just not that that I want the most …" "What's that?" Lola was unable to consider any one thing that Daniel Salvatore was not in possession of. "You know? Thee perfect girl. Someone to share it all with. You know? The lid that fits this pot. My mom constantly says that men are pots, and that there is a lid to fit each pot." "I don't think there is anyone perfect, but Tanita is pretty damn close. I can see her being your lid." Daniel was horrified, and thought Lola's assumption careless, "Seriously Lola? Tanita is not my type and she's definitely not my lid. I don't feel that way about her. I don't think I've ever loved anybody, if it actually exists?" Daniel responded with conviction. "So, Lola, what's your story? Some guy break your heart? You ever been in love?" Lola looked up and sighed, "No, nothing like that …" Daniel was unconvinced, "No ex-boyfriends walking around somewhere?" Lola burst out laughing, "No, I think this lid broke a long time ago. Nobody wants a broken lid."

She instantly recalled one of her many dreams, "You know, I do have the strangest dreams though. There's always a woman with long, blonde hair, and she's always telling me to go home, go find him … whatever that means? Perhaps I just read too much Steven King?"

Lola paused to let out a faint giggle, "I'm not kidding though, not about the dream. True story!" Daniel smiled forlornly at her and questioned once again how it was possible that Lola remained so contented on her own. "It's just that, I just haven't found anyone, and I want it all, Daniel. I want love. I want to love and be loved. I want someone and something real and honest, you know? Passion. All those things you read about, I want that. Not wealth or anything else, just love. Someone I can give myself to. I feel he's out there, and I think, or rather, I know I'll know who it is when I meet him. There just has to be someone out there, that one person you would give up your whole life for." "Yeah, but does it exist? True love?" Lola considered it for a moment, "It has to Daniel, or else I am stuck this way for the rest of my life! I suppose I'd better start getting my cats together. You know? The bag lady with the cats?" "In that case, I guess the only thing left for us to do is to make a pact. If we don't meet our soul mates within the next few years, we'd have to end up with each other, broken lids and wobbly pots and all." He burst out laughing and couldn't resist the urge to playfully tickle her.

Lola's cheeks were in agony as a result of her laughter. She could barely breathe, and when Daniel stopped tickling her, she found him on top of her, intently gazing into her eyes. She once again noticed his arctic blue eyes. It felt to her as though her heart was about to hammer out of her chest, and she was convinced that Daniel could hear the pounding. She had never been aware of her heart batter for a man other than Peter Storey, just before he was about to strike her. Lola couldn't understand what was happening to her. She was instantly aware of a hollow pulsation that had crept into her tummy.

Daniel had the strangest urge to kiss her at that very instant, but when he gazed into her eyes, he was certain that crossing the line at that very second would blemish what was gradually developing between them. They lay gazing at one another for what felt like an eternity, before Lola gently pushed him aside and hurriedly rose to her feet. "We'd better go, it's getting cold and it's a school night." Lola was taken aback and undeniably anxious as to what was budding between them. Daniel got up, and together, they walked back to the apartment in silence, sure that there was something inevitable going on that neither of them expected or understood.

Before leaving the apartment, Daniel turned to face Lola,

"So, thanks for the chat. See you tomorrow, and please, no cats just yet. I'm allergic." Lola laughed out loud again, "Me too, I just didn't want to say that. Thanks for coming, Daniel, I had a good laugh tonight." She waved him goodbye when all she wanted was for him to stay.

Alice VL

Lola's Secret

A NEW TOMORROW

With December rapidly approaching, it had been three months since Lola's first day at Salvatore. After her initial hesitation and concerns, she found herself eagerly rushing to work in the afternoons, and remaining behind until the last of the work was completed. Lola valued sperding her time at Salvatore, and happily discovered that it was a welcome escape from her daunting daily routine.

Dean and Lauren had become inseparable which made life a great deal simpler for Lola. He was picking her up in the afternoons, bringing her to Salvatore for lunch, and taking her home afterwards where he assisted her with homework, and staying with her for most of the time until Lola arrived home from work. Daniel was coaching Lola on countless new ideas at Salvatore as she grew increasingly interested and fascinated by his work. At any time, a new car would come in, Lola eagerly and animatedly watched him work while he transformed each and every car into a work of art. She would grow impatient at times, eagerly waiting for a project to be finalized. Daniel would just shake his head and laugh into his sleeve, each time Lola implored him to get a move on. Some nights, they would leave Salvatore after midnight. Lola had no interest in allowing him to continue working on a project without her.

Lola spent her afternoons completing her homework and when Daniel had free time, he would call her into his office and force her to study around the boardroom table while peppering her with questions afterwards in preparation for her tests.

Daniel Salvatore turned out to be a loyal and trustworthy friend to Lola and Lauren, and they equally enjoyed their afternoon lunches together with Dean. Tanita was growing progressively discontented with their working arrangement, and at school, she steered clear of Lola at all cost. Lola preferred it that way, especially since they had become ill at ease in each other's company.

When Tanita would stop by the workshop, Lola would hurriedly make her way into the filing room, and remain out of sight until Tanita had left. Although Lola would never admit to, or make her feelings known, she had grown extraordinarily fond of Daniel. Each time he walked in, her heart would come to a standstill for just a moment. At times when he smiled at her, she was forced to catch her breath. Lola was agonizingly aware of the fact that she was falling in love with Daniel, but she was convinced that he was way too far out of her reach. Most evenings while she was studying, Daniel would sit and run his hands through her hair, whispering almost habitually that she had the most beautiful hair in the world. Each time Lola smiled proudly. She was pleased that she decided against chopping it all off, delighted that it was the one little detail about her that Daniel evidently adored. Lola became increasingly contented as time went by, and all traces of hurt and resentment seemed as though it was a lifetime ago, and a million miles away from her. To her, Salvatore had become her second home, and Dean and Daniel became her closest friends.

Lauren was enamored. Dean had turned out to be her

pillar, and her knight in shining armor. The four of them regularly went out together, and when Dean and Lauren disappeared into their own little world at the theatre or at restaurants, Daniel and Lola would take the opportunity to converse about new projects. Lola felt as though she wasn't expected to pretend around Daniel. He was one of a small number of people who under no circumstances, criticized or condemned her. At the same time, Lola had closely befriended Gregory Pastor much to Daniel's dissatisfaction and displeasure.

After meeting with him on one occasion regarding her novel, they remained in touch and frequently spent evenings out. Daniel recurrently cautioned Lola against Gregory, but she explained that they were merely friendly. They enjoyed the movies together. He would often pick her up on a Saturday when she was alone. They would then linger and loiter in bookshops, or enjoy an informal lunch. When Gregory peeked in at Salvatore on occasion, it would drive Daniel out of his mind. He would flinch each time he witnessed Gregory embracing her, or taking her hand into his. Lola too became fond of Gregory, but it was Daniel she would rather retreat with.

Lola was devastatingly aware of the fact that she could never confess to Daniel how she felt about him out of loyalty to Tanita, but she secretly yearned for him. Tanita on the other hand, was reassured when it came to Lola's friendship with Gregory, and informed Daniel once that she considered them well suited. "Aren't they just so meant to be, Daniel?" Daniel was horrified each time, "She's just not the kind of girl who should hang out with him. She's better than that." "Why not? Gregory is a nice guy, successful, attractive, charming, what's not to like?" Tanita would liberally object to Daniel's assessment of Gregory.

"So, he's a little forward and rough around the edges or drinks a bit too much, but Lola needs someone like that. Opposites attract." Tanita would continue to defend the man that Gregory Pastor was. Daniel would persistently and aggravatingly turn away from her, and instead, maintained a watchful eye over Lola. "Lola is not his type. She's sensitive and sweet, but Gregory on the other hand, is crude and rude. He'll just end up hurting her." Tanita hated the fact that Daniel was so protective over Lola, "Well, I think its Lola's choice and decision who she sees. I don't get why you care?" "Here we go again. She works for me Tanita, she's a friend of ours. I'm just trying to look out for her, and you should too." Daniel lied while excruciatingly alert to the fact that he could not at all stomach seeing Lola with another man. "She can look after herself, she's a big girl, and in any case, she's not your problem or mine." Tanita would harshly strike back.

There was nothing at all until then that Lola hankered after other than to be the lid for Daniel's pot, the girl who claimed his heart. It was an impossible and unattainable dream, and even less of an expectation for Lola. She was utterly aware of the fact that she could never live up to Tanita's morals and ethics, and that her history was something she didn't want Daniel to be familiar with. Lola was ashamed and mortified by her past. She knew in her heart that it was a story she could never flee or hide from, nor did she possess the power to undo it. It did, in fact, happen, and for Lola, it was only her acceptance of her days gone by that supported her in moving forward with her future.

Lola's Secret

On a cool summer's evening, just after the sun had set, Daniel called Lola to the back of the workshop, "Hey ..." She hurriedly made her way over to him, dressed in a taut fitting t-shirt, and even tighter fitting jeans after braiding her hair into a French plait. "Hey, so Dean and Lauren are catching a movie and a late supper tonight. Do you want to have something here with me, or are you meeting up with Greg?" He was busy working underneath his latest project when he caught a glimpse of Lola, once again devotedly aware of how flawless and tiny Lola was. "Sure, I'd love to, no plans otherwise. Greg is having dinner with his parents." Lola was pleased that she could stay and watch him work, as opposed to being entirely alone at the apartment. "Cool. I still have a few things to do, so if you don't mind waiting? I shouldn't be too long. Urgh, won't you pass me the wrench over there please Lola?" With confusion written all over her face, she marched over to the workbench. She was instantly appalled when she realized that she had no inkling as to what a wrench was. She turned back to him with unmistakable perplexity on her face. Daniel sniggered when he slid out from under the car, and made his way towards her, "This is a wrench ..." Lola giggled timidly, agonizingly aware of how ridiculous she must seem to him.

He touched the tip of her nose before he burst out laughing, "You better get that overall on." She was handing him all sorts of tools, while attempting to memorize them as he needed them. It was almost an hour later when he slithered out from underneath the car again. He gathered all the tools, and began packing them away in order. Lola grabbed a few, and curtly followed him to the workbench, handing them to him one by one. When he turned to face her, he broke down in hilarity once again,

"Why are you laughing at me this time, Daniel?" Lola was instantly self-conscious. "Look here …" He signaled for her to look at her own reflection in the mirror. She was totally confounded when she noticed that she was covered in black smudge on her left cheek. She rigorously attempted to rub it off when Daniel turned her around to face him. "Let me …" He gentled swabbed the black smudge off her cheek. "That should do it, as good as new." He whispered affectionately while he ran his finger over her cheek. Her heart began to shudder when she became excruciatingly sensitive to her emotions, unable to place or understand what she was feeling at that very second. Lola bowed her head when she felt his frosty blue eyes on her. He placed his hand in underneath her chin, and lifted her head just enough for their eyes to meet. "You are so beautiful, Lola. You just have no idea how beautiful you are, do you?"

Daniel was promptly enamored by the way her skin felt on his hands, and the expression in her eyes confirmed to Daniel that she welcomed his touch. "I'm not …" Lola whispered hoarsely. He noticed the hazel spots in her eyes grow larger, and all he wanted at that very minute was to feel her lips against his. Lola had no idea of how to respond. She had at no point in her life, ever been in a position such as that before. Daniel lowered his head, and moved closer to her until his lips gently touched hers. She unwittingly closed her eyes, aware of the unanticipated need to entertain each sensation that had begun to torrent throughout her entire body.

She felt her heart thrash inside of her, before her legs began to quiver. He kissed her with exceeding vigor when Lola felt his arms around her. She reached out and placed her arms around him, and prayed that their moment, in no way ever ended. It was a feeling she had not in the slightest bit experienced before. A sensation that she had an unexpected desire to hold on to, yet it was an emotion she was sure she could not at all disregard. Lola could smell him into her soul, and for the very first time in her short life, he was undoubtedly the only man whose arms she hunted.

The distant buzzing of his cell phone hauled her back to reality almost at once. Lola was wholly and undeniably swept away by her emotions, which she by no means aimed to admit to. The feelings she was exploiting, was flawed, self-seeking and unjust towards Tanita. Daniel impatiently grabbed his mobile phone from his pocket, and realized in agony that should he refuse to take the call, it would continue to ring. When it became apparent that Tanita was the irksome caller, Lola had a sudden and remorseful urge to flee from Daniel. "Tan, hold on ..." Daniel clutched at Lola's arm just as she turned to leave. While holding onto her arm and signaling her with one finger to stay, Daniel turned his attention back to his mobile phone, "I'm just in the middle of something. I can't talk right now. I'll call you later." He abruptly ended the call, and tossed his phone onto his workbench. "Don't go, I want to kiss you again." Lola glanced back at him. She was agonizingly and excruciatingly aware that even though walking away from him was the right thing to do for Tanita, she didn't want to or irrefutably, had the courage to. "Tanita is my best friend Daniel." Lola tried to explain before he kissed her again. She hesitantly withdrew, while scandalously convinced that all she fiercely desired was to feel his lips on hers once more. "Daniel, she's my only friend here. You don't understand what it was like. When Lauren and I got here, she's all we have. I can't do this to her ..." Lola closed her eyes when he pressed his overpowering lips against hers one more time.

He swept her in his arms and held her firmly against him. Lola recognized each and every part of her body begin to quiver, and noticed with certainty that she integrated faultlessly into his arms. He cautiously hesitated for an instant before he took her hand into his, and led her to his office. Lola was unsure of what was about to take place between them, but she in no way at all, tried to caution herself. She sought Daniel in any way he willingly presented himself to her. She secretly prayed that he wanted her in the same way she did him. He gently laid her down on his couch, but instantly stepped back and gazed at her for what felt like an eternity. "I want to make love to you, Lola, let me. Ask me to. Ask me to make love to you …" He huskily whispered as he gazed intently at her. Lola stared back at him for just a moment, before she closed her eyes, "Daniel, make love to me. I want you to …" "Lay back Lola, close your eyes …" Daniel began to shudder slightly. He slowly undressed her, and intentionally memorized every inch of her body. "You are so beautiful to me, Lola …" "I've never, there's never been … I've never done this before, Danny …" Daniel abruptly retreated, stunned to hear what Lola had unexpectedly and unpredictably stated. "Don't stop Daniel …" "Are you sure, Lola?" Daniel was insufferably aware of his inexplicable need for her, but at the same time, he had a larger need to value her virtuousness. "Yes …" Lola was unbearably aware of every fraction of her body come to life as he gently ran his masculine hands over her.

Her entire body was aching, and Lola in turn, was unbearably aware of an insatiable hunger for him. She held forcefully on to him until she could no longer effectively control any part of her. In no way and under no circumstances, had a man been responsible for what she had sensed as her heart pulsated and hammered with each touch and with every thrust. It was the man she had unreservedly and liberally given herself to. He was the very first man she willingly shared her body with. At that very moment, she was indisputably certain that she would never again feel the same way at any other time, or with any other man.

Daniel had been with scores of women prior to Lola, but it was she who enforced his emotions of intimacy, and it was unlike anything he had ever experienced before. He had an irrefutable and incontestable correlation with her. He was in every respect aware of the fact that he had never felt the same way with any of the other women. He caught glimpses of her as they gently and devotedly made love, while anxiously anticipating Lola's endorsement. He powerfully clung to her, certain that the phenomenon between them was an incredible one. Daniel was sure that he would at no point in time, ever again experience the exact same familiarity with any other woman, but with Lola. Daniel's heart was trouncing. He wondered for an instant whether his lid hadn't been right in front of him all along without a hint, or perhaps, while he failed to pay an ounce of attention.

Daniel turned over and laid beside her while maintaining a firm hold over her. Lola had no indication of what to say to him, but was utterly and disturbingly convinced that she was plummeting hopelessly, although unwillingly, in love with him. Terrified that he might sense her emotions or detect her vulnerability, she summarily bolted to her feet, and inadvertently startled Daniel. "What's wrong? Are you okay?" Lola could barely look him in the eye. "Yes, I'm fine, but I must go." Daniel was entirely caught off-guard by her sudden urgency to leave. "Did I do something wrong? Should I say that I am sorry?" "No. Oh no, Daniel, I wanted this. I won't say anything to Tanita." "Tanita? Is that what this is about? Or is it really about Greg?" He sat up straight, and began clothing himself. Lola glared at him. She instantly questioned how any of what had just happened between them, could not be about Tanita or Gregory. "Lola, I wanted you. I wanted to be with you tonight, not Tanita. I knew exactly what I was doing." He placed his arms around her. "From the moment I met you, I wanted to hold you in my arms. When you walked into Salvatore that first day, I didn't want to let you go. There is just something about you. I don't know what it is, but I want to find out. I want to spend my lifetime looking at you, and listening to your laughter. I know that you have a lifetime of smiles in there Lola." He looked up and closed his eyes, "At prom, I had to control every part of my body. I so badly wanted to sweep you up and just hold you close forever. I've wanted you from that very first day, and when you walked into Salvatore, I knew it was a sign, and I just can't stand seeing you with him, with Gregory." "Daniel, I've never, nobody has ever, you're the first guy I've been with but, Tanita's my friend Danny. This is wrong and if I stay, damn it, Daniel. If I stay, how am I going to walk away from you? I'm already struggling ..."

Lola grabbed her keys and hurriedly made her way out to her car, while half-heartedly admitting to the fact that she couldn't deny the ecstasy and elation that had made its way into the very core of her. Her heart assured her that it was alright, but her mind rebuked her for her disloyalty to her closest friend. 'Tanita is your friend and it doesn't matter how you feel, you shouldn't have done this!' It erratically scolded her.

While driving home in an almost trance-like state, Lola had no doubt that she could still smell Daniel's scent on her, and each second that she blinked, she unintentionally envisioned their love making. But, instinctively, Lola's thoughts turned to Tanita yet again. She was horrified to recognize the enormous and terrifying dishonor that had swept through her entire heart. Tanita had been a brilliant and thoughtful friend to both her and Lauren. Lola was positive that her treachery would come at an enormous price that would ultimately cost her their friendship. It was never whether Daniel was in love with Tanita, it was important to Lola that Tanita was in love with him. "What have we done?" Lola whispered dejectedly as she pulled up to the apartment.

"Hey Dean ..." Lola hurriedly entered the apartment, and made a paramount effort of steering clear of them, and totally avoiding eye contact with Lauren and Dean at all cost. "Hey ..." Dean puckered a brow and glared pryingly at Lauren. Lauren jumped to her feet at once, and brusquely followed Lola into her bedroom. "You okay, sis?" "Yes, fine. Just tired. It was a long day." Lauren hesitated but instantly left Lola's bedroom to rejoin Dean in the living room.

Lola in the meantime, immediately ran a bath. While she lay soaking in the bath for what felt like forever, Lola was overwhelmingly aware of the fact that she could barely banish Daniel form her mind as she revived their love making over and over again. With an unintended grin on her face, Lola was certain of only one thing. Even though she possessed the determination and willpower, she would never be able to renounce their one night together.

Before climbing into bed, she took her mobile phone

from her purse when she noticed a flickering red light. She swiftly scrolled down to her text messages, and smiled when she read the first message, "So, I was your first? Really?" "Yes ..." Lola responded without delay. "I can't stop thinking about you. I want to do this again, just with you." The next text arrived right away. "Daniel, what about Tanita?" Lola hesitantly probed him in her message back to him. "I'm seeing Tanita tomorrow night and, I'm going to end it." Lola's heart began to hammer once again, "No!" Lola was instantly frenetic "Yes!" He responded without wavering.

Lola placed her phone on the pedestal beside her, unable to respond to his last text. She climbed into bed, and was thankful that Lauren had gone to bed straight away. Lola was sure that she wouldn't be capable of falling asleep anytime soon, but all she really wanted to do, was to lie silently, and relive their incredible night together.

Daniel sat in his office for hours after Lola had abruptly left with little desire to return to his apartment just yet. He had called Tanita earlier, and lied when he told her that he was ploughed in under a mountain of paperwork at the office, and that he wasn't able to see her that night. While aggressively attempting to focus his attention on the drawings that lay scattered on his desk, he finally surrendered when he realized that he could barely concentrate on anything at all, other than Lola. He irritably shoved the drawings to one side, and dismally reclined into his chair. He lucidly recalled the expression on Lola's face when he made love to her, and the look in her eyes was involuntarily and hauntingly impressed into his mind. He recalled every modest detail about the way she appeared. Her hair that had come loose from the braid, her lips that turned red and engorged, and her flustered cheeks. He was captivated by the way she looked while she lay beneath him, and he realized with a jolt that he had never quite taken the time, or had the desire to look at any other woman in the way he intently gazed at Lola while making love to her. Daniel sensed once more that there was something about Lola. He was staggered at how frantic he was to know all that there was to know about her. He thought back to her surrendering herself into his arms. It left him unexpectedly responsive to his hammering heart. Daniel was entirely and terrifyingly mystified. He couldn't at all recognize his emotions, and it frightened him to realize that even though he had no answer as to what he was feeling, he welcomed the opportunity to further explore his incontestable passion for Lola.

When they were handed their final test rosters at school the following day, Lola was tremendously nervous when she thought about the fact that her school career was about to end. She was almost crippled by the daunting reality that the finals had crept up on her far too quickly, and without warning. She tried her utmost to avoid Tanita when she tirelessly struggled to propel Daniel from her thoughts which was exhausting for her. She realized that her mind was playing tricks on her when she was convinced that Tanita somehow was suspect to what had taken place between her and Daniel the night before. She grew impatient, and could hardly wait for the last school bell of the day to sound, and found herself scrutinizing her wristwatch and mobile phone every so often.

When school was finally out, she rushed over to the workshop to find Daniel in the reception area, conversing with a potential client. When she walked in, her heart began to stagger almost at once. She became unexpectedly flustered, "Just going to change

..." Lola's voice had started to tremble as she made her way past Daniel. She let her hair flow loosely for the first time in what seemed like forever, and hurriedly made her way back to the reception area. When Lola glanced around her, the new client had left, but Daniel remained in the reception, lingering at her counter. She was anxious when she noticed the expression on his face. It was a look that she had under no circumstance at all, ever seen before and it made her shudder.

"Dean and Lauren will be here soon for lunch. We only have a few minutes, so I am just going to say what I need to say to you, Lola." He placed his hands on her shoulders and took a deep breath. Before he was able to say anything, Lola promptly interrupted him, afraid of what he was about to say. "Daniel, nobody has to know about last night. I'll never tell. We can pretend it never happened. We were both just vulnerable. I mean, I was. I don't know, maybe we just weren't thinking?" "Stop Lola, look at me!" He lowered his head just enough for their eyes to meet. "I am falling in love with you. I think I've fallen in love with you a long time ago, and I can't stop thinking about you, or about last night. I fell in love with you from the very first moment we met, and I don't care who you tell." He paused for only a moment, trying to identify the expression in Lola's eyes. "You can shout it out if you like, but please, please don't say things like we can pretend it never happened. It did happen, Lola, and I'm not sorry, and I don't want you to be sorry. I want to do it again, all over again ... again, and again." Daniel took Lola's hands into his, "I am begging you Lola, stop seeing Gregory. I am telling Tanita tonight. I don't know where this is going. I don't know what we're doing, but I do know that, whatever this is, I want to go there with you. I want to see where this takes us. I know we both have to take a chance on whatever this is." Lola's heart instantaneously leaped in delight, and her legs began to quiver yet again. "I don't know what to say, Daniel? Tanita's my friend, our only friend. She's all we have?" She was undeniably and disconsolately torn between her feelings for Daniel, and her allegiance to Tanita. Daniel squeezed her hands and gazed at them for a moment before he looked back at Lola, "You've got me Lola, and Lauren has Dean. Tell me you feel nothing for me. I'll walk away if there's nothing, but don't walk away from me because of Tanita. I didn't ask to feel this way." Lola grimaced slightly, nudged by her conscience, "I just, I can't betray her like this, she loves you." "Just tell me this, Lola, do you feel anything at all for me?" Lola knew that it wasn't hard to honestly respond to Daniel, "I don't know what I feel Daniel. I've never felt like this before, so yes, I feel something, but, I care about Tanita too. I don't want to do this to her. I am so torn Daniel, it just doesn't feel right like this. I'm not this person."

She grew quiet when she heard the shop door open suddenly. Lola instantly freed herself from Daniel, responsive to a prodding awareness that she was betraying all that was sacred to her. Lauren and Dean walked heedlessly into Salvatore, before Lola made her way around the reception desk, terrifyingly aware of the fact that she was apprehensive. Dean and Lauren glanced uncomfortably at one another when they both realized they had walked in on an awkward moment, and abruptly felt as though they could slice through the atmosphere with a sharp blade.

"Lunch!" Lauren hauled up a take-out bag, not sure of what else to say, but instantly alert to a state of affairs that had become entirely ill at ease between all of them. "Mmmm, smells great!" Daniel tried at once to alter the sudden somber mood, before he made his way to his office.

Lola, Lauren and Dean followed shortly behind him, while Lola scuffled to shake her discomfiture. When they found their seats around the boardroom table, Lauren and Dean instinctively began discussing their plans for the afternoon, while Daniel and Lola regularly caught glimpses of one another, unsure of how to act around the other one, and not entirely certain of what precisely was emerging between them. Daniel winked and smirked at her frequently, while Lola felt herself withdraw further each time he caught a glimpse of her. When he was sure that neither Dean nor Lauren were paying attention, he took her hand under the table, and gently squeezed it. Lola glanced around nervously, hoping that Dean and Lauren remained oblivious to what was going on right under their noses.

They had just begun to enjoy their lunch when Tanita unexpectedly marched into Daniel's office, "Hi!" She waved uneasily when she walked in. "Hey ..." Daniel greeted her, and instantly made his way towards her. "Can we talk?" Tanita seemed a little off and unnerved. "Sure ..." Daniel led the way into the workshop, Tanita hot on his heels. Lola felt intermittent horror seize at her heart when she saw them leave. She convincingly tried to veil her panic from Lauren and Dean. She was positive that Daniel might discover his mistake, and that Tanita was after all, all he really sought. More than that, Lola was horrified by Tanita's possible reaction if she were to learn of their deliberate betrayal. She was under immense pressure, and felt an enormous amount of accountability for the role she had played in the deceitfulness. Watching them in silence, Lola had no indication of what to expect from their conversation, and became relentlessly apprehensive once again. Dean was surveilling Lola the entire time during lunch, and could not, in all honesty, disregard the terror that was visible in her eyes. "You alright, Lola?" Lola smiled at him and nodded before bowing her head, forcing herself to continue her lunch, but glaringly aware that she had lost her appetite only moments earlier.

Daniel was at once despondent when he led Tanita to the workshop. He turned to face her, and found it enormously challenging to look her in the eye. "You've been avoiding me ..." Daniel was caught off-guard when he witnessed the tears well up in her eyes, almost as though Tanita instinctively knew what Daniel was about to say. He knew without a fraction of a doubt that he wasn't in love with her, and he was sure that the time had come to expose his true feelings, and tell her the truth.

For a split second, he questioned what his true feelings were, but when he turned to look through the glass window of his office where Lola sat quietly with her head bowed, he was convinced that it had everything to do with the way he felt about her, and at that very moment, while simply gazing at her, his heart began to thump erratically.

He turned back to Tanita, and unexpectedly grasped that he was so much more than just in love with Lola. He had no desire to face one more moment without her in it. "Tanita, you are a great girl, and you're going to make some guy real happy one day ..." He stumbled over his words, utterly unconfident of how to tell her that he was in love with Lola. "You're breaking up with me?" Daniel swallowed back while trying to maintain eye contact with her. "I'm not in love with you, Tan. I really, really like you, but you deserve more ..." "Is it Lola? Are you in love with Lola?" He lowered his head in disgrace before taking her hands into his.

Tanita furiously withdraw them from him, "Damn it Daniel, are you in love with Lola? Just tell me the truth. I deserve the truth!" Daniel once again glanced over to where Lola was sitting, and without a doubt, he knew he was obligated to be absolutely honest with Tanita. "Yes." "I knew it! You've been cheating on me with her?" "It's not like that Tan, it just, it just happened once. I was going to tell you tonight ..." She ruptured into tears, and irately brushed past him. Daniel stood watching her leave until he could no longer see her. He felt murkiness make its way into his heart. He had never wanted to intentionally hurt Tanita, but he could not refute his feelings for Lola. He was fanatical for a chance with Lola, and when he looked at her one more time, he was certain that he had made the only decision that was fair to his heart.

Tanita angrily marched into Daniel's office, and glared at Lola with obvious revulsion in her eyes, "I thought you were my friend, Lola?" Lola hesitantly got up from her seat when she realized that Daniel had told her of their one discretion. "I, I'm sorry, Tan. I didn't mean for this to happen ..." "Then why, Lola?" Lola knew that she could no longer hide her feelings for Daniel from her, "I, I'm in love with him. I can't help how I feel, and I didn't want to hurt you. I never wanted this to happen. I didn't plan it. I didn't want to hurt you, I swear." "Why did you have to go for Daniel? Why did you have to fall for him! After everything I've done for you and Lauren, you betray me like that? You knew how I felt about him!" Daniel walked in to find Tanita furiously confronting Lola. He was instantly aware that Lauren and Dean were both bewildered by what was going on around them. "Tanita, it wasn't like that. We didn't set out to ..." Daniel was frantic to explain before Tanita interrupted him, "No Daniel, it was like that and, I hate you. I hate you both!"

When Tanita stormed off, Lola had an inexplicable urge to run after her, but Daniel firmly anc resolutely held her back, "Let her go Lola." He was sure that there was nothing Lola could say to Tanita, to convince her that they by never intended to deceive her. Daniel took Lola into his arms, and held her protectively against him. For the second time in her life, she felt bliss like she had in no way imagined before. She at last felt hunted, truly wanted, and it pleased her immeasurably that Daniel explicitly flaunted the beginning of their very own love story. She was distantly reminded of her guilt and immense sorrow for Tanita, but Daniel's comforting arms convinced her that they would all be alright in the end.

Lola had no doubt that Tanita felt obliged to call Gregory and inform him of the turn of events that took place at Salvatore earlier. He heatedly stormed into Salvatore just as Daniel had made his way back into the workshop. She was horrifically sure that her heart had reached an almost abrupt halt when she noticed the expression on Gregory's face. "When were you going to tell me?" "I don't know what you're talking about? Tell you what, Greg?" "Don't act like you don't know, you and Daniel?" Gregory bellowed in aggravation when Lola made her way towards him. She was at once terrified of him, and had no idea of how to react to his apparent temper. "I am in love with you Lola! You knew that!" Lola was gob smacked by Gregory's admission, "No, I didn't …"

Daniel was disturbingly conscious of a commotion that echoed through from the reception area when he hurriedly set out to find Lola. "You and I, we're just friends, Greg. I never thought … I don't feel anything but friendship for you. I didn't know you felt that way?" Greg was barely listening to anything she was saying. "Did you sleep with him?" Lola dangled her head in indignity, and was once again unsure of what to say to him, but abundantly aware of the fact that she could not withhold the truth from him. "You fucking whore!" Gregory grabbed her by her arm when Daniel instantly seized him by his throat. "Don't you touch her Pastor. And don't you ever talk to her like that again. If I ever catch you near Lola, I will kill you." Lola was at once fearful when she noticed the shudder in Daniel's voice before Gregory released her arm. "Get out now, or I will make you regret ever walking into Salvatore." Daniel cautiously, but furiously freed Gregory from his grip. He stumbled forward, and as soon as he had regained his poise, he turned back to Lola, "You will come crawling back, Lola. You don't know Daniel Salvatore like I do." Gregory took in a deep breath before he continued, "He'll drop you just like he did Tanita when you came along, mark my words. There will always be someone else for Daniel Salvatore, you just don't know him like I do." He sniggered sardonically before he turned and walked out of Salvatore. "I'm sorry Daniel, I thought we were just friends. I don't know why he is acting like that?" She tearfully tried to explain before Daniel took her into his arms once again. He held her securely against him, and with no question in his mind, he knew that Lola Storey was the woman he was compelled to guard, be devoted to, and cling to until the end of time.

HODGKIN'S VALLEY

Lola had finally graduated from high school at the end of her last school year. She was relieved and eternally thankful that her days of classes and tutoring were at last over. She was spending the majority of her free time at Salvatore, but when she wasn't at work, she was with Daniel at his apartment. She spent the night often while Dean stayed over at her apartment with Lauren, but on occasion, Daniel too, would stay over at her place.

When they awoke one morning in Lola's apartment, Daniel was enthusiastic for them to establish a more regular routine, and to take their relationship to the next level. "So, Lola, this is getting a little crowded." Lola was not sure what Daniel meant, "What do you mean, crowded?" "Dean's over here almost every night. You spend most nights over at my place, why don't you move in with me? Dean could move in with Lauren?" Lola became nervous at the mere thought of leaving Lauren on her own, knowing she could barely take care of herself. "I don't know Daniel, what about Lauren? I still have to take care of her. If I let her live here on her own, they might take her away from me?" Daniel still had no clue of Lola and Lauren's past. "Who? Who are 'they'? She's a big girl, Lola. She can take care of herself, and she'll have Dean around. Plus, we are only two blocks away." Before Lola could counter him, there was an urgent knock on her bedroom door. "Come in!" Dean and Lauren casually strolled in carrying their morning coffee. "Thanks guys ..." "So, listen guys, Lola and I were talking. I've asked her to move in with me ..."

Lauren smiled and excitedly took Dean's hand into hers. "Cool!" Dean grinned and glanced over at Lauren, before he swiftly turned back to Lola, "I guess, I should have to move in here, you know? To keep an eye on Lauren?" "Is that what you want, Lauren?" Lauren flung her arms around Lola, unable to contain her excitement. "Yes!" "It's not that simple, Lols ..." Lola was cautious not to disclose too much information, but enough for Lauren to understand that she was still legally answerable for her. "I know sis, just trust me please?" In one single moment, it was determined that Lola would move into Daniel's apartment while Dean in turn, would live with Lauren at their apartment.

The two couples spent Daniel's birthday and Christmas with the Salvatore family in Hodgkin's Valley and for Lola, it was a magical time. A moment in time she never wanted to end. Lola was enormously anxious to meet Daniel's parents for the first time, and was instinctively frightened that they would in no way at all, endorse her union with Daniel, should they in any way discover the secrets of her past.

From the very moment they arrived in Hodgkin's, Lola was at peace and bizarrely at home, and extraordinarily comfortable around his parents. From the instant that Daniel and Dean introduced the sisters to John and Sarah, Lola was responsive to an immediate sagacity of calm and relief, a reality that she could certainly not experience around her own parents. "Mom, dad, this is Lola and Lauren Storey." Daniel turned to Lola and Lauren, "And these two, are our parents." "So, pleased to meet you ..." John extended his open hand out to both Lola and Lauren. "Hello girls ..." Sarah embraced each of them, making a vast effort to welcome them into her home. "We've heard so much about you Mr. and Mrs. Salvatore ..." Lola was in high spirits to finally meet Daniel's parents. "Please, you can call us John and Sarah." It was imperative that John create a comfortable and endearing environment for Lola and Lauren. On no occasion before, had Daniel or Dean brought their girlfriends home, or in no way, had the desire to introduce them to their parents.

John was caught off guard when he first laid eyes on Lola. Even though he could not place what it was about her, he knew there was something different, yet proverbial about her. He was enormously pleased to learn that they were well raised, well-adjusted girls with impeccable manners, yet he felt into the innermost part of him that there was more to Lola than they might ever discover. John was instantly fond of her, and later mentioned to Sarah that he was relieved that the boys had at last, found their lids, the women they wanted to share their lives with. They were equally overjoyed that Dean had ultimately settled down with one girl, but Sarah was saddened by the fact that her boys had finally matured into men. She glanced at Lola often, and admired her flawless beauty and engaging persona. Sarah too questioned whether she had perhaps met Lola before, yet she could in no way at all, place her at any moment in the past

Evening after evening, Daniel and Lola would lay under the stars, discussing and planning out their future. They spoke of their dreams and hopes, they indulged in extensive walks together, and they chuckled in delight at hearing stories about one another for the very first time. It persistently scratched at Daniel that Lola under no circumstances, discussed or mentioned her parents. It incessantly troubled him to such a degree that he was frantic to learn more about them when they strolled back from one of their evening promenades. "Lola, I've been meaning to ask you, you never mention your parents? You don't talk much about yourself?" Lola abruptly turned away and glanced up into the sky as they carried on walking. She maintained her silence for a moment, convinced that she was in no way at all, equipped to disclose the truth about herself just yet. "If you don't want to talk about it, you don't have to ..." Lola knew she had to say something. "There's not much to tell, they're just not around." Daniel noticed that she had become edgy, and without pressing her any further, they continued on their walk in silence.

Just moments before they reached the Salvatore house, Lola paused when they were about to pass by the house right next door to the Salvatore home. Lola stood gazing at it for a moment while trying to decipher why it was so dreadfully quiet and eerie. Who lives here?" "Nobody. I think. This used to be the Hudson house. It was such a long time ago. I'm sure they sold it, or, I'm not sure, but it's been empty for quite a few years. My dad gets people in to clean a little and maintain the garden, but nobody actually lives here." "It's beautiful. And such a shame that nobody lives here." Lola was in awe of the powder blue, three story home. "Yeah, I wish I could remember what happened to the people that lived here. I was still very young. I know we used to visit each other all the time, but I can't remember much." Lola smiled sadly, "Can you imagine raising kids here? Wow! Just look at this tree! I can just imagine sitting here, watching the sun rise ..." Lola turned to the large gum tree that stood firmly and pompously at the entrance of the drive way.

She closed her eyes, desperate to take in the aroma of the tree, and instantly felt the hair on her arms begin to rise. She opened her eyes at once, overwhelmingly convinced that she had done that once before. She scowled incessantly while standing there, trying her utmost to place that moment in her memories, but brushed it off just as swiftly when she realized that she had never set foot in Hodgkin's before. She smiled sadly while she glared through the branches to the moon that was peeking through. She was certain that an ancient tree such as that contained a lifetime of chronicles. Daniel too, was lost in thought for a moment, while vaguely recalling the many days he spent playing there as a child. It made way for a certain morbidity that had unexpectedly crept into his heart.

Dean and Lauren spent their days around the swimming pool and horse riding as often as they could. Lola favored Sarah and John Salvatore's company, while Daniel cowered at the tales they told her. She treasured their stories and adored listening to them. She heard tales of Daniel as a child, she listened to narratives of the brothers' mischievous mishaps, and she enthusiastically implored them time after time to repeat the story of how Sarah and John had started their lives out together.

Sarah grew to be immensely doting of Lola, but John could not shake the prod that there was something unusual about her, even though he could not quite identify with what it was. John was an intellectual man who judged people well, priding himself on the fact that he was an excellent arbitrator of character. He was certain that Lola hankered after a sense of belonging. He watched her closely as she eagerly sat listening to the hundreds of stories that Sarah was impressing upon her. John noticed how animated and anxious Lola became, eagerly anticipating the beginning of another story. John had a nudging feeling that somehow, she was attempting to create an improved past, or an incredible dream for herself, and it terrifically worried him that she would appear to be utterly distraught at certain moments. It was a breath of fresh air for him to find someone as young and spirited as her to be so thoroughly and honestly interested and willing to listen to what he had to say.

For the first time in years, he once again sensed a deep loss at never having experienced the absolute pleasure and elation of fathering a daughter. One evening at the dinner table, Lola pleaded with Sarah to tell her more about Granny Dolly, Sarah's mother. It was at that moment that John turned to her, "Tell us a little about yourself and your parents, Lola?" Sarah smiled, "They must be wonderful people." She responded instinctively when she realized that Lola had become unpredictably anxious. Daniel took her hand into his and squeezed it firmly, desperate to restore confidence in her. He was excruciatingly susceptible to the fact that her parents were nonexistent in her life, but his courage failed him each time he had the need to enquire about them. Lola glanced up at John while Sarah smiled nervously. "They, aren't around. I finished school only recently, and I'm not quite sure about what to do, you know? For the future?" John smiled sympathetically at her, and lightly nodded while squeezing her free hand gently. John turned to Sarah after a brief pause, "I just thought of who she reminded me of, love?" He took Sarah's hand into his. Lola was positive that she could detect a colossal amount of heartache in his eyes all of a sudden. "Molly and Liam Hudson? Their girls, weren't they Tallulah and Lucille? And a son, what was it?" He looked enquiringly at Sarah. "Manoli, and yes, she does remind me of Tallulah too, although, Lula was still very little at the time." "Oh yeah, I remember them! They lived in the house next door, what ever happened to them?"

Daniel was intrigued, and vaguely recalled the family next door. "They were all killed in a car crash when the girls were little." Sarah's voice was tremulous when she hurriedly explained. "That's so sad. Was that their house next door?" Lola was instantly eager to learn more. "Yeah, he was my business partner, but long before that, we were best friends." John paused to swallow back on an obvious lump in his throat. "With his help, Salvatore-Hudson was formed and well, it's just Salvatore now, but you have a striking resemblance to Molly and her daughter, Lula. It's amazing, even though it's been so many years, you just remind me so much of little Lula." John bowed his head for a second before he continued to explain, "We were god-parents to their children. Tallulah would spend hours sitting right here listing and begging for stories, just like you do. Daniel just adored her."

Daniel unexpectedly erupted into laughter, "I had such a crush on Tallulah! I think it was basically a crush on her hair! She had really long hair Lola, just like you. I carved our initials in a tree somewhere here, and promised to marry her when we grew up. Actually, I'm pretty sure it was that gum tree in the drive way next door ..." They all giggled while listening to Daniel, but Lola was agonizingly conscious of the devastating toll it had taken on Sarah, even after all the years. Sarah briefly told Lola the story of how she and Molly grew up together, and how Sarah had fallen in love with Liam's best friend, John.

Sarah mentioned how she longed for a daughter, but that Tallulah and Lucille crept so profoundly into her heart that she acknowledged them as her own from the moment they were born. There were moments and pauses where Sarah had to control her unsolicited tears, while John regularly placed a protective arm around her. Daniel admitted that he could barely remember much about the Hudson family, other than spending hours playing outdoors with Tallulah and Manoli. "It was a very sad day, son. They were travelling with friends on their way to some or other lake for the weekend. We never really found out what happened exactly, or what happened to the other people. It was just too sad. After the accident, I wanted to get in touch with the other people, but your mother and I felt it would just make things worse." John swabbed at a lost tear that had rolled down his cheek. "Do you remember this picture?" He cautiously pulled out a photograph from a cabinet drawer, and handed it to Daniel. It was a photograph of the Hudson girls posing with the Salvatore boys when they were barely older than six or seven. Daniel laughed once again and handed it over to Lola. "Man, I was so skinny."

Lola glared at the old portrait and felt her heart unexpectedly begin to hammer as she gasped for breath. She looked intently closer, and was almost convinced it was a manifestation of her and Lauren when they were younger. She stared and studied the photograph, but when she realized how long ago it was, and how much time had passed, she was certain that it could not be the two of them. "Lola? What's the matter?" Daniel was disturbingly susceptible to the fact that Lola had become ashen. "Nothing. I'm fine Danny, fine." She was ridiculously conscious of the blood that had instantly drained from her face before she handed the photograph back to John. "You look as though you've seen a ghost. Is something the matter?" Daniel was at once perturbed and enormously alarmed. "I, no … I don't know? This is just so sad. An entire family just, gone."

For the remainder of the evening, Lola was powerless to turn her thoughts away from the photograph, and how copiously the image had unnerved her. Her mind reminded her that she and Lauren were the daughters of Peter and Sally Storey, but her heart presented her with the uncanny resemblances they bore to Tallulah and Lucille, and how incredibly striking the similarities were. Lola was confident that her overwhelming need to exist as someone else was overpowering her, so she convinced herself that her mind was playing tricks on her. Still, she struggled to shake the feeling that she was somehow, acquainted with the girls in the photograph. Daniel watched her often, and questioned what it was about the photograph that entirely demoralized Lola.

After Daniel went to bed later that night, Lola made her way downstairs and back into the living room, unable to sleep and concerned that her tossing and turning might wake Lauren. She was pleased to find the log fire still smoldering, and quietly sat down in front of the warmth, still overwhelmingly troubled by the photograph she saw earlier. She failed to notice John come in, and was startled when she unexpectedly heard his voice behind her. "Lola, are you alright? Are you cold?" She smiled nervously at him. "A little, but I'm fine, thank you, John. I just couldn't sleep. It's so peaceful down here." John sat down on the sofa beside her, and gazed into the fire. "You look a little sad." "It's nothing, just the photograph earlier, it just made me sad. Families that just cease to exist. Just like that." John placed his hand on her shoulder before he stood up, and without responding, made his way back towards his bedroom. Lola sat in silence for a while afterwards, furtively wishing that it was her and Lauren in the picture, but sure that it could never be.

On the morning of Daniel's birthday, Lola woke Lauren early by gently shaking her, "Lauren, Lauren, wake up." While fuzzily opening her eyes, Lauren stared at Lola in confusion, "What time is it?" "It's just after six. Come help me make Daniel breakfast." Lola quickly changed into a summer dress. "Okay." Lauren begrudgingly climbed out of bed while rubbing her sleepy eyes. Lola quickly grabbed the gift she bought Daniel only a couple of weeks back, and realized once again how hard it was to get Daniel presents. She had found an exact leather jacket as the one he always wore, but which was starting to show signs of wear. She had a seamstress embroider the name 'Salvatore' on the back, and was pleased that she was able to give him, what she thought, was the perfect gift.

They tiptoed down the stairway while silently making their way to the kitchen, when without warning, they found Sarah already busy preparing breakfast. "Morning girls, why are you up so early?" Sarah hurriedly removed her apron. "Morning, Sarah." Lauren let out a soft yawn. "Morning, Sarah, we actually came down to make Daniel and Dean breakfast." Lola was disappointed that Sarah had begun setting the dining room table, who in turn, sensed her disillusionment, "I thought I'd get a head start and pack a little tray that you and Lauren could take to them?" "Thank you, Sarah." Lola took the tray from her and excitedly turned to Lauren, "Come on, before they wake up!" When they reached Daniel and Dean's bedroom, Lauren tapped softly on the bedroom door. "Yeah?" Lola heard Dean's sluggish voice on the other side of the door. "It's Lola and me …" She was almost whispering. "Come in." When they walked in, Lola realized that Daniel was still fast asleep. She made her way around to his side of the bed and paused for just a moment, hesitant to wake him, "Wakey-wakey, handsome …" Lola lovingly whispered before she gently kissed him on his mouth. Daniel gradually opened his groggy eyes, and smiled broadly when he saw Lola. "Happy birthday, good-looking!" Lola kissed him one more time. Daniel turned around and noticed that Dean and Lauren were seated on the other side of the bed, gorging down their breakfast. "Happy birthday, bro." Dean leaned in to embrace Daniel. Lauren walked around and gave Daniel a warm hug when he sat up straight in bed. "Happy birthday, old man." Lauren teased while giggling timidly. "Thank you, thanks my green-eyed angel ..." Daniel pulled Lola down onto the bed with him. She handed him his breakfast before they ate in silence. When they were all done, Lauren and Dean set off for the kitchen, giving Lola an opportunity to hand Daniel his gift. "Nothing extravagant, but geez, you're a tough one to buy a gift for." Daniel animatedly ripped it open, and was instantly overwhelmed by his new leather jacket. Inspecting it closely, he was proud and thrilled to notice the name 'Salvatore' printed on the back. He shoved it to one side before he pulled Lola closer to him, "Thank you beautiful, I love it. You know how much I love my leathers, it's perfect, just like you." He kissed her with concentrated passion while devotedly aware of an abrupt urge to feel her body against his. "Close the door ..." he whispered hoarsely. Lola retreated at once, "Not a chance! Not here in your parent's home." She bashfully resisted her own undeniable need for him.

Lola's Secret

Alice VL

TOGETHERNESS

When the New Year showed up rather unexpectedly and far too swiftly, Lola began feeling the pressure to secure a more stable arrangement at a company where she could be engaged in full time. She could no longer place the majority of the monetary burden solely on Daniel, and Lauren had only just entered her final year of school. She had saved funds which she had kept in her trust, wanting it to be available to Lauren should she decide to study further. Lola had no desire whatsoever to financially rely on Daniel for wholly contributing to their living expenses. It made sense to her that she searches for a higher paying job, even though she adored and cherished her job at Salvatore.

When she began folding the last of their laundry, Daniel snuck up behind her, and held her lovingly in his arms. It was something he did often, which she had come to adore. She felt protected, and for the first time in her life, she felt that she truly was in safe hands. "I've got something for you." Daniel turned her around to face him. In his hand, he held a beautifully wrapped gift, and as she unwrapped it, she once again realized how wonderfully sacred her life was at that very moment. She gently took out a gold necklace to find a four-leafed clover pendant dangling from the gold chain. "Daniel …" She excitedly flung her arms around him. "We are forever, Lola, and each time you look at it, you remember that. Remember that we are each other's good luck." He kissed her tenderly and firmly held onto her. "I am forever yours, Daniel. Wow, a four-leaf clover …" For just a moment, for a fraction of time and for a split second, Lola was once again aware of a familiarity in that moment, utterly convinced that she had done exactly that before. It was an inexplicable sense of recurrence, perhaps a memory, but certainly a reality she could not quite identify.

It hauntingly puzzled Lola that she was once again alert to a moment of tremendous de ja vu which frightened her, and left her reeling at once. Lola was speechless as she stared at the necklace, while agonizingly aware of all the questions in her heart. Daniel lifted her chin only slightly to face him, "I love you so much ..." "I love you more, Daniel, so very, very much more." When he turned to walk away from her, her thoughts were once again preoccupied by the pendant. She hurriedly banished it from her mind, and followed Daniel, eager to discuss the matter of their working arrangement. "Daniel, can we talk about something?" Daniel puckered a brow, and nodded in agreement. "I was thinking, with school that's over now, and with me being able to find a full day job that I couldn't before, and, I just thought that maybe, I should look for something more permanent. More full time?" "What do you mean by permanent and full time? Why? You have a permanent job at Salvatore." "I was just thinking, Lauren turns eighteen soon, and the trust fund I have is only enough to get her a car, and maybe college. I have to look ahead for the future, for Lauren's future, you know?" Daniel took her by her hand, and led her out into the dining room.

He sat her down at the table, his mind wildly beginning to race. Daniel could barely stomach the thought of having her elsewhere, but with him at Salvatore. He had become entirely accustomed to having Lola around him at work, and he was content with how efficiently she was administering the business.

He could not at all contemplate the proposal of someone else stepping into her shoes, and it terrified him to consider that she would find it necessary to search for a job someplace else. He needed her around him, yet, he was pragmatically sensitive to the reality that she cared for Lauren, and that her financial burden was tremendous. "Listen to me Lola, you don't have to look for a job anywhere else. I need you at Salvatore. Stay on full day if you want, you are there all day anyway. I make more than enough. Please, Lola, I will pay you more." "I'm there full day because I want to be, not because you need me fulltime, Daniel." "I want you there, all day long, every single day." He was determined to coerce Lola in realizing that she was indispensable to Salvatore, and to him. She smiled before she placed her arms around his neck, "Really Danny, so I can kiss you anytime I want?" Daniel said precisely what she wanted to hear, and there was no other place she would rather be. "No, Lola Storey, so I can kiss you anytime I want!"

A few days after they had finalized Lola's new and improved working arrangement at Salvatore, she glanced at her wristwatch, and noticed that the day had almost come to an end. Lola hurriedly gathered the job cards that had been captured onto the system, when her internal buzzer rang. "Daniel?" "Come to the back please, I want to show you my latest project. It's nearly done!" Lola was instantly confused, and utterly surprised that she couldn't remember a project that had come in recently. "New project?" Daniel hadn't mentioned a new project, and the last car had been collected earlier that morning. She could not recall booking in another one, and was frantic to recall whether she had made out a job card for it. She hurriedly locked the glass doors to Salvatore before she swiftly made her way into the workshop. Approaching Daniel, she was responsive to a new and shiny, big black car, and could barely restrain her pride for Daniel, and his work. She at once sensed that his latest project was incalculably extraordinary. Daniel's value manifested in the pride he took with each project, but for Lola, this one was different somehow. "Wow! The owner of this car is going to be so very proud. I don't remember you mentioning this project, or even remember the car coming in? It's beautiful, Daniel ..." She took his hand and excitedly squeezed it. "Oh wow! Oh wow, Daniel!" As though in a daze, she slowly walked around the car while attempting to take in all that Daniel had done. "Oh, it's just beautiful Daniel, and I have to say that this must be your best, best work yet."

Still inspecting the car, Lola lifted her eyes, and frowned, "How come I haven't seen you working on this car?" She was once again confused, but in awe. Daniel remained silent for a moment longer. "What else do you need to do here?" He was stunned by Lola's fascination, and smiled when he finally answered her, "Just the number plates. They're over there on that shelf." He pointed to a shelf at the end of the workshop. "Will you get them for me, please?" She took the registration plates from the shelf, and had just started making her way back to Daniel, when her eyes caught a glimpse of the license plate. She stopped and stared before she curiously looked up at Daniel. Lola lowered her head and gawked at the plates once more. She hastily turned back to the shelf, and noticed that there were no other registration plates. Once more, Lola gazed up at Daniel, still utterly confused while he stood glaring her, grinning from ear to ear. "These plates?" "What's wrong with them?" He made his way towards her, unable to straighten out the gigantic smile on his face, "Do they say 'Lola'?" She gazed up at him, unreceptive to the fact that she was grimacing, "Yes?" "Well, then they are the right registration plates." He took them from her, and without saying another word, Daniel made his way back to the car, and within five minutes, both registration plates had taken their place on the shiny new black car bearing the proud plates with the name 'Lola'. She had no indication of what he was doing, or what any of it meant as she stood glaring in silence.

He took the keys from his pocket and placed them in her hand, "I was thinking, instead of getting Lauren a new car, why not give her Bonnie? Dean will do some work on her, and she will be brand spanking new by the time Lauren gets her back. What do you think?" Lola walked around the car one more time, utterly staggered by his enormous gesture. "Daniel, this is so big, so much and so extravagant. I mean, first the job, now this? I can't take this?" He took her into his arms and whispered softly, "I love you. You deserve so much more. You deserve everything. You deserve the moon. Now, get in your car and let's go home." As he turned away from her, Lola grabbed his arm, and when he turned to face her once again, she flung her arms around him and kissed him. "Oh no, let's go into your office. I have to thank you properly."

Lola's Secret

Alice VL

SECRETS OF YESTERDAY

On a bright and sunny Saturday morning, Daniel was getting ready to leave for Salvatore, even though they barely worked at all over weekends. "I won't be long, babe. I just want to make a list of the parts for the new project. Do you want to go to the mall afterwards?" "No, I'll wait here for you, or, I can come with you?" "Why don't you finish up and meet me at Salvatore?" He gently kissed her on her forehead, "Alright, I won't be long." Lola was instantly attentive to the fact that she felt as though she had not slept a wink the night before. "What is wrong with me?" When she reached the bathroom, she stared at her reflection in the mirror, and realized that she looked as awful as she felt. After taking a quick shower, Lola didn't feel any better. "Must be something I ate?" She dismissed it, and made her way to the kitchen where Daniel had brewed fresh coffee. While she poured herself a cup, she unexpectedly became queasy, and swiftly ran back into the bathroom. "Must be my stomach." She swabbed her face down with a wet face cloth, before once again setting aside her sudden nausea.

When she entered the workshop a short while later, Lola noticed that Daniel was seated on a chair, jotting down a list of parts that were still needed for his latest project. "Hey." He at once noticed her walk in. "What's the matter?" He quickly made his way over to her when he recognized how ashen she had become. "Nothing, I'm fine..." "You look like you've seen a ghost. Are you sure you're okay?" Daniel had not once before seen her as pale, and if he hadn't known better, he could have sworn that she had no sleep at all the previous night. "Yeah, just something I ate, I think?" "Come and sit over here, I'm almost done." He showed her to his chair before he walked around the latest car, and continued listing the parts that were required. Every once in a while, he would gaze at her, and grew increasingly concerned by the realization that all was not well with Lola. "Let's grab a soda in the office, I have something for you."

He showed her to the sofa in his office where he nervously sat down beside her, "There are so many better ways to do this, but this is where all the important stuff happened for us. We made love here for the very first time, and then a thousand times after that. I fell in love with you right here. You changed my life right here, in this very office. I'm hoping that you can change it again today, for me." He paused to take in a deep breath while detecting the disorientation in her eyes. "I used to sit here and watch you while you were completely unaware. It was right here that I realized my life would never be the same again, that I couldn't and didn't want to spend another day without you. Your smile, your eyes, your beautiful hair, your touch, your laugh, your frown, and now, your confusion. I love you so much, Lola." He pulled out a tiny box from his pocket, and when he opened it up for her, the diamond ring staring back at her took her breath away. "Let's get married! Let's tell the world. Let's just do it!" Daniel paused just long enough to take in a deep breath, "You are my lid, Lola. I have found that someone that I would lay down my life for, I found you." Unexpected tears began to well up in her eyes, and as much as she wanted to shout out that there was nothing more she wanted, there remained far too much about her that Daniel was not yet acquainted with, that she had a responsibility to introduce him to.

For Lola, the moment had presented itself to ultimately let him know and understand fractions of her life before him, her life with her parents. She knew that she could no longer run from it, and in the innermost part of her, Lola realized that she no longer wanted to run from her secrets. She swore that no one person would ever know what had happened to her, but at that very moment, she was convinced that she owed Daniel the truth. "Daniel, I love you, so much. And, I want to say yes so badly, but ..." Her tears had, without prior notice, begun to shimmer in her eyes. Daniel was not at all equipped for her faltering, and at once felt terrifyingly insecure.

He loathed feeling that way, and again realized that no other person had the ability to make him feel the way Lola so effortlessly and inadvertently did. "But?" He took her hand into his, instinctively wiping away the tears that had begun rolling down her cheeks. Her tears were another thing he didn't quite understand. He thought that she would be happy, and that she would want to spend the remainder of her life with him, but her sorrow told Daniel an entirely altered story. "There are things, things you don't know about me. Things that you must know. These are things that you might not understand. When you asked me about my parents, I don't know how to begin, so I'm just going to ask you to come with me." She got up to her feet, "I want to show you something, and if you still want me after that ... Please just don't say anything until we get to the apartment, please Daniel. You don't owe me anything, just remember that."

They drove home in silence with Lola behind the steering wheel. She was no longer tearful, but prayed that Daniel would keep his questions to a minimum. Fear engulfed Daniel once again. He was absolutely caught off-guard by her sorrow, and had no clue of what to expect. Whatever it was that she had the urgency to reveal to him, convinced Daniel that it could negatively affect their life together. He knew that anything that was so imperative to her, frightened him possibly more than it did her.

Lola walked directly to her closet, and hesitantly took down a wooden chest she had kept securely hidden and protected. Daniel had caught a glimpse of it often, but it in no way occurred to him that something ghastly might be hiding in there. He not once considered that it could contain the secrets to her tears, or perhaps, the clues to her past. While reaching for the key, she nervously turned to Daniel, "Come, I want to show you something. I should've done this sooner. I shouldn't have left it so long." Her voice began shuddering again. "Daniel please, just try to understand. You might see me differently after this. It's not something that I wanted to hide from you, but it wasn't something that I could just blurt out either. There just never is a right time for something like this, but you deserve to know the truth about me, about who I am, and where I come from." She paused for a moment before she assertively wiped the tears from her eyes, "So, I'm rather just going to show you ..." Lola handed him a photograph after wavering for an uncomfortable second. "This is my mother, Sally Storey ..." Daniel took the picture of the woman with dark hair, bearing an unyielding expression on her face, before glancing enquiringly over at Lola. "This one, is my father, Peter Storey ..." Daniel pryingly stared at the man glaring back at him, and questioned why she was presenting him with the photographs. "This is a picture of my brother and sisters. I have a brother named Ford, and another sister named Melanie, and of course, you know Lauren."

She handed him one more portrait while excruciatingly sensitive to the fact that Daniel could in no way understand why she had never told him before. Daniel stared at the photographs and wondered why she had been hiding them from him, and what her reasons were for dismissing them in the past. "And lastly, this is a picture of me at the age of fifteen ..." Lola began to shudder before allowing her tears to flow unreservedly from her eyes. Daniel snatched the photograph from her, and was instantly and abruptly sickened to bear witness to the image of the woman he loved, staring back at him.

It was a photograph taken of Lola after being battered and beaten. A picture wherein Daniel could barely identify her, but a photo he now was certain he never wanted to see again, at any given time. He looked searchingly up at her, but was unpredictably powerless to ask her the question his heart so dreadfully needed an answer for. Lola glared at him as she tried to find the recognition in his eyes, before he swabbed the heart-rending tears from her cheeks. She hesitated for a moment before she turned away from him, abundantly aware of what she was about to say, but like a coward, unable to face him. "That was the last time my father raped and beat me, Danny ..." She erupted into tears and could barely believe what she had heard herself saying. It deafened her at once. Lola was staggered that the words had after all, surged from her mouth.

Daniel gasped for air when he understood what she had said. He was disgracefully aware of the tears that had begun to roll down his own cheeks. He desperately wanted to ask her if what he had heard was in fact what she had said, but he was in no doubt that he did not mistake a single word of what she had impressed upon him. He left her to weep. He felt a recognizable, restricting lump in his gullet grow larger. He could barely even begin to visualize what she had said to him only moments earlier. He stood up, and made his way towards her before he turned her around to face him. When he lifted her eyes to his, Lola recognized the enormity of all the questions in his eyes, an interrogation she had little to no desire for.

She abruptly wiped the tears from her eyes, painfully insightful to the sudden dishonor that had made its way into her core, "A neighbor took me to hospital the night that picture was taken." Lola wanted to tell him everything, she had nothing more to lose. "The police were called in, and then child services were called in. We were placed in a home, a place of safety. All of us, but eventually, Melanie and Ford were taken back to them. I wouldn't go, and Lauren wouldn't go back. If only I didn't fight him the way I did. But, that's why they're not around. That's why it's just Lauren and me, and that's why I couldn't tell your parents. That's why I couldn't tell you."

Lola began to sob again. She unremittingly told him that Peter and Sally denied the events that had taken place with Lola, and even though Lauren had enforced an uncompromising effort to persuade them that Lola was being truthful, it was Ford and Melanie's testimony that convinced the courts of their parents' innocence. They reached a decision to keep Lola and Lauren in the home, leaving them little room to cause any further heartache for the Storey family.

Daniel was appalled to hear Lola tell him about the

thrashings and how effortlessly she provoked him. While listening to her telling him about the Storeys, Daniel could barely imagine how she survived them. It made no sense at all to him why any single person would deliberately and without hesitation, want to inflict harm on Lola. Her sensitivity and vulnerability was evident for the world to see, and the suggestion that a man like Peter Storey was wounding her in such a way almost drove him fanatical. What especially angered him was the fact that Lola was accepting liability for the abuse. He could no longer consent to her, to surrender to her role in his antagonism. "I'm sorry, Lola. Man, how could he? I thought they were dead. I never imagined anything like this." Daniel furiously and irately thumped his fist through their bedroom door. Lola moved closer to him, and stood directly behind him before she timidly placed her hand on his shoulder. "Daniel, listen to me. I'm okay, honestly I am. I just needed you to know. I, I don't have scars Danny. I survived him. I wasn't going to let him be the end of me, and that's why I, Lauren and I, are here." Daniel gazed intently at her while in no doubt that there was still so much more that she wanted to say to him. "I am tough. I became strong, and I made it through. It was my choice to carry on, and it is my choice not to allow it into my life. I don't carry the scars of this, Daniel, but, I can't wear your ring with this secret, so if you don't want to, I understand, but Daniel, please don't pity me. I don't come from an upstanding family like you do. I'm not the university graduate that I should be, but I'm me Daniel. I love you. I do love you, and that's why I'm here today, telling you. You deserve to know." Daniel instinctively took her in his arms and held her forcefully against him. "I love you, Lola. I love you, and I want to spend the rest of my life with you. I don't care about your past. I don't care about any of that. What I care about is you. I want to keep you safe, and love you, and I want you to love me back. But, know this Lola, what happened to you doesn't make you a bad person. It doesn't make you unworthy of me." She gazed into his eyes, and held steadily onto him.

Her heart reminded her that with Daniel, was unerringly where she belonged. In his arms until the day he no longer wanted her, was where she had to be. Daniel slipped the ring onto her finger and gently kissed her. "I will never hurt you Lola, and I will never let anyone hurt you again. You have to believe me, okay? From this moment on, it's you and me. And the past is in the past. It doesn't matter Lola, I will protect you always. I will lay down my life for you. You are mine and I am yours. From this moment on, it's just us."

Lola dabbed at the tears on his cheek, before he took her hands into his and once again, he lovingly held her against him. "Lola, listen to me, this wasn't your fault. He had no right to hurt you like that. You know that, right?" Daniel needed her to accept and understand that she was in no way at all liable for the maltreatment. Lola smiled forlornly when she wiped a lost tear from her cheek, "I know Daniel, I know that now. I just, I just think you can do so much better than someone like me, Daniel. I have so much baggage, and you deserve someone better. More, you deserve so much more ..." "Lola stop! I deserve nothing more than you do. It's you I want. I don't care about your past. I care about our future together. Today it starts. From this day forward. I love you, Lola. I want to give you a life. I want to see your laughter every single day. I want to show you all the beauty in life. I don't want to do this life without you."

Lola packed up the photographs and locked them away

again, absolutely certain that she would never have to open up that chest again. Daniel sat beside her on the bed, grasping so much more about her, and indisputably convinced that he could not adore her any more than he did at that very moment.

Daniel immediately realized why it was that Lola was so utterly diverse to all the other women he had met before, why she was so significantly resilient and so much more grown-up than other women her age. Daniel valued her for the woman she had turned out to be, and enormously admired her enthusiasm to take her sister in, and unconditionally care for her. Wallowing in self-pity was not an option for Lola. She willed her survival, and she had an urgent need to come out the victor. She was engaged in an on-going battle with Peter Storey, and even though it was never a physical brawl, she had conquered the emotional clash. "What did he do to Lauren?" "Oh no, he never physically hurt Lauren, but she had to witness the abuse and it was hard on her. My father knew that it would break her, and that's what he tried to do. But we stayed strong, and drew strength from one another." Lola smiled sadly. "I was legally emancipated when I turned sixteen and with a little money my aunt left me, I was able to get the apartment and the car. I never actually understood why she did that? I never really knew her. We met only once. Lauren joined me just after she turned sixteen, and well, here we are ..." "Ford and Melanie?" "They remained with my parents. Ford and Melanie were able to stay out of harm's way. I suppose Lauren and I were too different to belong to that family, and perhaps too fair and too blonde." Lola let out a faint giggle. "You are my blonde, and I love you. Dean adores Lauren. This is your life now." Daniel protectively placed his arms around her. "I've always tried to understand why, Daniel? Why Lauren, and why me? I used to look at myself and try and be better for them, but it was never enough. So, if you had to ask me why it happened, I couldn't tell you. I just don't know why? I used to feel that Lauren and I were born by mistake into that family. That we were so different to them. But, I'm done with trying to find the answers, I can't do it. I don't want to do it with them anymore. Lauren and I, we're doing okay and we're happy. I do vaguely remember a time when things were different. I remember bits and pieces. I'm not sure exactly what I remember, but we were happy once. I don't know why it changed? I never knew how to love them anymore. Sometimes, I think I have memories of another time and another life, with other people in it. I know it sounds crazy, but I do remember a time that we were happy. I never, ever felt that I or Lauren belonged there with them."

In Daniel's mind, there could never be an adequate amount of enticement to do what Peter Storey did to Lola. In no way whatsoever, could she do something so horrific that it could rationalize his deeds. It was not her limitations, instead, it was clear that no matter how desperately she attempted to please Peter Storey, it would not at all have been enough.

Daniel and Lola were still caught up in a poignant embrace when they were interrupted by a light thud on their front door. Lola opened up the door to find Dean and Lauren standing there, which forced her to put on a hospitable smile. "Hey sis, what's the matter?" Lauren at once noticed that Lola's eyes were red and swollen, as were Daniel's. "Nothing Lols, how are you guys?" Lola made way for them to enter, before showing them into the living room. "Fine ..." Lauren replied devastatingly susceptible to the fact that Lola was being deceitful. "Anything to drink, anyone?" Daniel tried to pull himself together, but found himself lingering on Lola's words, 'I'm done with trying to find the answers, I can't do it.' It scared him to realize the enormous conflict within her. "Hot chocolate, I'll help!"

Lauren leaped from the sofa to follow Daniel into the kitchen. "Daniel?" She was hard-pressed to get to the bottom of their palpable wretchedness. Without turning around to face her, Daniel responded with hesitation, "Yep?" "What's the matter, what's wrong?" Daniel turned around swiftly, and placed a finger over her mouth in an attempt to keep her composed. "Daniel, what's wrong?" "I know, Lauren. I know about what happened, with your father and Lola." Daniel stepped back when he noticed the unexpected and alarmed expression in her eyes. Lauren's tears were instantly brimming in her eyes. "Please don't cry. I don't want her to know I told you that I know." Lauren hurriedly swabbed at her tears, "I can't believe she told you. She never wanted anyone to know? I can't believe she told you ..." "I'm glad she did, Lauren, and I'm sorry that it happened to her, and to you." Daniel impulsively held her against him. "But please, stop crying, it's over. I will never let anyone hurt her again, I promise, alright? I will love her, and protect her always, and I know Dean will never let anything happen to you."

Daniel reflected again on all that Lola and Lauren had gone through. He overwhelmingly realized that Lauren was hardly as strong as Lola was. He was thankful that Peter Storey in no way physically harmed Lauren, but at the same time, he was utterly beleaguered by the fact that Lola had to endure the entire wrath of her family. His mind wandered to his own parents, and for the first time in what felt like an eternity, he was deeply grateful that John and Sarah Salvatore were his parents. He was sorry that Lola never had the privilege or pleasure to experience the joys and commitment of a loving family.

When Daniel and Lauren reemerged from the kitchen carrying in the hot chocolate, Lauren was the first to noticed the ring on Lola's finger. "Lola? Is that an engagement ring?" Lola at once glanced down at the ring on her finger, before smiling broadly. With an enormous grin on her face, she turned back to Lauren.

Daniel was relieved by the infinite elation in Lola's eyes, followed by an enthusiastic endorsement on Lauren's face. "Yes ..." Lola whispered bashfully. "Bro, you bugger you. You never said anything!" Dean bolted to his feet, and animatedly embraced his brother. "Oh wow! Oh, that's great! The car, the ring ... you are spoilt, sis!" Lauren excitedly cuddled her sister. "When is the big day?" "We haven't talked about it. We haven't gotten that far yet. It all happened only just this minute." Daniel winked at Lola, "But, hopefully soon ..." "So, talking about weddings, have you heard about Tanita?" Daniel hesitantly shook his head while Lola glared inquisitively at Lauren. "She's pregnant! On purpose and with Tony Mueller's baby!" Lauren was hardly able to restrain her exhilaration. "Really?" "Yeah, Tony reckons she did it to trap him, especially after Daniel left her." Dean chipped in at once. "Oh man, bro, that's a bugger, poor guy!" Daniel chuckled before he shook his head. "That is so typical Tanita!" Lola smirked uneasily while hoping and praying that they would never, ever find themselves in a position such as that.

While lifting the hot chocolate to her lips, she unexpectedly felt nauseated again. Daniel watched her grow pale for the second time that day, and became concerned one more time. "Babes, I'm going to make an appointment with the doc for Monday. If it's the stomach flu, you better get something before it gets worse." Lola smiled at him, and turned her attention back to Dean and Lauren. Lola thought about Tanita, and was sad that it had happened to her. She knew that Tanita was distraught after Daniel left her, but the impact of Lola's betrayal was almost unbearable for her.

Alice VL

IN THE BLINK OF AN EYE

"Good morning, Dr. Stalting, how are you?" Lola greeted her medical practitioner before she made her way to an empty seat directly across from her. "Good thanks, you're looking a little worn today?" "I'm not sure, but I know there's a tummy bug doing the rounds although, I do feel a lot better today. It was Daniel's insistence that brought me here." "How is that fetching man of yours? Is that an engagement ring?" Dr. Stalting grabbed Lola's hand to admire her new engagement ring. "Yes, we got engaged on Saturday." Dr. Stalting congratulated her before she released her hand to focus her attention back to Lola, "Let's see, it could be the stomach flu. I've had a dozen cases in the last two days, but you seem a little anemic too. I'd like to take some blood samples, nothing too drastic." Dr. Stalting signaled for her assistant, "Two tubes, please Annie." She turned back to face Lola, "I'll call you, say, tomorrow if anything's wrong. In the meantime, take one of these three times a day, and if you don't feel better by Friday, you come straight back." Annie summarily took a sample of Lola's blood, leaving Lola relieved to find the whole procedure swift and painless.

When she returned to Salvatore, Lola found Daniel restless in anticipation of her return. "Hey Danny-boy ..." She placed her arms around him. "Hey, everything alright? What did the doctor say?" "Yes, everything's fine. I've got to take these, and you know how I feel about medication." "So, it's the flu?" "Yep, just the flu, and I'm feeling better already." "I've got breakfast in my office." Daniel was not quite convinced when he again noticed how ashen she was. "I'll be there in a minute. I just have to lock that cash in the safe." She noticed a heap of bank notes on her desk. "Oh yes, that was Frankie, he took his car this morning." When Daniel entered his office, the front doors to Salvatore unexpectedly swung open. Donovan Moodley, a regular client of Salvatore made his away over to the counter. "Hi, Mr. Moodley, can I help you?" Lola smiled broadly at the client she had come to know over the past few months. "Yeah, just bringing in my deposit." "Okay, let me just pull out your job card." She knelt down to open her job card drawer, and urgently flipped through the job cards to find his. "So, you married?" She heard Donovan's voice directly behind her. "Engaged." Lola was instantly aware of Daniel's voice which unnerved her almost right away. When she turned around, she noticed that Donovan Moodley had walked around the counter, and had almost pressed against her which instantly alarmed her. Daniel grabbed Donovan Moodley and hauled him up against the wall. "Engaged to me, and don't ever let me catch you looking at her like that again, understand?" "Sorry, I'm so sorry. I didn't know." Lola was immensely anxious when they both stood staring at her in an uncomfortable silence. Lola fumbled nervously for a receipt.

After hurriedly handing him a receipt for his deposit, Lola locked the front doors, and followed Daniel into his office. "Your favorite, scones and cream cheese." He smiled before handing her a scone. When Lola brought the scone to her mouth, she was once again familiar with the twinge of nausea that had showed up unexpectedly. She jumped to her feet, and frantically sprinted down the passage and into the restroom, afraid that she might not reach it in time. Daniel followed her closely, and when he saw her heave in the basin, he was convinced that she was still under the weather. He took her hair into his hands, and gently stroked her back while fervently hoping that she would recover soon. "Sorry Daniel, I guess I'm still a little queasy. Let me just wash my face and brush my teeth, and I'll meet you back in your office." Daniel watched her closely, and could not shrug off the panicky feeling that had started to build up inside of him. She looked severely pallid and exhausted. He had not once known Lola to be ill. He hoped once again that it would blow over, and that she would return to her usual self soon. "We have an appointment with Mr. H this afternoon, just some documents we need to get out the way." Daniel mentioned matter-of-factly when Lola re-entered his office. "We?" Lola was at once taken aback. "Yeah, just a few things. We can leave at about two, is that okay?" "Sure ..." Mr. H was the Salvatore attorney, and had been working with them for many years. It almost at once made sense to her that Daniel had drawn up a prenuptial agreement. It came as no surprise to Lola who had been expecting it, although she had no hesitation whatsoever to agree to the terms and conditions regarding Daniel's wealth.

When they arrived at Hart and Son Incorporated, Mr. H was eagerly awaiting them. Daniel led Lola into his office and firmly shut the door behind them. "Daniel Salvatore, good to see you again. And this is Lola?" He extended an open hand to her. "My beautiful fiancé, Lola Storey." "My pleasure, ma'am." Mr. H showed Daniel and Lola to empty seats across from him, "Alright Daniel, as requested, all the documents are drawn up. As per your request, 50% of Salvatore will be registered in Miss Storey's name. You will retain the remaining 50%, even though I'd feel much better if you kept the majority shares, but, it's your choice.

Dean will be entitled to complete ownership of 'Double D' which will give him full control over designs and ..." Mr. H carried on explaining the formalities of the business and ownership without pausing to take a breath. Lola was no longer listening. She was certain that they were there to agree on a prenuptial indenture but, as it turns out, Daniel was handing her half of Salvatore. "Daniel wait!" She frantically grabbed a hold of his hand. Daniel smiled and winked at her before he turned back to Mr. H. "Daniel, please, this is yours, your company, your everything. I don't, I don't want this!" Daniel turned to face her and firmly squeezed her hand, "Do you love me?" "Yes, more than anything, but you can't ..." "I will never leave you, Lola, and I hope you will never leave me. I want to share everything with you. Not just me, but my life too. This is how I do it. This is my promise to you."

Lola glared at him, unable to find the words to object to his proposal before she glanced at Mr. H. The world around her began spinning, and she suddenly felt as though she was falling just before the entire world went dark in front of her. She groggily opened her eyes to find Daniel kneeling over her. "Hey, welcome back, you scared me?" "What happened?" "I think you fainted, are you feeling okay?" "I'm fine, just too much excitement, I think?" She teased while letting out a faint chuckle. "You've got papers to sign ..." "Daniel ..." She protested once more before he placed a pen into her hand, and gently kissed her. Lola reluctantly signed the forms, scarily aware that he was signing an enormous portion of his life over to her, and that she too, was responsible for Salvatore, partly responsible for Daniel's dream.

Daniel reached the workshop early the following morning, eager to complete Donovan Moodley's car before the end of the week. Lola had a few errands to run, and told Daniel that she would be at Salvatore no more than an hour after him. While Daniel was drawing up a set of schematics for his new project, the ringing of the landline interrupted him. As though irritated by the disturbance, he abruptly answered. The soft-spoken voice was unfamiliar, yet harsh and proficient. "Good day, Lola Storey, please?" "She's not in at the moment, is there a message?" "This is Dr. Stalting, please could you get Ms. Storey to call me urgently. It is very important that she stop …" Daniel interrupted her while hurriedly scribbling down her name. "Dr. Stalting, right? She must stop what immediately?" "The antibiotics, she must stop taking them immediately." "The antibiotics? Why?" "Her blood work came back today." She began to explain before Daniel interrupted her once more. "You got the results of her blood work? Anything wrong?" Daniel was at once responsive to the trouncing of his heart, as all sorts of scenarios began playing out in his mind. "I can't say. Pregnancy test results are confidential." "I'm her fiancée, why can't you tell me? The results of her what test? Her pregnancy test?" Daniel was utterly astounded. "Yes, I know that you're her fiancé and yes, her pregnancy test." "Well, what are the results? Is she pregnant?" "Like I just said, I can only discuss this with Ms. Storey. Please get her to call me as soon as she gets in." "Alright …" Daniel stood holding the phone in his hand, entirely stunned by Dr. Stalting's evasiveness. While dialing Lola on her mobile phone, he tried to remain composed, and was enormously thankful that he had reached her voicemail instead. "Lola, Dr. Stalting called. She wants you to stop the antibiotics straight away. You can call her when you get here. I love you."

Daniel hung up immediately, panicky that she might pick up on the shudder in his voice. He sat back in his chair, and nervously fidgeted with his hands while assessing his conversation with Dr. Stalting. "Pregnancy test? Why would she have a pregnancy test?"

Daniel was startled to notice her walk in, and place her bag behind the counter, before she hurriedly made her way to his office. "Hey Danny, did Dr. Stalting say why I should stop the antibiotics?" "No, just that you should call her?" He got up from his seat and hesitantly kissed her. "Okay, I'll go call her then." "The number is on your desk." Lola found the note that Daniel had left for her, and anxiously dialed Dr. Stalting's number. She turned to check whether Daniel was still in his office, oblivious to the fact that he was watching her from a distance. "Lola Storey for Dr. Stalting, please …" Daniel was aware of the sudden trepidation that was evident on her face. "Stalting." "Hi doc, it's Lola Storey. You left a message for me to call you?" "Good morning Lola. Yes, I just wanted to discuss the results of your pregnancy test." "What? You did a pregnancy test?" She turned around quickly to ensure that Daniel could not hear her. "Yes, it's standard practice to rule out pregnancy. The good news is you are not ill, but you are pregnant, congratulations!" Lola sat down as though in a wandering haze, and rested her head in her hand. Daniel, who was watching her closely, instinctively knew what that had meant, and abruptly felt a nauseating panic grab a hold of his entire being. "Dr. Stalting, it can't be, really. I know a lot of women say this, but, it has to be a mistake." Lola made a brave effort to persuade Dr. Stalting that the test results had to be a mix-up. Dr. Stalting had the results of her blood tests in her hands, and she assured Lola that there was no mistake. Lola's tears began to brim in her eyes when Dr. Stalting explained regular check-ups and sonogram appointments for the future, but Lola was no longer listening. She was instantly reminded of Daniel's words when Lauren and Dean told him about Tanita.

When Lola ended her call with Dr. Stalting, she was unexpectedly terrified of having a baby. She was horrified by how Daniel might react, but more than anything else, she was terrified that he would walk out on her. Lola got up from her chair, careful that she in no way at all, raise suspicion which was likely, had she lingered for only a moment longer. She was in no doubt that Dr. Stalting would call her in a day or two, and inform her that they had made a mistake, perhaps muddled her results with another, and maybe they would both giggle about it. Lola was convinced that there was no point in upsetting Daniel until she was certain there was no slip-up.   "Is everything alright?" Daniel looked tensely at Lola when she walked into his office, aware of the sudden anxiety and fear on her face. "Yes, just fine Daniel. I'm just a little anemic, no biggie …" She avoided his suspecting eyes. "So, why do you have to stop the antibiotics?" Lola was terrified of Daniel's sudden curiosity. "I think, well, I don't know? I didn't ask."

He was convinced that she was lying to him. For the very first time, Lola was being dishonest, and it almost shattered his heart. His mind had convinced him that she was in dire need of processing the unexpected news. He was confident that she would tell him when the time was right for her. He kissed her gently, "I love you, Lola, always and no matter what." Lola felt as though someone had taken her lungs into their hands, and began squeezing them with all their might. "Daniel, I love you. I love you so much, and …" Daniel knew what she was going to say, and interrupted her before she could go any further. "You will never lose me, no matter what." She smiled wretchedly before she turned away from him, knowing in her heart that she could not tell Daniel about the baby, the one that Dr. Stalting would call her about in a few days, and tell her that the results were accidentally switched. Lola understood all of a sudden that she was running out of alternatives, and that there was only one thing left for her to do, just out of fear that the results were in fact, her own. "I'm just going to do the last of the filing ..." She did not look back when she walked out of Daniel's office.

He could barely stop thinking about it. If only he knew for sure, if she would just say something. If he could just hear her say it. But she never said a word, and he unpredictably became severely anxious by the abrupt detachment that was emerging between them.

Lola sat numbly, as though frozen and stunned. She kept replaying Daniel's opinion of Tanita's pregnancy over and over again. She knew that she could under no circumstances, break the news of their unplanned baby to him, but more than that, Lola was certain that she could not lose him due to a mistake she had made, although she had no idea how she slipped up so terribly.

She watched Daniel make his way to the workshop, and hurriedly found the number for St. Darla's, the only legal abortion clinic, a short drive out of town. She nervously dialed the number while her heart was pounding rapidly. "St. Darla's." "Hi, I, when can I ..." "Are you expecting, miss?" "Yes ..." Lola replied almost inaudibly. "Well, how far along are you?" "Seven, uhm, seven weeks, I think?" Lola hurriedly guessed how far along she was.

"And you want an appointment? For a termination? You want an appointment?" "Yes ..." "Okey dokey, tomorrow morning, can you be here at eight?" "Yes, that's fine, thank you." "No eating or drinking tonight. Your details please?" "Uhm, it's Lola, Lola Storey." She was conscious of the unanticipated tears that had begun to roll unreservedly down her cheeks. Lola ended the call after swiftly giving her a run-down of her medical history and personal details. She speedily swabbed away at her tears, and hurriedly wrote down the name of the clinic with the directions in her diary.

Daniel slid in under Donovan Moodley's car and lay stationary while staring straight ahead of him. His mind kept drifting back to Lola. It in no way mattered to Daniel what was happening in their lives, he loved her, and was confident that he intended to spend the rest of his life with her. "Daniel, I'm going to go home, do you mind?" She was powerless to look him in the eye, and her voice began to quiver again. Daniel slid out, and walked over to where she was standing. He gazed at her, and was once again sentient to the trepidation and apprehension in her eyes. "Sure, do you want to do anything tonight" "I'm tired. Maybe we could just go to bed early. Is that okay?" A terrifying and unsolicited thought crept into her mind that it might be one of their last night's together. Lola was absolutely convinced that Daniel would abandon her if he found out she was pregnant, and he would certainly in no way at all, pardon her for what she was about to do.

She knew that no matter which choice she made, it would indisputably tear Daniel away from her. All that was good between them had changed in the blink of an eye, but for the moment, Lola prayed that he would not find out about the baby, or the planned abortion. She hoped that it would be only a dreadful memory in the not too distant future. She was horrified by how effortless it was to reach the decision to slay her child. Her heart nudged her to keep their baby, but her mind convinced her that she could not. She knew that she should be confident with the idea that having their baby would keep them together for all eternity, instead, Lola was certain that it would rip them apart. "Oh crap, Dean and Lauren are coming over, should I cancel with them?" Daniel suddenly remembered that they had invited Lauren and Dean over later that evening. "No-no, not at all. Are we going to have Chinese?" "I'll pick some up on my way. Love you, Lola." Daniel pressed Lola firmly against him. She held onto him, fervently wishing that he would never let her go.

Daniel wanted to spend the night alone with her. He hoped that they could find a way to talk about their circumstances. He was frantic for her to tell him, but at the same time, he was pleased that Dean and Lauren would be a welcomed distraction for her.

Alice VL

Daniel had taken a quick shower while Lola set out the Chinese food in anticipation of Lauren and Dean's visit. She was enthusiastically aware that she was not allowed to eat any of it, or anything else that night.

Lola hurriedly walked into their bedroom, and was at once caught off-guard. She had to catch her breath when she saw Daniel, who had just climbed out of the shower. He was no doubt the most beautiful man she had ever seen. Her heart reminded her of that fact each time he walked into a room. She walked over to where he was standing with only a towel wrapped around his waist. Lola placed her arms around him, and smiled devotedly at him, "Daniel Salvatore, I love, love you. How did I get so lucky with you?" She whispered hoarsely as her tears began to shimmer in her eyes. Daniel stood in silence while gazing at her.

He was agonizingly aware of the sorrow in her eyes. He so desperately wanted to tell her that he knew about the test, that he instinctively knew what was happening to them, but Daniel was certain that Lola would confide in him the very moment she was able to process the information. "What's the matter, Lola? I love you too babes, don't you ever doubt that. No matter what happens, nothing Lola, nothing can change the way I feel about you. You're my lid. Don't you ever forget that. You can talk to me about anything, don't forget that, ever." "Nothing, it's just, what if I disappoint you somehow? What if something happens? What if it's so bad that it comes between us? What if there are things that can change us?" "Lola, you can never disappoint me. I love you. That alone will get us through anything. Nothing can change us or what we have. This. Have a little faith Lola, have a little faith in me."

When she heard a faint knock on their front door, Lola smiled and kissed him gently, "Dean and Lauren are here, shall we go?" Daniel hoped that he had convinced her of his loyalty to her. "I am just going to get dressed." Daniel was instantly downcast that Lola missed the opportunity to tell him about the baby.

"Hey guys, I hope you're hungry …" Daniel smiled when he casually strolled into the dining room. "Dean, will you get the wine?" "Uhm, not for me, Danny. I'll just have some juice. Still queasy, but only a drop, please." "Sure …" When Daniel got up to pour Lola juice, he was at once convinced that Lola was pregnant. "So, Lola, are you feeling any better? You're still very pale?" Lauren was notably concerned about her sister. "Much better, just a little anemic, but otherwise fine. Thanks for asking, Lols. I am just waiting for the vitamins to kick in." Dean at once turned to Daniel, "So, Daniel, have you heard the latest about Tanita. Oh, sorry Lola, I wasn't thinking …" Dean was instantly apologetic. "Don't be Dean, I don't mind talking about Tanita. How is she?" "She's getting married. They decided to give it a try, and it's great. It's not the baby's fault though, and Tony is a good guy." Daniel did not agree. "Yeah, but she shouldn't have done it on purpose, that just isn't right. You can't force love, or marriage." Daniel glanced over at Lola. "Don't you agree, Lola?" "Well, I agree, she shouldn't have done it on purpose but, maybe it wasn't on purpose, Daniel? Has anyone bothered to ask Tanita?" Daniel frowned, "Even so, she should've been more careful." He was adamant that Tanita slipped up. "They Daniel, they should have been more careful. And you know, sometimes it doesn't matter how careful you are, these things just have a way of happening, and then, what do you do?" "Accidentally on purpose! Come on Lola, how long have we been together? How long have Lauren and Dean been together? These things don't happen by accident, or ... do they?" Lola at once understood Daniel's apprehension, and that he would blame her for the rest of their lives, should he discover her pregnancy. "You're right, Daniel. There are no accidents. These things never happened by accident. Or at least, it shouldn't." Lola was unexpectedly overwhelmed by a confining lump in her throat throughout their entire meal. "Please eat something, babes ..." "Later Daniel, I'm not hungry right now, besides, I had something to eat earlier on." Lola lied to Daniel once again.

After Dean and Lauren left their apartment, Daniel helped Lola tidy up before she climbed into a warm bath. As was custom, Daniel regularly sat beside her where they both discussed the events of the day that had passed. He was hoping and praying that their moment alone would somehow encourage her to say something, anything to tell him that they were having a baby. "Daniel, I have a few things to do in the morning, and will probably only be in, in the afternoon, will that be okay with you?" "Sure, anything I can help with?" "No, just this and that, you know?" Daniel felt fear grab a hold of his entire being. "Are you really okay, Lola? Is there anything you want to talk about? Is there something on your mind? You look stressed and anxious." "I, Daniel, do you really believe things like that shouldn't happen, I mean, like with Tanita?" She was desperate to find a sign, an opening to tell her that he would be okay with having a baby. "I just think that, I know Tanita so well, and I know how she is. If it was us, it would be different." Lola felt a glimmer of hope inside of her. "What do you mean by different?" "We're together. We love each other, we're engaged and, we're living together. It's different. We're already starting a life together." "But they, they're in love. And Daniel …" She couldn't bring herself to utter another word. "Never mind, let me get out the bath, the water's getting cold." "Alright …" Daniel got up, and made his way into their bedroom. When Lola reached their bed, Daniel was waiting for her. She climbed in beside him, and turned to face him. He kissed her gently at first, before he kissed her a little more fervently. She felt him passionately against her when her body began to shiver at his touch. "Daniel, I love you so much." "And I, I love you so much more, Lola." Lola held on to him. Daniel was certain that he saw her tears escape from the corner of her eyes. He held her in his arms, and wondered for a moment whether he should tell her that he knew. For just a second, Daniel wanted to hold Lola, and tell her that they would be just fine and that they would get through this. It would all work out exactly as it should.

Instead, he gently kissed her after she had fallen asleep. He laid quietly beside her, staring at her long afterwards. He knew Lola well, and he was convinced that she needed a fraction more time to contemplate their unexpected situation. Daniel knew that Lola wasn't impulsive, and that she was probably coming up with a plan to break the news to him. He was sure that it would only be a matter of days before she would discuss her condition with him, yet, he could not block out the fear and anxiety he noticed in her eyes earlier. It frightened him to realize that the very idea of having an unplanned baby, terrified her.

They had been asleep for what felt like only minutes when Lola's mobile phone rang, abruptly waking Daniel. Daniel leaped out of bed to take the call before the ringing phone woke Lola. "Hello?" He was confused and wondered who would be calling at such an hour. "Hello, Lola Storey please." "Who? Lola?"

"Yes, can I speak to her?" "This is her fiancée, she's asleep. It's four in the morning, can I help you?" Lola was awoken by Daniel's voice after his feeble attempt at whispering failed miserably. "Who is it?" She groggily whispered before sitting straight up in bed. Daniel shrugged his shoulders, and turned back to the call. "Could you tell her to contact Mrs. Myburgh from Social Services. She has my number. It's about her father, Peter Storey. He was killed in a car crash last night, and the funeral is tomorrow. The family want him buried within 48 hours. Lola should attend, she will know what I mean." Mrs. Myburgh was careful not to divulge too much information. "Please give her the message, and if she is unclear about anything, she can call me. Sorry to have woken you." "Yes, I see, alright then ..." Was all Lola could hear Daniel say before ending the call. While he anxiously made his way over to her side of the bed, Daniel was in no way prepared for the phone call, and had no way of knowing how to approach her with the news. Daniel took her hand into his, before he lowered his head.

"What's the matter? Who was that?" Lola felt a sudden rush of anxiety flow through her entire body, positive that Daniel was struggling to find the words to tell her something that must be awful. "That was a Mrs. Myburgh from Social Services ..." Lola was at once wide awake and alarmed at hearing her name. "What did she want?" "Peter Storey, your dad, was killed in a car crash last night ..." Lola stared at him in stunned silence before she closed her eyes.

Daniel held her in his arms, unsure of how Lola was feeling, but aware of an inexplicable need to hold her close to him. "The funeral is tomorrow Lola, and Mrs. Myburgh thought you should go. She said you would know why?" Lola turned away from him before she pulled the bedcovers up to her shoulders. Daniel noticed that she had begun to shudder, and held her close to him once more. "For closure, I think. I'm okay, Daniel, really. Just cold." Daniel was astounded that he could find no traces of melancholy in her voice. He was once again reminded of her father's cruelty towards her.

Unable to return to sleep, they both remained awake and alert for most of what was left of the night, without saying much of anything to one another. Lola felt an enormous amount of culpability when she thought back to the many nights she prayed for his demise, when she was only a little girl. Even though the guilt was overpowering, she still could not explicate or understand the sentiment of relief that had entered into her core.

For Daniel, it too was a sense of reprieve that had entered into his mind. He was finally reassured that Peter Storey no longer left his footprint on this earth. There was an urgent need that Peter pay dearly for what he had done to Lola and Lauren, and he was delighted that it was now all in God's hands. "Daniel?" He turned to face her. "I don't feel sad. I don't feel anything?" Daniel took her hand into his one more time, and gently squeezed it. "I used to dream about this happening to him. At one point, I wanted this. I prayed for this for so many nights." She hastily dabbed at a lost tear that had rolled down her cheek. "It's alright, Lola, no-one can blame you."

They were out of bed an hour later when Lola decided to call Lauren and ask her and Dean to come over. After spending the morning conversing with Lauren about Peter Storey, and discussing their expected attendance at the funeral, Lola had no doubt in her mind that she would attend his final service. Even though she was persuaded that it was in all probability for the best that she did not show up, she told Daniel that she had fragmentary concerns with the Storeys.

The night before, Daniel was determined to discuss Lola's pregnancy the very next morning, but decided against it when he noticed the strain and tension on her face subsequent to the news of Peter Storey. The protective side of him had an unfathomable need to implore Lola to stay, but moreover, he knew that it was essential for Lola to deal with her family in her own way. Daniel immediately made all the travel arrangements while Lola, Lauren and Dean were gathered around the dining room table. "So, Lauren, do you want to go?" Dean asked nervously when he took Lauren's hands into his. "Yes. I want to be with Lola. I don't want Lola to go on her own." "Then we'll all go." Daniel interrupted after hanging up the phone. "We leave early tomorrow morning and should be there on time. I managed to get all the information from Mrs. Myburgh when she called back earlier." Daniel took his place next to Lola. She squeezed his hand, before she turned back to Lauren, "I don't know, Lauren? I don't think you should be there. You know what they do, you know what they're like?" Lauren was adamant, "I'm not letting you go without me, Lola."

Daniel handed Lola a cup of coffee before she once again, felt sick to her stomach. She sat quietly when she realized that if she stirred just a little, she would be ill. Daniel watched her growing paler, and was certain that the trauma of returning to the Storeys, along with her pregnancy were taking its toll on her. He wanted to hold her close and tell her that he knew about it all, but he could not bring himself so far as to say the words.

Alice VL

Lola's Secret

Alice VL

A MISTAKE

Almost inconspicuously, they entered the St. Bernard's Chapel in Dawn Hills just before ten on the morning of her father's memorial service. Daniel clasped Lola's hand firmly when he opened the car's door for her, "Are you sure you want to do this?" She nodded cautiously before she turned to Lauren, "You alright, Lols?" "I'm fine ..." Lola turned to Daniel and squeezed his hand gently, "I, I'm all right Daniel. We need to talk after the funeral. I have to tell you something, so we really have to find time to talk later. I wish I had spoken to you sooner, but later okay?" Lola smiled sorrowfully before she turned to the Church. Daniel knew intuitively that she had every intention of discussing the baby with him.

As they silently made their way down the aisle, Lola at once spotted Ford and Melanie who glared back at them in disbelief. In the row ahead of them, Lola saw Sally. She was instantly aware of a hollowness at the innermost part of her belly. Daniel held her hand tighter before he showed her to an empty seat. While glancing around nervously, Lola and Lauren noticed aunts, uncles, cousins, nieces, nephews and friends, all quietly sobbing while wiping away one another's devastating tears. There was not a dry eye in that Church that morning, and for just a second, Lola questioned whether she had perhaps, imagined all the abuse, or whether it truly was as awful as she deemed it to be.

The Priest hurriedly made his way to the altar, and after a short introduction, he gracefully thanked the mourners for attending the service for Peter Storey, a remarkable man. He continued to pay tribute to the life of a man Lola loathed, a man she feared more than anyone else, and a man she had run away from. The preacher told stories of how readily her father would assist in the community, and how greatly he was esteemed by each and all in Dawn Hills. He told of the extraordinary family Peter Storey had left behind, and subtly implied how two sinister rebels had strayed from them, and the community. Finally, he summoned a devastated Sally Storey to the altar.

When she stood up in all her splendor and magnificence, Lola could vividly remember an era when she strived in all earnest to be unerringly the woman her mother was. Sally Storey was marvelously tall, physically strong and absolutely beautiful. Lola wished on so many stars that her hair would turn as black as her mother's, and that her eyes would become as dark as her father's. As a little girl, she believed that she might wake up one morning, and resemble Melanie and Ford a little more, but to her utter disappointment, it never happened. Not for her and not for Lauren.

Shortly after she reached the altar, Sally promptly thanked the mourners for paying their respects to a man she dearly treasured. She spoke of her soul mate, the man she had married, and the man she prized. She spoke of his flawless heart and supple demeanor. Sally told tales dating back to when they were teenagers, but Lola could scarcely imagine any of her accounts. Lauren nudged her a number of times. Lola understood and acknowledged what her sister was attempting to express, that nothing she was saying about their father had any legitimacy.

Lola was distressed at once when she, without warning, heard her name being called out. "Finally, I would like to ask our daughter, Lola, to say a few words." Sally pointed her out to the congregation before she returned to her seat.

Daniel turned to Lola, "Don't do this ..." He whispered nervously in her ear. Each and every person in the Church had turned to glare at Lola. Lauren grabbed a hold of her arm. "Don't sis, you know what she is trying to do ..." Lola's mind was racing in terror when she thought back to her years as a child in Sally's home. She was excruciatingly aware of the reality that Sally was placing her in an uncomfortable position, and she surreptitiously hoped that Lola would fracture under the immense pressure.

Every person attending the service for Peter Storey was conscious to that, that Lola had accused him of, but they were convinced she had lied. She reluctantly began to rise to her feet, before she turned to face Daniel, "I'll be fine. This is what they do Daniel. I have to stand up, for me, and for Lauren. I have to do this." Lola nervously made her way down the aisle. When she passed her mother, who had returned to her seat, Lola was aware that her heart had begun to pound irrationally, and that her hands had begun to shudder frenziedly. Sally glared at Lola with unmistakable abhorrence. Lola was certain that she could feel it infiltrate her skin. She glanced over at Lauren who was staring questioningly at her. She was determined to be her sister's voice, and when she looked over at Daniel, she was no longer fearful.

She peered over at the man that was lying immobile in his coffin, and she felt her lower lip unpredictably quiver. She became unexpectedly poignant, distressed and sad for the man that gave her life. Lola was heartbroken that their lives had turned out the way it had, yet, she grew increasingly irate. She was exasperated by Peter Storey for wounding and damaging her. Angry that he never shielded or sheltered her, and annoyed that he had not once held her close to him. She was livid that they never guarded her, or kept her out of harm's way. She was bruised due to the fact that they took away her right of enjoying loving and caring parents.

Daniel watched her closely, and sensed at once what she was feeling. He detested the fact that she was standing at the altar in full view of the entire congregation while being mercilessly judged by all, but he knew he had to allow her to find the closure she so desperately needed after searching for it for almost her entire existence.

"I …" She whispered hoarsely after her initial hesitation and reluctance. "I, I look around and see so many familiar faces. Aunts, uncles, cousins, friends and family, and I listen to some of you bringing testament to my father's life. What a wonderful husband he was, what a doting father he was, what a great and generous heart he had …" She paused to look around at each and every face looking sternly back at her. "I look at him, and I realize that none of you really knew him. I loathed him. Peter Storey was a cruel and heartless man, and I am glad he's dead. I have waited to see him lifeless for most of my life." She paused once more when she was capped by the tremble in her voice. Her tears were shimmering in her eyes, and about to escape.

One and all became silent while Sally was shooting imaginary daggers at Lola. She turned away and bowed her head, gasping for breath before she gazed back over the congregation. "Why did you come today?" She recognized Melanie's familiar voice from below. Lola stared at her, and even though she felt downhearted for the loss of her brother and remaining sister, Lola was standing up to them for the very first time in her life. She cleared her throat before she started again, "I am here, only to see that the man lying in that coffin, is Peter Storey. I am here, to see his coffin closed and lowered into the ground. I am here, because for the very first time in my life, I am free. Free of him, free of my mother, and free of you all. I am here, because at this very moment, Peter Storey has to account for what he has done. He has sins to answer for. At this very moment, God is confronting him and that is, why I am here." She looked up suddenly to find Daniel standing right beside her. He could no longer bare her facing the congregation on her own, and decided that they had to leave. "Come …" He took Lola's hand before he led her away from the altar.

While they walked down the aisle on their way out, Lola heard mumbling and fussing, but she no longer cared, and was no longer intimated by them. She turned to Lauren who had been sobbing, and took her sister's hand into hers. Dean followed brusquely behind them, and when they all had left the Church, Lola turned and embraced her sister. "Oh, wow Lola, did you see mom's face?" Lauren sniggered through her tears. Lola smiled and turned back to Daniel. She wanted to bellow out, 'I did it! I did it!' but she remained silent, smiling forlornly at him.

Daniel was aware of the relief that reflected in her eyes, and he realized once again that Lola was the victor in one more encounter with the Storeys. Daniel gently kissed her and smiled proudly at her. He felt colossal satisfaction for Lola at that very moment, and understood for the first time how it was that she survived the Storeys.

They had just reached the car when they heard unanticipated rumbling and shuffling behind them. When Lola turned around, she noticed Sally, Ford and Melanie directly behind them, which unnerved her for an instant. "You!" Sally shouted out to her when Daniel stood directly in front of Lola, desperately afraid that Sally Storey would physically harm her. "Mrs. Storey, please …" Lola emerged from behind him before she interrupted him, "It's alright, Daniel …" "You are a disgrace to the Storey name! Who are you to come here and accuse dad of being cruel?" Ford carried on hollering where his mother had left off. Melanie moved forward, and looked Lola sternly in the eye, "When are you going to tell the truth Lola? Dad never laid a hand on you!" Lauren became irate before she burst into tears once again, "She is telling the truth! He raped her and beat her over and over again, and none of you did anything! I watched him do it to her over and over again. Mother! You knew, and you let him hurt her! You had to know! I know you knew!" Lola signaled to Dean to walk Lauren to the car before she calmly turned to face Sally, Ford and Melanie. "Ford, I turned to you so many times. You were my brother, the eldest, but you never believed me. Melanie and mother, you say what you like, but I never lied. You all knew and you did nothing, and as of this moment, you are all dead to me, just like dad is dead. You are nothing to me anymore." She turned back to Daniel, quickly swabbing the tears from her eyes, "Let's go." He opened up the door for her to climb in. Before making his way around to the driver's seat, Daniel turned to Sally Storey, "Stay away from Lola, and stay away from Lauren! I am not asking …"

' They had been driving for only a few minutes when Lola erupted into tears, sobbing into her hands. Daniel left her to cry. He understood that her tears were long overdue and far behind schedule. Sporadically, he stroked her back without saying a word about Sally or Peter Storey. When Lola suddenly and unexpectedly clutched at her belly, Daniel instinctively knew that something was wrong with Lola. He abruptly pulled off to the side of the road and ran around the car, forcing her door open in terror. "Lola?" "Daniel, oh God it's sore. I can't breathe!" Daniel ran around back to the driver's seat, and climbed back in. When he pulled away, he took out his mobile phone and speedily dialed for the closest hospital. Lauren had placed a protective hand on Lola's shoulder when she began howling in pain. While Daniel made his way to the recommended hospital, Lola was horrified by what was happening to her. She prayed for the pain to impede. She was agonizingly aware of the severity of the excruciating pain, and gasped for air often while gripping at her belly.

Daniel pulled into the emergency entrance of the hospital, and swiftly carried Lola out of the car. He looked down at her dress, and was horrified to notice that she was bleeding. Fear seized a hold over Daniel's heart as he rushed inside with her in his arms. "Help! Please!" Two orderlies noticed his distress, and immediately took Lola from him, before they rushed her into the emergency room. Daniel swiftly followed them, while Dean and Lauren stood quietly, fanatically attempting to identify with what was happening to Lola. An on-call doctor had been found almost straight away, and assisted Lola. "Daniel, there's something I have to tell you. I'm pregnant. I'm so sorry." "I know, Lola." He squeezed her hand, exceedingly thankful that the doctor had arrived almost at once. "What's the matter?" He turned to face Daniel. "I, I don't know. Her stomach. I think, I'm not sure, but she's pregnant." "Wait outside, please." "No, I …" The doctor was at once concerned, given Lola's circumstances. "Outside!" Daniel reluctantly turned to leave. He was devastatingly aware of an enormous fear that had made its way into his entire body. Lola fearfully took a hold of the doctor's hand, "I'm pregnant, seven weeks."

After a short examination and a quick ultra sound, the doctor turned back to Lola. "I'm sorry ma'am, there is nothing I can do. The baby is gone. I'm sorry …" He placed his hand on hers before he gently inserted an IV into her arm. Although the pain in her belly had begun to subside, the pain in her heart was mounting. "I want to keep you overnight just to make sure that no infection sets in. Do you want me to get your husband?" "No, please, not yet." Lola had no clue of what she would say to Daniel, or how she would explain herself. The doctor turned to the nurses who were attending to Lola, "Clean her up and move her into Ward D. I'll check in on her later."

When Dr. Mahoney found Daniel, the worry and strain was evident on Daniel's face. Daniel, Dean and Lauren bolted from their seats and speedily approached him. He at once noticed the questions in Daniel's eyes and knew that there was no straightforward way to say what he was about to tell Daniel. "Your wife is going to be fine, but we lost the baby. I'm so sorry." He placed a comforting hand on Daniel's shoulder. Dean and Lauren stood as though frozen in time, glaring at one another in astonishment. "She's being moved into Ward D. Give her a few minutes before you go in. I want to keep her overnight, but she should be discharged in the morning if no infection sets in."

Daniel made an incredible effort to gulp back on the lump in his gullet, but when Dean placed his arms around his brother, he began to sob uncontrollably. "Bro, we didn't know?" "She didn't know I knew ..." He carried on telling Dean and Lauren to find a hotel close by to stay in for the night. Dean hesitated at first, but was intensely attentive to the fact that his brother needed crucial time alone with Lola. While he watched them leave, Daniel despondently sat down on an empty seat in the waiting room. "If only we didn't come here. Peter Storey just keeps taking from her!" Daniel closed his eyes as the tears continued to roll down his cheeks, and he wondered how he was supposed to put Lola back together again.

When he walked into Ward D, Daniel noticed that Lola was the only patient in the ward. She was weeping softly, and when he placed his hand on her shoulder, she became restless at once. Lola sat up straight. She knew that he would want answers from her after she had kept the truth hidden from him. "Daniel ..." She began to explain through her tears, painfully aware of the quivering in her voice. "Why didn't you tell me sooner, Lola?" She bowed her head in disgrace, and realized that there was not much that made sense to her any longer. She placed her hand on her belly and closed her eyes while saying a silent prayer for her baby, the baby that Daniel had given her, but the baby she had lost. It was a fraction of him that would love her for all eternity, even past the day that he no longer did. Daniel embraced her and held her intimately against him. She cried in his chest, before he felt his own tears roll without restraint down his cheeks. She retreated, and gazed at him once again, "Daniel, how did you know? You said you knew?" She stared questioningly into the arctic blue eyes that had captured her heart from the moment she saw him for the very first time. "Daniel? I couldn't. I mean, I wanted to tell you, but I just couldn't ..." "You should've told me, Lola." She was agonizingly aware of the tears brimming in his own eyes. It crushed her heart to witness Daniel in such a state. "I know, I know how you feel. And I, I was scared ..." Lola tried to explain through her unlimited supply of tears. "I kept thinking that maybe it was a mistake, you know? Maybe Dr. Stalting was wrong. Maybe she mixed up the results with somebody else, and that she was going to phone me any day to let me know she made a mistake. All the maybes that I hoped for ..." She reluctantly removed the engagement ring from her finger, and handed it back to Daniel. "I'm sorry this had to happen to us, Daniel. If I could change it, if I could go back in time, I would. I just don't know how to fix this?"

Daniel became enraged. Angry that she was so intensely frightened to tell him, but most of all, he was irate at her for doubting the love he had for her. "How could you, Lola? How could you think I would leave you because of the baby? I have been waiting for days for you to tell me, but you didn't!" He shouted out in resentment as his tears continued to roll down his cheeks. "I was waiting for you to tell me, and while I was waiting, I was scared to death of losing you. You distanced yourself from me, and it crushed me. I love you, Lola, and I loved the idea that you were going to have our baby, but you? What was going on in your mind?" "I, you said about being careful. I thought you'd leave me Daniel." Daniel shook his head and held her against him one more time, "This was our baby. The best part of us. I saw her in your eyes the first time we met at Joe's. I could never, ever leave you, Lola." "Her?" Daniel smiled sorrowfully, "I hoped ..." He kissed her gently before he resolutely placed the ring back on her finger.

That night, Lola fell asleep with Daniel lying closely beside her. She felt foolish for not tell him the truth, and was agonizingly repentant for keeping the secret from him. Lola was instantly convinced that Daniel would never turn his back on her, and losing the baby was a little more challenging than she thought it would be. She at once regretted her decision of making the appointment at St. Darla's, and berated herself for almost going through with it.

Daniel too felt enormous sorrow for their loss, but was relieved that Lola was alright. Dean and Lauren had checked in on them earlier, but Daniel left Lola to sleep, assuring Lauren that her sister would make a full and speedy recovery.

When Dr. Mahoney stopped by early the following morning, he hurriedly examined Lola and was pleased to discharge her. They drove home in silence. Dean and Lauren held each other's hands a little tighter. Daniel held Lola's hand a little firmer, but no-one mentioned the baby or the sequence of events that led up to her losing their child.

Daniel dropped Dean and Lauren off at their apartment shortly after they returned to Sutherland, anxious to get home and put Lola to bed. "Bro, could you check in at Salvatore for me, please? I don't want Lola to be alone right now." "Of course, get some rest both of you." Dean embraced Daniel before he drove Lola home. After putting her to bed, Daniel climbed in beside her. He had an inexplicable urge to discuss the events of the previous day with her, but he had no thought of what to say to her, or precisely how to approach her. "Lola, it truly bothers me that you didn't tell me. Did you really think that I'd leave you? Don't you have any faith in us, in me?" Lola's heart was hammering in her chest, "I don't know, Daniel?" Daniel desperately needed answers. "I mean, were you trying to figure things out first? What Lola?" "I don't know Daniel. I was so confused, and it all happened so fast. I honestly didn't expect something like this to happen to us. I, I just don't know? I wanted to tell you, and then I didn't have the heart to. And then, I didn't want to go through with it …" "What do you mean? Not go through with it? With the pregnancy?" "I mean Daniel, I wasn't sure. I thought that, I just wasn't sure if you were ready for something like this, and then I starting thinking all sorts of things." Lola was nervous when she began to explain, before her mobile phone rang unexpectedly, interrupting their conversation. Daniel irritably snatched it from her, "Hello?" "Hello, this is Judy from St. Darla's …" "St. Darla's?" He noticed Lola grow ashen at once. "St. Darla's, the abortion clinic?" "Well, yes, is Ms. Storey in?" Daniel's heart began to hammer at an unprecedented rate, one he had never known before. "It's for you …" Daniel handed Lola her mobile phone before he made his way over to their bedroom window.

Daniel was bewildered and thoroughly distraught to realize that Lola had made contact with St. Darla's. He could barely fathom that she was capable of even considering terminating the life of their child. While he stood there gazing out over Sutherland, Daniel finally realized that she never planned on telling him about the baby, and that she continued to lie to him, even after she miscarried.

Lola sat with the phone in her hand for what felt to her like hours, hesitant to give an explanation for her circumstances even though she was abundantly attentive to the fact that she was compelled to take that call. She accepted the fact that Daniel was aware of what she had planned to do, and there was not much she could say to alter what he had heard when he answered her phone. Her heart began to thump ferociously when she realized that she alone was answerable for the mess she found herself in. "This is Lola Storey ..." "This is Judy from Darla's. You missed your appointment yesterday?" "I'm sorry. I, I should've called. I, I lost the baby ..." She began to sob into the phone before she ended the call without delay. Daniel glared at her. It felt to him as though he was looking at a stranger.

She slowly placed the phone on her bed, avoiding immediate eye contact with him. He stood in silence, and continually contemplated the idea that she was about to undergo an abortion.

He realized with a shudder that, if Lola had her way, he would never have known that she was pregnant. He finally understood why she was reluctant to tell him about the baby, and realized that she would certainly have kept it from him without hesitation. Daniel was confounded by the thoughts that were racing around in his mind. He suddenly felt that he could no longer control the unexpected rage that had begun to consume him. "Lola!" He shouted at her before turning around to face her which at once, terrified her. "How could you? That's why you never told me! You were never going to tell me!" He hollered while walking up to her. She glanced at him in fear, with nothing sensible to say to justify her unthinkable behavior to him. There was no explanation or reasoning that came to mind that would force Daniel to understand the vulnerability that overwhelmed her at the time.

At that very moment, it all seemed surprisingly and enormously foolish, and for just a second, she hardly recognized herself. "You lied to me! You arranged an abortion behind my back! If you didn't lose the baby, I would never have known, would I Lola? What the hell else is there that I should know about? What else is there, Lola?" "Daniel, you're not giving me a chance. I just wanted to tell you now, before the phone rang. I wasn't thinking! There's nothing else. That's what I wanted to tell you. I tried to tell you." Just as rapidly as she grabbed onto his arm, Daniel pulled away from her. Lola found it hard to look him in the eye, and turned away from him in dishonor. "You always think, Lola. You think everything through! You plan everything down to the last, don't tell me you weren't thinking! You always think! I feel like I don't know you. I feel like I never knew you at all. Who are you really? All these months, you were wearing a disguise! I thought I knew you! How the fuck could I have been so blind to you? You disgust me, Lola!"

Daniel was without a doubt, certain that he had to leave their apartment before he said much more of anything that he might regret later. He glanced at her one last time, before irately and abruptly walking out. "Daniel, you do know me! It's me, Daniel. Please don't, don't go!" When she heard the front door slam, Lola sobbed violently yet again. She had in no way at all, ever seen or known Daniel to act in such a way, and it frightened her.

He had launched a brutal assault on her heart even though she willfully acknowledged that she entirely deserved his wrath. When she laid her head down on her pillow, Lola sobbed herself to sleep while sensing into the very core of her, that Daniel would never pardon her for what she was about to do. She all of a sudden felt entirely alone and bare inside, but she accepted that it was all her own doing, and her very own fault. She suddenly understood that the biggest mistake she had made was not getting pregnant, it was the fact that she had withheld the truth from Daniel and worse, she considered slaughtering their child.

Daniel reached Salvatore shortly after leaving the apartment. He was relieved to find that Dean had left for the day. He made his way around to the reception counter, and slowly paged through her diary, hoping to find answers, hoping that there would be something to tell him what was going on in her mind. When he saw the name 'St. Darla's' scribbled in her handwriting, he closed the book and irately hurled it against the wall. Daniel sat, overcome with numbness, holding his head in his hands, continually questioning how she was capable of doing what she was about to do.

He could still see the desolation in her eyes play out repeatedly in his mind, but Daniel's heart was in no way ready to absolve her for her planned and unthinkable deeds. He sat defeated for what felt like hours at her desk before he made his way into the workshop. Daniel grabbed a hold of a hammer, and angrily began slamming it into his work bench over and over again until there was not much left to destroy or demolish. He thought back to Sally Storey and her cruelty towards Lola and Lauren. He recalled the way Peter appeared to be while laying stock-still in his coffin. Daniel was reminded of Lola's sorrow when she was told that their baby had died, and then he thought back to the phone call from St. Darla's. He was horrified by the fact that Lola was able to consider ending the life of their child with such an enormous amount of callousness.

Finally, he let the hammer fall onto the floor and wept quietly on his hunches in the corner of the workshop. Daniel was frantic to find valid grounds for why she felt so entirely compelled to abort their child, but his mind informed him that there was not even one that could validate any form of logic. He reflected back to the past couple of days once more, and was overcome with physical and emotional exhaustion. He again thought back to Peter and Sally Storey, and wondered whether the scars that Lola was adamant that she by no means was left with, weren't perhaps left by her parents after all. For the first time since they had started out their lives together, Daniel was convinced that he never truly knew her as well as he thought he did. It was far too easy for her to lie to him, and in the process, she destroyed a tiny fraction of themselves.

Daniel felt betrayed by the one person he loved more than anything else in the world. It was a kind of a deception he knew he could in no way exonerate. His heart brutally instructed him to admit that what they had once shared and held dear to them, was ultimately over. They had lost all that was important to them, and although he knew he still adored her with every single element inside of him, Daniel also knew that the nagging truth buried deep inside of him, was one that assured him, he could never, ever trust her again.

For the first time in his life, Daniel was excruciatingly aware of his own heart shattering, and it was something he was determined, would never happen again. The anguish and torment he was experiencing was inexpressible. It frightened him that he had become so enormously susceptible around Lola. He was desperate to hold on to her, but at the same time, he could never again risk the overwhelming soreness and betrayal he was sensitive to at that very moment.

Back at the apartment, Lola took a quick shower before she dressed herself in loose-fitting jeans and an oversized sweater. She was distraught over the expression on Daniel's face earlier, and had an inexplicable urge to find him, sure that he was almost undoubtedly at Salvatore. She was desperate to try and explain herself, and even though she feared Daniel's antagonism and resentment, Lola was frantic for Daniel to understand.

When she walked into the workshop, she found Daniel hunched in a corner. She quickly glanced around her in shock and disbelief. The workshop had been trashed, and for a moment, Lola was convinced that vandals had broken in. "Daniel?" She was afraid of what might have taken place at Salvatore. "Lola?" He stood up and turned to face her. "Are you alright? What happened here? Did you do this?"

She inspected Daniel to ascertain whether he had been hurt. He gradually began picking up the tools without explaining, abundantly aware of the fact that he alone was to responsible for the pandemonium at Salvatore. "Just go, Lola. Please ..." Daniel swabbed at the tears that were still wet on his cheeks. Lola walked up to him, and gently touched his arm. "Daniel, please can we talk?" "No, I don't want to talk. Not now. Not yet. You should be in bed, go home, Lola. I don't want to talk right now. I am so mad at you." Daniel hastily turned, and walked away from her. Lola followed him, anxious for an opportunity to explain. "Daniel please, this is going to change us. You're scaring me. You said nothing could ever change us?"

He turned around to face her before tossing the hammer

into a corner. "Do you understand what you've done? Or how it makes me feel? How can it not change us? How, Lola, how? I thought you loved me! I thought we had a life together?" Daniel became enraged once again. "I'm sorry Daniel. I didn't think that, I thought that, I just thought it was the right thing to do at the time. I wasn't thinking, Daniel. I didn't want to do this to you …" "The right thing? Do what to me Lola? Rip my heart out?" Lola placed her arms around his neck, anxious to hold him against her while recognizing the tremendous anguish he was in. Daniel gently pushed her away from him, and nervously held her hands into his for a brief moment. "Lola, not now. I want to be alone. Just leave me alone, please. I want to be alone. Just go." Lola moved closer and pressed firmly against him once more, "Daniel, please. I don't want to leave you like this …" She kissed him gently. Daniel responded by kissing her back, and took her firmly into his arms. She held onto him and ran her fingers through his hair before he retreated abruptly. "I can't Lola, I can't …" Lola looked questioningly at him before she moved closer to him one more time. "Don't Lola, just don't. Don't throw yourself at me like that! You are just like everyone else! I don't want you here, just get out!" Lola felt her tears sting in her eyes when she walked away from him. She knew in her heart that the love between them had been irreparably distorted.

When Lola returned to the apartment, she climbed into their bed, confident that all Daniel needed was time to process all that had happened between them in such a short while. She thought back to Sally Storey, and wondered whether Sally was perhaps exactly right about her all through her childhood, and if she was indeed the nuisance they would continually remind her of being when she was only a little girl. Lola fell asleep, exhausted by the events of the day, but even while she was asleep, she could sense that her connection with Daniel would never be the same, ever again.

When Daniel arrived home, he made his way straight to the sofa in the living room, and lay down with a heavy heart, painfully aware of the sadness that was overwhelming him. He had no desire to face Lola that night, and he hoped that somehow, he could awake the next morning without feeling as though his heart was cataclysmic. He was overcome with rage for Lola, and prayed that he could somehow, salvage what they had once shared, and feel kindly towards her once again.

Lola heard him enter the apartment, but after a while, she realized that he had no intention of climbing into bed with her. She quietly slipped out, and made her way into the living room where she found him asleep on the sofa, "Daniel?" He ignored her while feigning sleep. "Please come to bed?" She knelt down beside him, oblivious to the fact that he was pretending to be asleep, not wanting to face her just yet. Lola stood up and gently covered Daniel with an over-blanket before she kissed him on his forehead.

She leaned in to smell his hair, and silently prayed that Daniel Salvatore would come back to her, "I Love you, Daniel ..." She whispered softly, not wanting to wake him, before she made her way back to their bedroom.

Daniel opened his eyes after she left. He lay in silence and without moving a limb, thinking of Lola and his inner struggle with her betrayal. He felt his heart break over and over, giving it his best effort to stop the lump in his throat from entirely restricting his ability to hold back his tears.

TURMOIL

Lola was determined to step back from Daniel in an effort to allow him sufficient breathing space to process all she had done. She was hopeful that he would eventually pardon her for inexcusable betrayal. She was certain that time and distance was precisely what Daniel needed, and she hoped that once enough time had passed, he would finally excuse her, even though he no longer had any desire to discuss the baby. To keep herself busy in the evenings, aware that Daniel would intentionally arrive home long after she had fallen asleep, Lola threw herself into orchestrating Lauren's eighteenth birthday party, which was rapidly approaching.

Daniel and Dean had spent exhaustive hours at Salvatore, painstakingly working on Bonnie for Lauren, both keen for her to be perfect and new for Lauren's birthday. They had in every respect serviced the car, and had given it a complete re-spray. Dean insisted on a top of the range sound system for Lauren which he had meticulously installed for her, while ensuring that Bonnie was mechanically sound.

On the morning of Lauren's birthday, Daniel woke up to find Lola already in the kitchen, busy writing out Lauren's birthday card. "Morning Lola." He poured himself a quick cup of coffee, as he did on most mornings. "Morning …" "So, how do you want to do this today? Dean says that Lauren's birthday party is being held at the lake?" "I was thinking, we have to get to the lake at least thirty minutes before everyone else arrives. I can drive Bonnie to the lake, and then maybe drive home with you afterwards?" "Sounds good." Daniel nodded in agreement before he made his way into the shower. Lola ran up behind him, and placed her hand on his shoulder. He let out a disheartening sigh before he slowly turned around to face her, "Daniel, please can we talk before we go to the party? I don't want us to go like this …" "Not now, Lola, it's getting late, but don't worry, I won't say anything." Daniel quickly turned away from her. "Daniel wait, please just wait. I feel I need to tell Dean and Lauren, and maybe your parents. They are confused and don't understand what's going on with us. I really need to explain things, and seeing as we'll all be together today, I thought that maybe I should speak to them all together?" Daniel stopped and turned around to face her when Lola noticed the exact same incensed expression on his face that she had become accustomed to. "You won't tell them anything, Lola! As far as they are concerned, you miscarried! You will not embarrass me like this!" Daniel swiftly turned around, and walked away from her. "But, I did miscarry …" She whispered softly.

Daniel and Lola arrived earlier than the rest of the guests to ensure that the venue was flawlessly set up for Lauren's birthday party. Daniel quickly placed a ribbon around Bonnie, and parked her at the entrance of the Lake Club. Lola smiled gravely when she noticed Daniel replace the existing number plates with brand new 'Lauren' plates, just as he had once done for her. He adored and cherished Lauren as he would a sister. Lola was pleased that what was so entirely wrong between them, did in no way influence his affiliation with Lauren. "I hope she'll be happy?" Daniel was hesitant for just an instant. "She will love it,

Danny!" Lola instinctively grabbed his hand when she recalled her own excitement to a similar moment, but she let go of him almost immediately when she noticed his obvious discomfort.

John, Sally and Bo arrived shortly afterwards. Lola was relieved to have some form of distraction from Daniel. They both tried to put forward a united front in front of Daniel's parents, but it was apparent to the Salvatore's that there was a certain tension between Daniel and Lola.

When Lauren and Dean arrived, Lola took her sister's hand, and led her out to Bonnie. She proudly placed the keys in her hand, "This is from Dean, Daniel and me. I hope you will have many, many safe miles with her, and I hope you will appreciate the freedom she gives you." Lola was at once alert to diverse emotions when she, out of the blue, realized that her sister was growing up too fast. Lauren turned to face the Salvatore's when she unexpectedly turned sad, "Thank you, all of you. I love what you guys have done with Bonnie. Thank you, Sarah and John, for coming, it means so much to me, and sis, thank you for everything." Lauren embraced Lola who was fighting rigidly to hold back her own tears.

Once all the guests had arrived and the party was well underway, Lola and Daniel went their separate ways, as they had been doing for weeks while secretly in suspense that not a soul would discover their growing separation, at the same time as realizing that they no longer had much of anything to say to one another anymore. Just by catching a glimpse of him, Lola's heart would be submerged. She was devastatingly aware of the fact that they were moving further and further apart from one another, and as hard as she tried, there was not much she could do to alter it. It frightened Lola when she glanced around her, and noticed how many young, beautiful and single women were flirting audaciously with Daniel. She knew again that she could not contend with any of them, while her heart reminded her how fast she was losing him. When she gazed at him while he was caught up in laughter and banter with someone else, Lola was convinced that she would never be the one to bring laughter to his face again.

Daniel regularly hunted Lola, and noticed that she was steeling glimpses of him. He would calculatingly touch the arm of someone he was talking to, or gently stroke a beautiful woman's cheek, while flatteringly conscious of the frantic intention simply to wound Lola.

When she found it emotionally exhausting to be around him, Lola hastily made her way down to the lake, away from the crowd. She found the ache in her chest so excruciating and agonizing, that she could scarcely breathe at times. When she reached the lake, Lola could no longer prevent the tears that had started to flow unreservedly and without restraint down her cheeks. She was reminded once again of all that had happened, all that had gone so terribly wrong, and she silently wished that she could turn back the time, and mend her mistakes with Daniel. Lola was convinced that Daniel would never absolve her for betraying him in the way that she did. He would not at all have the capacity or motivation to understand how it was likely that she had become so severely distressed by her unexpected pregnancy. "Lola?" She was instantly plunged back to reality when she heard Lauren behind her. "Hey sis …" "What's wrong? Why are you crying?" Lauren took Lola's hands and glared at her with a fretful expression on her face. "Nothing. It's just, you're growing up so fast. You're not that little girl anymore ..." "It's Daniel, isn't it?" Lauren didn't believe her sister, and was confident that Daniel was the basis for her sorrow. Lola erupted into tears once again, defeated by the anguish in her heart. "I don't understand Lola? Losing the baby wasn't your fault?" "He, it's not that, Lauren, we're just, it just isn't working anymore. It's like, the harder I try, the more he pulls away from me?" Lauren could make no sense of what Lola was saying. "I see how he looks at you, Lola, he loves you. I know Daniel loves you. Maybe he's just trying to get over losing the baby? Maybe he's just hurting, sis?" Lauren was making no sense of what Lola was telling her. "It's more than that, Lols. I love him so much. It's just, it just doesn't want to work. He just doesn't feel the same anymore, and nothing I do or say makes any difference. I just love him so much, but I'm losing him. I did something. I did something so stupid Lols, so bad." Lauren held her sister close to her, attempting to fathom what it was that Lola had done, "What did you do Lola?"

While Daniel stood chatting to John, he was at once sensitive to the fact that he had not seen Lola around for some time. He frantically glanced around him, but could not find her anywhere in the crowds. He felt sudden dread well up inside of him, at the mere thought of not knowing where she was. As he was about to find Dean, he noticed her and Lauren down by the lake. His heart skipped a beat watching her. He realized with sudden wretchedness that he not at all noticed how beautiful she looked that day. She was dressed in a white summer dress with dainty straps that were hanging loosely over her shoulders, and her hair flowing down her back. Daniel realized for the first time how much longer her hair had grown and by the way Lauren was holding onto her, Daniel was certain that something was appallingly wide of the mark with Lola. Once again, he was alert to an unexplainable and unsolicited urge to be closer to her. He had an unexpected, and abrupt need to hold her in his arms. He was once again totally mystified and caught off guard by his erratic emotions for her, and it was disconcerting to him, once again.

He apprehensively made his way towards them, and as he approached them, he was conscious of an indignant expression that was evident on Lola's face. He utterly reviled seeing Lola so dejected, and he suddenly realized that it had been a while since he truly stopped to look at her. It had been a while since he noticed her beautiful smile. The distress in her eyes was unreservedly overpowering, and it occurred to him that she was growing more despondent with each passing day. Her sorrow told Daniel a thousand stories, but they were tales he could not mend for her, he didn't want to. He secretly yearned for the days that she would break out into laughter for no apparent reason at all, and he longed for the days she seemed so carefree and untroubled.

As he reluctantly made his way towards her, Daniel realized once again that it appeared as though Lola was hauling the entire world on her shoulders. He thought back to the day she told him about Peter Storey, and he felt his stomach turn at the paltry thought of what her father had done to her. When he reached them, Daniel was instantly and unpredictably miserable, "Everything okay here?" Lola swiftly retreated and hurriedly swabbed away her tears, unsure of how to respond to Daniel. "Yes, fine. I was just telling Lauren, she's growing up so fast, and I just, I wanted to tell her … I need to tell her … I have to tell her,

Daniel." Daniel touched her arm and gazed sadly at Lola, "It's going to be fine Lola, it happens, it's life. People grow up, people change, life changes, that's all there is to it, nothing more. There's nothing else to say, not today." He was adamant that Lola withhold the truth, and not tell Lauren of the intended abortion. "Lols, everyone is asking for the birthday girl." Lauren smiled nervously at Lola before she hastily made her way back to the party, but enthusiastically hoping that Daniel and Lola would sort out their issues. Lola gazed up at him, certain that she recognized the kindness she once saw, but almost forgot.

She tried to recall when the last time was that Daniel looked at her without abhorrence and resentment in his eyes. She took his hand, and gently, but nervously squeezed it, hoping that she could sense a little fraction of him again, instead, he slowly freed his hand from hers. It tugged at his heart to witness her so utterly disconsolate, but there was nothing that came to mind that he could say to make her feel better. He hoped that something would flow from his mouth, but nothing did. "Daniel, please just say something, please? What can I do to make things right with you?" Lola began to beseech him, almost able to see the invisible wall that had come up between them. "Nothing Lola, you've done enough. I don't want to do this with you. I don't want to talk about this now. Not here!" He at once turned to leave, feeling guilty immediately for not permitting Lola an opportunity to explain. Daniel was convinced that there were a number of things that were better left unspoken, and unarticulated. "Daniel, don't do this to me, I'm begging you. Don't walk away like that." Lola choked on her words through her tears when he carried on walking away from her. He abruptly turned to face her one more time, "I can't forgive what you've

done, Lola. I'm trying. It's just harder than I thought it would be."
He moved closer to her. "I look at you, and it's not the same. I
mean, sometimes, I feel bad, horrible for the way things have
turned out, and I want things to be the way they were because, I
miss you. I miss us, and then other times, I'm glad you're hurting.
I want you to feel what I feel. It's almost like I can't stand the sight
of you sometimes. Every time I look at you, I think of your lies and
deceit!"

Lola began weeping violently. She was in little doubt that
her heart could not splinter any more, than after hearing what
Daniel was so effortlessly and callously saying to her. "Stop crying
Lola! I can't deal with you when you're crying all the damn time!
Just toughen up for once! You want to talk? But, we can't talk
when you just fall apart like this! I just can't talk to you like this!
I don't know how to forgive you, Lola, but I am trying. I am
honestly doing my best. I just need time. You have to give me
more time."

He turned and walked away from her. Her stomach
twisted in a knot when she realized that they were both walking
away from one another, walking away from love. Lola quickly
wiped her tears, and hurriedly made her way back to the party.
Lauren was dancing with Dean, Sarah was dancing with John, and
Daniel was caught up in conversation with a beautiful and leggy
brunette at the bar. When Lola glanced at them, she wondered
why it was that Daniel had chosen her, when it was crystal clear
to her, that he could have chosen any other woman.

With sorrow and utter desolation, Lola realized that she
had never really deserved Daniel. He could have had better, and
it was undoubtedly, not Lola Storey. From where she was

standing, it seemed to her as though Daniel was lavishing in the mystery brunette's company. She was convinced that she had no right to feel aggrieved.

"So, Mr. Salvatore, where is that girlfriend of yours?" Samantha Darling tossed her dark hair loosely over her shoulders. "You've met Lola?" "Lola? So that's her name. I've heard about her, but no, I haven't met her. Where is she?" Daniel turned around, swiftly glancing over at the crowd, and when his eyes caught Lola seated at an empty table, he pointed her out to Samantha. "That's her. We're actually, we're engaged." "Wow! I heard the rumors, but wow! Daniel Salvatore, the famous bachelor getting married?" Samantha was thoroughly astounded and deeply disenchanted. "Yeah well, that remains to be seen." "Oh? What does that mean?" "Nothing, it means nothing."

Lola was still profoundly in thought and unaccompanied at the table when she heard a shuffle next to her. She was astounded to find Gregory Pastor right beside her, "A penny for your thoughts?" He lowered her hand from her mouth, when he noticed that she was chewing on her nails. "Gregory? Hey ..." Lola was suddenly in high spirits when she recognized a familiar, and friendly face. Without releasing her hand, he smiled at her. "Why are you sitting here all alone? You should be dancing. Did Daniel dump you already?" Lola bowed her head, not wanting to familiarize Gregory with what was going on between her and Daniel. "No, not exactly. Not yet ..." "Do you want to talk about it?" Lola smiled despondently at him, but shook her head. She just couldn't tell anyone what she had done, even though she desperately needed to be freed from the entrapment it had brought into her life. Daniel turned away from the bar after Samantha took to the dance floor. He glanced over at Lola, and noticed Gregory sitting beside her, still holding her hand in his. He felt a sudden burst of irritation come alive inside of him, but was determined to allow Lola to decide whether she was willing to have Gregory Pastor around her.

Lola and Daniel avoided one another throughout the remainder of the party celebrations, but Daniel consciously and intentionally remained close to her. He had an inexplicable need to keep a watchful eye over her, and by the time the evening had come to an end, he noticed that her inflamed and red eyes were almost insufferable for him. He was devastatingly aware that he alone, was the cause for her entire world diminishing right in front of her.

When most of the guests had left the party, Daniel found Lola at the bar with Gregory. Gregory had placed his arms around her. It was apparent to Daniel that he was whispering sweet nothings in her ear. She let out a faint giggle when Daniel noticed obvious delight on her face. He was hesitant, but he was almost certain that he detected abnormal behavior in Lola. As Gregory was about to kiss Lola, Daniel abruptly placed his hand on Lola's arm. "Lola, it's late. Everyone has left. We should go." Daniel took the drink from her hand, and placed it on the bar. She chuckled slightly when she turned around to face Daniel. The expression in her eyes was one that Daniel had on no one occasion ever seen, or recognized before. "No! The party just is getting started, where is everyone?" She hastily glanced around her, "Gregory, weren't we still going to dance?" "It's late Lola, and you've had too much to drink." Daniel became agitated, while glaring at Gregory. "No-no, I've just had one. Or two? Okay, maybe three. Besides, I don't want to go home yet …" She tittered stridently and winked what she thought was in secret at Gregory. Gregory too, had far too much to drink, and burst out laughing at Lola.

Daniel grabbed her by her arms, and brusquely pulled her out of the bar stool. "You've had enough and we're leaving!" He furiously turned to face Gregory, "Shame on you, Pastor!" "Oh, come on Daniel, she's having a good time. It's not like you've been anywhere in sight today. I'll bring her home when she's ready to leave." Lola sniggered out loud once again, "Yes. Yes, and you know why he hasn't been around?" Lola freed herself from Daniel's grasp. When she turned around to face Gregory, she almost fell over her own feet. "Oopsie daisy ..." Lola chuckled again. "Let me tell you why Greg, he can't stand the sight of me. Ask him. He said so, just now, down there by the lake. He said he can't stand me, that I've got to toughen up." Lola almost stumbled again. "He said that people change, that he can't forgive me. And do you want to know why he can't forgive me, Greg? Do you want to know how horrible I am?" Lola was slurring while trying to maintain her balance. Gregory snorted out while Daniel was horrified by Lola's conduct. "Tell me?" Gregory placed an arm around her. Lola moved closer to him, and instinctively threw her arms around him, "I made a stupid phone call. Oh wait, I'm not allowed to tell. I'm going to embarrass him." "You're coming home with me right now. Let's go!" Daniel grabbed her forcefully by her arm before she pulled away from him, and just about fell over her own feet again, "I am not going anywhere with you. I don't want to and I don't have to." She placed her arms around Gregory again, and buried her head in his chest. "You are behaving like a slut Lola!" Daniel picked her up and tossed her over his shoulder. "A slut? I'll let you know, Mr. Dictator, it's my body and I will do with it as I see fit!" She winked at Gregory who was laughing hysterically. "Yes Lola, don't I just know that. Didn't you just prove that?" Daniel grabbed her bag, before he shot a blank stare at Gregory, and turned to leave with Lola over his shoulders.

When they reached Daniel's car, he gently put her down, but Lola struggled to maintain her steadiness. "Oh, I don't feel so good …" Lola quickly placed her hand in front of her mouth. Daniel turned her around, and took her hair into his hands, leaving Lola to heave. When she felt better, Daniel took a hankie from his pocket, and wiped Lola's face with it. She stood silently with her eyes closed, completely ignorant to what was going on around her. After she was safely settled into the passenger seat, Daniel swiftly made his way around to the driver's seat. When he slid in, he noticed that Lola had turned the radio on. She was quiet and calm, but Daniel was certain that Lola was not quite ready to fall asleep just yet.

While driving through the streets of Madison, Lola glanced around her with profound admiration for the city lights. "I don't want to go back home. That prison, I hate it there." "It's late Lola, you need to go to bed." "Drop me off at Lauren's. It just sucks to be at the apartment." Daniel refused to entertain her request, and when they reached the apartment, he was confident that Lola would be asleep soon. When he opened the passenger door for her, Lola climbed out, aware of the fact that if she moved too suddenly, she would be ill again.

When Daniel closed her door behind her, he took a hold of her arm in an effort to keep her upright. She was agitated and tugged frantically to free her arm from him, "I'm fine. I can walk. See, two feet. I'm tougher than you think. I don't always cry, you know?" She mumbled almost incomprehensibly while pointing to her feet. When Daniel cautiously released her, Lola fell to the ground at once, before she burst out laughing again. "Uh oh! Alright then, maybe I can't. I've never been drunk before, you know?" Daniel chuckled softly before he picked her up, and carried her to the apartment. He led her into the bathroom, where he quickly drew a bath. Lola sat down on the toilet seat, waiting for Daniel to get her pajamas for her.

When he walked back into the bathroom, he noticed that Lola was slumped against the back of the toilet, not quite awake, but not quite asleep yet. "Lola, come, get into the bath quickly." Daniel was frantic for her to stand up straight. "I want to sleep. I am so tired." She unsuccessfully attempted to open her eyes. Daniel helped her up, and smiled unexpectedly when he recognized the humor in an intoxicated Lola. "Just quickly, then you can go to sleep, I promise." Daniel began undressing her while Lola stood silently. When he removed her dress, he reluctantly and unintentionally admired her exquisiteness once again. He turned her around to the bath, and with his guidance, Lola climbed in and laid back. Daniel could not take his eyes off her as she lay there with her eyes closed.

He had an indescribable desire to memorize the way she looked while lying there, afraid that he might forget what Lola looked like before she became so entirely broken. He slowly and gently sponged her down, before he washed her beautiful long hair at the same time as trying to keep her awake just for a little while longer. "You don't have to take care of me, Daniel." Lola whispered drowsily. Daniel smiled at her, abundantly aware that she was in no condition to take care of herself. "I'm just helping you, Lola. I don't mind …" He helped her climb out of the bath before he gently dried her off. After dressing her in her night clothes, he squeezed toothpaste onto her toothbrush, before Lola half-heartedly brushed her teeth. When she was done, he led her into the bedroom and opened the bedcovers for her. She climbed in and pulled the duvet up to her chin. "I saw you with her, Miss Perfect. I know you like her." She closed her eyes and fell asleep almost at once. Daniel sat down next to her, enormously anxious of how defenseless and vulnerable she had become.

When Lola awoke the following morning, she was excruciatingly aware of the brutal hammering of her head. She climbed out of bed, and swiftly made her way to the bathroom cabinet in a desperate attempt to find pain killers for the pulsation in head. She popped two in her hand and hurriedly made her way to the kitchen. She was stunned to find Daniel seated around the kitchen table, sipping on a cup of coffee. "I've made coffee ..." "No thanks, just these will do." She opened her hand to expose the painkillers. After she swallowed them, Lola realized that she could barely recall much about the previous night. "So, what happened last night?" "Nothing much, you got drunk and flirted with Gregory. Hung onto him like a tramp. You virtually blurted everything out to him, and then I brought you home." Daniel was at once irritated with her. "Shit. Sorry?" "Yeah well, you shouldn't get drunk, Lola!" Lola bowed her head in disgrace and remained silent. "You're a terrible drunk, you threw yourself at Pastor!" "Yes, well Daniel, I am lonely here. I'm all alone here, all the time. You're never home anymore. I go to Salvatore and I come home. You stay there, and when you do eventually come home, you ignore me. What do you want me to do?" Lola was slowly working up the nerve to fight back. "Even when you're here, you're not here. Last night, you were more interested in that Samantha woman than in me!" "I need time, Lola, I told you that." Daniel had calmed down just a notch. "Time for what, Daniel? Either you love me, or you don't. Either way, you should just tell me!" Lola had become unexpectedly snappy.

Daniel placed his empty coffee mug in the washbasin before he turned to leave for Salvatore. While she watched him walk away from her one more time, Lola decided to refrain from going into Salvatore that day, and opted to go out, and watch a movie instead. She greatly wanted to clear her mind, but more than that, she craved the silence and solitude of a movie theatre.

Alice VL

Lola sat inside the cinema in silence, thinking of Daniel and unable to focus her attention on the movie. She recalled certain moments of the previous night, and how he behaved towards her. Lola wondered if it was in fact only time that Daniel needed, or if it was perhaps, a pathetic excuse to distance himself from her.

At Salvatore, Daniel became rigorously alarmed when Lola failed to turn up for work. He dialed her mobile phone often, but reached her voice mail each time. After his umpteenth attempt to reach her, he hurriedly dialed Lauren, and was disappointed that she had not heard from Lola either. Daniel raced back to the apartment shortly after his phone call to Lauren, only to find that Lola was not there.

When the movie ended, Lola strolled past an old Irish pub that she had regularly seen. It was around the corner from their apartment, and after parking her car in the garage, Lola returned to the pub. When she walked in, she was relieved that there were only handful of people. Lola instantly made her way to the bar, and ordered a glass of wine. While she sipped on her wine, she once again thought of Daniel, and all that was going on between them. She sat in silence listening to music, unintentionally and without count, she ordered one glass of wine after another.

Daniel promptly closed Salvatore at six that evening, and hastily returned to their apartment. After parking his own car in the garage, he was relieved to find her car parked right next to his. When he reached the apartment, he was staggered and suddenly anxious that she again, was nowhere to be seen. Daniel again called Lauren, and once more Lauren informed him that she had not heard from Lola all day. When Daniel rushed downstairs, he had no idea of where to begin looking for her. He stood at the apartment entrance in a panic, unsure of what to do, or where to begin.

Lola had befriended an older man named Billy that had been in the pub with her all day. She found it somewhat daunting that she was so easily able to talk to him. She told him about Daniel, and what she had done. She became teary frequently, and he in turn, would soothingly rub her shoulders, and order her another glass of wine. By early evening, Lola knew that she had drank far too much and that it was time to go home, back to the apartment she was learning to loathe. Billy walked Lola out of the pub, and insisted on walking her home. When they reached the corner of the block, she burst out laughing when Billy told her that he would certainly and habitually crawl home, if he had lived as close to the pub as she did. Daniel instantly recognized her laughter, and when he saw her standing on the corner, he immediately made his way towards her. "Lola! What is wrong with you?" He inquisitively glanced over at Billy. "Oh hi. This is Billy …" "Hey …" Billy extended a hand out to Daniel. Daniel rudely ignored him while maintaining his focus on Lola, "Where have you been all day?" "I should go, Lola, thanks. I had fun. You've got my number if ever you want to talk." Billy politely kissed her hand. "Thanks, I had fun too. Thanks for listening."

When he walked away from them, Lola was convinced that Daniel was once again offended by her, and she was positive that he certainly thought the worst of her yet again. "Who was that?" "Billy." "Billy who? Who is he Lola?" "I don't know? Some guy I met at the pub." "You went to a bar? On your own?" Lola lowered her head in shame at once. It sounded awful when Daniel said it. "You're picking men up in pubs now?" "Well, if you put it that way? Then yes, but just so you know, and in case you couldn't see it, he's an old man." Lola abruptly walked past him before she hurriedly made her way up to the apartment.

When they reached the apartment, Daniel grabbed Lola by her arm after shutting the front door behind them. "What was that all about, Lola?" "Nothing! Just company, just conversation. That's all. Someone to talk to. Someone un-judgmental. Something you know nothing about!" Lola was fraught to free herself from his tightening grip. "Company? Really? Conversation, really? Un-judgmental isn't even a real word, Lola." "Yes, really Daniel, company! Someone to talk to! It's my word, and you know what I mean!" When he finally let go of her arm, Lola turned away from him, glaringly alert to the fact that she had incensed Daniel once again. "You are pushing me too far, Lola. What is wrong with you?" Daniel followed her into their bedroom. Lola stopped and turned to face him, "I am losing my mind here, Daniel. I can't talk to Lauren about any of this! You won't let me talk to anyone! You won't even talk to me!" "Do you want out, Lola? Is that what you want?" Daniel took her by her shoulders and as she lowered her head, the suggestion of their separation frightened her almost to death. "I want you, Daniel. I am so alone, and when you're here, I feel even lonelier." Daniel released her arm at once, "I can't, Lola. I told you, I need time. But, if you can't give me more time, we should, I should leave." "Do you want out, Daniel?" Her hands began to shudder when he lowered his head, unable to look her in the eye. "Daniel! Look at me!" Lola shouted at him before he lifted his eyes. "I just need more time, Lola." He sighed despondently before he turned his back on her again.

When August rolled by far too abruptly and unexpectedly, it was almost six months after Lola had lost the baby. Six months after Daniel had discovered the intended abortion, and six months since he had expressed one decent word to her. Dean and Lauren had grown closer to one another. It was only four months before she would graduate from high school.

For Lola and Daniel, nothing was as it once was between them. Daniel could not overlook the fact that Lola wanted to terminate her pregnancy, and Lola ultimately acknowledged the fact that he would never, ever absolve her. Daniel had increasingly distanced himself from her with each passing day, while hoping that somehow, time would restore their broken hearts. He was eager that the detachment between them might allow him the time he so desperately needed to toil through his own unidentified emotions. They barely spoke to one another anymore. Lola made daily attempts to repair all that was broken between them, to prove to him that she was the Lola he fell in love with, but for Daniel, it had brought an excessive amount of remoteness between them.

Lola eventually gave up on trying to offer Daniel an explanation for the scheduled abortion. She gave up on trying to submit a rationalization as to her reasoning behind that critical appointment. It was grueling for her, and at all times, ended in a quarrel between them where they would incessantly bellow at one another. "Daniel, you don't want to hear! You don't want to know!" "I don't, Lola. You're right, I don't! Because I just don't care!" The more of an effort Lola made to explain, the less Daniel was listening to her. He constantly reminded her that she had finalized her decision once she had scheduled the appointment. In turn, she tried non-stop to make him understand that she had acted out of extreme anxiety. They, under no circumstances, discussed the miscarriage that had wrecked Lola's heart. While she was struggling to deal with the loss of her baby, Daniel was certain that it was of no importance to her. He noticed her weep one night after he arrived home from Salvatore, and when Lola desperately tried to approach him about it, he instantly dismissed her. "Oh, come on, you were going to kill the baby anyways, what's the difference?"

As far as Daniel was concerned, it was the coward's way out for Lola. She was preparing to terminate the baby anyway, she had suffered no defeat. He barely touched her anymore, and Lola's heart shattered each time he would turn away from her. Lola would take his hand at the dinner table, but Daniel would pull back coldly. At night, on the few evenings that they were home together, she would try to make small talk with him, but he candidly ignored her most of the time. She placed her arms around him one evening, but he instantly unchained himself from her, and calmly turned his back on her.

When Lauren and Dean came around, she would see fractions of the old Daniel returning, but only until they left. They came by less, and in turn, Lola and Daniel would visit them independently. They very rarely went anywhere together anymore, and Lola found it tiresome to come up with excuses to Lauren. She would lay awake during the night, and quietly slip out onto the balcony of their apartment where she would shed silent tears. Lola willingly acknowledged that she alone was responsible for all that had turned out so wrong between them, but she prayed that he would love her as much as was necessary to eventually exonerate her.

At Salvatore, Daniel spent his days in the workshop taking on additional work while doing his utmost to take his mind off of her and their baby. Daniel worked longer and longer hours, hoping that Lola would be asleep by the time he arrived home at night. It was simpler for Daniel that way. Facing her had become one of the hardest things he's had to do. There were moments that he longed to seize her in his arms, and tell her that he incessantly loved her, but then there were instances that all he wanted to do was hurt her, and tell her that he found her loathsome. The idea of being unable to control his emotions was tremendously demoralizing, and shunning her had become the only alternative for him. He would often gaze at her when she was preoccupied. His heart would insist that they could get through their fierce blizzard, but his mind prompted him that there was not much to cling to anymore. Daniel pined for her. He longed to hold her, and he yearned for the old days at Salvatore. He was aware that his world had stood still, and that he had no hunch of how to move forward.

Dean and Lauren had detected the growing coldness between them, and were disconsolately saddened that they could not find a way to work out their unsolved crisis. Dean would repeatedly remind Daniel that his inflexibility towards Lola would certainly be the end of them. This would result in arguments between them and about Lola most of the time. Daniel never told Dean about the abortion. He could not convince himself that Lola could have been capable of going through with it, but at the same time, he had an inexplicable need to protect her from what people might think of her. He not once necessitated for Dean or Lauren to see Lola the way he did. It was imperative to keep her safe from other's perceptions.

Every now and again at night when she was asleep, he would stare at her while dreadfully trying to identify with what she was thinking. While asleep, she seemed completely guiltless and childlike, and he almost had a relentless urge to place his arms around her, and hold her safely against him. Some nights, he would wake up to find his arms around her, and he would instantly turn away from her.

On one specific night when Daniel had come home after drinking far too much at Joe's, he valiantly turned to face Lola, "Hey pretty, sad, lonely Lola ..." Lola was ardently aware of the stench of alcohol from a mile away, and was distressed to find Daniel in such an unknown state, "Have you been drinking?" "A bit." He chuckled while he undid the buttons on her blouse. "So, you're lonely Lola? Are you still hanging out in pubs while I'm at work? Picking up strange men?" "I am lonely, Daniel!" "Let me take care of that for you." He whispered raucously, but Lola was agonizingly convinced that it was the alcohol performing on behalf of Daniel. She longed frantically for Daniel, and had no desire whatsoever to stop him from undressing her. They made love for the first time since the miscarriage, and it solicited hope for Lola that there might still be a possibility for the love and life they were once united in. Daniel barely kissed her, and when Lola tried to kiss him, he turned away from her. When she placed her arms around him, Daniel shifted awkwardly. Lola had never before felt as second-hand as she did after he nonchalantly climbed out of bed when it was all over, and without saying a word, walked away from her. Daniel retreated from her, sensitive to the fact that he was responsible for making her feel inferior, but unable to convince himself that love had anything to do with what had just taken place between them. "Daniel, don't go ..." He stood silently, unsure of what to say to her, but in no doubt that he had made an enormous error in judgement. He turned around and gawked at her, devastatingly aware of the beseeching in her eyes. "This was a mistake, Lola. I'm sorry. I, I had too much to drink tonight." Lola grabbed the bed sheet, appalled by what he was saying, and attempted to cover up her exposed body, mortified by the way he had so readily made her feel. "Do you really mean that?" She had become instantly tearful and felt no better than a common vagabond. "It won't happen again. I didn't mean for it to happen, it shouldn't have. I don't know what else to say?" "Don't do this Daniel, please. Please, just think about what you're doing." "What do you want, Lola? Do you want me to come over and hold you? Do you want me to tell you that I love you? I can't do that, Lola, I just can't. I just needed to be with someone tonight, and it could've been anyone! Don't you get it? It meant nothing! You, you mean nothing! It could've been anyone." He stormed off irately when he realized that what he had just said was brutal and heartless. He was excruciatingly aware of the fact that he could never renounce what he had just told her. "I know I mean nothing anymore, Daniel, but you didn't have to make me feel like a whore!" Lola shouted out before she sobbed into her pillow. Daniel came to a complete halt at the doorway. She recalled once again what it felt like to be used by a man, and she was ashamed of herself for allowing him to humiliate her. Daniel stared at her and smirked, "Maybe you are one?" He was frantic for a retort from her. She climbed out of bed, and moved towards him while clutching the bed sheet in a feeble attempt to cover herself up, before she swiftly swabbed the tears from her cheeks, "You were my first time, and only one, Daniel, you know that?" Lola was inconsolable as she stood gazing tearfully at him. "No, I wasn't! You're damaged goods, Lola! I got you damaged, remember? And who knows who you've been with since meeting up with men in pubs!" Daniel grudgingly realized that he was being unrealistically vindictive, but he wrathfully wanted her to hurt more ruthlessly than what he was. Lola remained quiet, and angrily slammed their bedroom door in his face. She could feel the detachment between them when they had made love, but Lola did not care. She had a yearning to feel the way Daniel had made her feel once more. She was confident that their one night together would be the first step to getting back to where they once were, but, after he walked out on her one more time, Lola was convinced that love had nothing to do with their togetherness.

August 4th meant dinner dates as they had habitually and without fail fashioned as an institution when any birthday had come around. Lola had an early dinner date intended with Dean and Lauren, in an effort to celebrate her birthday. She secretly wished that Daniel would unite with them, but when she called him earlier at Salvatore, she knew that commemorating her birthday was the very last thought on Daniel's mind.

"Hey Daniel, it's me, Lola." "Yep?" Lola reluctantly sensed the utter annoyance in his voice. "We're going to dinner later at Joe's. Dean, Lauren and I. I just wanted to know, or rather ask, do you want to join us? Please come, Daniel?" Daniel hesitated for a moment, "I can't, Lola. I told Dean earlier that I just have too much to do at Salvatore. I can't. Sorry, maybe next time." "That's alright, bye." Lola was devastated and turned off her mobile phone. She was painfully conscious of how unreservedly redundant Daniel had made her feel. He declined the dinner invitation earlier to Dean, too exhausted and shattered to give an explanation that he could not face Lola.

It was an on-going clash deep within him, and each time he looked at her, he recalled and identified solely with her betrayal. He sat in his office at Salvatore into the long hours of the night, furiously attempting to get his mind off of her. He was terrified of the possibility of allowing her back into his heart, convinced that he could not surrender to her, and continue to exist with the same amount of disillusionment and discouragement, again.

Halfway through dinner, Lola ran into Gregory Pastor who was seated at the bar. "Hello gorgeous!" He was pleased to stumble upon Lola where she was waiting for the champagne she had just ordered. "Hey Greg! Haven't seen you in ages, how are you?" "Good, really good, where's Daniel?" Lola lowered her head, reluctant to divulge to Greg that Daniel Salvatore could no longer stand the mere sight of her. "Working …" "On your birthday? By the way, happy birthday. I saw them sing to you earlier." "Thanks Greg." "Word around town is, you and Daniel are having problems?" "Yeah, something like that." "Sorry to hear that, but I'm here for you if you ever need to talk. You know how to find me." "Thanks Greg, I better go, Lauren and Dean are going to start wondering what happened to me." She picked up the glasses filled with champagne, and returned to Lauren and Dean who were unwearyingly waiting for her.

Alice VL

Lola's Secret

Lola was unexpectedly disillusioned to discover that
Daniel had not arrived home yet after Dean and Lauren dropped
her off at the apartment almost an hour later. She quickly glanced
around at the empty and quiet apartment before she took her
purse and her car keys. She decided that she was not at all
prepared to spend her evening alone at the apartment, especially
not on her birthday. Without hesitation, Lola headed back to
Joe's after finally admitting to herself that she was exhausted and
worn out seeking redemption from Daniel, that was never going
to come.

When she walked back into Joe's, Lola found Gregory
still seated at the bar. She hurriedly made her way towards him,
and even though she felt a twinge of guilt, entirely aware of how
Daniel felt about Gregory, it no longer mattered as much to Lola
as it did before. She had a sudden impulse to let go, and disregard
all the abhorrence and detestation that Daniel was carrying
around for her. He had failed to recognize her birthday, and all it
did was substantiate to Lola that the love he once had for her,
had been lost, and that he no longer valued her. "Back so soon?"
Greg was astounded when he spotted Lola. "Yep, it's my birthday
and I refuse to spend it alone at the apartment. Buy me a drink!
I just want to forget about Daniel Salvatore and get drunk
tonight!" Lola removed her coat before taking the empty seat
right next to Greg. Gregory chuckled delightfully and cheerfully
ordered Lola a drink.

Daniel strolled into their apartment shortly after Lola had
left, and was stunned to find that she had not returned from her
dinner yet. He made his way into the kitchen, and promptly
poured himself a cup of coffee. While sipping on his coffee, he
felt a sudden pang of remorse for deliberately avoiding her

birthday dinner, and hurriedly dialed Dean on his mobile phone, "Hey bro." Dean answered almost at once. "Hey. So, listen, I finished up earlier than I thought I would, and I was thinking of maybe joining you guys after all. I feel bad that it's Lola's birthday and all." "Joining us? We left Joe's about an hour ago, is Lola not home? We dropped her off?" Dean was instantly mystified. "You dropped her off here? She's not here?" Daniel hurriedly walked through the apartment. "Her keys are gone. I'm going to go look for her." "Do you want me to help you look for her?" "Thanks bro, I'll pick you up in a few." He grabbed his car keys, and quickly made his way down the stairs and to his car. When he reached Dean and Lauren's apartment, Dean was anxiously waiting for him outside. "She might be at Joe's." Dean mentioned matter-of-factly, before Daniel turned the car around and without delay, headed straight for Joe's. "I don't know what's going on with her lately?" Daniel had become irritated at once.

When Daniel and Dean walked into Joe's, they noticed that the bar was almost vacant. They glanced over to the dance floor, and saw Lola slow-dancing with Gregory. His hands were all over her, and Lola seemed not one bit disturbed by his hands exploiting her. Daniel realized that she was not quite drunk, and decided to stay out of sight. He was eager to hear what they were discussing so intimately. "So, Lola, what's the story with you and Daniel?" "It's, it's a long story, Gregory, but I can tell you this, he hates me." "Wow! Has he even looked at you lately?" Greg held her a tad bit tighter before Lola turned away from him. She was utterly swayed that Daniel would never again look at her in the way he once did. It scared her to admit how revolting the mere sight of her was to him. Greg delicately turned her face to his, and gently kissed her.

Lola retreated slightly, and was astounded that Greg had unexpectedly kissed her. Daniel was compelled to do all he could to control his displeasure when he walked up to them, "Lola? What are you doing?" Lola was shaken to find Daniel standing there and stared forlornly at him, "I, nothing. I just didn't want to be at home." Lola turned back to Gregory, convinced that Daniel witnessed Gregory kiss her.

Daniel shook his head, and was once again certain that Gregory was in no way the kind of man to be around Lola. "I'm taking you home Lola, now!" Daniel instinctively grabbed Lola by her arm. "You can't tell me what to do! You go home! I'm not going anywhere with you! Not tonight Daniel, and not this time!" "Lola, you better get your things together and come with me." By the expression on Daniel's face, Lola realized that there was a side to Daniel she knew nothing about. "My apologies, Greg. I don't want to cause a scene. Thanks for dancing with me, and thanks for my birthday. Thank you for tonight." Lola smiled sorrowfully at Greg. "The car's out front." Daniel tugged at Lola's arm. "I'll drive my own damn car!" "Fine!" Daniel instantly released her arm. "I'm just dropping Dean off. You better go straight home! You better be there when I get there, Lola!" "Or what? Or what, Daniel?" Daniel grabbed her by her arm once again, "Do you really want to find out?" "I don't want to. I don't want to go home. I don't want to be there! You can't make me Daniel!" "Lola Storey, I will put you in my car, and drive you myself if I have to!" Daniel tightened his grip on her arm. "Do you hear what I'm saying? I mean it Lola, don't go there! You do not want to go there!" "You're hurting me, Daniel!" Daniel released her arm at once and stared jadedly at her, "You better not let me get there and you're not there." He turned away from her before she turned to Gregory and smiled, mortified by what had just taken place.

When Lola reached the apartment, she resolved to try one last time to engage in a civilized discussion with Daniel. It frightened her to witness his rage, and all that was left for her was to discover for once and for all, how Daniel truly felt about her, and whether they were included in one another's future. When she heard Daniel unlocking the front door, Lola quickly made her way down the passage to meet him. "Daniel?" She realized for the first time how drained and tattered he seemed. "Hey …" He shut the front door behind him. Lola was relieved that he had calmed down, and that he was no longer fuming. "So, some night, huh? I wanted to join you guys, but, anyways. Happy birthday, Lola, I'm sorry I didn't wish you this morning. Did I do that? Did I hurt you like that?" He noticed the bruise on her arm. "It's nothing." "I'm sorry, Lola. I didn't realize that I was hurting you. You just, I just, I just don't understand you sometimes. I'm sorry I hurt you." Daniel was devastated that she had once again brought out the worst of beasts in him. "It's alright, Daniel. It doesn't, hurt and it doesn't matter. But, we have to talk. I need to do this. I have to talk to you, and you don't have to say anything, but please Daniel, just let me talk. Just this once, and just listen. I won't ever ask again, but we have to do this tonight. Please, this can't go on. I can't go on like this." Daniel nervously sensed that it was the end of the road for them, "You're right, we can't carry on like this. I can't do this with you anymore, Lola. Just don't start crying, please." He calmly took a seat at the dining room table. "Daniel, I just want to know one thing from you, do you still love me? Please Daniel, just tell me honestly how you feel?"

Daniel turned away from her, and bowed his head. "Daniel, say something. Please. Do I carry on fighting for you, or do I stop? I don't know what to do, so just tell me how you feel. Do you still love me? If I just knew how you felt, I would know what to do, Danny. Just please tell me. I don't know where my place is anymore. This has been going on for far too long, for months already. Do. You. Still. Love. Me?" He gazed up at her, and by the expression in his eyes, Lola was sure that she never wanted to witness the look of complete and utter desolation again. It was a look of utter dejection and despondence, one of quitting and letting go. "I, I honestly don't know, Lola? I've been asking myself that question over and over again. I feel something, but it's not the same as before. It's not … love. And this, you and me, it's exhausting. It's just too much. I don't want you to fight for us anymore, Lola. I've given up, and you should too. I feel, I just feel it's not worth it. There's nothing left to fight for."

Daniel had no way of knowing how to categorize his feelings for her even though he indulged in a paramount effort to be entirely honest about it. He sat staring at her, positive that there was still something left inside of him, but convinced that it was not nearly enough. "You betrayed me Lola, and I've tried, really hard to get past that, but I can't. I just can't. Time isn't making any of this better. Time just isn't working. I care. Hell, I care so much, but it turns out it's not enough to forgive."

Lola bowed her head in shame, and made a severe effort to hold back her tears. "I know you don't understand, Daniel, but, if you could just try …" "I don't understand, Lola, and nothing you say can make me understand!" When he raised his voice at her once again, he was certain that he detested her so much more than he loved her. "I would've done anything for you. I would have given up everything for you. We could have been a family, but you never gave us a chance!" "I did give up everything for you, Daniel, everything, everything. The baby was everything to me! But I loved you more, and I didn't want to let you down. I wanted you to be with me, because of me, not the baby!"

Her tears began rolling without restraint and unreservedly down her cheeks when she realized that Daniel couldn't understand how much more valuable he was to her. "We made that baby, Lola. We were engaged to be married! How do you figure I would have been with you just for the baby?" She turned away from him. There was nothing more she could say to help him identify with her state of mind that day. She stood in silence for a moment before she finally walked up to him. She gazed into his eyes, and placed his hand over her heart, "I am so, so sorry, Daniel. I love you. Please, please just listen to me. Just give me a chance to explain, to tell you how I felt and to try and explain what went on in my head. If you could just give me a chance to do that, Daniel. Please. I wasn't seeing things the way you do." She instinctively, but hesitantly kissed him. Daniel reciprocated, and for just a moment, Lola thought that there might be a diminutive possibility to recapture his heart. Daniel retreated hastily, and at that very instant, Lola was convinced that Daniel was surrendering to his antagonism and abhorrence. "Daniel, don't do this. There has to be something. Just give me something to work with, anything Daniel. There must be something. I saw it at Joe's, don't hide it, please!"

She nervously reached out for his hand. He pulled back slowly, and gazed at her with wretchedness in his own eyes. "I can't, Lola. I can't do this anymore. I can't go on pretending that it didn't happen. I can't sit here and look at you without being reminded of what you've done." Daniel paused for just a moment. "I can't even look at you, Lola. I don't want to do this. I just can't. I can't even talk to Dean about this. I have nothing anymore. What you think you saw at Joe's, meant nothing. I don't care who you're screwing, but at the end of it all, I am responsible for you. We're still engaged, and I don't want the whole town to know that you are screwing Gregory behind my back." "Daniel, don't do this. I want to take it back. I want to fix this. I was in such a dark place then. You said you'd never leave me, but you've already left me. You said you'll never hurt me, but I am dying inside. Don't give up on us like that, Daniel. Don't look at it like this, please, let me just try and fix this." "You can't fix this, Lola. Not everything can be fixed! You Lola! You killed it for me! You alone hurt you, yourself. You did this! I don't trust you anymore! I will never trust you again. It's always about you Lola, and how you felt! What you were thinking! How hurt you were! I am so tired of your crying all the time. It was our child, Lola, ours. Mine and yours! You've been living your life so caged, when are you just going to wake up and look around you? How in the world does your mind work? I just can't figure you out, and it makes me crazy!" "Daniel please, you just don't want to listen!" "You're right, Lola, I don't want to listen. When I look at you, I look at you with hatred. I'm angry with you all the time. I just wish ..." "What? What do you wish for, Daniel?" Lola was desperately anxious about what he was about to say next. "I wish I never met you! I wish you never came into my life! I wish you never walked into Salvatore! I wish you would just stop! I wish this can just end! I can't take this anymore!" Lola felt as though he was grabbing a hold of her heart, and squeezing it with all his might, "That's easy, Daniel. How about I hand over all my birthday wishes to you. I can't change that you met me, or that I walked into Salvatore, but I can give you your one wish. I can end this. Now, tonight." Lola wanted to plead and implore Daniel to hold her and love her again, but instead, she turned and retreated into their bedroom. Daniel watched her walk away from him, and felt a sudden twinge of pain rush through his heart.

He slept on the couch that night, while Lola lay awake trying to outline what to do. She was devastatingly aware that the destruction they had caused one another could undoubtedly be undone. Lola accepted the fact that no matter how much time would pass them by, Daniel was at a standstill, and would under no circumstances, ever have the ability to forgive her.

Unable to fall asleep, she dressed quietly, and tiptoed her way out of the apartment. Lola drove around for what felt like hours. She could not spend one more night in the apartment with Daniel. It was at last over for them, and there was nothing she could do any longer, to force Daniel to understand, or to listen to anything she was saying. Lola knew that Daniel's heart no longer belonged to her, and when she pulled up at the beach, she realized how truly alone she was. When the sun finally began to rise, Lola was convinced that the day had come for her to move on.

She drove back to the apartment while deciding which way to go, and what she should do. She had no intention of imposing on Lauren and Dean, and immediately thought of Greg. When she reached the apartment without Daniel noticing that she had been gone all night, Lola gave Greg a quick call, hoping that she could stay with him for a few days after he previously mentioned a bedroom in his apartment that he wanted to let out. "Hey Greg, its Lola." "Lola?" He was flabbergasted to hear her voice at the other end of the phone. "You mentioned last night that you have a bedroom available for rent, has it been taken yet?" "No. Well, not yet. Technically not yet. Are you interested?" "Yes, please." "Sure. When do you want to move in?" "Today, if I can?" "That can work. Alright then. You know where I live, do you need any help?" "No, I don't have much. See you later then, and thanks Greg, I truly appreciate it." It was a decision that she never had the desire to enforce, but the antagonism and resentment she was facing with Daniel had become too excruciating for her to put up with any longer. Lola knew that should she leave, any possibility of her and Daniel salvaging their connection would be lost for all eternity, but the likelihood was slight whether or not she stayed.

She marched into the kitchen to find Daniel standing with a cup of coffee in his hand. She knew she had to inform him of the fact that she was leaving. "Daniel." He stood in silence, intuitively perceptive to what she was about to say. "I'm, I'm leaving. I'm moving out. You're right, we can't do this anymore. And you should have your place back. I don't belong here anymore, and I don't want to be here anymore. I haven't wanted to be here for a long time, and, you can tell Dean whatever you like. You can tell everyone what really happened, it doesn't matter. You don't have to protect me anymore. I don't want you to protect me anymore. What I did was wrong. Hoping you'll never find out was wrong, but my reasons were good, Daniel. And I would do it again, because, it's just, if I had to choose between losing you or losing the baby, I choose you, Daniel. You were my lid, and I'm trying so hard not to cry, so please, don't be mean about it. I can't help it. Besides, you won't have to deal with any of this anymore, after today."

Alice VL

He stood calmly while glaring at her. He was rigidly trying to find an indication, anything to convince his heart that he still loved her. "You don't have to leave, Lola. We both just need space. I'll go." "No, I'll go. We both know that this is your place. I don't want to stay here. This is your place Daniel, you should stay." "Where will you go? Are you going back to your old apartment with Lauren and Dean?" He was at once heartbreakingly aware of the finality of it all. "No. I am going to live with a friend for now. It's not fair to upset Lauren and Dean's life because of us." "A friend? What friend? Who?" "Gregory Pastor. I spoke to him early this morning and he, he's offered me his spare bedroom to rent. I, I'd just like to keep my job for now, until I can find something else, if that's okay with you?"

Daniel felt his entire world collapse around him. The idea of her living alone with Gregory was ripping at his soul. He was once again reminded of the fact that Lola ought to be kept away from a man like Gregory Pastor. "Just for now, until I find something else." "Half of Salvatore is yours, Lola. If you like, I will buy you out. You don't need to live there. I didn't know that you were so close with Gregory Pastor? Did he offer you a shoulder to cry on? Has he been comforting poor little you? I saw how you two carried on last night." "No. I don't, no, keep Salvatore as it is. I just want to keep my job for now. You know we're friends, Daniel, and no, I didn't cry on his shoulder. I just happened to run into him at Joe's last night." "Fine Lola, whatever, but Gregory? You're shacking up with Gregory Pastor?"

Daniel was growing disconcerted and restless by the minute. "I'm not shacking up with him, Daniel. It's not like that. He told me about a bedroom that's available at his place, and I'm taking it to rent. I am paying for it." "Really? With money, or with your body? And why should I believe anything you say? For all I know, you've been screwing him right under my nose. I don't have to believe anything you say! We all know Gregory Pastor, so please, don't bullshit me. Oh wait, maybe that's why you wanted to slaughter your baby. Maybe what you didn't want me to discover was that Gregory was the father? Is that it? Because honestly Lola, I have trouble believing anything that comes out of your mouth!" "You don't, Daniel, you don't have to believe anything I say anymore. And it shouldn't matter to you what my relationship with Greg is. You can believe what you like. You anyways always do, but I'd rather stay there than know you don't really want me here. The hatred you talked about, no, I have to go. And if it makes you feel better, if it makes this easier, and if it helps you feel better about yourself, then yes, I am screwing Gregory Pastor. I don't care what you think anymore, Daniel, I'm done trying to explain when you don't even want to try and understand!"

Lola was despondent and enormously sensitive to the fact that Daniel constantly thought the worst of her. She removed the engagement ring from her finger with a dejected heart, and placed it on the kitchen counter top before turning away from him. When she reached their bedroom, she fell onto their bed, and sobbed wretchedly. Her heart was crushed at the contemplation of her life shifting, and the knowledge that Daniel was no longer a part of hers any longer.

Daniel picked up the engagement ring, and stared at it for a moment before he finally placed it in the tiny pocket of his jeans. He made his way into the bedroom where he was vividly aware of Lola's desolation. Daniel was at once frightened of what the future might hold for them, and he secretly hoped she would stay one more day. "Lola, I know it's over for us. I know our feelings have changed, and I know that we can never go back to the way things were, but I don't want to end things like this. It doesn't feel right. Give me a few days. I'll find you a place, and help you move out."

Daniel was at once terrified of the shift between them. He never thought it could leave him so confused, and reeling all at the same time. "You don't have to live at Greg's place. I don't want that for you. I know I said a lot of things last night, but let me help you. I owe you that." He was appalled by the unexpected notion that he may ultimately lose her to Gregory Pastor. Lola sat up on her bed, her eyes red and engorged. She gazed questioningly at Daniel, and wished that he would ask her to stay, "No Daniel. You're not responsible for me. You don't owe me anything, and you never did. It's just best I leave now, today, you know? A clean break. I don't want your help, but thanks. It's just better this way. And it's not about what you want anymore. It's about what's right, and this, all of this, this isn't right. I should have done this sooner, I wish I did. I've known for a long time that it's over, but I just couldn't face up to it, so please, let me go on my own terms. Just let me go."

Daniel left the apartment without saying another word. Without considering the devastating truth that it was finally over between them. Daniel had an inexplicable desire to distance himself from Lola, and in no way exactly understood how terrifyingly diverse his life was about to become.

Lola quickly scheduled an urgent appointment with Mr. H, and forced him to nullify the agreement of the shares that Daniel had given her in Salvatore. He had summarily placed it back in Daniel's name by destroying the altered indenture which entitled Lola to half of Salvatore. Mr. H was puzzled when Lola instructed him to withhold the information from Daniel, but was bound by privilege to uphold her wishes.

She promptly moved into Gregory's apartment which overlooked the river running through their quaint and picture-perfect town. Even though it was tinier than the apartment she shared with Lauren, Lola thought it was the ideal place to put her broken heart back together, and to hopefully, recover from Daniel's detestation and resentment. She moved in a few of her belongings before contacting Lauren, and updating her of the sequence of events that had unfolded.

Lauren and Dean were both utterly distraught at the sudden turn of events, but they were certain that given enough time, Daniel and Lola would find their way back to each other. Lauren promised to check in on Lola during the week after begging her to move back in with her. "This is your apartment too, sis. Please come back here." "No sissy, it was ours, and now it's yours and Dean's. I'm fine, I promise." Lauren's apprehension was evident in her voice. "I'll check in on you later this week."

Gregory helped her settle in, and was secretly thrilled that Lola had moved in with him. He was certain that it would significantly disturb Daniel, and there was not much that could make him more contented than the idea of a frantic Daniel at that very moment. Lola nervously dialed Salvatore, and when Daniel answered without delay, her heart had unpredictably begun to shudder. "Daniel, hi, it's Lola …" "Hey Lola, what's up?" "I, I've left the keys to the apartment with the caretaker, and I'll leave the car with you tomorrow." Daniel's heart broke out into an uncontrollable gallop. "Just keep the car, Lola. I don't have time for this!" He abruptly slammed down the phone, and for just a moment, he considered calling her back. Into the core of his being, he was convinced that Lola still loved him, and he was sickened by the way he treated her. He picked up the phone, but before he could call her back, he was plagued by his own hesitation, and decided against returning her call.

Lola stood numbly, still holding the phone in her hand, horrifically persuaded that Daniel Salvatore could no longer stomach conversing with her.

When Daniel arrived at the apartment shortly after ten that night, he strolled into an empty apartment. He quickly glanced around, and realized that Lola had barely taken anything. Even so, the apartment felt bare and chilly. When he walked into the kitchen, he was agonizingly aware of a certain melancholy at the reality of not seeing Lola walk through their apartment door at any given moment, or ever again. It was a prospect Daniel could not eject from his mind, when he was unable to remember what his life was like before he met Lola Storey. A life he was fraught to get back to. He sat down on the sofa in the living room, and wondered if he had become so accustomed to having her around him, that her absence was almost insufferable.

Earlier that day, Dean reminded him of the fact that Lola had become an enormous fraction of his life, and that even though Daniel was swayed by the fact that he no longer loved her, he would miss her presence. Daniel thought back to the expression on her face of that very morning when she removed the ring from her finger. The sorrow in her eyes haunted him. He was unexpectedly concerned that he could no longer keep a protective eye on her. He noticed a handwritten note that Lola had left for him. He slowly opened it, and felt an unexpected throbbing in his heart as his hands began to tremble.

'Daniel, I know I let you down and I know there is so much you can't understand and can never forgive. It was never like that, and I never did it to hurt you. I am sorry for all the hurt I've caused you, but please know that it is still me, Lola. I can tell you this over and over, but I can never change the way you feel. I get that. I understand that, and it's not your fault, none of this is. Please forgive me, and know that I loved you so much. I wish so many good things for you, and I'm sorry that I'm no longer a part of your life. I hate me too. I love you still.'

He heatedly crumpled the letter and tossed it into the bin. Daniel felt bare inside when he began to agonize over her once again. He questioned Gregory's motives with Lola. It terrified him again that she could possibly fall in love with a man like Gregory Pastor. He hesitantly dialed Dean's number, frantic to know that Lola was doing all right. "Lauren speaking?" "Hey, its Daniel. Is Dean there?" "Hey Daniel. Dean's just in the shower, can I get him to call you back?" She instantly sensed misery in Daniel's voice. "I just wanted to know, is Lola alright? Have you heard from her?" Lauren was glaringly aware of the fact that her sister was inconsolable, but she in no way elected to choose sides between Lola and Daniel. "She's fine, Daniel, really, but I just have to say and I've been trying not to but, you lied to Lola too, Daniel." Daniel was at once caught off-guard by Lauren's bluntness. "I lied? What did I lie about, Lols?" "You said you'd never let anyone hurt her. That night in the kitchen, you promised me, and now you are the one hurting her. You are the only one hurting her. How does that happen? It wasn't her fault she miscarried, and maybe she just hadn't gotten around to telling you yet. It wasn't her fault she got pregnant, she didn't do it alone. And now because of that, she is living with Gregory. She won't even consider coming back to the apartment. She would rather live there, with him, Daniel!" Lauren was reduced to tears, but was adamant to remind Daniel of his promise to her. "You don't know everything, Lauren. I told her I'd help her find a place. Maybe she just wants to be with Gregory. Maybe it's what she's wanted all along. Talk to your sister, Lauren, there are things you know nothing about." He abruptly ended his call to Lauren, and slammed his mobile phone on the kitchen counter. Lauren was convinced that they still loved one another. It crushed her heart that they were both being incredibly inflexible, and unable to fully comprehend their state of affairs.

When Lola arrived at Salvatore the following morning, she was relieved to discover that Daniel and Dean were busy in the workshop. "So, Dean, have you heard from Lola?" Daniel pressed Dean for information about Lola. "Yeah, Lauren spoke with her yesterday. Apparently, she's moved in with Gregory?" "Yeah, she left. Seems like Gregory is where she wants to be." "Lola isn't like that bro, and I don't understand how things got so out of hand with you two?" Dean was outright puzzled, and could no longer avoid asking him the question that made no sense at all, "Are you guys still stuck on the miscarriage?" Daniel glanced over at Dean before a lump in his throat made its unwanted presence known, "Something like that …" "She loves you Daniel. You've just let the best thing ever get away from you, and you can't blame Greg for this. This is what you do. The moment someone gets too close, or the moment things get too serious, you back away. You always, always do this." "You have no idea what you're talking about Dean!" Daniel shouted after him before Dean abruptly left the workshop.

Lola made her way around the counter, and promptly filed paperwork that were stacked up from the day before. When she looked down at the documents lying scattered on her desk, Lola noticed that she was still wearing the four-leaf clover necklace that Daniel had given her. She quickly removed it from her neck, and lovingly stared at it for a brief moment. She once again vaguely remembered being given a four-leaf clover once before, but she couldn't remember when it was, or who it was from. Lola could distantly remember holding one in her hands, while gently rubbing it, but she could not evoke anything else about that moment, and as a result, it unreservedly mystified her. She rubbed it as gently as she did in her memory, but when she could remember nothing more, she knelt down and placed it in her handbag.

When Lola looked up again, Daniel had unexpectedly appeared on the other side of the counter. "Hey, Donovan Moodley will be in shortly. There's a problem with his car, will you just book it back in, please?" He was zealously aware of the fact that she had only moments ago, removed the necklace he had given her. "Of course." Before disappearing into his office, he turned around to face her, "So, you settled in okay?" She nodded and smiled before she turned her back on him, "Yes, thank you." Her heart was aching for him. She longed for his arms around her, but she was convinced that Daniel no longer loved her, and that the time had come for her to accept that he no longer wanted her around him. "Daniel, before I forget, we need to talk about the car ..." "What about the car?" "I, it's not mine. I want you to have it back." Lola was desperate to let him know that she wanted or needed nothing from him anymore, but her quivering voice stopped her. "And what will you do for transport? Oh right, Gregory." "No, Daniel. I can drive Bonnie when I need to. I've saved a little, you know that?" "Listen to me Lola, I gave you that car. If you don't want it, you can sell it, but I don't want it. Call it a pity payout if you must!" Daniel instantly became agitated. Lola was horrified to hear that he pitied her. "Wow Daniel, pity pay?" "Call it whatever you like Lola, I call it pity pay."

He abruptly turned away from her, and before Daniel reached his office, he turned to look back at Lola, satisfied that she could not see him. He was overwhelmed by the fact that she so dispassionately removed the necklace, and he despondently questioned how it was possible for her to accept their break up so readily, when he was struggling so much more than he ever thought was possible.

While watching her go about her normal day to day duties, Daniel felt his stomach turn. He was convinced that he was going to be ill. She remained the most beautiful woman in the entire universe to him, but she shattered his heart into a million fractions. He was crushed by unrecognizable emotions that he had never experienced before he met her. He no longer wanted her as an element in his life, yet he could barely visualize a life without her in it.

When Donovan Moodley walked in, Lola handed him the job card, ready for him to sign off on. "Hi Mr. Moodley, please sign here." He eagerly signed on the dotted line, and contentedly handed it back to Lola. "So, when's the big day?" Lola smiled nervously, unsure of what to say or how to explain that Daniel Salvatore no longer wanted a future with her. "Oh no, there's not

Lola's Secret

going to be a wedding." She was about to clarify when Daniel walked in, almost as a knight in shining armor. "Donovan, bring it around the back, and I'll see what I can do for you."

When Donovan left, Lola was thankful that she wasn't forced to explain to Donovan Moodley that they were no longer together. She was intensely aware of a proverbial ache in her heart when she realized that she was no longer Daniel's fiancé.

Daniel lingered in his office while he stood staring at Lola, and noticed for the first time how tattered and exhausted she appeared to be. He guessed that the end of their relationship had taken its toll on her, but he had no way of knowing how to be with her any longer. He adored Lola. His heart reminded him of that one truth over and over again, but his mind constantly told him of the hurt and rage he was carrying around, brought on by Lola. Daniel was immensely displaced and irritated by all the unexpected and abrupt emotions he was feeling and once more, he had no idea of how to deal with any of them.

Lola's Secret

Alice VL

SEPARATE LIVES

November appeared out of the blue and far too suddenly. It was also the month that Dean and Lauren had set aside for their engagement. Lauren had graduated from high school with honors, and Lola was hopeful that she would attend college, but Lauren insisted on taking a year off from studying. Lola had almost adapted to living without Daniel, but she was comforted by the fact that she was close to him during the day at Salvatore.

A week prior to the engagement, Lola scuffled at the mere thought of getting out of bed one morning, something that had hardly ever happened before. She awoke to immense queasiness on the morning of the engagement party, and unceremoniously suspected the reason behind her sudden ill health. She thought back to the one single night she shared with Daniel, and knew instinctively that a similar incident from the past was about to take place once again. Once again, it terrified Lola. She fervently begged to a higher power that she may be wide of the mark this time. Lola dragged herself out of bed, and made her way to the bathroom. She glared at her reflection in the mirror, desperately trying to place when it was that she developed the shadowy circles around her eyes. She looked appalling, and she felt even shoddier. Lola climbed into the shower, hoping that she would feel better afterwards, but by the time she climbed out, the nausea was overpowering.

She hurriedly dressed herself and ran across the road to the drug store, just a short distance from the apartment she was sharing with Greg. She quickly bought a pregnancy test, and dashed back to the apartment as fast as her legs could carry her. She sat quietly on her bed where she stared at the test for what felt like forever, secretly praying for the courage to take it, but deathly afraid of what it might tell her. When she glanced down at her wristwatch, she realized that it was almost time for her to leave for the engagement party. Lola decided to take the pregnancy test in an effort to get it over and done with, but when Gregory arrived home unexpectedly, she shoved it into her closet before the results were available, desperate for Greg to remain clueless.

The engagement party was hosted by the Salvatore's at Joe's which Lola unenthusiastically and half-heartedly agreed to attend. She knew she could not punish Lauren and Dean for her mess with Daniel. It was a beautiful evening. Lola was delighted that it turned out so wonderfully for her sister. It was fantastic to see Sarah and John Salvatore again. Lola spent hours locked into memorable conversations with them. Lola's heart turned grave when she realized how dreadfully she was going to miss their stories, but she was in high spirits to listen to them while she still could. Dean had declared his undying love for his gorgeous bride to be, and Lola was finally persuaded that Lauren would be in safe hands and loved by the Salvatore's.

Lola frequently caught glimpses of Daniel during the evening, but she engaged in a valiant attempt to steer clear of him as often as she could. She noticed him earlier on in the evening at the side of a striking brunette. Lola was excruciatingly aware of how taken she was with him. When Lola stared at her for just a moment longer, she recognized her as Samantha, the same woman who sat with Daniel at the bar on Lauren's eighteenth birthday. It wasn't hard to appreciate the fact that women were in awe of Daniel. Yet, he was still responsible for the galloping of Lola's heart each time she laid eyes on him, so it came as no surprise that he was closely shadowed by a soaring, and elegant beauty. When the guests took to the dance floor, Lola quietly made her way down to the beach, leaving Gregory behind at the bar.

It had grown crowded inside, and Lola became queasy once again. She was desperately hoping that the fresh air would keep her from getting sick. While standing on the beach gazing out over the ocean, Lola thought back to the last time she was standing there. It was the very night she met Daniel. She suddenly longed for those days almost as much as she yearned for him. Lola couldn't help but wonder what their lives would've been like, had she never scheduled that devastating appointment, and if Daniel had never taken that critical call. She restlessly deliberated on the pregnancy test shoved into her closet, and prayed silently that she was mistaken. More than anything, she was frantic to free herself from the unrelenting hold Daniel continued to have over her.

Lola was instantly startled to notice a shadow come up from behind, almost out of nowhere. She hurriedly turned around, and when she recognized Daniel, she was at once overwhelmed by a light-headedness. She instinctively grabbed at him the moment her legs gave away beneath her. "Lola, what's the matter? I didn't see you here on the beach. Are you alone here?" "I'm fine, sorry. I just lost my balance. You gave me a fright. No, I'm not alone. I'm here with Greg." She let go of Daniel as soon as she regained her balance. He took her by her arm, before Lola gazed up into his eyes. "Are you sure you're alright?" "I'm fine, Daniel, really. It's nice to see you again, away from work. You look good, and happy." She was dreadfully nervous that she might blurt out that she was terrible, that she missed him, and that she loved him with her entire self. "Thanks Lola, I am good and, I am happy. I just, I wish I could say the same about you." "But you can't, can you Daniel? You can't say anything nice to, or about me." Lola had no desire at all to stand in front of him, and willingly pay attention to his insults. As she turned to leave, Daniel was shocked to realize how much tinier she had become. He watched her make her way back to the bar, before he turned to gaze out over Sutherland.

Daniel too wondered what it would have been like, had they not lost their child. He repeatedly interrogated himself as to whether she would have gone through with the abortion. It bothered him immensely that he had no inclination as to what the truth was. Daniel accepted a small amount of accountability for all that had turned so appallingly bad between them, by blaming himself for not telling her that he was aware of the pregnancy right from the start. As disconcerting and unattainable as it was to pardon Lola, Daniel was finding it a tad bit harder to forgive himself. He turned around, and as he made his way back to the pub, he noticed her seated at the bar while Gregory Pastor was once again making his way over to Lola. "Hey pretty girl, a drink?" Gregory cheerfully sat down on the empty seat beside Lola. Lola smiled grudgingly at him, and was once again aware of the unchanged panic that so unpredictably enthralled the innermost part of her on each occasion that Gregory addressed her as provocatively as he did, and whenever he began to consume alcohol. "No thanks, Greg, nct tonight." Lola was once again hauntingly reminded of the pregnancy test in her closet. Gregory agreed to her appeal that she take the critical time she desperately needed to heal from her break up with Daniel, but every so often, he would test the waters with her. For Lola, it was grueling, and she habitually questioned how long it would be until Gregory Pastor lost his patience with her.

Daniel was irritated to see Gregory with Lola, and on the spur of the moment, he made his way directly towards them. He had made up his mind to pose only one question to her, a question Daniel was supposed to ask her a long time ago. On his way to the bar, he was hauled to one side by Samantha. "Hey handsome, come dance with me!" Daniel glanced over to where Lola was sitting, and almost overcome with resentment, he turned back to Samantha. "Sam, I just want to get a drink from the bar. See you in a bit, okay?" She glowered with disappointment before she reluctantly strolled back to the dance floor, before Daniel quickly made his way over to Lola.

As he approached her, he noticed that Gregory had his hands all over Lola, and even though she was in no way retreating from him, he could not restrain his annoyance, "What's going on here, Lola? Are you drinking again?" Lola was mortified to find Daniel standing so closely behind them, "Nothing's going on, and no, I'm not drinking. But anyway, what I do has got nothing to do with you!" "Dude, how is it any of your business?" Gregory took Lola's hand before Daniel grabbed Gregory on impulse from his seat and when Lola stepped back in horror, she was unsure of how to respond to his sudden and violent rage. "This isn't about Lola, this is about you. You just want to get her drunk again!" "What's your problem, dude?" Gregory was utterly befuddled by

Daniel's vicious and impulsive conduct. "Dude? Really? Dude?" "She's living with me pal, after you kicked her out, and if she wants a drink, she can have a drink!" "Lola can't handle her drink and by the way, she left on her own. You have no idea what you're talking about. I don't care what you two are up to, but you should just know this, don't ever knock her up, she'll destroy your soul! So, I'd think twice about feeding her all that booze!" Daniel turned to face Lola and glared at her in antipathy after Gregory had stormed off.

Lola was unexpectedly terrified of Daniel, but was nudged by her own rage accumulating inside of her almost at once, "Daniel, when did you turn into this huge asshole?" "Why do you keep getting into situations like this, Lola? How can you be so completely helpless? I'm not going to be around to save you every damn time! And look at you, you are fading away. When did you stop taking care of yourself? Or is it all the booze and Gregory Pastor?" "You don't have to save me, Daniel. I never asked you to save me! I never needed saving! What do you care anyways? I'm with Gregory now. I'm with him, and what we do has nothing to do with you." Daniel grabbed her by her arm when she quickly turned away from him. "You're with Gregory? What does that even mean? So, I was right about you, and you lied to me again. Does he know that you are an executioner? Did you tell him what you've done? Does he know that you will rip his heart out next? And don't lie to me, Lola, I want the truth. I want to know from you tonight, how you could have wanted to kill our child? Was the baby getting in the way of you and Gregory, or was Gregory the father? Which one is it?"

She looked up at him with unspeakable sorrow while wholeheartedly conscious of a dominant and debilitating fear that had devastatingly crept into her heart, but at the same time, she knew that she had little left that Daniel could take from her. She had, beyond a shadow of a doubt, lost the man she treasured more than life itself. She lost the child she wanted only to love, and she had involuntarily, and with complete and utter desolation, lost the will to fight him. "I tried telling you for months, but you wouldn't listen! Why now? Why here? Why now, Daniel? Do you want to humiliate me here, in front of everyone? In front of your parents, Lauren and your girlfriend? In front of Gregory? Will that make you happy? Is that what it takes to put an end to this? Do you want me to blurt it out here, where everyone can witness me admit to the fact that I am an awful person? Will that make you stop? Is that the peace you need?" Her heart could no longer tolerate the brutality of his vicious and unrelenting attack on her. Worn-out and defeated, she seized a hold of him, and began pounding at him with her fists, mustering up every ounce of strength that was left inside of her. "I don't know, I don't know! I feel like I could never have gone through with it, but then I remember how scared I was, and then I think I would've done anything to hold onto you, because, I just loved you so much." She couldn't predict or foresee how she would have felt, laying there, waiting to end the life of her unborn child. Lola wanted to cry out that she might be pregnant again, that they had one more chance, and that she could do it right, given one more chance.

While witnessing the fury and resentment on his face, Lola knew that until she knew, she could not reveal her suspicions to him. Daniel clutched her hands into his when he noticed the guests staring, but unable to suppress his rage. "You cut me out, Lola! You decided on your own! You made that appointment!

And then, conveniently, you miscarried! And when things got too rough between us, you moved into another man's bed, just like that! You left me, Lola!" Daniel was frantic to find anything in Lola's eyes to tell him that she would never have gone through it. But, all he recognized was hurt and antagonism, which puzzled him even more. "I was scared!" Lola shouted out through her unyielding tears. "I did, I cut you out! I did it, because I didn't know what else to do! I made that appointment, because I was confused! But yes, I did make that appointment! And yes, I would have done it! Is that what you want to hear? Are you happy now? Let it go, Daniel, and just leave me alone! Things didn't just get rough with us Daniel, things ended! You ended it! You left me, you left me, Daniel, long before I moved out, you left me!"

She paused to take in a deep breath before lowering her head while desperately trying to hide the tears that were rolling unreservedly down her cheeks, "Nothing I say, changes anything. Nothing is good enough for you. You turned your back on me when I wanted to fight for you. Why do you keep doing this to me? Now, even the miscarriage was my fault." Lola quickly swabbed at the tears on her cheeks.

"I never wanted that, how can you be so cruel? You referred to me as damaged goods when you know, you know better. You know what happened, Daniel! I told you! I never told anyone, but I told you, and you are making me pay for that as well. Gregory is kind. He doesn't try and destroy me like you do. How do you get to make me feel so unworthy? We're not together anymore, Daniel. You and I, it's over so just stop! Maybe now you will listen, I didn't want that baby, and I didn't love you. That's all that you'll believe so please, believe that, and just let me be! Let me get on with my life! Listen carefully to me Daniel,

I'm with Gregory now. I want to be with Gregory. I never wanted your baby, and I don't love you anymore. I am in love with Greg, not you. I hate you. I hate you, Daniel. I hate you …hate you …" The words she was choking on sliced into Daniel's heart like a blunt knife. Listening to her tell him how she found him loathsome made him feel sick to his stomach. He caught a glimpse of Samantha who was utterly confused by the commotion, but when he glanced back at Lola, he could have sworn that he could visibly make out how utterly shattered her heart was.

All the guests were staring at Daniel and Lola when Lauren ran up to Lola, and placed her arms around her while she sobbed unremittingly into her sister's arms. "What happened? What's going on?" Lauren was horrified to find her sister so utterly broken and deflated. "Lauren, I can't do this anymore. It's time I tell the truth. I can't hide this anymore. I don't want to. Daniel hates me, and so will all of you, but I just can't go on like this anymore." Lola quickly glanced around her before she looked back at Lauren, "I can't get up each morning and pray that I get through the day without being reminded of all my stupid mistakes. I can't live with what I've done. I don't want to do any of this anymore. I'm in love with Gregory now, my life is with him. I want to make it work, but I have to tell you something, all of you. I have to tell Greg." Lola turned to glance over at John and Sarah. She knew that what she was about to tell them all, would change the way they saw her. She was aware of a brand-new batch of tears ready to escape from her eyes, when she considered the reality of losing John and Sarah in the process.

Daniel nervously peered over at his parents, and had an unexpected, but urgent desire to protect Lola from their discontentment. He walked up to Lola, before he gently touched her arm, suddenly agonizingly sensitive to the fact that he had pushed her too hard. "Don't do this, Lola." Lola was once again stunned by Daniel's unexpected behavior. "No Daniel, I do. I do have to do this. I can't stand this anymore, and I can't stand hiding this. I can't stand the way you look at me anymore! I have to tell the truth for once. I must! This is precisely what you wanted, Daniel! You don't get to tell me no anymore! You don't get to attack me, and then protect me. You don't get anything, do you?" "It's private, Lola. We are dealing with it. It's between us!" "Us? There is no us anymore and maybe it's time that everyone knew what a horrible person I am." Lola looked around her one more time before she turned back to Daniel. "Maybe then, you won't hate me so much! Maybe then, one day, you can forgive me, because I just can't take this anymore! We are not dealing with anything, Daniel. I've tried, but you don't want to." Lola swallowed back on the lump in her throat, "You've pushed me away. I feel like I am a stranger to you. For months after I lost the baby, I tried to talk to you, but you weren't listening. I tried everything to make things right. I stayed much longer than I should have. I tried fighting for us. I tried to give you time but, you haven't said anything decent to me since, and the only time you ever touched me was when you came home drunk. And the way you used me that night, was worse than being treated like a whore. That, I can't live with. I look at you, and I see the hatred, the disgust, and sometimes, the pity. But, you won't say it, Daniel. But, I feel it, you pity me! That's disgusting! And then, you turn around and you hate me, all at the same time. I can't do this. I don't want to."

She glanced around her one more time, unsure of

precisely how to tell her sister of all she had done, convinced that she had to take responsibility for her cecisions. "Lola, not here. Everyone's staring. Let's go outside." Daniel became anxious all of a sudden. "I don't care Daniel, everyone can stare. It doesn't matter. I just don't care anymore. I will get up on that stage if I have to, I don't care. I've given up on us Daniel, on everything."

Daniel abruptly took her by her arm, and led her out onto the beach when he realized that there was nothing he could say to stop Lola from revealing the truth about all that had gone so wide off the mark between them. He had an inexplicable and unexpected need to shield her from the devastating facts. Lauren, Dean and Gregory followed curtly while John and Sarah remained indoors at the insistence of Daniel and Dean.

Daniel took her cold hand into his and gently squeezed it when he noticed that she had begun to tremble. "You don't have to do this, Lola. Nobody has to know. I want to listen now. You and me, alone. Let's go talk somewhere in private, just don't do this now." He was excruciatingly aware of his own tears that were laying shallow in his eyes, while recognizing for the first time, that the anguish had become intolerable for her. "No Daniel, no. What I need to say, I owe to Gregory now, and to my sister!" Lola became erratically panic-stricken, "It's over, Daniel. You and me, there's nothing anymore. I am nothing to you anymore, and it doesn't matter to me what everyone thinks. I don't care. I just want my sister and Gregory to know the truth. I don't even care what you think anymore, Daniel. You hate me already." Lola's world came crashing down around her when she noticed the remorse in Daniel's eyes. "You spent months bashing me, telling me that I'm a killer. And now? You want to keep me quiet? I don't get that, so no, Daniel, no more! You don't know what you want, and I don't know how to figure you out. And I pray that after this, we will never see each other again. I, Daniel, never want to see you again."

Daniel's world suddenly became much darker than he ever thought was possible. "I pray to God that you just stop, because I can't stand this, and I can't stand your pity. I've been through worse, but I've never wanted anyone's pity. You look at me with disappointment in your eyes, and I never, ever want to see that again. I never want to see you again, Daniel. I have nothing left anymore, so I no longer care. And Gregory wants a chance with me, and I, I want to give it to him, understand?"

Lola turned to face Gregory. "Greg, I know you and Lauren, and everyone else are confused by all of this. And I, I know you don't understand, and that you think Daniel is being unfair but, what happened between us, what went wrong between us was all my fault. It was never Daniel, or anything he did. This time, it wasn't him." Lola felt her heart begin to hammer erratically. She was unsure of how to carry on, but, she was committed to coming clean. "I did something really stupid. It had nothing to do with the miscarriage. Before I lost the baby, I made an appointment to have an abortion, and, and that's why Daniel is so angry. I never told him, and I hoped he would never find out. I was going to go the morning Peter, my dad, died, and then the funeral happened. And then I lost the baby. I lied to him. I lied to all of you, and yes, I would have gone through with it, so please, hate me or forgive me, but there it is. I just don't want to do this anymore. I know you think it was Daniel, but don't, it was me. All of this is me. I did this."

Lola turned to face Daniel, only to find his tears recklessly sloping down his cheeks. Lauren was stunned, and stood glaring at Lola, unable to fully grasp what she was saying, "How could you, sis? You went against everything you ever believed in. You loved Daniel. He loved you so much. I don't get it? Daniel never said anything about an abortion?" Lola bowed her head in shame. "That's what I want to know. I'm trying to understand. I loved her." Daniel hurriedly swabbed the tears from his cheeks. "How many times do I have to tell you, Daniel? I was scared. I didn't want to let you down. I didn't want you to look at me like I was trying to hold onto you. I didn't want to be Tanita. You said these things don't just happen. I didn't know what to do? I just loved you so much. The way you bashed Tanita and her pregnancy. How you said she trapped Tony, I didn't want you to look at me like that. I didn't want that."

Dean walked up to Lola and placed his arms around her while she sobbed hysterically into his chest. "I'm sorry Dean, I am so sorry." "That's okay, Lola, I get it. We all had something to say about Tanita. We're all responsible for this. This isn't all just you, Lola." Lola smiled despondently at him before she turned back to Daniel, "I made such a gigantic mistake. I want to take it back Daniel. I would do anything to take it back, but I know, I know I can't. I can't go back, but I never did it because I stopped loving you. I was so scared that I would never again feel the way I felt with you." Lola quickly swabbed at her tears, frantic to appear brave in front of Daniel. "And that night, when we made love, I realized you just wanted to humiliate me. That night I knew. I knew it was over." Lola brought both her hands to her face, and covered her eyes while sobbing into them.

She quickly regained her composure and faced Daniel again, "I didn't do it because I didn't want your baby, I just wanted you more, and I am sorry. I don't know what else to do, or how to tell you. I should have asked you what you wanted first. I just thought, I just thought that you'd think I'd want to use the baby to hold on to you, and I can't, not like that. And now, now it's over and there's nothing I can do. Nothing that can take me back. So rather, let's rather just get on with our lives. You go your way. I can't anymore, Daniel, it's just so sore ..."

Lauren placed her arms around Lola while Dean held a protective arm on her back. Lola was thankful that they didn't abandon her as Daniel had. When she glanced over at Daniel, Lola noticed the drenched tears on his cheeks, but she was certain that he was not yet ready to forgive her. "Its sore, Lola? After everything we've been through? You didn't trust me enough to rely on me with something like that? What was I to you if you couldn't trust me? We had a life, a future, and you stole that from us. You destroyed everything! It was our decision Lola, not yours alone, and you stole that from me too. I gave you everything I could. I gave you my heart, and you destroyed that so effortlessly." Daniel took in a deep breath when he bowed his head. "We, you and I made that baby together. You never trusted me. You hurt me, Lola." Lola glanced up at Daniel one more time, "But you're forgetting one thing Daniel, I lost our baby. I miscarried. The baby died. I didn't have the abortion. That doesn't seem to be as important as scheduling an appointment for an abortion, does it? You are stuck on the abortion, as though I actually went through with it!" Lola became irate instantaneously. "And, how well everything turned out for you, Lola ..." "How can you say that? Daniel, you knew I was pregnant, and you never said anything! What does that say about you?" "Lola! Don't do that! Do not play that card. I tried giving you space. I knew that it was something you had to deal with first. Little did I know that you were going to deal with it! It never even crossed my mind that you could do something like that! I never thought, I never thought it was ever an option." "Daniel! You think what you want! Nothing, nothing I say will make any difference to you! You have answers for everything and you just believe what you want to believe! I am the one that did this! Yes, that I know, and I'm living with that, every single day! I am taking responsibility for what I've done. I am damaged goods, Daniel, you were right! No, you weren't my first! Peter Storey had that privilege, but damn you for making it sound as though I wanted it, or that I had any control over it."

Lola did her best to hold back the tears for as long as she could. "Things aren't as simple as you think they are! You are so narrow- minded, but you know what? I can't do this, I don't want to anymore." She hastily turned to face Lauren, "Lauren, please. I don't want to fight, I just want to go home. I've said what I needed to say, and there's nothing more left to explain. He will never understand. He just doesn't want to, and whether you do or don't, it doesn't matter."

Lola turned to Daniel one last time, "I am done, Daniel. I have nothing more to say. You will hate me always. Just let me go, you won't see me again, I promise." Gregory stepped in between Lola and Daniel, "Let her go Daniel, she wants nothing more to do with you. I love her, and I will never treat her that way." Gregory took Lola's hand into his, "You abandoned her, just like I said you would, and just like you always do. You always find a way to push someone out, just like you did with Tanita, and now with Lola."

Daniel grabbed him by the shoulder, and looked him sternly in the eye, before instantly turning away from them. Lola wanted to flee from it all just as she had done with her parents. She wanted to hide, and under no circumstances, ever re-surface again, but she knew that she could no longer run. She was exhausted, and utterly alone. All she wanted was to leave them all behind her, and go to sleep while praying never to awake again.

Daniel watched her leave despite the fact that he was uneasily conscious of his own heart shattering into a thousand broken pieces. The idea that he may never see her again was an excruciating, and intolerable thought that frightened him almost to death. Hearing her tell him that she never wanted to see him again, carved like a sharp knife through his core.

Lauren had returned to Sarah and John, while Dean stood motionlessly and in silence beside Daniel. "Come on bro, you don't think she would really have done it? Don't tell me you don't get it even just a little?" "I don't know, Dean? I honestly don't, but I do know that she thought about ending it. That's how much she loved me ..." "Daniel, things are not always as black and white as it seems." Dean made a gallant effort to defend her. "I mean, look how you reacted towards Tanita. Don't you think that just maybe, just maybe she really was afraid of losing you? That maybe, you came first?" Dean placed his hand on his brother's shoulder. Daniel grimaced at the very suggestion that Lola was frightened of him. "We could've worked it out Dean, she knew that I loved her. She knows that I love her." "Put yourself in her shoes, Daniel, you left her anyways. Maybe she felt that you would leave her because of the baby. You haven't proved her wrong, but at the end of all this, the point you're completely missing is, she didn't abort the baby. She miscarried, and you are not being fair, bro. Lola was heartbroken about it, and you never let her grieve her baby." Dean was desperate to make Daniel see things as they were. "I hear her cry in Lauren's arms bro, and it has taken everything out of her. Lola is struggling, and all you see is the abortion that never happened. You're not around to see her sob into her sister's arms. You're not there to see her cry herself to sleep at night when she stays over. You just see what you want to see, Daniel." Dean hesitated for a moment before he continued, "Lola lost her child and then she lost you. If you ask me bro, you led her right into Greg's arms. Think about that for a second. And, you shouldn't have, you should have left Peter Storey out of it. That was low, Daniel. You know what Lola went through with her family and today, today you're punishing her for it. She is broken, Daniel. She survived the Storeys, but it doesn't look like she's going to survive you. You lied too, Daniel. You said that you'd never hurt her, that nothing could change?"

Daniel desperately wanted to believe his brother and identify with how Lola felt, but all he understood was the incredible heartache that had invaded his heart. His thoughts were instantly interrupted when Samantha appeared beside him. "D, you okay?" Daniel gazed at her and smiled despondently, "Yeah, always." He was still confused by the unknown emotions that were building up inside of him. Daniel no longer wanted to be at Joe's, and after saying quick goodbyes to his parents, Dean and Lauren, he led Samantha out to his car. "My place?" He was frantic to discard Lola, and all that had taken place only moments ago. "Oh? What have you got in mind?" Daniel laughed out loud before he drove out to the apartment in silence. When they walked through the front door, Samantha grabbed him, and pulled him close. She began kissing him while Daniel responded without hesitation.

Making their way into his bedroom, Daniel wavered for a moment, crucially aware that Lola was the last woman he had been with. He certainly, and in no way ever, considered the very suggestion that he would invite another woman into the bed that he had sacredly shared with Lola. At that very instant, Daniel came up with a verdict to disregard Lola, and all that had happened earlier at Joe's, for only one night. He pulled Samantha down onto the bed with him. He had an urgent need to break away from his reality, an escape from all that had gone so horrifically off-beam, a flight from his derelict heart. He had an awful urge to gaze into another woman's eyes. He was desperate to feel the intimacy of another woman's body against him. He gazed at Samantha, unable to ignore her stature and beauty, and even though he stared endlessly into her eyes, it was Lola's that played out like a nightmarish film in his mind.

When he closed his eyes, he was overwhelmed by the shattering that refused to let go of him, but he had no desire to drown in the waves that were building up inside of him. He was desperate to switch off all that was raging inside of him, and be the man he was before she had so carelessly entered his life, and trampled his heart into the ground. He kissed Samantha with undeniable enthusiasm and undressed her with excessive force and lust, once again indisputably alert to his anger and resentment. He hunted Samantha in a desperate attempt to discard and forget Lola, even if only for one night. It was essential for his survival to establish a sense of belonging again, but when he gazed into Samantha's eyes one more time, it was Lola's heartbroken and accusing eyes that were staring back at him. He was unexpectedly struck with an overpowering and crushing sense of guilt. He could not go through with it, and as hard as he tried, he could not make love to another woman.

Even though he so urgently desired Samantha's body, it was Lola who had captured, and held possession of his tattered heart. The Daniel from before was gone. His heart nudged him of the fact that he would be betraying not only Lola, but himself too, and he was in no way at all, equipped for the way the realization made him feel. He hurriedly slid off his bed, and instantly pulled his jeans back on. "Daniel?" Samantha was struck by bewilderment when she got up, and stood in front of him. "Sam, you shouldn't be here. This doesn't feel right. We shouldn't be doing this." "Why not? What did I do? Does this have anything to do with that girl at Joe's, the one you were arguing with?" Daniel had no desire to disclose that Lola utterly and thoroughly consumed his every thought. "No, she's no-one. I just can't." "I saw the way you looked at her, Daniel, who is she?" Daniel bowed his head, uncertain of what to say next. "Daniel? I saw what you did with Gregory, if she's no-one, then why? And what was all that drama outside about?" Daniel sat on the bed and buried his face in his hands for a moment, before he glanced up at Samantha who had begun dressing herself. "She is, was, my fiancée, Lola." "Oh right. I didn't recognize her. I thought it was over?" Daniel lowered his head yet again, sure that Samantha could sense the emotions that were causing havoc inside of him. "I thought it was over, Sam." She stood glaring at him in silence. "I don't know what to say to you." He took her hands into his before she angrily retreated, "How about the truth, Daniel?" Daniel had no way of understanding exactly how it was possible for Lola to trap him under her eyes, and under her breath. "I tried to stop loving her. I tried to hate her. I tried to forget her. Tonight, I wanted to tear her apart. I wanted everyone to know what she had done, and then all I wanted was to take her away from it all. I wanted to hold her, and tell her that I love her." "Daniel, you still love her!" Samantha yelled out in disgust. Daniel once again bowed his head, not ready to admit to it, but knowing that it was the truth. "You do! You do still love her!" "I don't know how I feel about her?" "What is really going on between you guys?" Samantha was desperate for an opening with Daniel. "I'm just so angry with her, all the time. I want to do this with you Sam, but …" He could barely continue.

Samantha gently stroked his face, "I get that Daniel, but I'm here now. She's with another man. Forget her, just for tonight. Do you think she isn't lying in the arms of another man right now? With Gregory Pastor? She is Daniel." She began undressing him once again, desperate to be in the arms of a man she fell in love with long before Lola appeared in Daniel's life. On impulse, he wanted to retreat, but he no longer wanted to feel so entirely alone. The mere thought of Lola lying in the arms of Gregory Pastor, gave way to a feeling of defeat and powerlessness. He was convinced that Samantha would successfully keep his mind from disappearing back to Lola. He convinced himself of the fact that one night with Samantha was all that he needed to escape the darkness that had surrounded him, even though he so frantically needed to be the man to hold Lola in his arms again. Daniel had an indescribable urge to feel her delicate skin against his one more time. He hunted her odor and the aroma of her hair, while he held her firmly her against him. Daniel willfully surrendered himself to Samantha, convinced that his lid had relinquished herself to another pot.

Lola's Secret

When Lola and Gregory returned to the apartment, Lola hastily and without delay made her way to her bedroom, before giving herself permission to sob fiercely on her bed. Gregory had retreated to his own bedroom, zealously aware of the fact that Lola was desperate for time on her own. She recalled the way Lauren stared at her earlier, and the look of pure disgust on her sister's face was almost unbearable for her. She could still hear Daniel bellowing over and over, but she was relieved that she was away from the crowd. Away from the accusations and the abhorrence she heard in Daniel's voice and saw in his eyes more times than she had ever intended to. She suddenly thought of the pregnancy test she shoved away in her closet earlier. Lola gradually got up from her bed, and hesitantly made her way to her closet, her heart hammering in her chest. She anxiously hesitated, but was agonizingly aware that nothing that was good, could come from a positive outcome on that test. She closed her eyes and said a silent prayer. She fervently prayed that there would be only one single line, instead of two. Having a baby at that point in time would have no divergence on her and Daniel, and it terrified her to consider how he would rebuff her, and begrudge her pregnancy.

She nervously opened her closet door, and slowly retrieved the test from under her clothes. At that very moment, Lola was certain that the tiny and insignificant stick had become her worst adversary. She stood staring at it for what felt like forever before she violently erupted into tears once again. Her worst fears had once again come true. The double lines confirmed that she was pregnant again. Lola could not make sense of why fate was being so immensely vindictive and cruel to her. She slowly walked into the bathroom, and stared at her reflection in the mirror. She was appalled and sickened by her appearance and without faltering, she grabbed a pair of scissors that was laying provocatively on her vanity.

With resentment and anguish in her heart, she began to slice at her hair. She continued to cut chunks of her hair until her bathroom floor was no longer visible under all her mane. With each hack, Lola unrealistically imagined each burden that she was compelled to carry, and cut faster and more enthusiastically. She recognized all the wrongs and all the twists that had crept up on her, and she continued to snip away as though she bore an endless supply. When there was no longer much left to cut off, Lola placed the scissors back on the vanity, and slowly ran her fingers through what was left of her hair. Lola had never once worn her hair short, and for the first time in her life, she could barely run her fingers through it. She smiled when she realized that she felt a tad bit lighter. She was aware of an unexpected feeling of exhilaration, and Lola delighted in the way she felt all of a sudden.

She gazed at her reflection in the mirror once more before she turned around, and made her way back into her bedroom. Lola laid calmly on her bed while staring blankly at the ceiling, aware of the thumping of her heart. She was remorseful for lashing out at Daniel, and annoyed at herself for accepting the invitation to Joe's. She had shed far too many tears over Daniel Salvatore, and even though it was her own imperfections that had led to all her heartbreak, Lola knew that she had to become stronger. She was aware of the fact that they would regularly and habitually have to face one another following Lauren and Dean's union, but she could no longer keep her job at Salvatore, alongside Daniel.

She had no plan in mind of how to prepare for the baby, but Lola knew that she was forced to tell Daniel of the sudden turn of events at once. She wanted him to understand that the time had finally come for them to go their separate ways, and change direction even though she was pregnant. The torment that she felt each time she was in Daniel's presence, was tearing her apart. The agony of witnessing him with another woman was something that Lola knew, she could never witness again. Lola decided that the only way for them to come out of their disastrous relationship with their hearts intact, was to wholly and entirely disconnect from one another. She was anxious to tell Daniel that she was having a baby, but that she could no longer be with him at Salvatore. She needed him to know that she had no intention of hiding her pregnancy from him again. Lola peered at herself in the mirror one more time before she made her way to her car. She was eager to face Daniel with the unexpected news before her courage failed her.

When Lola reached Daniel's apartment after a short drive, she was sure that she had heard voices through the door of his apartment. It left her trembling when she recognized the horror inside of her, knowing that he wasn't alone. When she reached out to knock on his front door, she was abruptly fearful of what she might find on the other side. She hesitated for an instant, but she was certain that her nerve would fail her if she didn't go ahead, and face Daniel that very night. Whatever it was that was waiting for her on the other side of his door, was a reality that she could not hide or scurry from. Lola's mind forced her to face whatever it was head on, no matter what it was, and even though she was dismayed at the very thought of finding Daniel in the arms of another woman. Instinct nudged her to turn around and run, instead, she knocked delicately and waited impatiently for a response.

After standing there in silence for a moment longer, Lola tried the door handle and was surprised to find it unlocked. Her heart began to hammer ferociously when she quietly slipped in, and again, she heard voices and soft moans. She was certain that it was coming from their bedroom. As though in a wandering haze, she slowly made her way to Daniel's bedroom, unable to turn around, and desperate to know how effortlessly Daniel had discarded her. When she reached his bedroom, she reluctantly and anxiously peered around the corner. She was horrified and revolted by what she was witnessing. She moved into the doorway, powerless to understand what was taking place right before her very eyes. Daniel was caught up in a passionate embrace with the same woman she had seen earlier at Joe's, and judging by the amount of clothing that was left on his body, Lola was devastatingly swayed that Daniel had unreservedly and without restraint, surrendered himself to another woman. The expression on his face was one Lola knew well, and it confirmed that she had ultimately, lost him forever.

Lola stood motionlessly as though frozen in time, unable to move a limb while her tears were cutting in her eyes. Her legs had grown weak and the familiar, yet restricting lump in her throat had grown enormously, while the mere movement of swallowing past her tears was unattainable. At that very moment, Lola was sure that there was not much more in the entire universe that could measure up to the excruciating distress she was feeling at that very second. There was nothing, other than death that could make her heart endure the agonizing and unbearable ache it was feeling as she stood watching Daniel. She could not move an inch of her, even though she was desperate to summarily escape the drama that was unfolding before her very eyes. It was a vision that she was certain, she could in no way at all, survive, and it carelessly and fluently tainted and destroyed her soul. Every part of her body had begun to shudder. She was overcome with intense nausea, accompanied by a hollow twinge that felt as though it was shredding her belly into a thousand pieces. She placed her hand in front of her mouth in a desperate attempt to remain silent, before her tears began streaming unreservedly down her cheeks. Lola was powerless to stop the valley of tears that had opened up inside of her. Her heart was hammering at an intense rate, and she could barely breathe. She gasped for breath while continuously swallowing past the confining lump in her throat, "Danny?"

Daniel was horrified to hear Lola's broken voice, and unexpectedly caught a glimpse of her standing in the doorway. He at once pushed Samantha back when he saw her standing there, devastatingly aware that Lola's heart was being ripped out from inside of her. He could not take his eyes off of her when he noticed the raw emotion on her face, and was instantly appalled that she had walked in on them. "Lola? Oh, God Lola ... fuck!"

He at once bolted from his bed, before he hurriedly pulled his jeans back on without taking his eyes off of her, even for a moment. Samantha had pulled the sheets up to cover herself, still unclear as to why Lola was standing there. Daniel let out a sigh and dejectedly ran his hands through his hair, instantly aware of the entire world that had crash landed on his shoulders. "Lola? What are you doing here? How did you get in?" While repentantly gazing at her, he had an urgent desire to take her into his arms, and beg her forgiveness. He wanted to ease the pain he could no longer bear to witness in Lola.

"Your front door was, it was open. Shit, Daniel. This hurts. How could you? How could you? How can this be so easy for you? This hurts so much, Danny." She bellowed through her tears, debilitated and incapable of moving.

"Lola, please, just listen," He cautiously moved closer to her before placing his hands on her shoulders. "No, Daniel, no. I don't want to hear it, and you know what Samantha?" Lola turned to face Samantha, "You can have him. I don't want him anymore." Lola finally felt the ability to move, and quickly turned away from them, wanting to escape the apartment, and knowing at once that it was an enormous error in judgement to have pitched up unannounced. The piercing pain in her heart told her of the truth that Daniel Salvatore was the biggest mistake she had ever made.

When she reached the hallway, she could hear Daniel frantically call out behind her. "Lola, wait!" She had no need to turn back to him, and felt a second flood gate of tears open up inside of her. When Daniel caught up to her, he grabbed her by her arm, and abruptly turned her around to face him. He could see the heartbroken tears roll down her cheeks as though she had an endless supply. Daniel was certain that they were not prepared to dry up any time soon. His heart thumped in agony when he witnessed her in such anguish. He in turn, was instantly mortified by what she had seen only moments ago. "I suppose now you're gonna tell me that you can't deal with me when I'm crying?" Lola was shaking, struggling to take in even a breath of fresh air. He held firmly onto her arm, desperate to say something to her, but nothing to validate or rationalize what he had done, was reaching his mind.

"Lola …" Lola stood glaring at him when she once again, noticed pity in his eyes. She reviled at the idea of pity, and became insanely livid at Daniel. "You slept with Samantha, Daniel! You humiliated me twice in one night!" Daniel pulled her closer to him, desperate to make her understand that his heart continued to belong only to her. He was frantic to assure her that he could not go through with it earlier, and that it was her eyes that captured and imprisoned his mind the entire time. "Nothing happened, Lola." "Nothing happened? What did I see, Daniel, if nothing happened? What was that in there? In our bed? In our place? Daniel! What was that? Gregory was right about you! Your hatred towards me has finally reached a new low. But then again, this should make you happy, because that's what you wanted! I mean nothing to you anymore, do I? After trying for months, you have finally broken me. That's what you wanted all along, isn't it? You tore me apart tonight at Joe's, just like you wanted to and now, now this? You are no better than I am Daniel!"

She freed herself from his grip, and as Daniel struggled to keep her close, he noticed her short hair for the very first time. "Lola no. I never wanted you to, I would never do this to you. Nothing happened, Lola." He knew that what Lola saw, was entirely in contrast to what he was saying. "I don't hate you. I'm so sorry, it's not what you think. I am so sorry. Your hair? Why did you cut your hair?" "You would never do this to me? You just did, Daniel, you just did." Lola abruptly swabbed at the tears on her cheeks, before she turned away from him once again. "Lola! Why did you come here?"

Before she reached the front door, she turned back one

last time, "I came here because I needed to talk to you, one last time. I needed to tell you something. Something important, but, I can't now, not tonight. Go back and finish what you started. Go back to her. I'm glad I saw this tonight, and I hate you for it Daniel. It makes what I need to do so much easier. I truly hate you, and I know now that it was never about forgiveness. You just wanted me gone. You're a coward Daniel, making this all about me when it's actually you, and what you wanted. You should just have told me the truth." Lola was growing increasing angry at herself for allowing Daniel to hurt her. "For months, you broke me down and made me feel entirely worthless, when all you really wanted was your freedom. You should have just said so. We'll talk another time. I don't even want to look at you right now. You Daniel, you were the biggest mistake I ever made. Not making that phone call. All your promises, and all the shit that came out of your mouth. I can't stand you right now. All your judgements and your talks of betrayals. You are no better, Daniel Salvatore!" She shouted out before finally slamming the door behind her.

Daniel stood glaring at the closed door for a moment, desperate to run after her, yet consumed by the culpability of his betrayal before he impulsively dashed out to find her. When he reached the ground floor, he caught a glimpse of her running across the road in a frantic attempt to reach the car he so amorously given her. It was pouring down with rain, and by the time he reached her, the rain had come crashing down on both of them.

Lola was struggling to unlock her car when he took a hold of her arm, and noticed that her tears had continued to pour relentlessly and unremittingly down her cheeks. Her short hair was soaked, and her wet clothes were clinging to her body. "Lola, please wait. What's wrong? Something's wrong. I know you, something happened Lola. Please talk to me. What was so important that you had to drive out here unannounced?" "Not now, Daniel!" Daniel was not ready to surrender. "Lola, I would never deliberately hurt you like this. What you saw, and I know how it looks, but nothing happened. I couldn't do it. I thought I could move on, but I couldn't. You stopped me. It's always been you, I realized that tonight. I know something's wrong. You came out all this way at this time of the night without Greg. Something's wrong. Please Lola, tell me. Nothing, nothing happened, you have to believe me. What I said about Peter Storey, I am so sorry Lola. I don't know why I said that. I know things weren't like that. You have to hear me, Lola. Just listen to what I am saying and give me a chance." Lola glared at him through her tears.

She noticed the rain pour down his face and knew that if she failed to tell him at that very moment, she would never be courageous enough to tell him at all. That would mean that Daniel was right about her, and after all the months of desperately trying to prove him wrong, she resolved to spit out the truth, even though they were standing in the middle of the road with the rain crashing down on them. "So, Daniel, you're saying that you deserve a chance to explain, but I never did?" Lola was still angry, but immediately swallowed her retort in an attempt to tell Daniel why she was there. "I came here to tell you, I had to tell you, I know it's going to screw up everything again, but, I'm pregnant again, Daniel. I don't want to be, but that one night, the mistake night, the last time we were together, and I was scared that if I didn't come tonight, I'd never have the courage to tell you, but if I'd known about her, about you and her, I wouldn't have come here at all. I tried to do it right this time, but look, just look at this mess. Look how well this worked out. I hate that I'm standing here telling you this. I hate that I am facing you with this, and I hate what I saw with you and Samantha. I hate that I'm pregnant, and I hate you, Daniel. I hate everything about us. I hate that this is happening."

Daniel gasped and stared at her with mystification and perplexity in his eyes. "What? What are you saying?" "I'm pregnant, Daniel! It was that one night, the night we both want to forget! The night I whored myself out to you, remember? You probably don't even remember, do you?" Daniel released her arm at once, and ran his hands through his wet hair in disbelief. He thought back to their one final night together since the miscarriage. He was instantly aware of the galloping in his heart, and eerily conscious of the fact that it took only the one time to bring a baby into their lives again.

Lola stood staring at him, unexpectedly disenchanted by the expression on his face. "Are you sure?" Lola reached into her bag, and handed him the pregnancy test that proudly displayed two unmistakable lines. Daniel stared at it, and was once again overwhelmed by the evidence he was holding in his hand. "Are you sure I'm the, father? I mean, Gregory, are you sure it was that night? Fuck Lola, how?" Lola glared at him with total repugnance and couldn't understand how he could ask her such a question, "I should have known you'd say something like that. It only takes one time, Daniel, but don't worry about it. Don't even give it another thought. I'll do what I do best, and just so you know, whether or not you care, Gregory and I haven't, we haven't, it's not like that. He can't be the father so, go back to your new life with her, and just leave me the hell alone. I should never have come here. Oh, and Daniel ... screw you, from the bottom of my heart, screw you!"

She tried the key to her car one more time and to her relief, it unlocked straight away. She did not turn to look back at Daniel, and by the time she had pulled away, she began sobbing again. Her heart was broken, her entire body had begun to quiver. When Daniel could no longer see Lola, he turned to go back into the apartment.

Daniel was unexpectedly irritated with himself. He was crushed by what Lola had told him, and devastated by the fact that she had walked in on him and Samantha. "Was that her? I thought she had long hair?" Samantha was baffled by Lola's unanticipated presence. "Yes." He reached for his shirt. "You have to go, Sam. I just, I want to be alone." "So, she saw us, big deal. You're not together anymore, Daniel." "She's pregnant, Sam, and I still love her, so it is a big deal to me."

After Samantha had stormed off in anger, Daniel removed the sheets from the bed and lay on the bare mattress staring at the ceiling, replaying the night's events over and over in his mind. He thought back to the night they made love for the very last time, and reluctantly accepted that it had to be the night they unintentionally conceived their child.

He instinctively reached for his mobile phone, and nervously dialed her number, unsure of what to say to her, but desperate to hear her voice. When she answered, Daniel was sure his heart would batter right out of his chest. "Lola ..." Lola remained silent, frantic not to choke on her own words "Nothing happened Lola. I swear, it wasn't what it looked like. I never meant to treat you like a whore. You were never that, never to me. I didn't know that I made you feel that way, I am so sorry." "It doesn't matter Daniel, I don't care. It's your life, and I don't care. Screw whomever you want, I just don't care anymore." "When did you find out about the baby?" "Tonight, when I got home." She continued to dab at the tears that were recklessly rolling onto her cheeks.

Daniel remained silent when he thought back to the clash between them at the engagement party. "I don't want it, Daniel. I just wanted to tell you. I wanted you to know. I didn't want it to be like the last time, but I'll take care of it. No-one has to know. I just don't want it." It felt to Daniel as though she had taken the wind out of his sails. "What do you mean, Lola? What do you mean, you don't want it?" Daniel became apprehensive and perturbed at once. "You know what I mean, Daniel. I do not want this baby. I don't want your child. I don't want to see you again. Ever. I have to go. I need to talk to Greg. We'll talk in the morning when I collect my things at Salvatore." She abruptly ended the call, and tossed her mobile phone on her bed.

Lola knocked tensely on Gregory's bedroom door, hopeful that he had not yet fallen asleep. "Come in." He sat straight up in bed when Lola cautiously walked in. Gregory was sensitive to her eyes that were red and inflamed, and at once startled by the fact that her hair had been cut short. "Can we talk?" She nervously sat beside him on his bed. "Sure." "I've just come from Daniel's place," "You went to see Daniel?" "Yeah, I had to tell him something. I don't know how to say this, but, I'm pregnant, Greg." She was unexpectedly and enormously embarrassed when Gregory turned away from her. "I'm sorry, Greg. It was one night before I left, and I, I only just found out tonight." Gregory turned back to face her. "What are you going to do?" "I don't know, but it's over between us, me and Daniel. I don't really know what to do?" "Well, you can stay here as long as you need to, Lola. I just, I'm just not ready for this, you know? Another man's child, Daniel being the father. I think you know what I'm saying ..." "I know Greg, I know. I'm so sorry. You've been so good to me." She quickly kissed him on his cheek before she made her way back to her bedroom. Lola picked up her mobile phone, and noticed several missed calls from Daniel. She lacked the vigor or valor to deal with him, and instead, she was anxious to hear her sister's kind and familiar voice.

She hesitantly dialed Lauren's number when Dean unexpectedly answered, "Dean?" "Hey Lola, you alright?" "Yes, I just wanted, I wanted to say sorry about what happened tonight. I was hoping to speak to Lauren?" "She's asleep, but I could wake her." "Oh no, please. I'll talk to her in the morning. Sleep tight." "What's the matter, Lola? Are you sure you're okay?" Lola remained silent, unsure of what to say him. "Lola?" "I'm fine, Dean. Sleep tight, love you guys so much." "Sleep tight, Lola." Dean whispered after she abruptly ended the call. He quickly dialed Daniel's number, troubled by Lola's untaught demeanor. "Dean?" "Hey, sorry. I know it's late ..." "I'm still up." "So, Lola just called. It sounded like she was crying, do you know why? I mean, have you seen her since the party? Or spoken to her?" Daniel was lost for words and dithered at once. "Daniel?" "She walked in on Sam and I tonight. She came to the apartment, and, nothing happened, but it didn't look that way. Fuck." "Oh, man bro, seriously?"

Dean was at once infuriated with Daniel. "Nothing happened Dean. Lola, she's, Lola's pregnant. She came here to tell me she's pregnant again." Dean was stunned to hear Daniel tell him that Lola was pregnant. He suddenly had no idea of how to respond. "I just don't know? It happened only once, just before she left. I was out drinking, and when I got home, it just happened. It happened only the one time since her miscarriage." "Seriously Danny? You think Lola is lying?" "I don't know what to think. I mean, why now?" "Daniel Salvatore, you are so full of shit! You know that Lola would never lie about that. She would rather hide it than lie about it. You know better!" Dean responded in irritation and aggravation. "I don't know if I can do this. We're not in a good place right now, Dean." "Find a way, Daniel. You find a way, and you make it work!" "I don't want to be a father, not like this. She doesn't want the baby either." "Daniel, listen to me, that kid did not ask for this, and now you and Lola must find a way to make it work. Do you understand?" "Yeah, I know, but, we can't even be alone in the same room. She hates me. Sometimes, I hate her even more. How are we going to bring a child into this?" "Daniel, you have to listen to me. You loved her once, and she loved you once. Things went bad and shit happened, but you have got to put that behind you, and think of the baby now. You can't just leave Lola, it's your kid, bro." "Yeah, I know. See you tomorrow, my head is spinning!" Daniel responded hoarsely after a long silence, and hung up almost immediately.

Daniel took a beer from his fridge, and made his way out onto the terrace where he sat staring out over the ocean, grudgingly recalling the events of the night while agonizingly aware of how Lola had suffered the degradation of the confrontation between the two of them, and then again with Samantha in his arms. When he closed his eyes, he could not get the image of her standing in his doorway out of his mind. Daniel's heart ached for what Lola had witnessed, and he knew that no matter how much had gone wrong between them, he never wanted to hurt her in such a way.

Alice VL

When Lola reached Salvatore the following morning, Daniel was seated in the reception area anxiously awaiting her arrival. Lola noticed that Daniel seemed edgy, but she was unwavering in ending the constant conflict between them, for once and for all. "Daniel? I wasn't sure if I should've come here this morning after what happened last night, but, I must speak with you. We have to end this today, and it's better that I face you with this, although, if I'm honest, I'm not really feeling as brave as I was last night." She hurriedly made her way around the counter.

Daniel was again saddened by the fact that she cut her hair short. It made way for sudden and unexpected horror when he realized how all that was good between them, had turned crooked. He walked towards her, but before he could utter a word, Lola interrupted him. "Do you have any clients coming in, or can we talk in private?" "Not right now. Do you want to come to my office?" He turned to lock the doors of Salvatore. "Yes, please." Daniel nervously made his way to his office while Lola followed brusquely behind him. When he took a seat behind his oversized desk, Lola sat directly across from him, and instantly felt like an outsider.

She nervously glanced around her, and recalled all the memories they had made in his office, and how it was mostly filled with affection and better times. She remembered how often he would finish paperwork while she studied into the long hours of the night. She thought back to the day he asked her to become his wife, and it saddened Lola to realize how close she had come to being someone's lid, and how it slipped away almost unnoticed. She abruptly felt stupid and naïve at the mere thought that she could find her happily ever after with a man like Daniel

Salvatore. "This is it, isn't it Lola? This is where you tell me how fucked up everything is." He leaned forward, but what he really wanted to tell her was that they gave up far too quickly, and that missing her had become intolerable.

Daniel was desperate to beg her to give their love one more chance. He had a smoldering need to tell her how remorseful and repentant he was for the way in which he had dealt with her, and their problems. He wanted to convince her that he couldn't make love to Samantha, simply because his heart had reminded him of the love he held for Lola, but when he opened his mouth, his voice begrudgingly failed him.

"Yes Daniel, everything is a mess right now. But I really just want to apologize too. I am truly sorry about what happened at the party for the way I fell apart and treated you. I am sorry. I am sorry I hit you, everything just sort of fell apart inside of me, and I guess I just, I don't know, maybe I just snapped a little." Lola began to fidget nervously, "And then, for pitching up at your place last night, and how I again acted towards you. I know that you're right about most of the things you said, and I know I made such a fool of myself. I shouldn't have behaved that way in front of your parents." Lola stopped, but only for a moment. "To be honest with you, I am glad that everyone knows now. We should never have hidden the truth. I felt so horrible carrying it around with me, and the guilt just festered inside of me. The thing is, I can't control my feelings when I'm around you and that's why, I can't work here anymore. I have to leave here. I know it's what you want too, even if you're too polite to say it. I'm so sorry for pitching up at the apartment unannounced. It won't happen again, and, it's none of my business what happened between you, with you and Sam. Most of all, I'm sorry that I'm pregnant again. I don't understand why this keeps happening to us." Again, Lola paused only to take in a deep breath. "I'm sorry that I can't tell you that Gregory is the father. I'm sorry that it happened to us. We were together only once, and you probably can't even remember that night. I wish it never happened. I hate that night. I hate that it happened, and I hate that you had to be drunk to sleep with me. I just hate, hate everything about us right now, and I just wish that I could make this all go away."

She paused to take in a bottomless breath, but careful not to allow Daniel an opening to interrupt her. "I don't know, you know? The first thing that came to mind was to have an abortion. Last night, I had made up my mind, but this morning, I'm not so confident." Lola bowed her head immediately. "I know choosing that route will be better for both of us, but I am struggling to make that decision while I'm feeling this way. I need to know that I can live with myself if I go ahead and do it, but if I do keep the baby, I don't expect you to feel like you have to play the daddy role."

Lola was desperate to convince herself that she no longer needs Daniel in her life. "I think I can do this on my own, but there are other options too, like adoption." Lola was weighing up their options, on a pay-as-you-go basis. She was making it up as she went along, unsure of how to have her one final conversation with Daniel. She knew she was mumbling, and she knew she barely made any sense. "I only told you about the baby because you'd find out anyways, and it would just be something else for you to hate me for, so it doesn't matter. I just wanted you to know, and I knew that if I didn't tell you last night, I'd never have the courage to tell you and that's why I just pitched up like that. I didn't plan on getting pregnant again, and if it is going to be too hard for us, then we should rather talk about terminating the pregnancy." She bowed her head, insecure and nervous of Daniel's probable retaliation.

Daniel was heartbroken that she was once again considering an abortion, and recalled yet again how all that had gone wrong for them had begun with her intended termination. He felt his eyes blaze unexpectedly, and made a desperate attempt to shut off his sorrow, aware of the lump in his throat restricting any chance he had to tell her that he was deeply remorseful for the role he played in her unhappily-ever-after. "I can't do this, you and me, Salvatore. Nothing is going to change what I did, and you're always going to hate me for it. I'm always going to hate me for it, but I can't change it. I just want us to stop hating each other so much. You want answers from me that I can't give you."

Lola refused to give him a gap until she had said all she wanted to say. "I am trying so hard to remain composed, so please Daniel, don't interrupt me. You want me to say I wouldn't have done it, but I can't say that, Daniel. I just can't see you hate me like this forever, and this baby, it was a mistake, a really big one. It's like I just keep making things worse. The harder I try, the more knocks I get, you know? I can't do anything right anymore, Daniel." "Salvatore is half yours, Lola." He made one desperate and final attempt to keep her with him at Salvatore. Lola remained silent, entirely unprepared for Daniel to find out that she had been to see Mr. H, and that Salvatore again, belonged only to him. "I loved being here at Salvatore. I love the work that you put out here, but I don't want it, Daniel. I want nothing from you, and I want nothing more from Salvatore. I'm not saying that because I'm angry Daniel, it's just too hard." She got up to her feet, satisfied and entirely contented that she had said all she intended to say, even though she mumbled through it.

Lola was surprisingly overwhelmed by the vigor she felt waking up inside of her. When she reached the door, she turned and glanced back at him where he had just begun to get up from his seat. "I just want to get through the day, Daniel, knowing that I got through it, and not feeling like you carried me through it. I used to be good at being on my own, and I want that back. You said yourself, you can't keep saving me, and I don't want you to save me." She wanted to tell him to pay attention to the fact that she didn't burst out crying, but instead, she kept it to herself. 'Maybe that's why I lost the baby. Maybe we were never really meant for each other, and this baby, this baby was a mistake. I have to carry on now, on my own. I've seen a side to you that scares me, and you've seen a side to me that disappoints you. It's not right that we keep doing this to each other. Do you know what I'm trying to say, Daniel?"

Daniel gazed at her and understood for the first time the sheer torment she had unwillingly endured. He knew that what he needed to say to her was much too little, and much too late for her to hear. His heart ached for her again. He was instantly faced with unreserved grief for all that went so wide of the mark in their lives. "Do you understand what I'm trying to say, Daniel?" "I am so, so sorry Lola." He walked up to her, and lifted her eyes to meet his. "I treated you unkindly, and for that I am so sorry. I said so many things I didn't mean. Even though you don't believe me, I never meant some of the things I said, and I don't hate you. I am sorry about last night, you walking in on Sam and I, but I swear Lola, nothing happened. I know what it looked like, and I wouldn't believe me either, but nothing happened. I'm sorry that

I never listened before." He was desperate to fit in all the apologies he had missed over the last few months. "I realize that you tried, and that it was mostly me. I know you were fighting so hard for us, but the hurt and anger just overwhelmed me. I've never known feelings like this before, and I've never had to deal with any of that. I'm sorry that you're pregnant now, again." Daniel swallowed back on an invasive lump in his throat. "You didn't do this on your own, and it's not your fault. I shouldn't have taken advantage of you that night. I wanted to be close to you, and then I wanted to hurt you. God, Lola." Lola took his hand and squeezed it firmly. "It doesn't matter, Daniel. I could have said no. I should have said no. I don't care about the things you said anymore, it doesn't matter. Honestly Daniel, I want you to know that I will never forget you, and I will always be thankful for what you meant to me. You brought something back into my life that I lost, that I missed, that I never had. The time I had with you has been of the happiest moments in my life, and I don't regret even a second of it." She smiled sadly before she lowered her head. "I just think that there are things we can't work through together and I, I have to move on. You have to move on. We need to put all the bad behind us now. I can't do this with you. I am not your lid, Daniel, I know that now. You came into my life, and you changed it. You made it better and I guess, maybe I just had to have some of that. You made me braver than I was, and you made me see the good in life. It felt good while it lasted. I am no longer that frightened nineteen-year-old that hid behind my hair anymore." She smiled and looked up at Daniel again. "You made me realize that there is a place for all of us in this world, even for me, and that I don't have to hide forever. You gave me a glimpse into a world that I didn't know, Daniel, so how could that have been bad? I just don't want to walk out of here without telling you that." She smiled sadly. "No matter what we have done or said to each other these last couple of months, the good was really good. I want you to know that." Daniel swallowed, desperately to shut off the tears that were welling up in his eyes. "Please don't have an abortion Lola." Daniel blurted out unexpectedly and caught Lola off guard, "I'll be here for you and the baby. I know why you feel you have to, but don't. It doesn't have to be this way. I don't want you to have an abortion, Lola. Please don't do this Lola."

He was dreadfully ill-equipped for the abrupt trepidation gripping at his heart at the mere notion of Lola destroying what might be the only thing left to save them. "I need to let go, and start again. I don't want to have an abortion, but I'm afraid of how it's going to tie us together, Danny. We should think about that, and that can't be good. We can't even talk to each other without arguing or fighting anymore. There are just so many walls between us now. We've become strangers, Daniel, and that's no way to bring a child into this world. I don't want the baby to grow up the way I did." "We can work it out, Lola. Lots of people do it, they work it out, and so will we. We'll find a way, I promise you. I will make it work even if only for the baby. Even if that's the only way to make it work. I will do anything you want, Lola, anything. I honestly wish, wish that I can take it all back. Everything I did and everything said to you. God Lola, how did I do the things I did?" "I just don't know if I can make anything work with you anymore Daniel, or if I want to. Our spoken words can never be taken back. Nothing we said can ever be unsaid, and we're not lots of people, Daniel. It's you, and it's me, and I need space, and I need you to let go of me, and all the wrongs. I want this baby, but I don't want to fight anymore. I don't want this child to grow up with two parents resenting each other all the time. If I do keep the baby, I'd rather raise him without you, away from Sutherland, you know? But I'm not even thinking about any of that now. I just have to be on my own, and clear my head." "Where does Gregory fit into all of this?" "I spoke to him last night after leaving your place. Greg doesn't want me like this. It's over between us, not that anything really had a chance to start. He's just not ready for all of this, and I know that it would be unfair to expect anything from him now. He's not prepared for another man's child especially given the history between you two, and I honestly can't blame him for how he feels. He has been so kind to me, Daniel, and I just want him to be happy too." "I'll give you space Lola. I can do that, and I swear to never talk about the abortion again if you give your word never to do it again." He exclaimed in extreme anxiety as she was leaving, desperate to induce Lola not to go through with the termination.

She turned around to face Daniel one last time, and smiled sadly, "But you see, that's just the thing Daniel, I didn't do it the first time. You are so stuck on that, and this time, I cannot make you that promise." Again, Lola felt as though her heart was being gutted into a thousand shards right before her very eyes. "I am so confused, and I am terrified. I am so torn. It's a tug of war the entire time. I'm just not thinking clearly right now, and I don't know what I want. I just know that I don't want to have a baby like this. It's such a mess. That night, I felt like, I just felt like you didn't see me. Like you said, it could have been anybody. You were drinking, and I knew that it meant nothing to you, but I still allowed you to make love to me. Now, this child was conceived like that, and everything just feels wrong. I don't want to do this, and I can't talk about this anymore. I must go now, Danny. I'm just so tired of all this. I have just started coming to terms with what happened the last time, and now it's happening again. I just don't know which way anymore." "Lola, don't do this. Give me a chance to show you it can work." He watched her bow her head and leave almost as though she had never been there.

He wanted to run after her, to seize her in his arms, and put all the shattered pieces of her back together again. Daniel wanted to tell her that he still loved her and that he never ceased pining for her. He was desperate to implore her to stay, but he was glaringly reminded of the nerve she had finally plucked together to stand up for herself. He betrayed Lola by rejecting and abandoning her, and he broke the only promise he had ever made to her, his promise of never allowing any one soul to harm her again. It was with immense dishonor and sorrow that he understood how he was the only one hurting her up until that very moment.

Lola glanced back at Salvatore one last time before she slid into her car. The lump in her throat she had become so accustomed to, had once again made its presence known. While wiping away her tears, she drove off, occasionally glancing in her rear-view mirror until Salvatore could no longer be seen. In her heart, she had hoped that Daniel might still feel a small amount of affection for her, and plead with her to stay, but Lola was convinced that Daniel Salvatore no longer loved her. When Lola reached Greg's apartment, she went straight to her bedroom, and fell helplessly and utterly hopelessly onto her bed.

While she lay there attempting to identify all the confusing emotions that were rushing around inside of her, she noticed a blinking envelope on her laptop, and pulled it closer.

She saw at once that it was an email from Daniel. 'I am so sorry Lola, for everything. There is so much that has happened, and I am sorry for it all. I am sorry for the things I said, and I am sorry for the things I didn't say to you. I just don't understand the way I feel most of the time, and I am honest when I say that I have been at war with my emotions. But, what I do know is that I don't want you to go through with an abortion. If you don't see chance, please give me an opportunity to raise the baby. Please, just give me that chance. Please don't have an abortion, please, Lola. I am so sorry that things turned out like this. I never wanted it to end like this. I am sorry that you felt so badly that night. I didn't realize that I made you feel like that. Please can we talk some more?'

Lola read over the email once more before she irritably hit the reply button and began typing almost as if in a daze, 'Daniel, I don't want to talk about anything anymore. We've said what we needed to say. I can't deal with you anymore. I don't want to see you again, and should I keep the baby, we will come to some sort of an arrangement after it's born. If not, it won't matter. I am mad at you, and I am mad at myself. But, it's over now and I cannot live like this anymore. Please, don't contact me again. I will get in touch to let you know when I've decided.' She hit the send button and shut her laptop without wanting to give it another thought.

Alice VL

Lola's Secret

JONATHAN

Daniel Salvatore marched into Mr. H's office just before noon on a cold Friday morning, a few days after Lola had quit her job at Salvatore. It was important to him to remunerate Lola for her shares in Salvatore, which was after all, a legal and binding contract, and even though Lola had indicated that she wanted nothing more to do with Salvatore, Daniel could not risk having the company's affairs in such chaos. "Mr. Salvatore, what a surprise!" Mr. H. offered Daniel an extended hand as he made his away across the room. "How are you?" Daniel took a seat on one of his comfortable and luxurious leather seats. "Good, good. What can I do for you today?" "I want to take back complete ownership of Salvatore. If you could calculate the cost of doing so by reimbursing Ms. Storey for her shares, then ..." Daniel began to explain before Mr. H swiftly interrupted him. He slowly removed his spectacles and peered down at his desk for an instant. "Just a minute ..." "Is there a problem?" "No, Daniel, no problem. Salvatore belongs to you already. Complete ownership is yours, and has been for months already. Ms. Storey had it reverted back into your name a couple of months ago."

Mr. H was suddenly aware of the bewilderment in Daniel's eyes. "She came to see me a few months back. It was her wish to destroy the transfer of ownership documents, giving you back complete ownership of your company. Thankfully, I hadn't filed them yet. It was legally her shares, so she had every right to make a request like that. She swore me to secrecy, but, well, here you are."

Daniel abruptly stood up, and vigorously shook his head. He could not understand how it was possible for Lola to take such radical steps behind his back, and became incensed at once. "What is the value of the company, H?" Mr. H pulled out the file on Salvatore, and after making a few quick calculations, he gave him a rough figure of Salvatore's net worth. "That excludes property belonging to Salvatore, uhm, to you." "Listen to me H, get a hold of Andrew and get a check ready for half of that, and see that she has it by no later than Monday morning." Daniel was visibly shaken before he stormed out of Mr. H's office, angry and frustrated that he had remained one step behind her, while she caught him by surprise once again.

Lauren and Dean were both grief-stricken by the fact that Daniel and Lola made no discernible effort to give their relationship another chance, more than ever now that Lola was pregnant again. It was horrifying for Lauren to witness her sister go through the sorrow of carrying their baby, and pining for Daniel all at once. Dean was enormously perceptive to the unrelenting torment in Daniel's eyes, but on every occasion that Dean tried to approach Daniel about Lola, he would become enraged and horribly pungent. "I wish I never met her!" Daniel would shout out in anger and resentment at times. Dean would remain silent and shake his head, certain that no other woman had ever brought out a side to his brother that he never witnessed before. Lola vehemently avoided Daniel even though Lauren would beseech her to give him one more chance.

Sarah and John too, were distressed by their break up, but were thrilled and tremendously animated in anticipating the birth of their very first grandchild. They silently prayed that the baby would somehow reunite them, even though Lola and Daniel knew they had no desire to reawaken what was lost between them.

Daniel would repeatedly question Lauren on how Lola was coping, and even though she would check up on Lola regularly, she was excruciatingly aware of the fact that her sister was heartbroken and pining for him. She chose to withhold the truth from Daniel, and secretly wished that they would work out their issues before the baby was born.

Shortly after the frenzied confrontation between Daniel and Lola, Dean met up with Daniel at Joe's one night for drinks after Lauren decided to spend a quiet evening with Lola. Dean found it insufferable to see Daniel in a state of total disarray, and once again attempted to discuss his situation with Lola, "So bro, how are things really with you?" "Let's not go there." Daniel immediately gulped down his beer. "I know you guys can work this out bro." "No, we can't. She doesn't want to. Lola doesn't even know whether or not she's going to keep the baby, and as usual, I have no say in any of this." "She won't do it bro. I know she won't. She's just overwhelmed by it all." "This is our last chance Dean. After this, it's over, for good. There'll be no going back after this." "But you love her? I know you do." "How do I take back all the things I said and accused her of? How can she ever trust me again, Dean? I broke every promise I ever made to her and yet, when I look at her sometimes, I just want to hurt her more. I can't stop myself from saying the things I say to her." Dean sipped his beer, and shook his head despondently while sensitive to the fact that their affairs had become chaotic. "She tried for so long bro. I never told you this, but before she moved out, God ..." Daniel realized once again that he had behaved like an utter fool. "She asked me whether I still loved her, and I couldn't answer her. She asked me to give her a reason to fight for us, and I told her there wasn't one, and that she shouldn't. I screwed up so badly bro."

Dean got up from his seat after hurriedly finishing his beer before he turned to Daniel, "Just forget all that shit and work it out Daniel. Listen, I've got to go. I'm picking Lauren up from Lola. Are you going to be alright?" "I'll be fine, have a good evening."

Three weeks subsequent to Lola having left Salvatore passed almost in the blink of an eye when she grudgingly and unenthusiastically called on Daniel early one morning, convinced that he was still asleep. "Daniel here?" "Daniel, it's me, Lola. Are you asleep?" "Lola? No, I'm up. What's the matter?" "Nothing, everything's fine. Can we talk? Do you have time?" He could at once sense her apprehension and exigency, "Sure. Do you want to meet up somewhere?" "We can talk on the phone. I'd rather we talk on the phone." "I'm at the apartment if you want to come by. My battery is low, or do you want me to come over?" He was desperate to see her one more time. Lola hesitated for a moment before she cautiously agreed to meet him, "I'll come by, say in an hour?" "Alright, see you then." She hung up quickly, aware of the brand-new pounding in her chest.

Before reaching his apartment, she was agonizingly susceptible to the fact that what she was about to say to him, would be of the most challenging words she would ever be compelled to pass on to him. When Lola nervously knocked on his front door, she was aware that she had begun to shudder slightly. Daniel opened up almost without delay, and smiled anxiously when he saw her standing there, noticing at once how weary and worn she appeared to be. "Hey Lola, come on in." She smiled apprehensively and tried her utmost to avoid eye contact with him. He showed her to a sofa where she sat down cautiously. "Is everything okay? It sounded serious when you called." "I'm fine, thank you. I just wanted to tell you, I wanted you to know that I'm, I'm not going to keep the baby. I am going ahead with the abortion. It's just better this way. It can't work any other way." Lola was rambling again when she realized that she was trying to make herself feel better when justifying her reasons. "We have to make a clean break from one another. I want you out of my life Daniel, and this baby, this baby is just going to tie us together, and make it hard for us to carry on. You know, to begin again?" Daniel grimaced involuntarily as her words ripped into his soul, listening to her while she was engaged a heroic effort to explain how she didn't want their child. "Lola, we can work it out. Let me take the baby after it's born for a while, or for as long as you need. Please, let's just try and figure something out?"

He made a valiant effort to gulp down on the bulge that had suddenly formed in his throat. "No Danny, we can't work it out. I know that, and I feel that we should put all this behind us. Keeping the baby will make it so much harder. I can't work this out with you. I've made up my mind, and I've scheduled an appointment. I am asking you to support me. Support me, just this once. I know we can't go back, but I also cannot do this at this point in my life. You'll forget soon. It's just better this way for all of us. I can't carry this baby for another six months and just hand him over to you afterwards. I don't see chance for that."

She was about to get up from the couch when he suddenly stopped her. "Wait Lola, don't leave yet. Can we just talk for a minute, please? Do you want something to drink? Have you had breakfast?" "Some juice if you have. It's all I can keep down at the moment." Daniel quickly made his way into the kitchen, and poured her a glass of juice before he casually handed it to her, "Lola, are you sure about this? Have you really, really thought it through?"

Lola placed the glass on the coffee table, unsure of how to explain what was going on in her mind, and ripping through her heart. "Can a person ever really be sure, Daniel? I, I've been thinking about it constantly and this is the only, only way I know how to deal with it all." "It's not, Lola. It's not the only way. I'm here. You can move back in, and we can try and work it out. I know we can. I'll be here for you and the baby. Please, let me just try. Doesn't anything from our life together count here?" "No, I, no Daniel. I can't, and I don't want to live here again. I don't want our lives to be on hold like that. You'll always find a way to make me pay for all my wrongs, even if you say you won't. You find a way, you always do." She was certain that it was what was best for both of them. "I don't know how things are going to work out, but I can't come back here. It won't work, and in the end, we're going to have a child that is going to struggle because of us. That's not fair, Danny. The fighting and the arguing all the time, that's not fair." "I just thought, given some time, that you might feel differently. That maybe we could put what happened behind us. Are you and Gregory together again?" "No, but he's been a good friend to me and he's standing by me. He supports my decision." Lola hurriedly got up again, "I must go, Daniel. I just wanted to tell you. I don't want to live here with you again, so please don't try and talk me out of it. Please Daniel, just forget me, and forget everything about us and what we once were." "Lola please, just think about what you are going to do. Let's just talk about it again, please Lola."

Daniel was desperate as he frantically begged her to change her mind. "No, Daniel, I can't. It's hard enough as it is. Things are starting to come right again, and you and I, it's just hard. It's been the hardest thing to deal with in my life, and it shouldn't be like that." "Lola, listen to me, just give yourself more time. I know it's asking a lot, and I know you don't trust me anymore, but please, just take a little more time." "I don't need more time, Daniel. I need to put this behind me. Besides, I don't really have any more time to think about it. I only have this week left before I'm in the second trimester. I have to do it now."

Lola was saddened by the reality of her termination, and was excruciatingly aware of the indisputable misery in Daniel's eyes. "When will you be doing it?" "Tomorrow morning." Daniel turned away from her. He was certain that his heart was about to thump right out of his chest. "Let me come with you, Lola please?" Lola initially hesitated, but realized that having Daniel with her might bring closure to what was taking place between them. "It's almost an hour's drive. I have to be there at 7am. You can come with me, but please Danny, this is what I want, and this is what I've decided." He smiled sadly when she turned to leave. Daniel was overcome with despondence when he realized that they had missed their one last chance.

When Lola reached the apartment, Gregory was anxiously waiting for her in the living room. "Lola, where did you run off to so early this morning?" "I went to see Daniel."

"Daniel?" Lola took a seat on the sofa across from him, unable to look him in the eye. "I went to tell him that, that I'm not keeping the baby, Greg. I had to tell him that it cannot work, and that it's over for us." She quickly wiped a lost tear that had unexpected rolled down her cheek. "Oh. You know, its better Lola. Daniel abandoned you, and you would have had to raise this baby on your own." Lola's heart shattered into a million pieces when she heard him say exactly what she had been thinking. "Maybe you and I, maybe we can move forward after this?" Gregory was blissfully ignorant to the immense pain and sorrow that she was experiencing. "Maybe Greg …" She smiled distraughtly before she got up, and made her way to her bedroom. When she laid down on her bed, she could no longer control the pitiful tears that had unreservedly begun to stream down her face. Lola had finally lost the only man she could, and would ever love. She was giving up the baby she so dreadfully wanted to keep, yet, all it did was remind her of Daniel's revulsion and antagonism for her. She thought back to all that had taken place between them. Lola suddenly wished that tomorrow would come soon, in a desperate attempt to put it all behind her, and move on without Daniel.

Daniel walked into Salvatore shortly after Lola left the apartment. He could in no way at all, shake the feeling that Lola was about to make the single largest mistake of her life. Daniel had no way of knowing exactly how to deal with Lola, or how to handle the reality and the finality of the intended abortion.

Dean was busy taking stock when Daniel marched in, inconsolable and disoriented. "Hey bro, you alright?" Dean was aware of an unmistakable expression of destitution on Daniel's face. Daniel nodded his head, and quickly made his way to his office. Dean followed curtly behind him, certain that all was not well with his brother. "Daniel?" Dean took an empty seat directly across from his brother. Daniel could barely utter a word, and after clearing his throat, he stared straight at Dean. "Lola came by the apartment earlier. She's going to do it, Dean, she's not keeping the baby." Daniel choked despondently over his words, and vigorously shook his head while overcome with disbelief. "Why? I don't understand?" Dean was surprised by the events that had taken place all of a sudden. "And the best of it is, I'm actually going to be taking her tomorrow." Daniel burst out laughing when he recognized his own foolishness. Dean made his way over to Daniel, and sympathetically embraced his brother, convinced that nothing they say or do, could alter what was about to happen. "I'm going to, I'm just going to go and clean up the tools." Dean left Daniel's office while in a state of total disbelief.

When he reached the workshop, he dialed Lola from his mobile phone at once. "Hello, Lola speaking." "Lola, its Dean," Lola sensed that he was irritated. "Everything okay?" "No Lola, everything is not okay. Why are you doing this to Daniel? What is wrong with you? I took your side before, but this? What are we supposed to think now?" Dean was horrified by Lola's decision. "Don't do this to Daniel, please Lola. I'm begging you, don't do this. We, Lauren and I can take the baby, or my parents can, just please, don't do this." "I don't care what anyone thinks anymore, Dean, I'm damaged goods and your brother will always see me like that. Besides, it's between Daniel and I, and I have to do what's best for the baby. I am not discussing this with you, or anyone else, it's over. I've told Daniel how I feel, and that's all. There's nothing else to say or to talk about anymore."

She instantly ended the call with no desire to clarify herself any further to Dean. Dean kicked at the tools lying on the floor, agonizing over the fact that Lola had made up her mind, and that not much he could say would adjust what had already been decided. When he looked back at the office, he noticed Daniel seated with his head in his hands. Dean was devastated by the fact that there was nothing he could do to rescue his brother, or salvage the love they once had for one another.

Lola had just climbed out of the bath when she heard the doorbell ring. Gregory had left for Valley Falls earlier, and would return only in a few days. She hurriedly wrapped a towel around her, and made her way to the front door. While slowly opening the door, she peered from behind and was delighted to see Lauren standing there. Lola invited her in at once, while in high spirits to see her sister. "Hey sissy, so nice to see you." Lola quickly closed the door behind her. Lauren did not respond, but walked straight over to the sofa in the living room. Lola summarily followed her when she noticed that her sister was undoubtedly troubled, "What's the matter, Lols?" Lauren burst into tears almost at once before Lola took the seat next to her, and placed her arms around her. "How could you, Lola?" Lola felt the reputed lump in her throat make its attendance known once again. She was certain that Dean had told her about the scheduled abortion. "I can't do this Lauren." "It's your child Lola, your baby, your flesh and blood." "I know, but it's more than that." Lola made a desperate attempt to defend herself. "It's not more than that, Lola. You always say that, but that's all there is to it!" Lola turned away from her sister, unexpectedly sensitive to the feeling of indignity for what she was about to do, while knowing that she was doing precisely that, that she swore to herself she would never do when she was only a little girl. "I can't face Daniel anymore, Lols, and this baby, how can I begin again with this baby? I can't raise this baby on my own. I can't give it to Daniel. I don't want to go through all of this." "Lola, I know you're hurt, and I know you're confused, but please don't do this. Please, sis. Daniel will never abandon his child. Dean and I are here for you. Please Lola, I am begging you." Lola gulped down on her tears, "Please go, Lols. I don't want to get into an argument with you. I love you so much, but I don't want to talk about this anymore. I've made up my mind, and for me, it's the only way." Lola got up from the sofa and made her way to the front door, opening it for Lauren to leave. Lauren walked out without uttering another word, but Lola felt her entire world crumble around her.

Lola arrived at Daniel's apartment just before sunrise the following morning, and was surprised to find Daniel waiting outside for her. She pulled up next to him and switched off her car. "Hey, Lola." He greeted her while opening the door for her. "Hey Daniel, shall we go in my car?" "No." He replied curtly in a fraught attempt not to say much more that might start up a quarrel once again. Lola was aware of the expression on Daniel's face, and suddenly questioned his presence at the clinic, "I've been thinking, maybe I should rather just go on my own?" "I'm going, Lola." Again, Daniel did his best to remain composed. Lola quickly buttoned up her coat when she realized that it had unexpectedly become cold. "You cold?" "A little." When they pulled away, Lola turned to Daniel, "I don't want to talk Daniel, please. Can we just be quiet? Please don't try and change my mind." Daniel nodded and looked straight ahead of him while anxiously hoping and praying that she might reconsider, and change her mind before they arrived at the clinic. They drove in silence for what felt like for hours, and when they reached St. Darla's Clinic, Lola began to quiver slightly.

When Daniel switched off the ignition, he turned to Lola before taking her hands into his. "Lola, your hands are ice cold." He tried to warm them up by rubbing them gently. She slowly pulled her hands away from him, and smiled nervously, "Yeah, just getting cold, and maybe a little nervous." "Listen to me, Lola, you don't have to go in there. You don't have to do this. Please don't do this. Let's go get a cup of coffee, and just talk. I just need to go through all that's happened again. The things I said to you, just one more time." Lola lowered her head, certain that she had made the only decision that was right for them both. "We talked about this Daniel. There's nothing else to talk about. What happened between us is in the past. The things we've said to each other, it's in the past. This has to happen now, here, today." She hurriedly slid out of his car before. Daniel quickly followed her as they made their way into the clinic.

He found an empty seat when Lola walked in to the reception area. "Hi, I'm Lola Storey," She hesitantly announced herself to the nursing staff at the reception counter. "Oh, here we go. Just fill out these forms, and Doctor Strachan will be with you shortly. You didn't have anything to eat or drink yet?" "No." Lola anxiously made her way to where Daniel was sitting in silence. She nervously began filling out the medical forms, and began shuddering once again. Daniel placed his arms around her shoulders, and after completing the forms, she handed them back to the receptionist and smiled. When she sat down beside Daniel once again, he took her hand. "Lola?" He whispered huskily. She was at once caught off-guard by the desperation in his voice. When she turned to face him, she was agonizingly aware of his tears, brimming in his eyes. "Don't!" Lola swabbed at a tear that had rolled down onto her cheek. She was convinced that they could not go back to the way they were before. They sat in silence for only a moment longer when Lola heard her name being called out. "Lola Storey?" She hurriedly made her way to where a nurse was waiting for her. "Lola, please Lola, don't go in there." Was all Daniel could say before ultimately accepting that they had reached their point of no return.

Lola followed the nurse into the doctor's consulting rooms where she was chilly again. "Dr. Strachan would like to consult with you first, he'll be here shortly." The nurse had just left the consulting room when Dr. Strachan walked in, and made his way around his desk. "Lola Storey, pleased to meet you. I am Dr. Strachan." Lola smiled nervously at him. "How far along are you?" "About 14 weeks." "You know, we don't abort after 14 weeks, which leaves me with only one question, why did you wait so long?" She couldn't tell him how she struggled to reach the decision, knowing it would finally be the end of the road for her and Daniel. "I, I don't know?" "In my experience, Ms. Storey, waiting this long is normally an indication of hesitation and doubt." "I did hesitate Doctor Strachan, but I am sure now." "Do you have a partner? Have you discussed it thoroughly with him, because once it's done missy, it's done." "No, I don't have a partner, and I'm sure. I want to do this. Can we just get it over and done with, please?" Lola was terrified that if he had asked her any more questions, she might change her mind.

A nurse entered the consulting room, and showed Lola into a small dressing room at the end of the passageway. She handed her a hospital robe, and instructed Lola to change into it before she made her way to an adjacent surgery. Lola slowly got undressed, again aware of how cold it was. She began trembling so severely, that she was barely able to undo her jeans. When she placed the robe around her, she nervously and hesitantly made her way onto the bed in the room next door, and laid down quietly. While lying there, her thoughts rushed back to Daniel, who was in the waiting area. She thought about the baby she was about to slaughter, but feverishly attempted to convince herself that she was doing the right thing. She was still deep in thought when Dr. Strachan walked in. "Nurse Jen will be administering local anesthetic. You won't be out cold, but you won't experience any pain either, at the most, a little discomfort. Are you feeling okay?" He gently rubbed her hand. "Fine, thanks." Lola turned to Nurse Jenny who was struggling to find a vein in her hand. After trying unsuccessfully for several minutes, Nurse Jenny turned to Dr. Strachan. "I can't find a vein?" She irritably handed the needle to Dr. Strachan. He patted Lola's hand gently, and was finally able to insert the needle. Lola was still watching Nurse Jenny who was about to inject the anesthetic into her, when she unexpectedly felt a flutter inside of her. Lola had never felt anything as powerful before. She was instantly convinced that her baby was alive. Feeling him stir inside her for the very first time, left her horrified to realize that she could not go through with it. She slapped the needle from Nurse Jenny's hand, and bolted from the bed, before turning to Dr. Strachan. "I can't, I can't do this. I am so sorry, Dr. Strachan. I just can't. I'm sorry I wasted your time. I cannot do this. I felt the baby ..."

Lola was almost hysterical when she ran into the next room, desperate to change out of the hospital gown, and back into her own clothes. While getting dressed as quickly as she could, Lola began shaking ferociously. She knew with certainty that she could not go through with slaying her child. After putting her sneakers back on, she sunk to her knees on the floor in a corner, and began weeping softly, instantly aware of the fact that she would not at all have been capable of going through with the termination the first time. She felt immense reprieve at the mere realization, and knew that she finally had a truthful answer for Daniel, Dean and Lauren. She smiled sadly, while wiping the tears that had begun to flow unreservedly down her cheeks.

Daniel had remained seated in silence while watching women come and go. He nervously watched the door which led out to the surgery, and prayed that Lola would come running through them, telling him that she was making a gigantic mistake. When some time had passed, Daniel knew that Lola had made up her mind, and that she was never going to come out through that door with their baby still inside of her. He closed his eyes, and prayed silently for God to step in and take control of the chaos they had found themselves in. He silently prayed that Lola would realize she was making an enormous mistake, and he begged for all of this to happen, before it was too late. Daniel was praying non-stop as though his life depended on it when he realized that he couldn't sit there in silence without putting up a courageous fight. He had to stop her. He had to try one last time.

Daniel suddenly jumped up, and ran through the same doors that Lola had gone through earlier. He sprinted down the passage when a feeling of powerlessness overwhelmed him. He had no idea of which door to burst through, so he began to call out her name in desperation, "Lola! Lola!" Nurse Jenny heard him call out, and cautiously made her way to the passage, where she found him frantically calling out for her. "Are you looking for Lola

Storey?" "Please, I have to find her. I have to stop her!" Nurse Jenny didn't have time to calm him down by telling him she couldn't go through with it. "She's in there." Daniel tugged at the door, and found Lola crawled up in a corner while sobbing inconsolably.

He had never seen her in such a state of disarray before. It seemed to Daniel that Lola was only moments away from entirely falling apart. She was clutching at both her legs which were pulled up to her chin, her face buried in her knees, rocking back and forth rigorously. "Lola, oh God, Lola?" Lola was at once startled when she looked up and saw him standing there, the horror evident on his face. Daniel walked up to her and knelt down in front of her, before placing his arms around her. He let her sob into his chest, while lightly stroking her hair. "Daniel." Lola was inconsolable. She surrendered to Daniel as he held her protectively. "Is it over? What happened? What did they do to you?" Lola could barely breathe between her hysterical crying, but wanted to tell Daniel that she couldn't go through with it. "I am such a bad person. I don't want to live anymore. I can't live like this. I just want to die, Danny. Please, can we go now. Can we just go, please Daniel? I have to get out of here. I can't breathe here. I want to go home." Daniel helped her up, and held his arm around her, leading her out of, and away from St. Darla's.

When they reached his car, Lola turned to face Daniel and smiled at him, overcome with sorrow, her eyes red and enflamed. "What happened, Lola?" Lola gazed at Daniel, submerged in desolation, but certain that she had to tell him she could not rid herself of the child who was alive inside of her. "Daniel, I was laying there. I was getting so cold, and they were struggling to find a vein. I kept thinking, I kept thinking that I couldn't do it. I couldn't go through with it, and then, I felt him move for the very first time, and I knew. I knew it was just something I could never do. My baby is alive, and I'm about to kill him. I couldn't do it. You can hate me always, and I would have to fight you always. I know that, but I just couldn't do it. He shouldn't have started moving yet. I still had this week. He shouldn't have started moving, but I felt him. I felt him, Daniel, and I don't care how he was conceived. I didn't care while I was laying there. All I cared about was saving my child's life. I can fight you Daniel, for the rest of my life if I have to, but I want my child to live, even if you're his father." She stared at Daniel as her tears continued to roll enthusiastically down her cheeks. Daniel moved closer to her, and placed both his hands on her shoulders. He stared at her, but he could think of nothing to say to her. "While I was getting dressed, I was thinking that I would never have been able to do it the first time. I know that now. In my heart, I know that. You never really know until you lay there, waiting to end the life of your child. Then you know. It just hits you, you know? I felt a presence there with me the entire time, and I kept getting that feeling of getting out of there. I don't know how to explain it to you. You wanted to know before, Daniel, and now, now I can tell you. Now I can tell you that I could never have done it the first time. I know that now, finally, and that's my answer. I know, I know now. I could never have. All these months you wanted to know from me. My answer is no, Daniel, I'm not that person. I'm not the person you thought I was."

She smiled sadly through her tears, and secretly hoped that he would be proud of her unexpected revelation. Daniel smiled at her, before he held her firmly against him. By the way he was holding her, Lola knew that, for the first time in an extremely long time, she did one thing right in Daniel's eyes. "I was so scared, Lola. I lost you. I didn't want to lose my child, our child. I can't lose you and my child Lola." Daniel whispered while holding her as rigidly as he possibly could, aware that he could once again, breathe without restraint. Lola retreated slightly, "I know it's going to be hard, Daniel, for both of us, but you can have the baby. You take the baby, and you raise him. I can't do this on my own, and if you feel that you can, if that's what you want, then, take him. I know that your mom will be there to help, and Lauren will help too, and maybe Samantha. I know you can do this better than I can, I know that. I can live with that, because, you're a good person, Daniel. We're just not good together. You're going to make a great dad. You're stronger than I am, you can do this." "You're not alone, Lola. I am here for you and for the baby. You won't do this alone, we can do it together. We'll figure it out. Just don't walk away from us like that. I want to do this with you, and even though you don't think so now, we were great together, Lola. We were happy once, and we had the best of times together." "No Daniel, not me, not us. You walked away from me a long time ago, but you never walked away from your child, so, you have to do this. I don't see chance for it. I'm not ready for this. I just want to leave Sutherland, and put all this behind me. I can't stay here anymore, and I know now that I should never have come to Sutherland in the first place. I know that now. I know you'll raise this baby right, Daniel. I know you will love him, despite who his mother is." She was devastated to hear herself tell Daniel that she wanted no part in raising their child. Daniel felt a wrench tug at his heart when he realized how broken they still were, but he was certain that the baby was a new beginning, and a brand-new promise for them, a colossal step forward from the past. "How would this work, Lola?" "I don't know, Daniel? I haven't thought that far yet, but, it can't be so complicated. Just take the baby. I'll stay until after it's born. I don't want to be a mother. I don't want to be a part of that. I don't want to look at the baby every day, and be reminded of this. I don't want to. This is not the right way to do this."

She slid into the passenger seat of his car. Daniel was content in allowing her the detachment that he was convinced, she needed. While driving back home in silence, Daniel prayed unspoken prayers, thanking God for hearing him, and for preventing Lola from taking their baby away from them. On the drive home, he regularly caught glimpses of Lola smiling, it made him happy to see her beam again. He was thankful to finally have the answers he needed from her, but, he always knew in his heart, that Lola would never have gone through with the termination the first time. Lola was oblivious to the smile that seemed like a permanent fixture on her face. She was proud of herself for realizing that she would never have been able to have an abortion, and even if no one person ever believed her, Lola was certain, and nothing else mattered to her at that very moment.

When they reached his apartment, Lola climbed out of Daniel's car, and without saying a word, walked over to where her car was parked. He followed closely behind her, and before she climbed in, she turned around to face him. "I remember that night, Daniel. It was the one night that gave me hope again." She smiled sadly, before taking his hand. "I don't regret being with you, but, this baby shouldn't have been conceived like that." Daniel bowed his head, and felt intense disgrace for how shoddily he had treated her that night. She quickly dabbed at a lost tear on her cheek, desperate to hide her sorrow from Daniel. "I don't hate you for it, Danny. I just wanted you to know that it meant something to me." She placed her hand on his chest, and gazed up into his eyes, "Please tell me that you believe me when I say that I would never have been able to do it, Daniel?" Daniel smiled, wanting to seize her in his arms, and kiss her again. "I do, Lola, I do believe you. I never thought you could do it, ever." He was desperate to hold her in his arms, and tell her that he never stopped loving her. He had an urgent desire to tell her how remorseful he was, but he was immensely embarrassed by the man he had turned into. Lola climbed into her car, and while he watched her drive away, Daniel had a disconcerting sensation that he had lost the only person he could ever love.

When Lola reached Greg's apartment, she knew that he would be dissatisfied with her decision to keep the baby. She walked in to find him seated on the sofa, distracted by the local newspaper. "Lola? Back so soon? My trip was cut short too, but I'm definitely not complaining." Gregory was surprised to see her standing there. Lola hesitantly sat down beside him, unsure of how to tell him that she could not go through with the abortion. "I couldn't do it Greg, but Daniel and I talked. He'll take the baby, and if you still want, we can see how it goes afterwards. You and I?" She cringed at the thought, but felt she owed Gregory a chance. "But, I have to leave Sutherland, I can't stay here anymore. I have to get away from him." Lola began babbling, her tears shimmering in her eyes. Gregory took her hand, and squeezed it gently, "We'll talk, Lola."

The following morning, Lola quickly called Dr. Stalting to schedule a sonogram. She was pleased to hear that they had an opening later that same afternoon. She immediately confirmed the appointment. Shortly after she ended the call to Dr. Stalting,

Lola excitedly called Lauren. "Hey, Lola!" Lauren was pleased to hear her sister's voice after their confrontation earlier. "Hey beautiful!" Lola felt lighter, and more at peace for the first time in months. "How are you? Do you want to grab lunch? I'm just helping out at Salvatore, but I should be free in about an hour or so?" "I can't. It's a long story, but I'm having a sonogram this afternoon. I'll explain when I see you. Can we do lunch tomorrow?" Lola was excited to tell her sister all about what had taken place in the last day. "Oh, okay. Do you want me to come with for the sonar?" Lauren was delighted to discover that Lola hadn't gone through with the abortion. "Yeah, that would be nice. It's at three, should I pick you up?" "No, that's alright. I'll meet you there. See you later!"

When Lola ended the call to Lauren, she quickly made her way to Daniel, who was working through paperwork in his office. "Can I come in?" Lauren hesitated before she knocked on his door. "Yes, please come in." "So, I've just spoken with Lola." Daniel frowned at once. "Anything wrong?" Lauren grinned, "No, everything's fine. She just, I was going to go with her for her first sonogram this afternoon, but I forgot that Dean and I made other plans, and I don't want her, uhm, you know, to be alone? I thought that maybe you'd, that you'd go in my place?" Lauren was terrified that Daniel might discover what an appalling a liar she was. "I, did you arrange it with Lola?" "Yeah! She's cool with it. 3pm at Dr. Stalting's office!" Lauren explained quickly before she hurriedly walked out of Daniel's office.

When Lola walked into the reception area of Dr. Stalting's office, she was irritated to find that Lauren had not yet arrived. She promptly dialed Lauren's number, but reached her voicemail almost at once. "Lauren, where are you?" Lola impatiently left her a quick message. "Lola Storey, how nice to see you again. Are you here for your first sonogram?" Dr. Stalting was excited to see Lola in the reception area. "Yes, I am." "Are you alone today?" Dr. Stalting quickly looked around. "I'm waiting for my sister. I'm sure she's just running late." "No problem. I'll have Rose show her in when she gets here. You can come through." Dr. Stalting led the way for Lola to follow.

Lola quickly changed into a hospital robe, and climbed onto the bed while Dr. Stalting prepped for the sonogram. Lola was anxious to see her baby for the very first time, and had no idea what to expect. "It's a little cold." Dr. Stalting explained as she gently applied gel onto Lola's belly. "You're starting to show already. Where's Daniel?" Lola just wanted to answer her, when there was an urgent knock on the door, before Rose appeared in the doorway. "Mr. Salvatore here for Ms. Storey, can I send him in?" "Yes, just in time." Dr. Stalting smiled when Daniel walked in. Lola was horrified to see him walk in, and felt her heart begin to gallop. "Sorry I'm late, Lola. The traffic was a nightmare, did I miss anything?" Lola was stunned and could hardly breathe when Daniel took her hand. "No, we were just about to start." Dr. Stalting turned back to the monitor while Lola glared at Daniel, who in turn, smiled broadly, and gently squeezed her hand.

After navigating around her belly a couple of times, Dr. Stalting stood inspecting the image on the monitor, while measuring and scrutinizing. Lola had no idea what it was she was doing, or what it was she was searching for. After continuing on for a couple minutes more, she turned back to face Lola, "Everything looks fine. You're almost eighteen weeks along, so you're a little further than we initially anticipated, but everything looks just fine. The baby's weight is a little low, Lola. You have to try and eat properly."

Lola was aware of a reproachful tone in Dr. Stalting's voice. "She doesn't, she hardly eats anything." Daniel became alarmed at once. "No, it's not that. I'm just struggling. I just can't keep anything down." Dr. Stalting frowned, realizing at once how pallid Lola was. "I'll give you something to take with your vitamins to help with the nausea, but you have to eat better." Dr. Stalting responded harshly.

She had just begun to show Lola the printout of her baby, when there was another loud knock on the door. Rose once again appeared in the doorway, "Goodness, train station this morning. Gregory Pastor here for Lola?" Daniel let go of Lola's hand almost at once. Gregory marched in, and was stunned to find Daniel standing there. Dr. Stalting remained quiet, but noticed that Lola was mortified by Greg's arrival. "Did I miss anything?" Gregory made his way to the end of the bed. "Greg, what are you doing here?" Lola was edgy at once. "I didn't want you to come here alone." Daniel immediately walked out, leaving Lola was once again saddened to see him go. Dr. Stalting promptly allowed Lola to listen to her baby's heartbeat, before leaving her and Gregory by themselves. "What's he doing here?" Lola could sense the annoyance in Greg's voice. "I don't know? I think Lauren told him about the sonogram? But, it is his child, after all. Would you mind waiting in the reception area while I get dressed?" Lola was desperate to escape both Gregory and Daniel.

She met up with Greg in the reception area just as Dr. Stalting handed her a new script for the vitamins and anti-nausea medication. She quickly looked around her, but couldn't find

Daniel anywhere, and was instantly saddened that he had left.

When they reached the parking area, Lola quickly kissed Gregory on the cheek before he left. She turned to unlock her car, and was suddenly anxiously aware of a familiar voice behind her, "Really, Lola? You invited Greg here?" Daniel was standing behind her. Lola could at once sense his downright antagonism. She dropped her keys, and at once bent down to pick them up again. "I didn't invite him here, Daniel. I don't know why he came? You shouldn't have come either." "I just wanted to, I wanted to be here for you. Lauren said you knew and I wanted to come." It suddenly made perfect sense to Lola. "You don't have to. I'd prefer if you didn't. I'd rather you just stay away, Daniel. Lauren lied. Can't you just wait for when the baby comes?" Lola was reminded of the fact that her heart was in no way at all, geared up to disregard what they had been through only a short while ago. "Yeah, if that's what you want." Daniel turned around, and walked away from her.

When Lola climbed into her car, she at once called Lauren, "What are you doing, Lauren?" Lola was fuming. "I just thought, it's Daniel's baby too, Lola." "And he gets to keep the baby Lauren, forever. I want nothing more to do with him, don't you understand that?" She shouted out before she hung up, and drove back to the apartment.

Reaching the apartment, Gregory was anxiously awaiting her arrival, "Choose Lola, you have got to choose between me and Daniel." Lola could sense the irritation in his voice. "I didn't know Daniel was going to be there. I just need to get away from here, Greg, away from him, and away from all of this." Lola was left wounded by the entire situation with Daniel. Gregory walked up to Lola, "I told you, Lola, if we're going to move forward after the baby comes, you have to let go of Daniel." Gregory placed a firm hand on her shoulder. "I know, and I'm trying." Lola was caught between keeping the peace with Gregory, and her love for Daniel. "I have to get back to the office, will you be alright?" Lola nodded, and smiled desolately as Gregory left the apartment.

Lola never again invited Lauren along to any of her doctor's appointments after that day, and reclusively remained indoors for fear of running into Daniel. She would call Lauren once a week, yet, she found an excuse to avoid her sister whenever she could. For Lola, it was exhausting and challenging while attempting to convince Gregory that what was between her and Daniel, was over. At the same time, it was grueling to live without Daniel and the baby she had fallen hopelessly in love with. Lola was terrified of the future, but she was content that as long as the baby was still inside of her, nothing could change yet.

Lola was almost seven months pregnant when Lauren called her one evening just as she was getting ready to work on her manuscript. Lola hardly saw much of Lauren, but she chose the elusiveness as a way to steer clear of Daniel and thankfully for Lola, they never spoke again since their brief encounter at Dr. Stalting's office. Lauren was sure that the more time that passed them by, the less likely it would be for them to reunite. "Hey sis!" Lauren was ecstatic to hear her sister's voice. "Hey Lauren, what's up?" Lauren hesitated for just an instant, "Dean and I would love to have you for supper tonight. I miss you. You never come around anymore." "I don't know, Lauren? I'm so tired lately, and just trying to get through the next few months. Greg's working tonight anyways." "Please sis, it's only dinner. I've made your favorite desert." Lola hesitated for a moment but realized that she too, longed for her sister. "You know what? I would love to; can I bring anything?" Lauren was instantly relieved, "No nothing, is seven'ish alright?" "That's fine." Lola replied before hanging up.

She walked towards the mirror hanging from the wall in her bedroom, and realized that she was showing a lot more than she did the previous week. Lola placed her hand on her belly when she felt her baby move, and smiled broadly. She was keenly aware of the fact that she had fallen in love again, even though she was convinced that it would never be in the cards for her. A thought crossed her mind that if she had kept the baby, she would forever have a part of Daniel with her, and even though he no longer loved her, their child would always. Lola considered the idea for an instant, but just as quickly determined that the baby too, would keep Daniel in her life for a lifetime, and she was not prepared for the reality of that frightening notion. She would never be geared up for Daniel Salvatore again. Handing the baby over to him, was all she could do to keep her heart intact, and she hoped that he would shower their baby with enough love for both of them. When Lauren tossed the mobile phone onto the sofa where Dean was sitting, after hurriedly inviting Lola over for dinner, she smiled broadly, "Your turn, call Daniel!"

Dean smiled, and enthusiastically dialed Daniel's number, while at the same time, panicking that he would become distrustful of them, "Hey bro, where are you?" "Hey Dean, just finishing up a few things at the workshop. Trying to square things out before the baby comes." He could hear Daniel was preoccupied. "So, listen, Lauren is cooking up a storm tonight, and she wanted to know if you'd like to join us for supper tonight?" "Tonight?" Daniel flinched at once. "Oh, come on. You know how Lauren gets when she cooks and nobody pitches, besides, we haven't really seen you outside of Salvatore?" Daniel sat back, and felt guilty for avoiding Lauren and Dean for so long, away from Salvatore. "Yes fine, but I can't stay long. I have an early meeting in the morning." Daniel accepted their dinner invitation before hanging up almost immediately. He had just cleaned his hands, when he secretly admitted to himself that he was pleased they had asked him over. He was spending far too much time at Salvatore, and loathed having to go home to an empty apartment. Daniel reviled at the idea that Lola was living with Gregory, and cringed at the thought of having him around her, and his child. He knew Gregory Pastor well, but made reluctant peace with the fact that he no longer had any authority over Lola.

He had not seen or spoken to Lola since the incident at Dr. Stalting's offices, and he was struggling to come to terms with the fact that they were no longer together. He missed her. He was shattered that they could not raise their child together, but he was also keenly aware of the painful reality that he no longer knew how to love Lola. He had not at all imagined that loving someone could be as hard as it was to love Lola, and he realized again that their love was toxic, and did nothing more than destroy each other. He was excited to raise his child, and he desperately hoped that the baby would fill up the barrenness that Lola had left behind.

Lola arrived at Dean and Lauren's apartment just before seven, and was thrilled to see them. Dean embraced her, and placed a protective hand on her belly. "Lola, you look beautiful. Do you know what you're having?" Dean was at once excited at the prospect of becoming an uncle. Lola was instantly self-conscious, and at once felt overweight and hideous, even though Lauren insisted that she was beautiful. "Yes, a boy." Lola smiled and responded bashfully. "Wow sis, congratulations! Does Daniel know? Have you told him?" Lauren clapped her hands in animation. "No, we don't talk. Can I help with anything?" Lola swiftly followed her sister into the kitchen. "You can keep me company, if you like." "How is Daniel?" It slipped out, but Lola wanted to know that Daniel was okay. "He's fine, or so he wants us to think. Just working all the time, trying to get as much done as he can before the baby comes. He never comes around anymore." Lauren glared at Lola, "How's living with Gregory going?" "I'm not living with Gregory, Lauren. He's just given me a place to stay. You sound just like Daniel." "And he doesn't mind having a pregnant roommate around?" Lauren grimaced curiously. "I told him I'll be leaving Sutherland when the baby is born, and that we can see how it goes."

Lola was abruptly and unexpectedly aware of voices that were coming from the living room. She gawked nervously at Lauren. Lauren knew that Lola would be irritated when she discovered her and Dean's scheme, and hurriedly took the salad out to the dining room. Lola listened cautiously, and was shaken to realize that it was Daniel's voice she was hearing. She could barely move, and felt her tummy turn when she realized that Lauren and Dean had set them up.

Dean waltzed into the kitchen, desperate to get Lola out to the dining room. "Dean, how could you? You and Lauren did this on purpose!" Dean pretended not to hear, and after picking up the dinner plates he turned back to Lola, "You two need to talk. Will you bring the knives and forks please, Lola?" He turned away from her as swiftly as he could, and strutted back into the dining room. Lola stood for what felt like forever, desperate to regain her composure.

She tensely picked up the knives and forks, and reluctantly made her way into the dining room, where they all had taken their seats around the dining room table. Daniel was as stunned as Lola was when he saw her, and grimaced when he realized just as Lola had, that they were being set up. He watched Lola place the knives and forks on the table, and noticed for the first time that her belly had grown enormously. Her hair was still short, but he couldn't imagine her more beautiful than at that very second. Lauren had mentioned to him earlier that she was a little skinny and exhausted, but that she was coping wonderfully with the pregnancy.

When Lola finally took a seat, she turned to Daniel, "Hi, Daniel. I didn't know you were coming? I'm sorry they did this."

Alice VL

She made a courageous attempt to hide her awkwardness. "That's okay, Lola. I know what my brother is capable of. So, how are you feeling? Are you doing alright?" He smiled sadly while attempting to take in all that enchanted him about her. She shifted uncomfortably in her seat. She wanted to blurt out that she was terrible. She wanted to tell him that she pined for him, that she missed talking to him, and she had an inexplicable need to tell him all there was to know about their child, but her heart reminded her that she had no right to expose her needs to him any longer. "Good thanks, trying to cope with the changes, you know? Getting fat, and hormones all over the place." She giggled timidly. "You're not fat. A little skinny, but not fat. How's, how's the baby?" "Lola just found out that it's a boy!" Dean breathlessly and impatiently blurted out that they were having a son. Daniel felt his heart begin to gallop, and was unexpectedly disappointed that Lola withheld the news from him. "Wow! When did you find out?" "A couple of weeks ago. I didn't want to know, but Dr. Stalting slipped up when she did the sonogram." "Wow, seems so real now, a boy? Wow!" Daniel was thrilled, but again, he couldn't shake the disappointment for the fact that he had to hear it from Dean. "It does feel real and scary, although, not as scary as for you, I'm sure." "I'm nervous, but not scared. Actually, I'm starting to get excited. Does he move around a lot?" "Oh yes, he never stops and hardly lets me sleep. You should see when I'm in the bath, he just loves the warm water, I think?" "Wow, can I feel? Is he moving now?" Lola didn't want his hands on her belly, afraid of how she might react to his touch. "He's quiet now, but I do have a picture from a 4D scan that was done yesterday." She instantly reached for her purse, and handed the photograph to Daniel.

He stared at the image, and became dispirited almost at once. "Are you ready for this, Daniel? I mean, really ready?" "Yeah, I think so. My mom's coming down for a month or so. Wow, a boy huh?" Daniel was mesmerized, and couldn't take his eyes off the picture. They all sat in an uncomfortable silence for a while after, until Dean and Daniel began discussing their new projects at Salvatore. Lola instantly realized how desperately she longed for her days at Salvatore, and silently wished that she was still there, and that things were the way they once were. "So, Lola ..." Lauren stumbled slightly when she realized that Dean and Daniel were profoundly caught up in their own discussions. "Are you excited about the future? Have you guys thought of a name?" Lola glared at Lauren, mystified by what the future may hold for her. "I've made some plans, just not sure yet. Daniel should name him." "Surely some names have popped up in your mind? Are you going to breastfeed?" Lola was astounded by Lauren's questions. She had made it clear very early on that Daniel would be raising their child without her. "Why are you doing this, Lauren? You know that I'm not keeping the baby." Lola was irritable at once when she caught a glimpse of Daniel listening intently to her. "Sorry sis, I just thought that, maybe you'd change your mind. So, what kind of plans have you made?" Lola did her best to regroup, not wanting Daniel to notice her discomfort all of a sudden. "I, I'm a little scared, and nothing definite yet, but I'd like to start working again soon after the baby comes, and get my own place. Gregory said he'd help me find something, possibly in Pine Valley. He might open up a branch there, but there are still a few months to decide, so we'll see. It's not too far from here." "You have money, Lola. You don't need Gregory for anything. What I don't understand is, why you haven't gotten your own place yet? Are you seriously going to move forward with Gregory after the baby is born?" Daniel abruptly lashed out at her. She lowered her head, convinced that he was referring to the money she received from Salvatore as a payout, but unsure of how to tell Daniel that she wanted none of it. "That's not my money Daniel. I don't want it, and I'm not shacking up with Gregory. He's good to me, but he doesn't want me like this. You know that. I've told you that everything is on hold for after, after the baby comes."

Daniel was surprised to hear that she was living off what was left of her trust fund, and grew increasingly irritated. "So, you'd rather shack up with, and depend on Gregory Pastor, while carrying another man's child before you swallow your pride, and take the damn money? You should be around Lola, for the baby. You shouldn't run away from us like that!" Daniel heatedly raised his voice. "I'm not running away Daniel. I just don't want to live here anymore. I told you, I told you I couldn't do it. I can't do it, Daniel. Nothing has changed, and we agreed to this. Pride has nothing to do with it. It's not my money, and no matter what you say, I will never use any of it! How could you, Daniel? Nothing ever happened between Greg and I, but you, you can't say the same, can you?" "Lola, your pride is making you egotistical! I told you nothing happened between Sam and I!" Lola was not about to allow Daniel the upper hand this time, "Yeah right! So now I imagined what I saw with my own eyes?" Daniel was not prepared to back down either, "Just remember one thing Lola, you're the liar here, not me!" Lola lowered her head in shame when she realized that Daniel was right, she was the one that lied to him, and nothing she could ever say will enforce his belief in a single word she would ever say again. "I know how things are going to end with Gregory. And it's going to be nothing compared to you and I! Don't come knocking at my door later, demanding to see my son. It's not going to happen as long as you are with Gregory Pastor! He will chew you up, and spit you out, Lola." "Funny, he said the same thing about you." Lola whispered softly, before she turned to face Daniel, "And what do you call what you did? You didn't just chew me up and spit me out, you crushed whatever was left of me!" Daniel got up, unable to control his temper any longer, "You think that's what I did? You have no idea, Lola. I got your feelings hurt a little, it's nothing compared to what Gregory will do to you!"

Lauren and Dean had left the dining room, but could not avoid hearing them squabble from the kitchen. Daniel walked over to the window of the dining room, desperate to calm himself, afraid of what he might say next. Lola was saddened to witness him in such a state, and cautiously made her way to him. "You're wrong Daniel, nothing can hurt me more than what happened between us, than you. You didn't just hurt my feelings, you almost destroyed me." Lola paused to take in a deep breath, desperate to contain the lump in her throat. "I know you're going to take care of the baby, and I know you don't believe me, but I will never come back for him, I promise you. I'll start my life over somewhere else, and you'll never see me again. I promise Daniel, I will never come back for him. You have to believe me." She gently placed her hand on his shoulder. Daniel turned around, and grabbed her by her arm, keenly aware that his anger had in no way subsided. "Lola, look at you! You are skinny and pale. You don't eat properly, you're not taking care of yourself or the baby!" "It's not on purpose, Daniel. I'm sick and nauseas all the time. I'm trying to do what's best for the baby. I don't skip meals, it's just, I can't keep anything down. I've been back to the doctor, and she's given me more medication. I'm not doing it on purpose. I am trying, my hardest, Daniel. I am." "Rubbish Lola! You're not taking care of yourself! And Gregory Pastor is not what's best for you, or for the baby right now! Are you drinking?" Daniel tightened his grip on her arm before Lola erupted into tears.

It shattered her heart that Daniel found her so entirely despicable, and failed to place any confidence in her. Yet, through all the lashing out, she realized again that she respected and loved him so much more than she thought was possible. "No, Daniel, I'm not drinking. What do you want from me?" Lola looked up at him, afraid that he might condemn her for her tears. While doing her best to swallow back on her excruciating pain, her desolation turned to anger without warning or prior notice, "I wish you weren't his father! I wish I wasn't pregnant! I wish I never met you! I wish I never decided to keep this baby! I can't do anything right with you! I am doing the best I can, I am trying, but I don't know what is right anymore! I am trying to be independent. I am trying to get my life in order! This is exactly why I wanted the abortion, but you don't see it. You think I'm such a bad person and always, always think the worst of me!" "You shouldn't be a mother! I should've left you to go through with it. How can you turn your back on him like that?" Daniel at once felt remorse for what he had just said to her, and abruptly realized that he was lying to himself. "But, Daniel, I won't be his mother. I am nothing to him. I don't feel anything, not for you, and not for him." She lied while sobbing uncontrollably. Just as she was hurting, standing before him, she wanted Daniel to feel pain as she did.

Through her tears, she felt a sudden grip around her belly, an excruciating and unexpected twinge that made its way from her back, and all the way across to her belly. She grabbed a hold of Daniel, afraid she might collapse. Daniel held onto her, and realized at once that all was not well with Lola, "Lola?" He panicked when he realized that her legs were giving way under her. "Lola!" He yelled out, desperate to keep her on her feet. Lauren and Dean came rushing in, to find Daniel holding onto Lola with all his might. "Oh, God no, not again. It's happening again, Daniel! It's happening again!" Lola frantically cried out through her tears. "She needs to get to a hospital!" Daniel signaled to Dean for help. While carrying her to the car, Lola erupted into violent sobbing, at the same time as clutching at her belly, and moaning out in pain. When they had safely placed her on the backseat of the car, Daniel turned to Dean. "Please drive, bro, I want to sit with Lola." He slid in beside her, and placed his arms around her. "Lola, please be okay. I'm sorry, I'm so sorry for the things I said. Please be okay." "It hurts. I can't breathe. I don't want to do this again! It hurts, Daniel. It's too soon, please make it stop!"

Carrying her into the emergency room, Daniel felt intense guilt make its way into the innermost part of him. He was convinced that he was solely to blame for Lola's early labor, and knew that if anything went wrong with Lola or the baby, he would never be able to absolve himself. They admitted her to the maternity ward without delay. Daniel in turn, refused to leave her side. Dean and Lauren made themselves comfortable in the waiting room, but both were miserable that it was happening all over again. The doctor examining Lola was tensed and concerned. He hurriedly explained that there was a faint heartbeat, but that Lola was frail. He quickly explained that they would keep her overnight to monitor mother and child. He turned to Daniel, and placed a comforting hand on his shoulder, "Let her rest. Everything is under control now. We just need to get some fluids into her, she's a little dehydrated. She should be okay in the morning. The baby's heartbeat is very weak. I don't know, I honestly don't know if he's going to make it, but if he makes it through the night, chances are good. He's in severe distress at the moment."

When the doctor walked out of the ward, Daniel glanced over at Lola who had fallen asleep. He hurriedly made his way to Dean and Lauren, and was at once abruptly aware of unfathomable guilt that had crept into his heart. "Hey bro, everything alright?" Dean took Lauren's hand into his. "Yeah, they're going to keep her overnight, but they're not sure about the baby. You guys go get some rest. I'm going to stay for a while." Daniel felt as though the entire world had come crashing down on his shoulders. Lauren placed her arms around him, and tightly embraced him before she gently whispered in his ear, "It's going to be okay, Daniel. Lola is stronger than you think." Daniel whimpered softly before he turned away from them, anxious to return to Lola. When he walked into her ward, he was overcome with defenselessness and despondence. He made his way into an empty seat beside her, and clasped her hand in his, overcome with agonizing remorse for all that had taken place earlier. Lola groggily opened her eyes and turned to face Daniel. "Daniel?"

She croaked hoarsely as she struggled to sit up straight. "Shhh …" He signaled for her to lie down. "It's going to be alright." He gently squeezed her hand. "The baby?" "He's fine Lola, he's going to pull through. He has to, you have to be strong, and make him strong, Lola. Please be strong." Daniel begged her before taking her into his arms. Lola held onto Daniel and said a silent prayer for her baby. "I'm sorry Lola. I'm so sorry, for everything. Everything I said tonight, and everything I've ever done to you. I keep doing this, and I don't know why? I am so sorry." Daniel was ardently aware of the tears that had begun to roll down his cheeks while Lola glared sorrowfully at him, "It's not your fault, Daniel. You were right. You're always right." "No, I'm not, Lola. Doc says if he pulls through, you can come home in a day or two and I, I want you to, I'm begging you, Lola, come home with me. Please." Lola was wholeheartedly perceptive to the guilt that had begun to overwhelm him, "No, Danny." "Please, Lola. Even if it is just until after the baby is born. It doesn't have to mean anything. I just want to be there. Please Lola, let me do this. I never meant what I said. I know it's hard, and I know that you're trying. I know you're doing the best you can, and I want to help." She began to sob softly when Daniel held her in his arms again. "I need you to be alright, Lola." He whispered as he held her firmly, and protectively against him. "You need the baby to be okay, Daniel." Lola corrected him. "No, Lola, I need you. You need to be okay, you have to be alright. I choose you, Lola. You are my lid. I choose you."

Before Lola could respond, she was once again aware of an immense tightening around her belly. She began to shake uncontrollably, and cried out in pain once again. Daniel bolted from his seat, and shouted out for a nurse who had found Lola curled up on her bed. The same doctor that attended to her only moments before, came rushing in, followed by a couple more nurses who instantly took command over Lola.

Daniel stepped back in horror, painfully aware that his entire world came crashing down on him, when he instinctively realized exactly what was about to happen. Daniel dialed Dean's number, and hurriedly informed him of what was going on before abruptly hanging up. Lola was quickly examined by the doctor, and after establishing that there was too faint of a heartbeat on the monitor, he turned to Daniel, "I'm sorry. The baby, he won't survive if we don't get him out now." Lola was sobbing, and Daniel felt a floodgate of tears rupture inside of him, all the while he recognized the familiarity of what was about to take place, one more time. "What now, doc?" "Well, unfortunately she is still in labor, and because she has completely dilated, she would have to give birth naturally. It's not going to be easy, but there is no time for a C-section. If there is any chance for the baby's survival, Lola has to give birth now."

Daniel despondently made his way over to Lola, and could barely imagine how she would survive going through the trauma of giving birth to a baby that might never breathe the air they were inhaling. "Lola, hold on. Please be strong. I'm here, but you have to do this now. There is a chance, but you have to do this now." He clasped her hand firmly in his, "It hurts, Daniel. I can't do this!" "Lola, can you start pushing?" Their doctor was ready for Lola to give birth as swiftly as possible. "I can't!" "Lola, please, push!" An assisting nurse begged Lola to push as rigidly as she possibly could. Lola closed her eyes and took in a deep breath before she pushed as hard as she could. When nothing happened, she was certain that she could not survive the pain that was overwhelming her. "Daniel, help me! Don't let them do this. The baby isn't ready! Danny, please!" Daniel had in no way ever, felt as powerless as he did at that very moment. "Again, Lola!" The doctor was anxious for Lola to keep trying. Lola pushed again, and again nothing happened. Lola felt her breaths become shorter. "Lola, once more, just one more!" The same nurse yelled out after noticing the baby's head crown. Lola pushed with all her might, and was at once relieved when the contractions began subside unexpectedly. She was holding on to Daniel, and was instantly thankful that she could breathe a little easier. The doctor seized the baby into his arms, and hurriedly turned away from Lola before he hastily wrapped their baby in a hospital sheet, and handing him to one of the nurses.

She immediately placed him in an incubator, while the doctor focused his attention on the newborn. Lola unwittingly grimaced when she realized that he had not started crying yet, and knew instinctively that her son would not survive being born as prematurely as he did. Her child had not developed as he should have. Yet, she hoped and prayed for a miracle. After frantic attempts to save their child, the doctor turned around, and shook his head when he caught a glimpse of Daniel. Daniel knew intuitively that their child had died, and was at once aware of an intense, razor-sharp sting entering the very core of him. He leaned over Lola and held onto her, unable to entirely comprehend how it was possible that their son had just ceased to exist. His heart had shattered into a thousand pieces, while Lola sobbed brutally in his chest.

The doctor placed their son on her chest. Lola held snugly onto him while Daniel stroked his cheek, and felt his tears torrent down his own. Lola swabbed away at her tears, desperate to absorb each diminutive detail about their son. "Jonathan, his name should be Jonathan. He looks just like your dad." Lola smiled forlornly before she turned to face Daniel. Daniel began to weep uncontrollably, and hung his head in shame for all he had done and had accused Lola of. She gazed back at Jonathan and finally understood that a child was never in the stars for her, as was a future or life with Daniel. She handed him to Daniel, and pulled the blanket up to her chest, before turning away from them. She was angry and overwhelmed when she realized her heart was rupturing into a million fractions.

Daniel strolled over to the window holding Jonathon protectively in his arms, and powerless to take his eyes off his son. He counted his fingers and toes over and over again, and could barely grasp how flawless his little boy was, yet he wasn't able to take in one single breath. A nurse walked up to Daniel, holding her arms out to take Jonathan from him. Daniel was not ready to give Jonathan up just yet, and gently kissed on his forehead. When he handed his lifeless son over to her, he sobbed inconsolably, all the while, devotedly aware of the fact that he would never hold his little boy in his arms again.

Shortly after the doctor and nurses had all exited the ward, Daniel sat silently next to Lola. The doctor had informed Daniel just a few moments earlier that there was no chance for the baby to survive, and that Lola would not have carried him full term at all. For Daniel, it was the son he had always dreamed of, and the very thought was enough to entirely crush him. The doctor continued to explain that Lola was extremely fragile, dehydrated and seemed utterly tensed and strained. These were all factors contributing to the still birth, leaving Daniel to once again recognize the enormous guilt he had entertained at that very moment. "This is all my fault, Lola. I kept hammering at you. I kept going at you. I made you feel bad about yourself, and I blamed everything on you. I was devastated when I found out you were pregnant. I wasn't sure that I ever wanted this baby, and then I never wanted you to have this baby. I kept thinking it was a mistake to stop you from having the abortion, but today, I truly failed you, and I failed our son. You were right, I chewed you up, spat you out, and crushed you."

Lola frowned when she listened to him accept absolute responsibility for their son's death, and even though her own heart was wrecked, she never wanted Daniel to experience the tremendous amount of guilt he was feeling. "It's not your fault, Danny, these things happen. It's no-one's fault. It just wasn't meant to be. The baby just would have complicated things for us both, and I just wanted you to carry on like before, without me. I know the baby was a mistake, but it's over now, Daniel." "I was so hard on you Lola, and I kept saying how the baby was a mistake, but he wasn't. I do remember that night. I remember everything. I remember making love to you, and never wanting to let you go. It was all just an act, Lola, and I was foolish not to admit it. He deserved to live. It should have been different. I did this. I wanted you to feel bad. I wanted to punish you, but all I could think of was that night. Our little boy was conceived that night, and I would do anything Lola, anything to take back what I said to you, or how I made you feel. I wanted to make love to you, but I didn't want to admit it to you. I wanted you to think that it meant nothing. I pretended to be drunk. How could he be a mistake? How could I ever have said that to you? That would mean we were a mistake, Lola, and I could never, never give you up. I would never change having you in my life. How did I ever say those things to you?"

Daniel was overwhelmed with remorse, and was anxious to let her know how that one night, was one filled with unreserved importance and immense enchantment. "He was a mistake, Daniel, and even though my heart is so sore, and even though he was so beautiful, I know that things happen the way they are supposed to. Maybe you were right. Maybe this life wasn't what was best for him. You and me fighting all the time, and Jonathan growing up with just one parent. I never wanted that for him, so this is for the best, Daniel. And at least, he will never know how much you hated his mother. Now we can both start over, and you can have a real family, with someone else. There's no baby standing in your way, Daniel. Just please, stop hating me. Please, stop punishing me, and just let me just go." Lola choked on her words as a fresh batch of tears rolled down her cheeks. "Lola, I don't hate you. I don't hate you. I've never hated you. God wouldn't have sent us Jonathan if we were a mistake. I love you, so much. Too much, and I think that's why I kept hurting you. I could never, ever let you go, Lola." He wanted her to know that he adored her so enormously, but just as Dean and Lauren walked in, his words fell silent.

Dean embraced his brother before he hugged Lola. Lauren stood sobbing at the foot of her bed. "I'm so sorry, Lola. I'm so sorry that this happened to you guys again." Lauren stuttered through her tears, certain that any chance of the baby bringing them back together, was lost forever. "That's alright, Lauren, it's better this way. It's better. It's going to be okay, sissy. Tomorrow, things will be better again." Lola was desperate to comfort her sister. Dean embraced Lauren, and Lola was once again pleased to encounter a man like Dean who wholeheartedly, cared for, and loved her sister. She wanted to tell Lauren how proud she was of her, but she smiled instead, when she realized that the confining lump in her throat would not allow her to speak. They sat together in silence for what felt like forever, before Dean and Lauren finally left. Daniel sat beside Lola, unsure of what to say to her, but happy to linger in silence around her.

He tried to discover ways to convince her of how entirely apologetic and remorseful he was, and he hoped that she would give him an opportunity to show her his undying love for her, but while Daniel was utterly lost and distracted by his thoughts, Lola had fallen asleep.

Daniel stared at her for a while trying to understand how they had reached that exact moment, and how it was possible to engage in so many avoidable mishaps. Daniel was determined to mend fences with Lola, but as he let her sleep, he prayed that all would appear better for them in the morning.

A nurse came in a little while later, and gently touched Daniel on his shoulder, "Go get some rest." Daniel was not ready to leave her side, "I want to stay." "She's going to be asleep for a while. Doc has given her something to help her sleep. Go home, get some rest, and have a shower. You need to be here for her, but not like this." Daniel got up from his chair, and gently kissed Lola on her forehead before he took his jacket, and reluctantly left the hospital.

When he reached his apartment, Daniel sat out on the terrace in sheer despondence, traumatized by the sudden turn of events. He gazed out over Madison, and thought back to all the events of the day that led them to that very moment. He thought of Lola, and how distressed and wounded she was. He thought of the moments she tried her very best to talk to him, but he was stubborn, and refused to listen to her. He recalled the night they made love for the last time. He was utterly mortified by his role in her heartache, one that left Lola feeling so entirely unworthy of him. Their son was conceived that night, and yet it was a night that Lola would to a certain extent, hate for the rest of her life. A night he often referred to as a mistake. It was a night that brought new life and eternal optimism to him, yet Daniel's words forced her to repel that night. "Please forgive me, Dear Lord!" Daniel cried out while wondering whether God was in fact, trying to teach him a lesson.

His heart was devastatingly crushed as he dabbed at the tears that were rushing down his cheeks once again. Daniel held his head in his hands, and sobbed liberally and relentlessly. They had lost another little element of themselves. He was certain that this time, he alone was answerable for their loss.

Lola's Secret

The following morning, Lola awoke just as Dr. Stalting had entered her ward. "Lola? I saw your name on the admissions list. I am so sorry." Lola smiled sorrowfully just as her tears began to sting in her eyes again. She quickly glanced around her, and realized that she was left alone in the ward, and was at once disappointed when she noticed that Daniel had left her there. "Can I go home?" "Yes, but please, rest. Take it easy, and if there are any complications, you call me at once. I want to see you in about two weeks. In the meantime, bed rest." Dr. Stalting hurriedly signed her discharge papers, and instructed a nurse to help Lola get dressed. "Thank you, Dr. Stalting." Lola was thwarted that Daniel was absent when she woke up, but acknowledged instantly that nothing between them had changed. She reluctantly dialed Greg's number, feeling vulnerable by the fact that he was the only one left to call. "Greg, it's me, Lola." "Lola, are you okay?" "Can you come and get me please. I'm at St. Mercy's. I'll wait outside." "Sure, I'll be right there." She was waiting at the entrance when Gregory arrived curtly after she called him, pleased that the nightmare of yesterday was finally over.

Daniel awoke to the realization that he had fallen asleep out on the balcony. He hurriedly glanced at the time, and was certain that Lola was awake. He was at once unbearably aware of an overwhelming urge to be with her. He dashed into the shower, frantic to reach the hospital before the doctor had arrived. He didn't want Lola to face him on her own. He quickly slid on a pair of jeans, before he threw a shirt on, and grabbed a pair of socks, and rushed downstairs to his car. He was instantly thankful that the traffic was only slightly congested as he tore through the streets of Madison in a frenetic attempt to reach the hospital in the shortest time.

Daniel sprinted into her ward, and was horrified to find her bed vacant. With utter confusion, he marched over to the nurse's station, desperate to find Lola, "Lola Storey. Her bed is empty?" "Let me just, oh here, Dr. Stalting discharged her an hour ago." Daniel was surprised that she had left in such a hurry, but at the same time, he was entirely crushed to realize that she had in no way at all, attempted to call him to pick her up. He at once dialed Dean's number, sure that they had picked Lola up from the hospital. "Hey bro, is Lola with you?" "No? I'm at Salvatore with Lauren. Isn't she still in hospital?" Daniel was at once disappointed. "No. Not to worry, I'll call Lauren on the landline." Daniel ended the call at once, and realized that Gregory had taken her home.

He climbed into his car, and stared straight ahead of him. He suddenly remembered why he had fallen in love with Lola, and for the first time since she left his apartment, he was aware of an enormous sense of loss that he was feeling since she had been gone. Daniel was overwhelmed by the realization that she asked nothing from him, but love and respect. All she wanted was love that escaped her as a child. Love that she so frantically needed from him, but never demanded, yet, she not once hesitated to surrender her heart to him. Daniel at once realized that it was her greatest gift to him. He berated himself for all the hurt and anguish he had brought into her life, intensely sensitive to how she had suffered at the hands of her father. She waged the ultimate price for him, and for the first time since losing the baby, Daniel understood why she had made that harrowing appointment the first time. Lola was terrified of losing him, yet by doing what she thought was right, she lost him nonetheless.

Daniel realized that he never once paid attention to the caution in her eyes, and understood for the first time, how utterly alone she must have felt. He again realized that he could never surrender her up to another man, his heart belonged only to her, and that no deed would in any way distort the love he had for her, just as he once swore to her. Daniel was desperate to see her, and beg her to come back to him. He prayed that it was not too late, but convinced that he would do whatever it took to bring her home to him.

When he started up his car, he quickly called Lauren on the landline. "Hey Lauren, its Daniel." "Hey Daniel, what's up?" "I need to get in touch with Lola, do you have her address? She was discharged from the hospital earlier this morning." "Already? Please don't fight, Daniel. Haven't you guys fought enough?" Daniel was horrified that Lauren thought all they ever did, was fight when they were together. "I don't want to fight, Lauren. I have to fix this. I have to fix things. Please, please just give me her address? I love her, Lols." Daniel was pleading with Lauren, before she reluctantly gave him her address. After entering her address into his navigator, he found the apartment building effortlessly. While climbing the stairs, Daniel was horrified to realize how run down the old apartment building was, and he cringed at the thought of Lola living there. When he reached the apartment number Lauren had given him, he hesitated for a moment, unsure of what to say to her. He had no idea of where or how to begin, but he had an inexplicable urge to convince her that he had no way of living without her.

After knocking twice, he heard distinct footsteps on the other side of the door. Lola slowly opened the door, and was entirely unprepared to find Daniel standing there. "Can I come in?" He walked past her, without waiting for permission, and after letting himself into the apartment, Lola closed the door behind him, as Daniel stood glancing around. "How are you feeling, Lola? Are you alright?" He turned around to face Lola. She was at once relieved when she noticed the indisputable concern in his eyes. "I'm fine, Daniel. At least, I will be. Doc says just a day or so, and I'll be back to my usual self, thank you for asking." The traces of hurt in Lola's eyes was almost too much for him to bear. "I'm so sorry, Lola. I hurt you." Daniel was about to tell Lola that he couldn't live without her, when Gregory walked in, without prior warning. Lola smiled uneasily. "Gregory?" She whispered softly, knowing that his presence at any given time, infuriated Daniel. "Our PA resigned this morning, so I have to run." Daniel was horrified to witness Gregory walk in, who instantly made his way over to where they were standing. "You again?" Gregory turned back to Lola, "Are you seeing this guy again?" "No." Lola whispered nervously. "You're not going back to Salvatore, are you?" "No." Daniel's heart splintered when he picked up on the desolation in her voice. "Good. I have a great position at my company. As soon as he leaves, we'll talk, and now that there is no baby, I see no reason why things can't turn around for us, and you can head out to Pine Valley with me." He smiled while gently rubbing her arm.

Lola smiled uncomfortably, and nodded without saying a word. Daniel could no longer control his temper. He could no longer stand by, and allow Lola to slip into the clutches of Gregory Pastor. He grabbed Gregory and punched him directly in the face. "She's just had a baby, Gregory, who died. Does that mean anything to you? Get out, just get away from her!" "Daniel! Stop!" Lola shouted as she tried to move in between them. "Stay out of this, Lola!" Lola was horrified by Daniel's sudden anger, "No, Daniel! This is his apartment! You can't tell him to get out? I need this job! Why do you care anyways? The baby is gone, Daniel! There truly is nothing anymore, and you shouldn't even be here!" Gregory pulled himself together, and irately turned back to Lola, "You know what, Lola, forget it. It's just too hard with you. I want you out! I've had enough of you and the Salvatore's. You deserve one another!" Gregory straightened his shirt, and left his apartment in a huff. Daniel glared at Lola who was standing quietly in her nightgown. He noticed once again how fragile she was. She had not a drop of lipstick on, and yet she still managed to make Daniel's heart soar. "Daniel, why are you doing this? What do you want from me? Why can't you leave me alone? The baby is gone, there is nothing for us anymore." She was mortified, unreservedly humiliated by what had just played out between Daniel and Gregory. "I needed that job! I have nowhere else to go! Don't you get it?" The despondence was unmistakable in her voice. Daniel walked up to her, feeling as though his entire world was at a complete stand still. "I've just come from the hospital. Your bed was empty, and it just scared me. Also, that thing with Mr. H that I haven't had a chance to speak to you about," "You really want to talk about that now?" "You went to see him behind my back, Lola. Of course, I want to speak to you about it." "I didn't want Salvatore, Daniel. I told you. I tried to stop you, but you wouldn't listen to me! You never listen." Lola was ready to give up on trying to explain when Daniel interrupted her. "Salvatore was ours, Lola, for you, and for me. For our future. For our children one day." He took her trembling hands into his, "Salvatore is you, Daniel, you! And your children one day, with what's her face. We will never, it isn't meant for us. Twice, it's just not for us Daniel!"

Her heart was shattered by the mere thought of the babies she had lost. Daniel turned around, and sat down on the only sofa in the apartment. He placed his hand over his mouth, and sat stock-still for what seemed like forever. Lola nervously sat down beside him, "Daniel, I didn't mean to go behind your back, but things were just not the same between us anymore when I changed it back, and I …" She gently placed her hand on his shoulder. "I didn't want Salvatore, Daniel. I didn't want to take that from you. You owed me nothing." Daniel glanced over at Lola, saddened to witness the grief in her eyes. "It was just that, after the miscarriage, then the abortion, and then you getting pregnant again …" She stood up to walk away, but swiftly turned back to face him, "Yeah, I know, there was a lot going on. I know it was a rough time, but it's over now, Daniel, and I promise you that I will leave your life for good. I promise. I just wanted to put things right for you again, but I couldn't even do that right."

She burst out crying, her tears were unanticipated, "I wanted that first baby so badly, Daniel, but I wanted you more. My heart broke when I made that appointment, and it broke again when I lost her. It was worse than any beating I have ever received from my father, but your anger and hatred towards me is crueler than all of that put together. Why didn't you tell me that you knew the first time? Why couldn't you just say something, anything? And now, this baby, Jonathan. I just couldn't face life like this anymore. I just wanted your life to be the way it was before we met, like you once wished for. I tried putting things right, Daniel. I tried to do what was best, but it just feels like the harder I try, the worse I make things." She sat back down on the sofa before burying her head into her hands, and sobbing uncontrollably. Daniel kneeled in front of her before he took her hands into his, "Lola, I was wrong about so many things. I was wrong. It's my fault mostly, and then losing Jonathan. It just made me realize that I was the one, you know? I was the one that just made things worse, not you. I don't want my life to be the way it was before we met. I was nothing before we met, Lola. I just, I just can't go back to that." He gently pulled her up, and held her firmly against him, when Lola began to sob again. "Nothing else matters anymore. You matter. I need you, Lola, I need you so badly. I choose you, Lola. I wanted this baby so much. I thought he could save us. I thought that, maybe after he was born, maybe you wouldn't be able to give him up. Maybe he would bring us back, and now he's gone, and my heart is wrecked. My son is gone Lola, and I don't, I don't want you to leave my life. I don't want to lose you. I am so sore, Lola, and for the first time, I understand how you felt, and I understand how I made you feel, and I am so, so sorry. You took so much from me, but, I didn't see it. You are so much stronger than I am, Lola. Jonathan was my son Lola, my boy. He was the best part of me. I, I don't know how to cope with losing him. I don't know how?"

Daniel paused to take in a deep breath. "When I found out you were pregnant the first time, I felt you distancing yourself from me, and it drove me crazy. It was all such a mess, Lola, I was a mess. I wanted to talk to you, but then Peter died, and things just turned ugly after that. I became so ugly after that. I lashed out at you. I treated you so badly, and you just stood by me. You always stood by me. You fought so hard for us, and I just let go." The tears were rolling unreservedly down his own cheeks. Lola looked up at him, and swiftly wiped her tears away. "When I asked you, that night, before I left, if you still loved me?" Daniel interrupted her at once, horrified that she thought he didn't. "I did love you, Lola, I do. I will love you tomorrow, and the day after. I was just so angry, that all I wanted to do was hurt you. I was so sure that you no longer loved me, and then I saw you and Gregory at Joe's on your birthday. You were hanging on to him, and, and I was so angry. I didn't want you to give up. I was fighting for you Lola, just not the way I should have. In the end, I just pushed you away."

He gently placed his hand on her cheek. "Come back to me, Lola, to Salvatore. Come home, Lola, so that we can bury our son together, as his mom and his dad. I love you so much, and I can't, I don't want to live without you. You are my lid, Lola. Let me make this right with Jonathan. Let me love you. Let me fix things Lola, please, please give me another chance." He gently, but firmly kissed her. "Salvatore means nothing to me without you. I just can't face another day there without you. I think, I thought that this baby would fix things, given a little time. I never, ever stopped loving you, and even when I thought I hated you, I adored you, Lola. I loved you even more. It's always just been you, and I know you were trying to tell me that. I know that, and I wouldn't listen. I just never thought you'd leave, and then Samantha came along ..." Lola opened her mouth, but Daniel quickly placed his index finger on her lips. "I thought just one night with her was what I needed, but I couldn't do it. I kept seeing and feeling you, and then you saw us, and then everything after that was so screwed up." Lola placed her arms around him, and for the first time in months, she didn't feel as though her heart was shattering. "I can't go back Daniel. I love you so much but, we've hurt each other so much. We've said so many things to hurt one another, and did so many things. Things will never be like they used to be, and nothing will ever be the same again. I can't feel this way again. I can't go through this anymore. Things will never be the same again." She swabbed at a lost tear that had unexpectedly rolled down her cheek. "No Lola, it won't be the same again, it's not supposed to, but, it could be better. We are stronger. I am stronger. Jonathan made me a better man, and I know the mistakes I made cannot be undone, but I want to try. I want to be the man you deserve, the one that promised never to hurt you. I want to, because I love you, but also for our son. I just fell in love with that boy, and I will never be able to make things right with him. Let me make things right with you. Let his life mean something. Let me be his father Lola, please." "Daniel, you're hurt, we're both hurt. We've just, it's just been a hard two days. Let's not do this now. Let's just give it a few days. Tomorrow things might look different again."

Lola held on to him, afraid that he might change his mind, but Daniel laid her down gently, and held her protectively in his arms. He was desperate to make up for the moments they had lost, while praying that somehow, they could get through this crucial stage in their lives together. Daniel knew with certainty that he could in no way ever, love another as he so unreservedly loved Lola. While Lola lay nestled in his arms, Daniel lifted her chin just enough for their eyes to meet. "She didn't mean anything, she meant nothing to me. Nothing happened, I swear. I never betrayed you like that. I couldn't do it, and I'm sorry you saw what you saw. That was the worst mistake I've ever made." Daniel was frantic to reassure Lola that nothing went on between him and Samantha. Lola placed her hand on his cheeks, "I believe you, Danny." She did believe him, but she was unable to discard the image of Samantha and Daniel in her mind. "Daniel, everything is just a mess, and Jonathan, my baby boy, I have nothing now." "You have me, Lola. You will always have me. I never left, and that's why I wanted Jonathan. I could never let you leave. Keeping him was my way to hold onto you."

A short while later, Daniel accompanied Lola back to their apartment after she packed up her belongings at Gregory's building. When she walked into their bedroom, Lola turned away at once. She caught a glimpse of their bed, and was painfully reminded of the fact that Daniel had shared her space with Samantha. Lola was unable to abandon the image of witnessing them together. "I'm going to stay in the spare room, you should stay in your bedroom." Daniel stood behind her, wrapping his arms around her, zealously alert to the thoughts that were rushing through Lola's mind. "Nothing happened, I swear, Lola. You can stay here. I'll stay in the spare bedroom." She smiled wretchedly at him, but quickly walked out, and hurriedly made her way to the spare bedroom. Daniel followed closely behind her in a desperate attempt to avert her from entering the bedroom, "Don't go in there, Lola." Lola grimaced, and was at once puzzled. "Why not, Daniel?"

When she opened the bedroom door, Lola stood back and gasped for breath. She quickly glanced around her, and at once understood why Daniel was frantic to prevent her from going inside. He had painstakingly converted the spare bedroom into a nursery for Jonathan. As if in a haze, Lola took a step inside to take a closer look around. Daniel stood limply at the door, powerless to follow Lola inside. She walked up to the crib that was placed under the bedroom window, and noticed a mountain of soft toys that were lovingly scattered inside. She caught a glimpse of the dresser, and was instantly distracted by a framed photograph of her and Daniel with the words 'Family' written all over the frame. Lola was at once sensitive to the immense sadness that had crept into her core when she turned to Daniel, who stood in the doorway as though frozen in time. "I, I'm rather going to get my own place, Daniel. It's too soon. I just feel we need some time to ourselves, apart from each other. I can't be here." "Stay here, Lola. I want you here. I'll pack up this stuff, and move the old furniture back in. I'll stay in here. I'll give you all the space you need." "I can't, Daniel. So much has happened, and I think that we're both just hurting at the moment, clutching at straws. It's just, I don't want to fall into that again, you and me. We've just lost our son, and not you or I are thinking clearly. Jonathan is clouding our judgement. We're not thinking, Daniel." Lola had no way of explaining to Daniel that she could never risk her heart again, not even once more. "I'll make things right, Lola. We belong together. There is nothing for me to think about. I don't need time, I need you. I love you. We've been apart far too long." Lola walked up to him, and took his face into her hands. "It's not enough anymore, Danny. If we're meant to be together, it shouldn't be so hard. This shouldn't be so hard. Everything is against us, Daniel. Everything is turning us away from each other. There is nothing left to keep us together. All that's really left is just what I feel for you, and, it hurts." She placed her arms around him, and held him tightly against her.

Lola's mobile phone rang almost unnerving her. She cautiously took the call when she realized it was Lauren. "Hey sissy?" "Where are you?" Lauren was at once worried since Lola was discharged from the hospital so soon. "I'm here, with Daniel at his apartment." "How are you feeling?" Lauren was instantly relieved that Lola was with Daniel. "I'm okay thanks, just a bit sore still. Daniel and I, we just need to sort things out with the funeral for Jonathan." "I'm sorry Lola, can I help with anything?" "No, that's alright, but thank you sis. I'm sure Daniel and I will sort it out." Lauren remained silent, unsure of how to break her own news to her sister, "So sis, I know my timing sucks and I know, I feel bad. I just wanted you to be the first to know." "What's wrong?" "Nothing, nothing's wrong. I, I just found out that, I'm pregnant, Lola." Lauren nervously choked on her words.

Lola burst out laughing, leaving Daniel surprised to see her laughing, while her tears were silently flowing from her eyes, all at the same time. "That's great, Lols! I am so happy for you and Dean! Congratulations! It's going to be great. I'm so happy, Lols! Can we talk in the morning? I am exhausted, and the meds are starting to kick in. We'll talk tomorrow. I'm happy for you sissy, bye!" She abruptly ended the call before she burst out into tears. Lola turned to face Daniel who was completely stunned by Lola's erratic and unexpected behavior. "That was Lauren." Lola swabbed at her tears, desperate to gulp down on the restricting lump in her throat, "I'm not sad, Daniel. I'm crying because I'm happy. Maybe a little sad, but mostly happy. They're, they're having a baby. Lauren just found out she's pregnant." Daniel took her into his arms, and held her closely once again, convinced that Lola was reflecting back on their son. The little boy that virtually tore them apart, but the baby they so desperately needed to bring them back together again. "I'm so sorry, Lola." "Don't be, Danny. It's a good thing, it really is. Things are different for them, not like with us. Lauren and Dean are creating a new life together. One out of love, and not the way we did it. They want this, and they deserve this." "We did it just fine, Lola. I wouldn't change anything about how Jonathan was conceived, about you and me, us." Daniel held her tighter. Lola gently freed herself from him,

"Danny, I don't want a funeral for Jonathan. I want to cremate him, only you and I, alone. I don't want anyone there. It's just too sad, especially now that Lauren's having a baby. I don't want to do that to her. I want this to be a special time for them." Daniel nodded sadly, "I get it Lola. I'll call the hospital. We can take it from there."

Lola could hear Daniel on the phone with the hospital discussing their options and specifically requesting a cremation for their son. He sadly agreed that the cremation would take place on a Thursday morning, two weeks from that day. Lola's heart was crushed as she listened to the inevitability of the arrangements. When Daniel ended the call, he walked over to Lola who was seated on the sofa. "Don't you want to lay down, Lola?" "Yeah, in a minute. Is everything arranged?" Lola gazed up at Daniel, unaware of the utter devastation in her eyes. "Yep, we're going to do it on Thursday morning, two weeks from now. I just need to collect his birth certificate, and then, then they'll give us his, his death certificate."

Lola got up from the sofa, and hastily made her way into his bedroom before she collapsed onto the bed, engulfed in misery. She thought of Jonathan and his beautiful face, and perfect little body. She thought of his ten fingers, his ten toes, and it tore into her soul. Lola cried herself to sleep, but Daniel was thankful that she had finally fallen asleep. He could not bear listening to her sob so heartbreakingly, and when he went to check in on her later, he found her curled up in the center of the bed, fast asleep. He gently covered her, careful not to wake her before he dabbed at the tears that were still wet on her cheeks. He held her firmly against him, and thought of Lauren and Dean. He could not shake the feeling that life was handing them a brutal hoax.

Alice VL

Lola's Secret

The next two weeks were the same for Lola. She would cry desolately and sleep uninterruptedly. Daniel tried his utmost to console her, but Lola had withdrawn from him, and the world. He would open up the bedroom curtains in the mornings, but as soon as he left for Salvatore, Lola would get up, and close them again. He brought her breakfast and dinner, but would take the trays back to the kitchen untouched. From time to time, he watched her sleep, and would on occasion, hear her cry in her sleep. Daniel anxiously wondered whether Lola was finally surrendering to her despair. When she was awake, she would lay in bed flipping through the channels on the television with a blank and wretched expression in her eyes.

For Lola, it felt as though her world had come to an abrupt end. She constantly thought of Jonathan and the way he looked when she held him for the very first time. She persistently thought of all that had happened in such a short while, and she was convinced that she could not face the future, while overcome with such intense pain, resentment and despair in her heart.

Daniel would often walk in when she was awake and try to talk to her, "Lola, please talk to me." He would plead almost unceasingly. Lola would turn away from him, engaging in a courageous effort to focus her attention on the television screen. Daniel would get up and walk out, certain that Lola was inconsolable, but convinced that he was unable to mend her broken heart. He would sit quietly in the kitchen, and weep silently in a desperate attempt to hide his emotions from Lola.

On the third night after Lola had brushed her teeth, Daniel tried once more to have a conversation with her, "Lola, please eat something. Tell me what to do? What can I do?" "Stop Daniel! Just stop!! Leave me alone! I don't want to talk about it! I don't want to!" Lola would shout at him, before climbing back into bed, and lifting the covers over her head. "Lola, please! Don't give up like this." He would plead with her, but she wasn't listening. Daniel felt utterly powerless, and he questioned whether Lola would at all get up again, or if she had perhaps, finally let go, and ultimately given up.

Lauren and Dean came by on the fifth day to check up on her, but Daniel was unable to convince Lola to engage with Lauren. "Lols, your sister is so happy for you, but she's still in pain. The doctor gave her medication that make her sleep all day. Just give her some time, please?" Daniel was desperate to shield Lauren from the reality that Lola was deliberately avoiding her.

On Wednesday evening before the cremation, Daniel had just arrived home from Salvatore when he noticed Lola was missing from his bedroom. When he made his way down the passage, Daniel was at once aware that the door to the nursery was opened. He instinctively knew that Lola was in there, and cautiously made his way down the passage. When he walked in, he found her seated in a chair he had placed beside the crib. Lola sat back with her eyes closed. Daniel's heart was crushed by the mere sight of her.

Lola had fallen asleep in the chair earlier, and dreamed about Jonathan. She dreamed she found him in the arms of another woman whose face she couldn't recognize. Lola was certain that it was the same woman she had been dreaming of her entire life, even as a little girl. In her dream, she walked up to her, frantic to take Jonathan from her. The woman placed her index finger on Lola's lips in an effort to silence Lola. Lola peeked down at him, and noticed that he was sleeping peacefully in her arms. The woman gently stroked Lola's cheek when she began to cry. "Don't be sad. Don't be afraid, my girl." She calmly whispered to Lola. "I miss him. Please give him back to me." Lola became desperate, and sobbed feverishly. "Oh, pretty girl, he's fine right here. He's just fine. You have to let him go." "I can't. I don't know how?" Lola was pleading with the mystery woman to teach her how to carry on without her baby. "You have to find a way. Your sister needs you. Daniel needs you to be alright again." "I'll never get over this. I don't want to live anymore, like this, without Jonathan. I want to be with him. I don't want to live like this." "But, you must live, you must carry on. Your sister is having a baby, and she needs you. Daniel needs you. He's not strong like you, my angel." She wiped the tears that were lying wet on Lola's cheeks, "You are so much stronger than you think my baby girl, but you have to get up, and place one foot in front of the other; one second at a time. And then a minute, and then an hour at a time. Then a day, and a week. That's how you do it. Now go, go find your reason for living. I will take good care of Jonathan. You just have to find your place again. Do it for your son, my baby girl." "You keep calling me baby girl, why? Who are you? Why won't you let me see your face? Who are you?" Lola tried to catch a glimpse of her face. "Not now my girl. One thing at a time. When the time is right, you'll have your answers. There's so much more out there for you to find. Go home, go find yourself. Remember who you are. Remember the little things, just like you remembered the four-leaf clover. Remember us. Go home, my angel. You have to find us." "Where is home? I don't understand?" Lola was instantly overwhelmed by the utter mystification in her heart. "The truth is out there, Lula. You will find it, my angel. Just not today, but when you're ready. Now get up Lola, this life may not be exactly how you planned it to be, but it's the only one you have, and you will get up, understand? You will carry on. Just don't fall apart, not now. It will mean that everything was for nothing, that Peter Storey was for nothing, that everything you fought so hard for, was for nothing. Now get up Lola!"

Lola awoke with a startle, recalling at once that the mystery woman had called her Lula. She abruptly opened her eyes, and was staggered to find Daniel standing in the doorway.

"Hey, you're back? I didn't hear you come in. I must've fallen asleep." Lola was utterly aware and entirely overwhelmed by her dream. "Yeah, I wanted to finish up early. I thought we could do something together, maybe ask Dean and Lauren over? They need to see you Lola. Lauren needs to see you." "I know, Daniel. I just wanted to sit here, just for a moment. Just to feel if I could feel him. Maybe feel a little closer to Jonathan. I just wanted to sit here for a moment. I feel so lost, Danny." Lola had an intense need to explain herself.

Daniel walked up to her, and kneeled in front of her before he took her hands into his. "You can sit here anytime you want, Lola. Whatever you need to do, you do it. If you want to sit here and cry, then you cry. If you want to stand here and shout, then you shout. You need to do whatever it takes to feel better again." Daniel gently squeezed her hands. Lola smiled sorrowfully, and again, a floodgate of tears opened up inside of her. "I'm never going to get over this, Daniel. I'm never going to feel better again. I just want to die. I wish I died with him. Why didn't I rather die? Why him, Daniel? Why did this happen to us again? I don't want to live with this. I don't want to be here anymore." Daniel held her protectively against him, "I know, Lola. I've always known that you loved him. I never for one moment thought you could walk away from him, but you have to get up again, Lola. You must. Don't give up like this. You cannot let this destroy you. You have to live. For me, for our son, for your sister, and for everything you fought for. You have to, Lola." Lola was at once taken aback by his words, and couldn't help but hear her mystery woman's voice, repeating exactly what Daniel was saying.

When they got up to leave the nursery, Daniel glanced around one more time, all the while making a firm mental note to pack any and all evidence of Jonathon away. He was at once saddened when he thought back to the day he started on the nursery. He had an enormous amount of hope for their child, and the certainty that Jonathan would bring them back together again, someday. It was a room filled with hope, promise and new beginnings and now, all it felt to Daniel was a reminder of increasing hurt and excruciating pain, a life he felt they didn't deserve.

When they reached the kitchen, Lola warily turned to face Daniel, "I heard about a place, Daniel, it's across from Lauren and Dean. I want to be near my sister especially now with the baby. I have to snap out of this, and be there for her now, Danny." Lola had no intimation of how to tell Daniel that it was time for her to leave. She had contacted an estate agent earlier that morning, and was pleased to find an available apartment immediately. "Lola, please don't go, not yet." Daniel was intensely aware of the fact that he needed crucial time with her. "No, Daniel, I haven't climbed out of bed in two weeks. I haven't eaten. I cry all the time. I have to snap out of this. I have to move on. I've been avoiding Lauren, and it's not right. It's not her fault. I have to go and try to find my place again. I just have to get back up, and you have to let me go, Daniel. I have to do this on my own. I know you're doing the best you can, but so am I. I just have to, I have to pull myself together. You're right, I cannot give up like this. I need time to work this out, Danny." Lola was unexpectedly reminded of her dream. "When do you want to leave?" "Tomorrow, after the cremation, when it's all over. I think its best we just put all this behind us, like it never happened, eventually."

Daniel lowered his head and felt immense sadness creep into his heart. Hearing her say the words 'it never happened,' tore into his soul. It felt as though his heart had shattered into a thousand pieces. Lola held him forcefully against her, before she eventually turned away from, convinced that her life with Daniel had come to an abrupt, but expected end.

The following morning, Daniel and Lola had Jonathan secretly cremated. Following the cremation, they were both convinced that nothing could make them feel better again. "He's gone, Lola. I should have saved him. I should have done more, something. I should have been able to do something." Daniel was grief-stricken as he held her in his arms, before they left the crematorium. Lola wiped the tears from her cheeks, and realized at once how cold and dreary the day had become. "There's nothing you could have done, nothing would've saved him. He's an angel now Daniel, he's where he should be. I am trying so hard to believe that, and you have to try too, Danny." "No Lola, he belongs with us. He should be with us. Why does this keep happening to us?" Daniel could not accept that Jonathan was gone, and Lola at once sensed the acrimony in his voice. "I don't know, Daniel? But, I have to believe and trust that everything happens, as it should." While walking back to their cars, Daniel knew that the time had come to say goodbye to Lola again.

It shattered him to realize that their life together had finally come to an end, but he was certain that nothing could mend all the damage that had been done, the wounds that continued to overwhelm them. "I, I have to go now, Daniel. Thank you for the money, thank you for everything. Thank you for being there for me. I just want you to know that you made things right for me, Daniel. Even though things turned out like this, I wouldn't change anything. Things have never been right for me, Daniel, but you made it right, and deep down, I will always love you for that." Lola reluctantly accepted his offer when Daniel insisted that she keep at least half of the Salvatore money he gave her. "You know where to find me, Lola, I'm not going anywhere. If you ever need anything, you know where I am. I meant what I said, I'll always be here for you. You have me, always. Here, you should have this." Daniel handed Lola Jonathan's birth certificate. She stared at it before she quickly folded it, and placed it in her handbag. "I'll be okay, Daniel. Take care of yourself, and be happy. I am truly so sorry about everything, but I have no regrets. I'm going to miss you." She made a colossal effort to hold back her tears. Daniel was aware of the tears stinging in his own eyes, but accepted that there was nothing more he could say to make her change her mind. "What are you going to do, Lola? I mean, your job is still there for you at Salvatore." "No, thank you, Daniel, but no. I'm, I'm going to start writing again. I've spoken to a few publishers a while back, and, I think it can work." Daniel placed his arms around her one final time.

"Good luck, Lola. I know you can make it work. I'm sure we'll still see each other, you know, with Lauren and Dean?" "Yeah, we're godparents now! Can you imagine? You and I godparents?" Lola let out a faint giggle, "Maybe we'd be better at that." She held him closely before she turned away from him.

Alice VL

TO BEGIN AGAIN

Lola moved into the apartment across from Lauren and Dean, overlooking the ocean of Madison. Although she felt entirely alone in the beginning, she was thrilled to be closer to Lauren who she made an effort to see daily. Lola began writing, and found it a welcomed escape from reality for her. It was a reality she could by no means break away from, and allowed her entry into a fictitious world that freed her from Daniel, and their memories.

Lola spent her nights writing when she found it challenging to fall sleep. She often had to resist the urge to call, or message him. It saddened Lola that it was a part of her life that was truly over, but she never once experienced regret for one single moment she spent with him. Lola would pass Daniel in the hallways of Lauren's apartment building once in a while. Either she was coming, or he was going, but they would smile courteously and wave at one another. It was always the usual hellos and goodbyes, but they refrained from stopping, and having a conversation with each other. They made a distinct effort to avoid being at Lauren and Dean's apartment at the same time, it was easier for them to deal with one another in that manner. Lola was slowly beginning to get her old, but altered life back again. The sting of losing Jonathan and Daniel, was subsiding, while spending almost every waking moment writing.

Daniel threw himself into work at Salvatore, and would

frequently decline invitations from Dean and Lauren. He would keep busy at Salvatore into the early hours of the morning, and sleep on his sofa most nights. The next morning, he would rush back to his apartment just to shower and eat something. It became his own escape from reality. Even though Daniel was relieved that he too, had started healing from the incessant anguish of losing his son, he still pined for Lola. She would often receive a text from Daniel which mostly read the same each time, "How are you?" In turn, Lola's responses were always the same, "Fine, thank you, how are you?" Daniel not once responded, and Lola never pressed him for an answer.

Early one morning, Lauren called Lola to let her know that Daniel would be bringing the new license disc for her car by. Lola was yet again reminded of how Daniel took care of the little details she would totally disregard. It wholly annoyed her that she overlooked the fact that the car license had expired the previous month.

She rushed over to Lauren's apartment to get the new disc, convinced that Daniel had left by then. She ran through Lauren's front door in a frenzy, before she hurriedly made her way into the living room. "Where is the most beautiful sister in the world? I didn't even think about the license disc! Trust me to forget that the license has to be renewed yearly! Daniel must think I'm such a twat!" Lola exclaimed loudly before she caught a glimpse of Daniel. Daniel burst out laughing, followed by Dean and Lauren. "Daniel doesn't think that. Lola, you're looking good. Wow!" Daniel was caught off-guard by Lola's sudden appearance. Lola bashfully ran her hands through her hair, and was instantaneously mortified. "Thanks Daniel, you too. You look nice, as always." What Lola in actual fact wanted to say was how breathtakingly handsome he was, dressed in his trademark jeans and black t-shirt. His eyes bluer than Lola could remember, and his dark eye lashes almost darker than his hair. Daniel smiled at the sight of Lola, barefoot, dressed in only an old t-shirt and scanty shorts. She was beginning to look like her old self again, and it brought Daniel much consolation and relief to see her that way.

Lola's hair was beginning to grow longer again and Daniel was surprised to catch glimpses of the girl he once fell hopelessly in love with. "I'm sorry, Daniel, you spoilt me with things like this. I promise, I'll take care of it next time." "It's no big deal, Lola. I don't mind." "Thank you." Lola smiled bashfully at him. He was once again aware of how effortlessly Lola's smile could brighten up his day. "You want some coffee sis?" Lauren nudged, delighted that Daniel and Lola were in the same room together. "No thanks, pretty girl. I'm in a bit of a hurry. Anyhooo, I can see you guys are busy, and I have to run! See you later, Lols?" "Yeah, cool." "Okay then, bye!" Lola took the license disc, and swiftly made her way to the front door. "Bye Lola, be good."

Daniel waved when she turned around. Lola summarily turned back to him, "Or good at it?" She giggled softly before she ran off. Daniel burst out laughing when he recalled that he once told Lola the exact same thing. "Wow! I haven't seen Lola like this in ages." "Yeah, she's full of life. She's happy, and she's writing. She hardly ever leaves the apartment though, but I watch her sometimes. She's in there dancing to her iPod, headphones plugged into her ears. You just have to see her, it's so funny. She's right across from us, but I don't think she even realizes that." Lauren giggled at the thought of how she and Dean would watch Lola, and break out into hysterics.

Alice VL

Daniel laughed at the mental picture Lauren was able to form for him, but was a little gloomy that he had failed to be the one to make Lola laugh again. "Oh bro, that is funny stuff!" Dean too, burst out laughing, along with the rest of them.

"I'm just glad she's happy again, Lols. For a moment there, I never thought I'd see that again. I was so sure she had finally given up." Lauren took Daniel's hand, "It's not, she misses you, Daniel. It's not because you're not around. Writing has done her good, and she's let go of the past. It's not you. That's how Lola copes, she always gets up again. That's how she does it. Even when she was a little girl, she switches off the bad, eventually." "I wish I was more like her. Anyways, I gotta go. You two have fun, and Lauren? You have got to let go of the coffee." Daniel rose to his feet and playfully kissed Lauren on her cheek. "I know, I know, geez!" Dean nodded in agreement and glanced accusingly at Lauren. Instead of climbing into his car, Daniel made his way into Lola's apartment building. He was ecstatic to witness her so incredibly youthful and vivacious again. Daniel was overwhelmed by a dire need to check up on her one last time, and when he reached her apartment, he was surprised to find her door standing wide open. "Lola?" He anxiously called out to her before slowly entering through the front door. "Lola?" He was unable to see her, but when he peered around the corner into her living room, he noticed her dancing to what seemed like utter silence to Daniel.

When he looked closely, he noticed the earphones plugged into her ears, and the iPod in her hand. He stood watching her for a while, and smiled when he realized that Lola had disappeared into her own little world. He laughed out loud when she started singing along. Daniel had a sudden urge to grab a hold of her, and dance with her. She turned around and stopped abruptly when she noticed Daniel unexpectedly standing there. Lola yanked the earphones from her ears, giving away the fact that she become bright red in the face.

Lola stood stock-still before Daniel burst out laughing again, realizing at once how inhibited Lola had become. She smiled back at him, hoping that he didn't witness too much of her performance. "Daniel? Shit you scared me." Lola whispered. "Your door was wide open. I called out your name." Lola peeked around the corner, and realized that the front door was in fact, wide open. "I am so ditsy today. See what seeing you does to me?" She giggled softly. "You need to be more careful, this town is full of weirdoes" "Yeah? Like those that sneak up on you?" She chuckled while poking him in the stomach, and at the same time, wondering why he was there. Daniel chuckled again, "I wanted to see your place." Lola smiled at him, "Its nice here." He caught a glimpse of a small staircase behind her, "What's up there?" He slowly made his way towards the staircase. "The study. I, I'm actually in there all the time, writing. It has the best view of the ocean!" "Can I go see?" "Sure." Lola led the way upstairs. When they reached the top of the stairway, Lola stepped aside for Daniel to enter. He strolled in, and hastily glanced around him.

Lola's desk was placed directly in front of a window with a magnificent view of the ocean, and against the wall, she had placed a large couch with a neatly folded throw and a cushion. On her desk, was a contract she was perceptibly busy with. Daniel quickly realized that it was an agreement for her novel. He was surprised to find the name 'Pastor Publishers' printed on each page, and glowered when he realized that Gregory's company was about to publish Lola's book. "This is nice. I see what you mean about the view." "I'm in here all the time and sometimes, I just don't bother going downstairs to get into bed." She paused for a moment, "So, would you like something to drink?" Daniel smiled enthusiastically, "You got a beer by any chance?" "I do, actually." She hurriedly made her way downstairs, Daniel followed narrowly behind her. "There we go." Lola handed him an ice-cold beer. "You're not having one?" "No thanks, it's too early. Besides, I only have a ginger beer now and again. That beer must be in there for weeks already. I keep it for when Dean and Lauren come over. You know, I don't do too well with alcohol." Lola giggled again, recalling her drunken evening at Joe's.

They made their way into the living room where Daniel sat on a sofa across from Lola. He glanced around, and realized how much effort Lola had put into the apartment to make it her own. When he gazed over at the wall unit, Daniel froze for an instant. He noticed a framed photograph of Jonathan. Daniel was once again aware of the agony that made its way into his heart. "Where did you get that?" "I, the hospital gave it to me when, when I was discharged." "I've never seen it before, is that the only copy?" "No, I have a smaller one. Keep this one." Lola was pleased to hand Daniel the photograph of their son. "I'm, I'm gonna have to go, I've been putting it off, but I'm gonna have to go and get his ashes." Lola lowered her head while fighting with all her might to avoid becoming emotional in front of Daniel. "Any idea what to do with it?" "I, I don't know? Do what you think is best, Daniel." Lola was unsure of what else to say to him. He became distressed at once when he realized that Lola wanted no part in it. He wondered for a moment how it was possible for Lola to let go so readily. She was instantly aware of what he was thinking, "Daniel, it's not that I don't care or anything like that.

It's just, it's over. I'm in a good place now. I don't want it to drag me down again. I trust you, so do what you think is best, and whatever that is, I will be fine with that." "If it was up to me, I'd just keep it." Lola made her way over to him, and sat down beside him on the sofa, "Don't do that, Danny. You have to let it go. Take him to Hodgkin's and scatter him on your parent's farm, or, in the ocean, but don't hold onto it. You have to close off that part of your life, you have to turn the page, Danny." "I don't know if I can?" Lola took his hand, and gently squeezed it, "Let it go. When you're ready, you will know what to do, but don't let it drag you down. He's not coming back, Daniel, but you're still here. You have to carry on." Daniel rubbed her hand with his thumb, "Will you come with me if I take him to Hodgkin's?" Lola let go of his hand, and took his face into her hands. "I've let go, Danny, it's over for me. That day I walked out of the crematorium, I put it all behind me. I had to. I was in a very dark place as you know, and I know now that nothing will bring him back. I know he's not really there, and that his soul is in Heaven. I don't want to put myself through any of that again, not now. I'm happy now, and I just cannot slip into that again. It's been such a tough fight, Daniel."

Daniel nodded dejectedly when Lola released him. He got up from the sofa while helping Lola to her feet. He firmly embraced her before she closed her eyes, realizing that she could not at all discard the way Daniel's arms felt around her. She hugged him tighter, and was once again aware of how familiar and perfect Daniel felt against her. "So, thanks for the beer, and put that license disc on, or come around to Salvatore and we'll do it for you." "Thanks, I think I can handle that." Daniel shut the door behind him, and as he left, Lola stood glaring at the closed door. She had a sudden and inexplicable urge to ask him to stay.

When she yanked the door open, she found Daniel about to knock again. They both burst out laughing after realizing what the other was thinking. "You forget something?" Lola was surprised to find him still standing there. "I don't know, did you?" Daniel grinned from ear to ear. "I did actually. I wanted to ask you. I mean, I was wondering, are you doing anything tonight?" Lola was determined to pluck up the courage to ask him over for dinner. "Not sure? I suppose it depends on why you're asking?" Lola hesitated for just a moment. "I was thinking that maybe, I mean, I've been dying to have a picnic on the beach, and, it's no fun on my own." She became inhibited at once. "Lola Storey, are you asking me out on a date?" Daniel moved closer to her. "Maybe?" Daniel couldn't say much, but grinned from ear to ear. "Meet you there at 7pm?" She smiled in agreement and closed the door again when Daniel walked away.

Lola unexpectedly jumped for joy before she grabbed her iPod and earphones, and began dancing again. When Daniel reached his car, he looked up at Lola's apartment, and was once again certain that Lola Storey was the girl who made it all real for him. He was excited to see her again, and he could hardly wait for night to fall.

When Lola reached the beach just after sundown, she glanced swiftly around her, and noticed that the beach was almost entirely abandoned. It was a beautiful summer's evening with merely a soft, gentle breeze that was scarcely blowing. She hurriedly shook out the blanket, and laid it out for her and Daniel to sit on. She placed the picnic basked in the center, and sat down to gaze out over the ocean. For Lola, it was a perfect evening. Daniel strolled down the path to the beach and noticed Lola stare out over the ocean. She looked beautiful while deep in thought, so much so, that Daniel hesitated for a moment. He was at once conscious of an inexplicable need to absorb the way she looked at that very moment. When he finally began walking towards her, he noticed that she was wearing a powder blue summer dress, and that she was barefoot.

He cherished seeing her like that and once again, he was certain that she was the most beautiful woman he had ever met. Lola was so completely lost in thought, that she barely noticed Daniel come up behind her. He placed his hand on her shoulders, before she quivered slightly. "Hey." He slowly sat down beside her. "Hey, you too. Are you hungry?" "Actually, I brought wine. Can I pour you some?" "Do you want to get me drunk, Mr. Salvatore?" Lola winked timidly. Daniel laughed out loud before he poured them each a glass. While sipping on their wine, they both gazed out over the ocean in silence. "It's so good to see you like this, Lola." Lola smiled at him, and turned back to the ocean. "It's not always like this, you know? I have my rough days and every day is a struggle, but seeing you again, now that makes me happy." Daniel smiled desolately, "I'm so glad we're doing this." "So, how are things at Salvatore?" "Good, really good. We're getting someone in from Monday to help out, you know, the invoicing and stuff?" Daniel explained matter-of-factly. Lola knew that it was just a matter of time before she was replaced at Salvatore. It was utterly taxing for her to imagine someone else in her place, but she understood that Daniel and Dean could barely cope with all the work on their own. "What else are you up to, Lola?" "Nothing much, I'm very boring actually, but I get to throw Lauren's baby shower soon, and I can't wait!" Daniel became gloomy once again, and was surprised to realize how often he thought of Jonathan.

Alice VL

Lola heard giggling around them, and turned to find two women walking by. Daniel immediately noticed that one of them was Samantha, enforcing a sense of edginess at once. Samantha instantly recognized Daniel, and swiftly made her way towards them. When they stood in front of Daniel, Lola recognized her at once, and could in no way at all, banish the image of Samantha and Daniel in their bed, from her mind.

Daniel got up uneasily, intensely aware that Samantha was responsible for Lola's uneasiness. "Daniel? I thought, I thought we were getting together later?" Lola glared at Daniel, unsure of what Samantha was saying. "I'll, I'll call you later, Sam." Samantha kissed him on the cheek before she turned to face Lola. "Lola, nice to see you again." "I unfortunately, can't say the same, Sam, although, I hardly recognized you with all your clothes on." Lola snapped back at her, before Samantha snorted, and turned away from her, waving Daniel goodbye.

Daniel sat down again, and gazed enquiringly at Lola, trying to decipher how she was feeling. Lola bowed her head, and realized that it was all still much too hard for her. Daniel had no inkling of what to say to her, and he hoped that Lola would say something soon. She knew she had to say something, but instead, she was agonizingly aware of the recognizable hurt and anger that had made its way back into her heart. "I can't do this Daniel. I thought I could, and I thought I'm okay to do this, but seeing Samantha has just stirred up all those feelings I fought so hard to get rid of." Lola began to explain, not sure that she was making any sense. "I know nothing happened, I believe you, but I just cannot get that picture out of my head, and it's hard. I'm not ready for this, you and me. I'm just not ready." She rose to her feet while packing her picnic basket. "Lola." Daniel took her hand, unsure of what to say next. "I mean, really, Daniel? You're meeting up with her later? You come here with me, but you've also made plans with her? You see, I don't get that?" +"I made plans before, Lola. Before you and I. I am just trying to move forward, and I would cancel all my plans with anyone else, just for a moment with you." "It's not you, Daniel. I'm not mad at you. Keep your plans with her. I don't want to be here. This was such a bad idea." She hurriedly picked up her basket, and abruptly turned to leave.

Daniel stood watching Lola until he could no longer see her. He instantly berated himself, and was keenly sensitive to Lola's repulsion of Samantha. Daniel feared that Lola might never be equipped for them again, and when he turned back to the ocean, he felt into his soul that it was finally over between them. There were countless of fragmentary and unresolved issues between them. A mountain of unspoken words, yet, he was convinced that their life together had at long last, come to an abrupt ending. Lola would under no circumstances be ready to love him again. While standing on that beach, Daniel lost all hope, certain that nothing between them will ever be the way it used to be.

Alice VL

Lauren was almost five months into her pregnancy when Lola resolved to throw her a baby shower. After calling the Lake Club and Joe's, she was disappointed to learn that both had been reserved months in advance, and the only date available would be after their baby was born. While holding her mobile phone in her hand, Lola stared blankly at her laptop screen. She researched venues in Madison, but after making another few phone calls, she was discouraged that again, there were no venues available.

While trying to find an appropriate solution, her phone rang unexpectedly, jolting her back to reality. It was Sarah Salvatore. Lola was surprisingly apprehensive about taking her call. "Hello, Sarah?" Lola was astounded by her sudden excitement to hear Sarah's voice. "Hello, Lola. I thought I'd give you a call. We haven't heard from you in a while, since, well you know?" "I'm sorry, Sarah. I've been trying to find a venue for Lauren's baby shower, but every single place has been booked, and I'm completely stumped. I don't know who else to call." "Oh? Well, that's no problem. You can host it here!" Lola could sense the sudden excitement in Sarah's voice. Lola considered it for a moment, but was not entirely convinced that she was ready to face John and Sarah so soon. "Lola, it's perfect! I'll have Maria cater the event. You know that Lauren loves it here, and at least I will get to see the boys again. Please Lola, let me do my first grammy job. Besides, we'd love to see you again, we miss you."

Lola knew that it would be exactly what Lauren would want, and if she was to be utterly candid with herself, Lola would wholeheartedly admit that she was desperate to see them gain. "Sure, Sarah, of course. I miss you too. I was hoping for next weekend, does that suit you?" Lola was convinced that no matter which date she presented Sarah with, Sarah Salvatore would formulate and execute all the details necessary to make it work out. "Wonderful, perfect! I will arrange everything. Shall we keep it as a surprise for Lauren? I will arrange with Dean to come through Friday night, and they can spend the entire weekend here. Oh, this is so exciting! Will you come on Friday too, Lola?" "I, no. I don't know? I think maybe ..." "Lola, please? Don't punish us for what went wrong between you and Daniel. John and I love both you girls, even you, Lola." Sarah interrupted her before she could come up with an acceptable excuse. "Sure, Sarah, I would love to." Lola at once regretted her decision. "Peaches! I shall expect you on Friday then, bye love!"

Sarah abruptly ended the call. Lola sat back in her chair, and felt her heart hammer into her throat. She thought of Lauren again, and knew that regardless of how she felt, or how much she intended to avoid the Salvatore's, she had to continually remind herself that it was what was best for Lauren. Sarah excitedly called Daniel shortly after her conversation with Lola. "Hey mom!" He was truly happy to hear his mother's voice. "Hello my boy, how are you?" "I'm alright mom, thanks for asking." "Good. Now listen, the reason I'm calling, I just spoke to Lola, and we're having Lauren's baby shower here next weekend. I expect you will join us?" Sarah was desperate to set Daniel and Lola up, together in one place. "Sure mom, will Lola be there?" "Yes, of course. So, I will see you on Friday night?" "Yes, mother, I will see you on Friday night." "Good. Bye my boy!" Sarah responded excitedly before ending the call. Daniel smiled at the obvious enthusiasm in Sarah's voice, and her excitement of becoming a grandmother for the very first time.

After her conversation with Sarah, Lola took a quick

shower and towel dried her hair. She climbed into bed, and switched on the television before opening up her laptop. She immediately noticed the flickering envelope on her screen, and opened up her emails straight away. Her heart soared when she saw his name, and almost closed the laptop at once. 'Hi, Lola. Mom just called about Lauren's baby shower. Apparently, it will be held in Hodgkin's, and she's making arrangements for next weekend. I thought that maybe we could make the trip together? Regards, Daniel.'

Lola was bowled over by the formality of his email, but she was certain that she would not have the courage to take the long drive with Daniel. After deciding almost immediately, she hit the reply button, 'Good evening, Daniel. Thank you for the offer, but I'd prefer to drive on my own. Why don't you bring Samantha along? Bye (not regards, dammit … sheez, by the way), Lola.' Before sending the email, she inserted a smiley emoticon, knowing at once that it would totally bewilder Daniel.

She realized again how effortlessly Samantha got in under her skin, and was hesitant to admit that she truly despised her. Without receiving a reply from Daniel, she opened up her manuscript, and carried on writing, hoping that it would distract her from him. When Lola realized that it was impossible to eject Daniel from her mind, she closed the laptop, and laid her head down on her pillow, aware that sleep was all that she needed at that very moment.

When Daniel received her reply, he shut the laptop instantaneously, realizing that Lola was being sardonic. He opted not to reply to her message, and instead, climbed into bed, desperate to fall asleep soon.

Friday arrived far too swiftly for Lola, but she immensely appreciated the fact that Daniel had resisted contacting her again. Lauren was utterly animated when she learned that Lola would be joining them for the weekend at Hodgkin's, and she was blissfully unaware that her baby shower was the basis for their visit. Lauren and Dean had taken to the road before lunch on that Friday morning, but Lola decided to leave just before sunset.

While driving to Hodgkin's, Lola was nervous about seeing the Salvatore family again, but reluctantly accepted that it was something she would have to get accustomed to. She knew that she could not at all penalize Lauren or Daniel's family for the aloofness between her and Daniel. It wouldn't be fair to expect Lauren to experience all her firsts on her own. Lola decided that she would be unconditionally accessible to her sister, and put whatever feelings she had for Daniel, aside. She had moved on with her life, and the past had been buried along with Jonathan.

When Lola reached Hodgkin's, it was heartwarming to see that all the Salvatore cars were parked in the driveway, and that all had arrived safely. She remained seated in her car for a moment longer, desperate to pull herself together, but sure that facing Daniel for the entire weekend would be heart-wrenching. It was simpler to face him for five minutes, than be around him for a jam-packed weekend. Lola knew that somehow, spending time with Daniel would reopen several of the old wounds, and she lacked the courage to deal with any of those fractions just yet. Just as she switched off her car, she heard her door open and was at once, staggered to find Daniel standing there. "Hey, I thought I heard you pull up. Did you drive okay? It's late, I hate that you drive at night, Lola." Daniel held open her car door for her to climb out. "I did, thanks. I left later than I planned to." Lola smiled nervously in an attempt to avoid a pointless argument with him. Daniel smiled, and picked up her overnight bag from the backseat of her car before leading the way into the Salvatore house. "So, everyone's here already. Lauren still has no idea, and mom and dad are so excited to see you." Daniel whispered before he opened up the front door.

When she walked in, Lauren and Dean elatedly met her at the doorway, both warmly embracing her, "So happy you came, Lola!" Lauren was overjoyed that Lola had agreed to join them, but Lola wondered whether Lauren secretly suspected that they were throwing her a baby shower. "Lola, what a sight you are!" She heard John's engaging voice, and turned to find him. While walking up to her, he had his arms stretched out to her. She unintentionally questioned how it was possible for a family to allow her to feel so undeniably welcome. Lola smiled at him as she placed her arms around him, squeezing him snugly. "It's so good to see you again, John. I missed you and Sarah." Gazing past John, Lola caught a glimpse of Sarah who was making her way towards them. "Lola, you're here! I am so glad you made it!"

Sarah screeched excitedly when she took Lola into her arms. Lola was contently aware of a certain inexplicable warmth enter her heart, and was at once thankful that Lauren would become a part of a warm, and wonderful new family. "Daniel, please show Lola to her bedroom while I finish up with supper." Sarah signaled to Daniel while nudging his arm. "Sure, mom, this way, Lola." Lola followed brusquely behind him, desperate to ensure that she remained a safe distance behind him. He opened her bedroom door for her, and stood aside, allowing Lola to enter. "Thank you, Daniel, see you later?" Daniel nodded in agreement before she hurriedly shut the door behind her, afraid that if she gazed at him for only a moment longer, she would end up inviting him in. After unpacking her luggage, Lola heard a faint knock on her bedroom door. She hesitantly opened it up, and found Sarah in the doorway. "Can I come in?" Lola stepped aside to make way for Sarah to enter. "So, Lola, everything is arranged. The shower will start at two tomorrow. I've arranged with Dean to take Lauren out for the morning. They will have breakfast in town, a movie, and do a little shopping. That will give us plenty of time to set everything up. I've arranged with Daniel and John to stick around in case we needed some muscle tomorrow. Or man power? Or how do you kids say it? Is that alright with you?"

Lola could at once sense Sarah's excitement at the prospect of becoming a grandmother for the very first time. Lola giggled quietly as she listened to Sarah, "Of course, Sarah, it's perfect. Just like you." Sarah was utterly ecstatic at hearing Lola's affectionate words. "Oh, Lola. You do me well. Come to think of it, my friend, Molly, used to say that. Well, supper is almost ready, say in about five minutes." Sarah smiled contentedly before she turned to leave. "Sarah, wait! Before you go ..." "Yes?" "I just, I just have to say, I want to say thank you so much, Sarah, for everything. For welcoming me into your home and for being so good to Lauren. We don't deserve you. Lauren, is so lucky to have you as her family." Lola was unpredictably distraught, certain that she would never be a portion of the family she had fallen exclusively in love with. Sarah walked up to Lola, and placed her arms around her. She whispered sympathetically, while holding her securely against her, "We love you girls, Lola, both of you. You're a part of this family too. Every single family has its up's and down's. Of course, you deserve us." Sarah squeezed her arm before she walked out of the bedroom. Lola smiled sadly, but was unable to shake the despondence that had crept into her heart.

When Lola made her way into the dining room, she was at once caught by surprise to find the Salvatore's seated, patiently waiting for her to join them. Lola promptly found an open seat next to Daniel, and sat down almost immediately before she summarily apologized, "I'm sorry, I didn't realize you were all waiting for me." Daniel winked at her, and John smiled broadly. After punctually saying grace, Sarah and Jill, who had been employed by the Salvatore's for almost a decade, served their dinner. Lola got up from her seat to assist Sarah, and after each plate was placed down, she hurriedly made her way back to her seat. "Lola, my friend Patricia at Pastor Publishers mentioned something about you writing a novel?" Lola was self-conscious almost straight away, "Yes. It's more or less done. I am just waiting for the editing process, but it's very exciting, I must admit." "That's just wonderful." She smiled proudly at Lola. "How are things at Salvatore, son?" John turned to Daniel who was silently eating his supper. "Busy pops, but it will get better now that Sam, now that we have someone working there again." Daniel started to explain, but realized too late that Lola had heard him mention that Samantha was helping out at Salvatore. Lola was horrified. Her heart was submerged almost at once, and she was instantly aware of an overwhelming and unexpected fear that gripped at her heart. She swallowed back with difficulty, not wanting Daniel to notice that it had upset her, annoyed at herself for allowing it to disturb her. "Oh? You've employed someone?"

John at once noticed Lola's disgust. "Yep, we had to." "Samantha, the Samantha? She's working for you guys now?" Lola was unable to avoid posing that preposterous question to Daniel. He declined to respond, and Dean had no problem glaring at Daniel. "Do you know her, Lola?" John stared at Lola with utter confusion in his eyes. "Yes, she's Daniel's girlfriend." Lola snapped, but instantly regretted saying it out loud. "Oh?" John glanced over at Sarah. There was suddenly a welcomed knock on the front door of the Salvatore home, one that at once interrupted the uncanny silence that had all of a sudden surrounded them. John instantly rose to his feet in an attempt to answer without delay. Lola felt instant remorse for reacting as unpredictably as she did, and made a mental note to apologize the moment John returned. "It seems we have another houseguest." John murmured when he returned to the dining room. Lola immediately caught a glimpse of Samantha who was following him, and was at once aware of a hollowness in the pit of her stomach. She glared at Daniel before glancing back at Samantha. "Hi guys!" Samantha waved cheerfully. Daniel got up from his seat, and walked over to greet her. Lauren stared at Dean, who in turn, glanced at Lola. Sarah too, caught a glimpse of Lola, but the silence between them was almost deafening.

"What are you doing here, Sam?" Daniel was entirely unnerved and overwhelmingly anxious when he reached Samantha. "You said something about spending the weekend with your parents. I wanted to join you. I miss you, and I would love to be here for the baby shower." She whispered, not wanting Lauren to hear before she quickly kissed Daniel on his cheek. Daniel turned back to the dinner table, and swiftly introduced Samantha to the family, undoubtedly uncomfortable. Lola was intensely aware that he was overwrought all of a sudden. "Oh, Daniel was just telling us about you." John shook her hand. "Have a seat Ms. Darling." Sarah showed Samantha to an empty seat next to Lola. Lola was once again scratchy, and was annoyed at Daniel for introducing Samantha into their lives. "Lola, you're here too?" Samantha was instantly puzzled to find Lola in their presence. Lola smiled cautiously, but had no intention of responding. Turning to face Daniel, Lola realized yet again, how irritated she was with him, "I wish you told me she was coming." Lola whispered almost inaudibly. "I didn't know she was coming." "You know? Actually, Daniel, it's none of my business." "No, it isn't, Lola." Lola had at once lost her appetite, and hastily excused herself, unprepared and unwilling to face Samantha for a moment more. "I'm so sorry, please excuse me. I just, please excuse me." She got up from her seat, and hurriedly headed out into the back yard. She stood in silence and found it immensely awkward to hold back the tears before she became livid at Daniel once again.

She didn't choose to be there. She didn't elect for Daniel to continue to have a heart-wrenching effect on her. She failed to own the courage to be around Samantha, and she never opted to spend an entire weekend with the Salvatore's, and with Samantha. Lola reluctantly resolved to conduct herself in an acceptable manner for Lauren's sake, and make a distinct effort to act as if Daniel did not get in under her skin.

When Lola walked out, Daniel was painfully aware of the fact that Samantha was to blame for distressing Lola as unexpectedly as she did. Turning to Samantha, he became irritated almost straight away, "I told you this was a family weekend, Sam." "Lola's not family?" "She's my sister, Samantha, so yes, she is family!" Lauren snapped at her without consideration for John or Sarah. "I asked you not to come. You knew Lola would be here, you knew Sam." He pushed back his chair and angrily placed his serviette on the table, "I'm going to find her, you stay here!"

"Lola Storey." She was startled to hear Daniel's critical tone in his voice behind her, and quickly turned around to find him making his way towards her. She let out a faint sigh, aware of the fact that she was compelled to apologize for her less than perfect behavior. "I'm sorry, Daniel. I don't know why I walked out? She just, I just don't like her. She just brings out the bitch in me." Daniel smiled hearing her refer to herself as a bitch. "I'm not sleeping with her, and she's not my girlfriend. But in all fairness Lola, I have to get on with my life too. Whether it's with Sam, or whether it's with someone else. I am trying to turn that page, trying to let go, like you said I should." "I know, and it doesn't matter, you don't have to explain. I just wish you told me. She's just a sore point, that's all." "I didn't know, Lola, and I didn't invite her. I know it's hard being here, you, me and now Samantha under one roof, and with Lauren being pregnant, but can we just be friendly just for this weekend please?" "Yes, of course, Daniel. I promise to behave myself. Your parents don't deserve this." Lola sat down on the grass before Daniel sat down beside her. She instinctively gazed up at the stars. "Exciting times for Dean and Lauren, they're going to make great parents." Daniel blurted out all of a sudden. "Things are just so easy for them, natural, you know? They love each other." Lola smiled sadly. "Yeah. So, you seeing anyone?" Lola glanced appallingly at him, and although she was utterly tempted to lie to him, she did not have the heart to. "No, I don't have time. There's a deadline on the manuscript and no, just not interested right now. I definitely can do without the complications. You and Sam, there's really nothing?" Daniel shook his head, "I told you, Lola, there's nothing. She lost her job at Corridors, and she's just helping out at Salvatore temporarily. Lauren has agreed to step in after the baby comes, and then Sam leaves. Nothing more. I don't know why she came this weekend, I mean, we've been out a few times, but that's all. She's starting work on Monday, but nothing has ever happened between us, and nothing ever will." "That's how we started, you know? You were seeing Tanita, and then I started working there." Lola thought back to the beginning, a point in time that seemed so magical to her. "That was different, Lola. I fell in love with you." "And what if you fall in love with Sam?" Lola was suddenly and unpredictably terrified of the notion. "It just happens once, Lola. After that, it's different. Maybe a different kind of love, but definitely different." "Maybe, but it could be a better different?" Lola was instantly apprehensive. "No, nothing is better than, than what we had. Besides, you, Lola Storey, seduced me." Daniel winked playfully at Lola. "I did not!" She burst out laughing before gently punching him on his shoulder. "Oh, please Lola, that day you were wearing the overall with the oil smudge on your cheek and those big green eyes looking up at me, whatever." "Whatever! Although, I must admit, you were hard to resist that day." Lola smiled bashfully at him. "I was hard to resist?" Daniel wanted to hear her say it. "Yeah, those come-to-bed arctic blue eyes and your please-kiss-me lips. Oh, my word, Daniel! This is entrapment!" "I'll have you know, Lola Storey, this body has never disappointed." Lola stridently laughed again, "You're telling me this? Seriously? As if I didn't know that already! I just look at you, uhm, just don't go knocking anyone else up, okay?" "Well, to be honest, I think I fell in love with your hair way before I fell in love with you." Daniel gently stroked her hair. Lola sat timidly next to him, unsure of whether he was being serious, or whether he was simply engaging in useless conversation. "You seduced me, Mr. Salvatore, and don't deny it!" Daniel smiled and let go of her hair. They both sat in silence for a while after that, devotedly insightful of what the other one was thinking.

"There you are!" They both heard Samantha behind them and when Daniel turned back, he noticed her walking towards them. Lola and Daniel reluctantly got up from the grass when she reached them. "Lola, can we try and get along for the weekend?" Samantha held an extended hand out to Lola. Lola glared at her, convinced that she could in no way at all, ever get along with Samantha Darling. Samantha reminded her of the night she found Daniel in bed with her, and she could not disregard the way she felt when she saw them together. "Let's just rather avoid one another, alright, Sam? I mean, after all, you've had your claws out for Daniel from the very beginning. You being here, is just another way to sock it to me. I know what you're trying to do, even if Daniel doesn't." Lola was unapologetic for her brusque disrespect towards Samantha. "Let's go inside Lola and Samantha. It's getting cold out here." Daniel instinctively held his hand out to Lola.

Lola categorically ignored him, and walked ahead of them, while avoiding Daniel and Samantha, but trying her utmost not to be discourteous or bad-mannered. When they reached the dining room, Lauren had taken the seat next to Lola, and held her hand firmly underneath the table.

After supper, as each one went their separate ways, Lola

went in search of John in his study. She knocked gently on his door, hoping that she was not intruding. "Come in?" When Lola opened the door, she found him behind his desk, smiling at her. "John, I am so sorry about tonight. I misbehaved, but I promise that it won't happen again." "That's fine, Lola, I understand." "Thank you." Lola turned to leave, careful to not disturb him any longer. "You and Daniel, are you two going to be decent this weekend?" "Yes, we've agreed to be friendly this weekend." When she turned to leave again, she noticed a photograph displayed on John's credenza. She picked it up slowly, and once again felt familiarity when she gazed at the family she had seen before, the night John showed her a photograph of the Hudson's, the very first night they met. John got up from his seat, and made his way over to her, "We miss them so much. It still feels like I lost my brother." He was visibly devastated when he stared at the photograph over her shoulder. "Yeah, so sad." Lola placed the framed photograph back on the credenza, before closing the door behind her.

Lola determinedly made her way into the living room where she found Sarah and Lauren excitedly discussing the baby's arrival. "Lola, come. We're discussing baby names!" Sarah made way for Lola to sit beside her. Lauren smiled elatedly and took her sister's hand, "Oh, Lola, this is so exciting!" Lola smiled, delighted to witness her sister's exhilaration. They were distracted by reading out names from a book Sarah had given Lauren when Dean, Daniel and Samantha walked in. "What are you guys doing?" Dean took a seat next to Lauren. Daniel and Samantha made their way to an empty couch across from Lola. He smiled broadly when he noticed the book in Sarah's hands. "We're going through baby names!" Lauren exclaimed breathlessly. "Well, as long as you don't name him Bruno or Bambi, or if it's a girl, Brandy or Barbie!" Dean laughed out loud before he kissed Lauren on her cheek. All that were present erupted into laughter, and when Lola caught a glimpse of Daniel, she was pleased to notice the elation on his face. "This is such a special time." Sarah turned to Lauren. "A baby, a new life. That's what makes us get up every day, you know?" "You are the most beautiful baby mama out there, Lauren." Dean held Lauren protectively against him. "Just like her sister." Daniel blurted out suddenly, unaware of the fact that he had said it out loud, before Lola lowered her head in mortification.

They spent the remainder of the evening discussing babies, grandmothers and god-parents. Lola often caught unexpected and unintended glimpses of Daniel. She would regularly catch him glancing at her, which enforced the ferocious thumping of her heart each time their eyes would meet. Lola tried desperately to discard Jonathan from her thoughts, while Daniel was excruciatingly aware that she was pining for him, even though she excitedly joined in the discussions about Lauren and Dean's child, and conscious to the fact that she was fraught to mask her own pain. Lola tried to pretend that Samantha was absent from their conversation, even though she could not avoid glancing at her every now and again. "This is so exciting Lauren, you are going to be such a good mommy, sissy." Lola warmly embraced her sister. "I can't wait, Lola, and you're going to be the best aunty ever!" Lauren gushed. "Is it painful Sarah? I mean, giving birth?" Lauren abruptly turned to Sarah. "Oh yes." Lola interrupted as though in thought, without realizing that she had said it out loud. Lola glanced around her when everyone grew silent. "Sorry." Lola bowed her head in chagrin once again. "Oh, that's right Lola, you do actually know. I mean, twice isn't it?" Samantha snapped, unable stop herself from rubbing it in Lola's face.

Lola lowered her head once more, and was instantly humiliated. Lauren looked to Daniel, while Dean squeezed her shoulder. "Sam, please." Daniel sighed before Sarah Salvatore interrupted him. "It is as Lola says, but the enormous pride and joy you feel when they place that baby in your arms for the very first time, you just forget it all." "That's true, it just changes everything. Your whole life changes in a second. Everything changes." Daniel was unable to remain silent. Dean turned to his brother, "Was it like that for you, bro?" "Dean!" Lauren bellowed in horror. "That's alright, Lols. I don't mind talking about it. Everyone tip toes around me when it comes to Jonathan, but I can talk about it." Daniel responded without hesitation. Lola felt the bulge in her throat return when she listened to Daniel. "When you see that face for the very first time, your first thought is, I did that. He's mine. We did that, you know? Two people creating a brand-new life, and then, watching him being born. The miracle of birth."

Daniel huskily explained before he felt the tears shimmer in his eyes. "It's the most amazing feeling you will ever feel bro, and you know then that your life didn't exist before that. It's a kind of love that you've never felt before. Different, but unconditional and strong. You feel different, and you're just never the same after that. Everything changes and nothing is more important than that little person in your arms." Daniel hurriedly swabbed a tear from his cheek. "When Lola held Jonathan for the first time, wow! I'll never forget that, or what she went through bringing him into this world, yet, still knowing what was about to happen. He was just so perfect. I have never seen anything more perfect than at that very moment. And for just a bit, my life was perfect. Nothing and nobody else mattered. I knew that there would never be enough time to hold my child in my arms. We didn't have enough time." Daniel whispered, his voice was breaking, unable to take his eyes off Lola, and desperate to tell her that he will never, ever forget, and how intensely he loved Jonathan. Lola was at once displace when her own tears rolled onto her cheeks. She vigorously tried to swab at them, not wanting anyone to notice, but certain she could no longer listen to Daniel talk about her son.

Lola swallowed with immense complexity, agonizingly aware that the lump in her throat was restricting her. "Daniel, don't do this." Was all she managed to say while gulping down with extreme intricacy. "Lola, I can't, I just, I can't forget him. I don't know how to go back to before? I have tried for so long to be the strong one. He was my moment. Jonathan was a promise that was so cruelly snatched away from us. I look at you, and I want him back. I can feel him inside of you somewhere, and I still see him in your eyes." Samantha unexpectedly embraced Daniel, "It's over now, babes. It's all going to be okay. Things like this happen for a reason." She made a courageous attempt to console Daniel. "Reason? Things happen for a reason? What possible reason could there be to give birth to a dying child, Samantha? What possible reason could there be to love and hold your child, who has never had the privilege of taking in even one little breath? Where is the reasoning in that? What could the possible reason be?" Daniel stood up and yelled inconsolably at Samantha.

Lola bolted to her feet at once, crushed by the reality that she was no longer as brave as she used to be, powerless and entirely unprepared to witness Daniel's heart ache for Jonathon. "I am exhausted. It was such a long drive here. I'm going to bed. See you all in the morning." Lola hurriedly excused herself before making her way to her bedroom.

They all felt immense pity for Lola, but Daniel more than anyone else, especially knew that her heart was shattering just as his was. Lola kept her heartbreak hidden inside. That was her way of coping, but for Daniel, it was easier to talk about it. Wanting to check up on her, Daniel excused himself shortly after she left, "I'm going to bed, mom. Will you show Samantha where to sleep please?" Before Samantha could object, Daniel had disappeared down the passage. When he reached Lola's bedroom, he nervously knocked on her door. "Daniel?" Lola was taken aback to find him standing there. He noticed that her tears were still wet on her cheeks, and was once again aware of his own devastating heart.

"Can I come in?" Lola stared at him. She was sure that her heart had shattered into a million pieces. "Oh God, Danny, I didn't know?" Lola's tears rolled unreservedly down her cheeks. "This hurts so much. You hurting like this, I am dying inside, Danny. I didn't know you felt so strongly, that you still, I didn't know that it was still so hard for you. I wish you told me, Danny. I didn't think you were having such a hard time with it. I wish you told me before." He made his way to the end of her bed, and despondently sat down, before Lola sat down beside him. "I didn't want to. You were struggling, and I just didn't want to take you there again. I'm not like you, Lola. I need to talk about him. You and I have never really gone there and talked about Jonathan, and it hurts so much. I don't want to talk to anyone else about him, I need to talk to you. You're going through this too, and watching Lauren and Dean, I know I mustn't, but I feel it's so unfair. I lost everything, Lola. You and Jonathan. I'm not coping with this, it's hard." "I know Daniel, but I can't. I can't talk about it the way you can."

She choked on her tears while swabbing fiercely at them. "I'd rather pretend that it never happened." "It did happen, Lola, how can you say that?" "That's how I cope, Danny. I can't bring him back. I've tried bargaining with God, but I know, I know Jonathan is in a good place." Daniel shook his head, "I want him back, Lola! I do. I'll do anything to bring him back. I'd give up my own life, just to bring him back to you." Daniel sobbed wretchedly. "Don't say that, Danny. I'm doing okay, but you need to find a way to get closure too. We cannot change the past Daniel, we just have to find a way to live with it." Lola placed her arms around him, and held on firmly while realizing for the first time that Daniel was crumbling and falling to pieces. "You shouldn't just have to do okay, Lola, you should have your child back. We should have our son back. I needed him so much. I needed to hold on to what we had." Daniel was fiercely trying to make Lola understand that he was struggling bitterly to carry on without her.

She began to sob once again. Not for her pain of losing Jonathan, but rather for Daniel's immense sorrow. Lola had never witnessed him so utterly heartbroken, and simply by looking at him, she felt sick to her stomach. Instinctively, Lola placed her arms around him again, and held him protectively against her before Daniel wept violently into her chest. Daniel glanced up at Lola who was vigorously attempting to hide her own unrelenting tears from him. He gently wiped the tears on her cheeks, but she could not prevent the next batch from flowing so utterly defiantly.

She gulped down with all her might, but surrendered when she realized there was nothing she could do, to put an end to her sudden misery. "I, I can't see you like this Daniel. I never knew, I didn't think, I didn't know that it was so hard for you. Please forgive me, Danny, please forgive me?" Lola was devastated when she gazed into his eyes. He moved closer to her, and kissed her gently. Lola closed her eyes, all the while hoping to shut off the tears, but realizing at once, how dry her lips had become. She kissed him back, aware once more that he was the only man she could love so entirely. The one man that her heart refused to abandon. Daniel seized her into his arms, and pressed her firmly against him, kissing her just as he did in the very beginning. Lola did not wrestle with him. She was desperate to feel him close to her one more time. She ached for him, and she desperately yearned for him. Her life seemed worthless and insignificant without him.

"I. Love. You. This year without you, I don't know how I got through it. I love you so much, Lola. Let me in again, I need you. You need me. I can't do this anymore, not without you. I need a reason again. I know you love me still, I can feel it. Don't give up, Lola, I am begging you. Fight for us again. I want you to fight for us Lola, like you used to want to. Just like you once wanted to. Oh God, Lola." Daniel kissed her again before Lola flung her arms around him, convinced that she wanted nothing more than to feel Daniel's lips on hers again. He retreated suddenly and gazed at her. She noticed how red his eyes were, and prayed silently that he would stay. "Daniel, make love to me again. I need you more than you need me. I need to feel you again. I need to feel connected to you again. You are the glue that holds us together, Daniel. I want you to make love to me, and tell me that you love me. I love you so much. I want to fight for us again. I will fight forever if I have to. I will go to any war for you, Danny. I will fight until my dying breath, if that's what you ask of me. Please Daniel, take me away from here." Lola whispered gruffly, terrified that Daniel might turn away from her. Daniel got up, and stood in front of her. Lola's eyes followed him, unsure of what was about to happen. He laid her down gently, and slowly climbed on top of her, before he overpoweringly, kissed her again. Lola's body came alive once again, and dreadfully ached for him. She needed him to end the misery in her heart. She was desperate to feel alive again, and she was certain that only Daniel had the authority to make her feel what the innermost part of her had forgotten.

Daniel watched her intimately, and dreadfully hunted a feeling other than torment. Lola was the girl he could not live without. He involuntarily chased his own worth, even if for just one night. He longed for the smell of her hair, and for the way her skin felt when he touched it. As if in a trance, he slowly undressed her and again, she didn't struggle with, or oppose him. She undid the buttons on his shirt, and pulled it off him as fast as she could, until she felt his warm body on hers. For Lola, it was a feeling she could never grow accustomed to.

She craved the way Daniel's skin felt against hers, and she sought after the obsession that made its way into her body. Daniel made unfaltering and earth-shattering love to her, the tears still wet on his cheeks, while the tears were continuously flowing from Lola's eyes. They intently gazed at one another the entire time without uttering a single word, instead, their eyes told each other a thousand tales. Daniel held her forcefully. Lola held onto him, and for a moment in time, it felt to her as though no single person mattered, and no-one else existed. They had escaped back into a world that only they were familiar with. They spent each second relishing in the beauty and wonder of one another. With each breath, they held on tighter as they danced together in their own alternate universe. When it was over, Daniel laid quietly behind her, holding her in his arms, unable to release her. She desperately held onto him, frightened that if she let him go, she would never feel the way she felt at that very moment. "I love you, Lola. I miss you. I can't do this without you." Daniel whispered huskily into her ear. "I love you too, Danny, I want to be your lid." She turned to face him. "Danny. I know I'm asking for much too much, but we just have to forget about Jonathan, just for now, and for just this weekend. For Lauren and for Dean. We must, Danny." "I can't Lola. It feels like nobody remembers him." "No Danny, it's not that. People just don't know what to say around us. They know it hurts us, but they're doing the best they can, while we, you and I, we're doing the best that we can." He kissed her gently, before they fell asleep, fervently holding onto one another.

When Lola awoke the following morning, she was displaced at once when she discovered she was alone in bed. She sat up immediately, and was not sure whether she had imagined her night with Daniel, or if they had in fact spent the night together. Lola vividly recalled the smell of his skin while they made love, and was sure that it was not just a dream. Impatient to find him, Lola hurriedly showered before slipping on a pair of shorts and a t-shirt. She headed straight for the kitchen, where she found Lauren and Dean enjoying their morning coffee.

"Morning guys! Lauren, you have got to let the coffee go!" Lola playfully tickled her sister from behind. "Morning sis. I know, I know! You're in a good mood!" "You sleep okay, Lola?" Dean too, was unprepared to find Lola in such an accommodating frame of mind. "I did, thanks. It must be the fresh air here in Hodgkin's. So listen, have you seen Daniel anywhere?" "Yeah, he's out at the stables." Lauren smiled suspiciously at her sister. "Where is she?" Lola glanced around quickly. "No idea?" "Okay then. So, are you two off to town?" Lola peered through the kitchen window, hoping to catch a glimpse of Daniel. "Yep, do you want to join us?" "Oh, no thanks." Just before she disappeared out the door, Dean grabbed her by her arm, "Are you going to be okay with Sam here?" "I'll be fine, thanks Dean. You worry too much." Lola waved them goodbye before hastily making her way to the stables.

When Lola reached the stables, she found Daniel engaged in somber conversation with Samantha, while brushing The Colonel. Daniel loved the Persian horse his dad had bought him a couple of years back, but found it poignant that he scarcely had the time to ride him as often as he would like to. She retreated in silence when she noticed Samantha standing in front of Daniel. She moved a little closer, desperate to hear what they were discussing, but unwilling to announce her presence. "You're asking me to leave?" She heard Samantha tearfully ask Daniel. "Yes." "Why?" "Listen to me, Sam. You've got to listen to what I am saying. I love Lola. I do, and I want to try and work things out with her. It's a little hard to do when you're around. You shouldn't have come here. I asked you not to." Daniel turned away from The Colonel, and gently placed his hands on Samantha's shoulders when she began to weep. "Daniel, just forget her. It will never work, you know that? When are you going to open your eyes to her? Just give me a chance to show you that I can make you happy. Give me the same chance you gave Lola." "Sam, I don't love you. What happened that night, it shouldn't have, but I'm glad Lola walked in when she did. If she didn't, who knows what would have happened? And it would have been something I would come to regret for the rest of my life." "We both wanted it Daniel, you know that?" "No Sam, I was messed up. That's not what I wanted. I wanted Lola, and when I closed my eyes, all I could see was her. I have to try and fix things with her." "She just makes you so unhappy, Daniel. You're never happy when you're around her! You have a short memory. You forget all the lies she told you." "I love her, and she didn't make me unhappy. What happened between us did. I took things too far with her. I pushed her too hard. It was my fault too, Sam, please try and understand. You weren't there." He realized that Samantha wasn't listening. "Please, Sam, we've just lost Jonathan. She is the mother of my son, and I love her. I want to be with her, and after last night, I know, I know we have to try. We have to get this right. Please understand, Sam." "Daniel, Jonathan is dead. I'm not going to hang around and wait for you forever. What do you mean after last night? What happened last night?" "I don't want you to hang around for me. That's not what I am asking you to do. Last night, Lola and I talked. We want to try again. I want to try."

Daniel turned back to The Colonel, aware of the fact that there was nothing more he could say to Samantha that could make her understand. Samantha stormed off, and passed Lola on her way out. "You, why you?" She bellowed out before running off. "Lola! Good morning, my green-eyed angel." "Good morning handsome. Am I interrupting anything?" "No, not at all. Would you like to go for a ride with me on The Colonel?" He placed his arms snugly around her. "I can't, I promised your mom I'd help setting up the baby shower, which you should help with too. But maybe later? This evening? That's if, she isn't around?" "That's a date. Sam's leaving. She's going back to Sutherland. So, before you go, do you want to talk about what happened last night?" Lola became inhibited almost at once, "No." Lola held him firmly against her as though to tell him that she had no remorse for their night together. "I heard you talk to Sam." Lola glanced questioningly at him. "Did you mean what you said?" "With all my heart, Lola Storey, every word. I want to try. I want to get it right, and I love, love you." Daniel gently kissed her. "Why Danny? Why me? Why me over Sam?" Daniel retreated slightly, still holding Lola close. "Because, you're the first person I want to see when I wake up, and you're the last person I want to see when I go to bed. Because I love you, and because you are my lid. You are Jonathan's mom, and because there is something there that just, we just belong, Lola, we do. I don't know how to explain it, but I was made for you. It feels like you have been a part of me long before I met you. My soul knows you ..."

Daniel smiled and turned back to The Colonel. "And this, Colonel, is why love makes the world go round!" "Wait, you're in love?" "Head over heels." Daniel burst out laughing. Lola was delighted to witness his uninhibited amusement once again. "I'd like to meet her, you know?" Lola responded playfully. "Can you handle it? She's smoking hot. Green eyes, blonde hair, and she rocks a pair of jeans!" Lola laughed out loud before she turned away from him, and made her way back to the house, hoping to find Sarah.

Alice VL

Lola, Sarah, Daniel and John spent the entire morning preparing for Lauren's baby shower. It had to be nothing less than perfect according to Sarah, but John on the other hand, would sigh and shake his head often. Sarah was absolutely overwhelmed by becoming a grandmother for the first time, and John was secretly ecstatic to witness Sarah's excitement.

He winked at Daniel often, signaling for him to indulge his mother. When they were alone, John was anxious to speak to Daniel about Jonathan. Sarah had mentioned earlier how distraught Daniel was the previous night, leaving John to realize that he hardly understood the magnitude of Daniel's loss. "Mom tells me you spoke about Jonathan last night, and that you were upset? How are you doing, son?" Daniel smiled sadly, unsure of what to say, but not wanting to spoil the mood. "It'll get better, you'll see." John squeezed Daniel's shoulder while from across the lawn, Lola noticed the misery appear on Daniel's face.

Daniel placed his arms around John and embraced him warmly, "I know pop. I'm just having such a hard time. I'm struggling to let go and the blame, man, the guilt is tearing me apart." "It wasn't your fault, son. God has plans, and we have to trust Him with them." "I just don't understand it, dad? I love Lola, and I know that she loves me, I know it. I just don't understand why we couldn't have had Jonathan. I know that he would have fixed things with us." "It doesn't work like that my boy, and you and Lola, you'll find your way back to one another. She's struggling too, just give her time." "I actually wanted to talk to you pops, about Jonathan." "Sure son, anytime." John stared at Daniel, overcome with sorrow. "I've, I've got his ashes here, and I was thinking, I was hoping to scatter them here in the river, if that's alright with you?" "Of course, son, do whatever it is you need to do. Do you want the family with you?" "No, I don't, no. It's Lauren's baby shower, and I just wanted to do it, on my own. I don't want to spoil the atmosphere around here, pop. I just wanted your permission, dad." John embraced Daniel once again, and held his son firmly against him. Lola smiled with relief as she stood watching them, but was once again sad that she had in no way ever, experienced the same intimacy with her own family.

As the guests were about to arrive soon, Lola hurriedly excused herself in an attempt to change into more appropriate dress for the party. Laying out a summer dress that she had chosen, Lola felt sudden excitement make its way into her heart, and for the first time since arriving in Hodgkin's, she was happy that she had decided to spend the weekend with them. She had just begun to undress when she noticed her bedroom door open. Daniel strolled in almost unnoticeably, smiling broadly at her. "Should I have knocked first?" He walked up to Lola who was clutching a towel in an attempt to cover herself up. "Yes, Mr. Salvatore!" Daniel seized her in his arms, and held her steadily against him. "Daniel, don't start." She was aware of the sudden racing of her heart. "I know, but you're just such a sight. I just wanted to remind you that I love you, and that we have a date tonight." Lola smiled, excited for more alone time with Daniel. "See you now-now."

Alice VL

The baby shower was an enormous success. Lola was delighted to witness Lauren's astonishment and absolute joy. She kept a close eye on her sister all through the afternoon, and was once again indebted to the Salvatore's for coming into Lauren's life. Lola was flabbergasted at the unexpected bliss she was feeling, and was deeply thankful that the tears of misery had become tears of pleasure for the remainder of the afternoon. She glanced at Daniel often, and was again struck by his incredible good looks. He had changed into a fresh white shirt, and a pair of jeans that were slightly torn. Lola audaciously admired his masculine beauty.

It terrified her to consider once again, how incredibly good-looking women found him. It was clear to Lola that women threw themselves at Daniel. She would often notice them flirting with him when they thought she wasn't looking. Sarah and John were overjoyed at the prospect of becoming grandparents, but it saddened Lola that Jonathan would never experience the joy of having grandparents such as Sarah and John.

After the last of the guests left, Lauren was exhausted and excused herself by telling Lola that she could barely keep her eyes open, and she was desperate to climb into bed. Dean accompanied her to their bedroom, while Sarah and John made their way into the living room. "How about that ride?" Daniel suddenly appeared right beside Lola. She smiled gleefully at him, "I thought you'd never ask. I can't wait to be alone with you again."

When they reached the stables, she climbed up behind Daniel when he mounted The Colonel. They leisurely made their way down to the river in silence. When they reached the river,

Daniel helped Lola down, and threw out a blanket he had brought for them to sit on. Lola sat down beside him, and gazed out over the river. It was a warm evening with not as much as a breeze blowing. They sat in silence, gazing out at the waters for a long time, before Daniel finally turned to her. "We should talk about last night." "Daniel, there's nothing to talk about. I wanted to, and I meant what I said. Everything that I said, I meant it. I love you. I want to be your lid, and I want you to love me back. I want to begin again." "I want our old life back. I miss you. I'm sorry that Sam pitched up here." "I miss you too, Danny. I miss the beginning of us. I miss what we had before, before everything went so wrong." She leaned forward, and gently kissed him. Daniel willingly reciprocated when Lola placed her arms firmly around him. She laid him down, and kissed him avidly before slowly climbing on top of him. He placed his arms around her waist, and pressed her powerfully against him. "I love you Lola, so much." Lola retreated abruptly and stared directly into his eyes, "I love you. I've always loved you. I never stopped loving you. You are the reason I breathe, Daniel. I am your lid, and I don't want to lie to myself anymore." She leaned down to kiss him again. Again, they made love, this time under the stars. Lola thought about nothing else except Daniel, and Daniel in turn, never wanted their moment to end.

After lying silently beside one another, Daniel turned back to Lola. "Come back Lola, come home. We can make it work. Let's just forget everything, and start over. Let's begin again." Lola stared at him for what felt like forever. She was convinced that she was finally prepared to take back her life with Daniel, "Yes, I can do that now. I want to now, Daniel, but Sam's just got to go!" "Jealous!" Daniel roared excitedly before kissing her enthusiastically. "And just so you know, I am never, ever letting you go again. You cannot run from me, Lola Storey."

When he walked back to The Colonel, Daniel retrieved a small vase from the saddle. He hesitated before he made his way back to Lola, and held the vase out in front of him. "I want to let go, Lola. I want to scatter his ashes here, in the river. Just you and me. You said last night that I needed to find a way to get closure and, this is my closure. That's what I'm trying to do. I am trying to begin again, to close off all the bad, and make way for the good to come back to us." Daniel staggered miserably.

Lola bowed her head, and became sad at once. "Let's end this, Lola. Let's put the past behind us, and let's start again tomorrow. Let's just let go. Let's remember the good, and throw out all that went wrong." Daniel had no intention of saddening Lola again, "But, Lola, I don't want to do this alone. I want to do this with you. Jonathan was our son. I was his father, and you were his mother. Let's do this, together. Let's start living again. I know that he's not coming back, and I want you to let go too. I don't want you to wake up one day, and regret never doing this, never saying goodbye, because we must. You have to, and so do I." Glancing up at him, Lola was excruciatingly sensitive to Daniel's eyes that had turned red. As brave as he appeared to be, his tears were lying shallow, ready to escape his eyes. She took the vase from him, and turned to the river. She closed her eyes, and at once understood why it was that Daniel was anxious to scatter his ashes in the river. It was calm and peaceful, almost magical. She was positive that Daniel had chosen exactly the ideal location.

She understood at once that she would live to regret not

participating in their goodbyes, and realized once more that Daniel knew her better than anyone else did, better than she knew herself. Daniel stood next to her, and took her hand. They stood in silence, unsure of how to go about it, or of what exactly to say. Lola turned to Daniel and handed the vase back to him, "You're his daddy, Daniel, you do it." Lola failed to muster up the courage to open up the vase. Daniel took the vase from her, and cautiously opened it. "We should say something to him, Lola, something we'd want him to know, something we never said." Daniel whispered distraughtly. "Lola, you go first. Just say what you feel. Tell Jonathan how you feel." Lola turned to face the river, and vigilantly attempted to identify with her emotions. She felt a nagging and restricting lump in her throat return without warning, but she knew she had to remain strong for Daniel. "Danny?" Lola began to sob almost at once. "I love you so much. I'm so sorry I couldn't take care of you." Lola whimpered through her tears. "I can't, Daniel." Lola sobbed in Daniel's chest, convinced she could not carry on.

While holding Lola steadily against him, Daniel turned to the river with the vase in his other hand. "My boy, there's so much I want to say to you, and so I wish it could be while holding you in my arms. I lost you too soon. I was so ready for you, and had so many hopes and dreams for you, for us. But, I know God's plan doesn't require our approval, and I can live with that. I'm sorry for not taking better care of mommy. God knows I loved her, but I hurt her so much, Jonathan, and I hope you can forgive me for that. I am so sorry for not being a better man, or a better father. I know that losing you was all my fault. We will never forget you, my boy. You made me a dad, and you made your mom a mother, and I am so proud to have had you as my son. Just please, please Jonathan, please send us signs that you are still with us. Tonight, I am saying goodbye to you. We are saying goodbye, but we will never, never forget you. I love you." Daniel choked on the tears that again ran liberally down his cheeks. Lola placed her arms around him, and held him intimately, desperate to ease Daniel's excruciating pain. "Daniel, let go of the guilt. It was never, ever your fault. Don't do this to yourself. We did the best we could."

While standing in silence for just a moment longer as he tried to reflect on Jonathon one last time, he leaned forward and vigorously shook the ashes from the vase, and into the river. The wind had begun blowing gently. They both stood back, and witnessed the river carry Jonathan's ashes away from them. Both Daniel and Lola began to cry desolately. "Goodbye Jonathan." Lola whispered her son farewell. "Goodbye my boy, dad loves you." Daniel quickly wiped the tears that were rolling down his cheeks. He grabbed Lola's hands as they both watched the river carry their son down the stream. Lola turned to Daniel, and embraced him firmly, "I love you, Daniel Salvatore." "I adore you, Lola Storey."

They returned to the Salvatore home directly after placing The Colonel back in his stable. Daniel and Lola walked hand in hand while smiling at one another the entire time, content that they had chosen the river to send Jonathan off in. Lola was grateful that the Salvatore's had retired earlier than usual. She was anxious that they in no way at all, witness their sorrow. Lola pulled Daniel with her into her bedroom. She had no intention of being apart from him, even for only one more night. They climbed into bed together, and held onto one another until they had both fallen asleep. Lola dreamed of Jonathan, but this time, it was a dream filled with joy and love. She dreamed she saw him in the arms of the same woman whose face she could never see. Only this time, the woman had remained silent, leaving Lola disappointed that she had elected to linger quietly throughout her dream. She dreamed of how she sang to him, and how utterly safe and content Jonathan was in her arms, and for the first time since Jonathan died, she felt no sadness or anguish in her heart.

When Lola awoke on their last morning in Hodgkin's, she was in high spirits to find Daniel fast asleep beside her. She smiled contently while gazing at his sleepy face, and wondered how it was possible that a man like Daniel could love her as fiercely as he did. She was undoubtedly blessed and favored, and knew once again that her life had barely any significance without Daniel in it. While staring at Daniel, she heard a faint knock on her bedroom door. Lola was panicky all of a sudden, and gently shook Daniel, "Daniel, Daniel, wake up." "Good morning, beautiful." He groggily opened his eyes. "Someone's at the door, and you're here, with me." Lola's anxiety was enhanced just as a second knock on the door was heard. Daniel grinned, not entirely awake yet, "So? Are you ashamed of me? Are you scared people will see us together, and wonder what we did?" He burst out laughing before he slid out of bed, and hurriedly pulled his jeans on. Strolling over to the bedroom door, Daniel opened it while smiling from ear to ear. "Lauren! Come in, your sister's still in bed." Lola was mortified at once. Lauren walked in, and almost fell onto the bed, glaring straight at Lola, staggered to find Daniel in her presence. "I'm not even going to ask!" Lola burst out laughing, and for the first time in an incredibly long time, she felt justly energetic again. "We're leaving, and wanted to know if you'd like to drive in convoy? However, I see you've got that covered." Lauren teased Lola mercilessly.

Daniel had just climbed back into bed with Lola, when Dean marched in. He at once stopped dead in his tracks when he noticed Daniel in bed with Lola, "Oh, wow! Okay, oops?" He chuckled while staring at Daniel and Lola. Dean was thrilled to witness the indisputable and unadulterated joy on their faces. "Well now, I'm not even going to ask!" "That's what I said!" Lauren giggled before Daniel and Lola burst out laughing again. "Seriously? It's been like a year, are you guys alright now?" Daniel took Lola's hand, and gently kissed it. "We're good, we're going to be." Daniel smiled at Dean. "Where did you two run off to last night?" Lola lowered her head and strongly squeezed Daniel's hand. "We actually, we scattered Jonathan's ashes last night, down by the river." Daniel hurriedly explained while pleasantly surprised to find that it no longer hurt as badly when he mentioned Jonathan's name. Lola smiled when Lauren glanced at her, but by the look on Lola's face, she knew that her sister was going to be just fine. Dean and Lauren were thrilled to find Lola and Daniel together. They were convinced that their love for one another would carry them through any trial and any tribulation that may be in store for them. They were overjoyed while chatting loudly when Sarah walked in, "Good morning, kids, so lovely to hear laughter in the house again. Oh my, I see Hodgkin's hasn't lost its magic? I knew it would work …" Sarah grinned gleefully when she discovered that Daniel had spent the night with Lola. "What do you mean, mom?" Daniel frowned before turning back to Lola. "Hodgkin's is just what the doctor ordered, but how would you know that, mother?" Daniel lovingly kissed Lola on her forehead, before he glared at Sarah. "Never mind that. Daniel, dad said that you wanted, that you had Jonathan ... that ..." Sarah was unsure of how to carry on. "We said goodbye last night, mom. It's going to be fine." Sarah smiled sadly before she hurriedly walked out of the bedroom, ardently aware that her presence was creating discomfort in Lola.

When Dean and Lauren left shortly after Sarah did, Daniel turned to face Lola, "So, we can drive together in convoy as Lauren says, clear out your apartment today still, and get yourself back to our apartment where I can hold you and kiss you anytime I want to!" Lola laughed unreservedly and pulled him playfully down onto the bed with her, "Daniel Salvatore, take me home! I wanna kiss you anytime I want to!" She shouted out while letting out a giggle, and folded her legs forcefully around him. Daniel kissed her gently and held her compellingly, "Lola Salvatore, I mean Storey, I love you more!" She squinted her eyes and frowned at once, "You can't." He slipped her engagement ring back onto her finger which left Lola utterly staggered that Daniel had brought it along to Hodgkin's, and for the first time since meeting Daniel, she understood how profoundly he loved her. "You are mine, the love of my life. You're just going to have to marry me one of these days." "Really? And what about that smoking hot blonde you were talking to The Colonel about earlier? And what about promising that Tallulah chick that you were going to marry her when she grows up, huh? I'm just going to have to kick her ass!" "Lola Storey, you are my lid. Don't let me get you pregnant again, and compel you to marry me!"

"Don't go there, Salvatore!" She took his face in her hands, "I want to marry you Daniel, and I am terrified that we just might never get there, but I want to step aside for Lauren now. You are my very first love, my twin flame, my pot, and nothing will change that. I have to trust that. We have time. There's no rush." "I love you." Daniel kissed her gently. "Alright, if you say so. Just so you know, if you get knocked up again, we're eloping! We're just not going through this shit again."

Alice VL

PIECE BY PIECE

It was early spring when Lola sat quietly behind her desk, reflecting on Lauren. She was merely weeks away from welcoming her baby into the world, and although Lola and Daniel were in high spirits for them, they continued to struggle to put aside all they had been through not too long ago. Daniel grew increasingly protective and shielding of Lola, while she in turn, depended more on him for almost everything.

They hardly spoke about what had taken place between them, but Lola and Daniel were wounded, and the damage had left invisible scars behind. Although they loved each other dearly, it had become a continuous and on-going battle to rebuild their lives together. Dean and Lauren had planned a spring wedding in Hodgkin's. It was while preparing their documentation for the wedding that John called Lola early one evening. "Hi Lola, am I disturbing?" "John, hi. No, not at all." Lola was baffled by his unexpected call. "Sarah and I are just finalizing the last of the wedding arrangements, but we can't seem to find a birth certificate for Lauren. Pastor McDermott needs it for his paperwork. Do I have your permission to get hold of it on Lauren's behalf?" "Yes, of course, John. Is there anything I can do?" "No, no problem. I will get it sorted out. Bye love, see you this weekend." John hurriedly ended the call before Lola could thank him. "Who was that?" "Your dad, he's trying to get hold of Lauren's birth certificate for the wedding."

When Daniel and Lola arrived in Hodgkin's the Friday evening before the wedding, Lola felt exhilaration and extreme anticipation build up inside of her. She was elated for Lauren, and thrilled to be back in Hodgkin's again. The Salvatore's had gone through enormous pains to give Lauren the wedding she had always dreamed of, and no expense was spared to make their day wonderful and flawless. Lola was pleased to see Sarah and John again, and was animated to spend time with Lauren before the wedding. "Come in you two, the others are in the living room." John welcomed Daniel and Lola as soon as they arrived. Lola walked into the living room to find Lauren and Dean inspect last minute details. Lola was happy to bear witness to all her sister's dreams that were being realized. "Hey guys! You ready for tomorrow?" Lola could no longer contain her excitement. "Yes, I can't wait!" Lauren screeched, her own enthusiasm evident in her voice. "You do know you're spending the night with me, and Dean will be spending his with Daniel?" Lola laughed out loud when Daniel grimaced. She embraced Daniel warmly, "Bad luck for the bride to see the groom the night before." "Lola, can I see you? Alone in the study for a second please?" John had walked in, and as he peered over his glasses that rested on the bridge of his nose, it was clear that he was anxious to speak to Lola. "Sure." Lola grew increasingly nervous while getting up to follow him. "What's the matter pop?" Daniel could sense his father's restlessness. "Oh, nothing son. Just formal documents, you know? Wedding stuff." John hurriedly turned back to his study. "I'll be right back." Lola smiled and followed John to the study where he closed the door firmly behind them. "Take a seat please, Lola." "Is everything alright?" "I'm not sure, Lola? I've tried to contact the Storeys, your family, but I am unable to get hold of anyone. It's almost as though they are deliberately trying to avoid me.?" "Why would you want to get hold of them?" Lola was abruptly horrified. "Well, I managed to get hold of your and Lauren's birth certificates. Yours for should you and Daniel decide to get married later on, and when I tried to verify it on the system, it maintains that there are no such records and no such birth registrations of you or of Lauren?" The mystification was unmistakable on John's face. "These are legal certificates, and could just be a glitch, but then I checked Lauren's blood tests which she had taken when they ran cross-checking for the baby's medical, and ran it against Peter Storey's. It wasn't a match." "Not a match? I mean, he's not her father? What does all this mean, John? I'm not sure I understand?"

Lola was aware of the hammering of her heart. "I took the liberty of running Lauren's DNA, and it came up as a match to people who were deceased over ten years ago, but back then, they sealed records older than five years, so there's no way I can trace it yet, but I've got somebody looking into it for me. Don't be too worried Lola, you and Lauren are definitely sisters. I would just like your permission to look into this a little more so that we can get to the bottom of all this." Lola was overwhelmed by all that John was telling her, and could in no way at all, make sense of any of it. "Yes, yes, of course. Could that mean that the Storeys weren't our parents? Were we adopted?" Lola felt goose bumps make its way through her entire body. "I'm not sure? Without Sally Storey's DNA, there really is no way to tell, but I will do my best to find out, for you and for Lauren." "Does this mean that Dean and Lauren can't get married tomorrow?" "No, not at all. Everything will go ahead as planned. All her documents are legal. I was just curious." John made a noble effort to reassure Lola. "I am too. Please don't say anything to Lauren, John, not until we are sure, or at least know what's actually going on. Not to Daniel either, John, please? He worries too much." "I won't. Now go and enjoy yourself with the others while I finish up here. I'll let you know the moment anything pops up, alright?" "Thank you, John, for everything." Lola smiled before finally leaving the study in search of Daniel, who was caught up in conversation with Lauren and Dean.

When Lola reached the living room, Daniel noticed that she had grown ashen almost immediately. Lola took a seat next to him, and smiled nervously, aware that she had begun to quiver. "What's the matter?" "Nothing. Everything's fine. Promise" She quickly kissed him and smiled. When Lauren and Dean said goodnight, Daniel took Lola by the hand, "Did my father say something to upset you?" "No, nothing like that, I promise." Lola shook her head, "Just wedding stuff, documents, things like that."

Lola kissed Daniel goodnight after they enjoyed their final mug of hot chocolate. "Meet me at the stables later." "No! I have to keep an eye on Lauren, and make sure she doesn't sneak out to Dean. And you Mr. Salvatore, you need to watch your brother!" Lola winked at him. Even though she was entirely puzzled by the conversation with John earlier, she managed to eject the questions from her mind, and celebrate Dean and Lauren's joining together. Daniel glowered once more when Lola went in search of Lauren. When Lola and Lauren climbed into bed, Lola could sense that Lauren was panicky. "You are going to be the most beautiful bride in the whole world, Lauren." Lola gently stroked her sister's curls. "Lola, I am so glad that you and Daniel are working things out. You should be together, he loves you so much." "I know, and I love him too, Lauren. I know it's going to be better now. Things are different now, we're different. We've begun again, and it feels like it's all for the very first time."

Lola laid back while staring at the ceiling and reflected on her sister's wedding day. She tried to picture it in her mind, when she suddenly realized that Lauren was about to walk down the aisle on her own. "Lauren! Who's walking you down the aisle?" "I, I was going to walk down on my own?" Lola frowned disapprovingly, "No sis, that's not the way to start marriage. There has to be someone you'd want to give you away?" Lola was completely discontented with the suggestion that Lauren would stroll down the aisle on her own. Lauren sat in silence before turning back to Lola. "I was thinking about John. In the beginning just when we started making the arrangements, but I didn't think it appropriate to ask? I can't ask Daniel, he's Dean's best man and you are my matron of honor, so I don't know?" "You can still ask him, Lauren. If you really want John to walk you down the aisle, why don't you just ask him?" Lola stared questioningly at her. "Isn't it too late, Lola?" Lola slid out of bed, and hastily threw her nightgown around her before handing Lauren hers. "It's never too late, we can ask him now." Lola took her sister's hand, and headed down the passage. Walking down the corridor, they tiptoed silently to John and Sarah's bedroom. Lola peeked in under the door, and noticed that a light was still burning. She was relieved that they weren't asleep yet, and knocked softly, suddenly nervous about the possible imposition. "Come in." After opening the door hesitantly, Lola and Lauren walked in before shutting the door behind them. "What's the matter girls?" Sarah peered over her reading glasses. "We're so sorry to intrude like this," Lola began apologizing. "No intrusion, come, sit. What's the matter?" Lola and Lauren sat down at the foot of the bed when Lauren turned to face John, "Lola and I were talking. I, I don't want to walk down the aisle on my own, and John, you are the closest I have to a father. I was wondering, I was just thinking, actually hoping that maybe, maybe you would walk me down the aisle tomorrow?" John removed his glasses and smiled at Lauren before Sarah wiped a tear from her eye, "I would be so honored Lauren. I was hoping you'd ask." Lola embraced Lauren and was at once pleased that her sister's wedding would now be perfect. After saying quick goodnights to Sarah and John, they tiptoed back to their bedroom, desperate not to alert Daniel or Dean of their intrusion.

Dean was nervously flipping through the channels on the television while lying in bed. Daniel was zealously aware of the fact that his brother was fiercely attempting to re-route his mind away from the wedding. "Are you nervous?" Daniel peered over at Dean. "I can't sleep just thinking about tomorrow, and worrying that Lauren might not pitch up, or dump me at the altar, things like that." Daniel burst out laughing, "That's ridiculous! You guys are having a baby, you're getting married and she loves you, bro!" Daniel was adamant to calm Dean's nervous tension. "I know, but I also know how things can change. I mean, look at you and Lola?" Dean placed the remote control on the bedside table. "That was different Dean. Lola and I, we were both, I was just being stubborn. Things could've been different, but I was such a dumb ass." Daniel bowed his head before shaking it, "I would give anything to be in your shoes, bro. To have Lola marry me, and start a family with her. Don't worry about things that will probably never happen." "You and Lola, you just got to get it right, Daniel." "We will, we are. She's my lid." Dean sighed, "I so want to see my lid right now." "Lola will skin you bit by bit, rather not. You know how traditional she is, and I'm supposed to watch you so don't make me tie you to the bed!" "Whatever!" Dean mumbled before he let out another despondent sigh.

Lauren left early the following morning with Sarah to Hodgkin's Valley Guesthouse where she was to prepare for her wedding. Lola awoke shortly after they left, and made her way into the kitchen where she found Daniel and Dean conversing over a cup of coffee. "Good morning, beautiful." "Morning handsome, you guys are up early?" Lola excitedly embraced Daniel. "Oh, I missed you last night. My brother had me up before five this morning." They hurriedly ate breakfast together, before the Salvatore house was invaded by caterers, flowers and waiters.

Alice VL

Lola's Secret

The wedding was beautiful. Lola was forced to swallow back on her tears a couple of times during the ceremony when Pastor McDermott spoke of Lauren and Dean, and their new life together as man and wife. Lola listened carefully to what he was saying, and smiled often when she caught glimpses of Daniel. She was wearing a turquoise dress that clung snugly to her body. The beautiful bride wore an off-white Travis Barker creation. Lola gazed dreamily at her sister during the ceremony, and could not discard the pride and joy that had engulfed her entire being. Dean and Daniel were dressed in black tuxedos with turquoise ties that brought out their eyes, and made them both look incredibly handsome.

At the reception which was held under a large marquee tent, Lola was devotedly aware of how exquisite and magical the day was, and how flawless it all turned out. The tables were laid with beautiful white and turquoise cloths, while stunning center displays almost drew the attention away from the bride. After each guest was seated, Lola swiftly glanced at the bride and groom's table, and could not shake the sorrow that Lauren's only family present, were the Salvatore's.

Dean rose to his feet, clutching a glass of champagne when all the guests became silent at once. "I just want to thank everyone for coming today and for joining us for this, the most important day of our lives. I want to thank Lola for bringing Lauren to me. It was, after all, because of her that we met. So, thanks sis." Dean lifted his glass to Lola. Lola smiled, thinking back to the day they met for the very first time and was once again convinced how every little action at all times, took place for a distinct purpose. "And my brother, Daniel. Thank you, you called it bro when you talked about finding a cute sister, you called it!"

Dean raised his glass to Daniel. Daniel laughed breathlessly, clasping Lola's hand in his. "My parents, thank you so much for everything. For being such wonderful and caring parents, for welcoming Lauren into the family, and for hosting this beautiful wedding. I love you guys so much. And Bo, bro, you're the designated baby sitter!" Dean became nervous all of a sudden, "And then finally, to my beautiful bride. You are so beautiful, Mrs. Salvatore." Dean glanced over at Lauren, "I can't wait to begin my life with you. I can't wait to become a daddy. Thank you so much for coming into my life, and for becoming my wife today. Mrs. Salvatore, I love you." Dean sat down and gently kissed Lauren. Lola witnessed the apparent and obvious love between them. It left her feeling happy, and utterly contented.

Shortly after Dean's speech, it was Daniel's turn. He got up quickly, holding his glass of champagne out in front of him. "As Dean's brother and best man, take note, best man, I would like to make a toast to the best brother in the world. Dean, may your life be filled with blessings. May your bride be ever as beautiful as she is today, and may your new baby, may he or she fill you with happiness all the days of your life. Lauren, sissy, welcome to our family. I love you guys!" "Cheers!" All the guests applauded in unity. "I just have to say that I couldn't be prouder of my brother even if I tried, and Lola, I love you. I hope you'll stick around with me, and I hope this will be us soon. I love you, and technically Lola, you are my sister-in-law now. Oh boy!" Lola laughed out loud when all the guests joined in, in laughter.

Lola anxiously got up from her seat, and nervously picked up her champagne glass. She quickly glanced around her, and lowered her head when all became silent. She turned to face Lauren before she smiled sorrowfully, "Lols, it's always just been you and me, since we were little girls. Today, all that changes. I want you to know how proud I am of the woman you have become. It was so easy with you, and I wish you so much happiness with your new husband, and your beautiful new baby. Thank you so much to all the Salvatore's, especially John and Sarah, who welcomed us into their family from the very beginning, flaws, fights, disruptions, heartaches, headaches and all. We have finally found a real mom and dad, and for that, for that, we both are exceptionally thankful."

Lola gallantly tried to steer clear of becoming emotional. Turning to Dean, Lola hurriedly dabbed at a lost tear that had fallen on her cheek, "Dean, you are an amazing man, and you are a fabulous partner for Lauren. I am asking you today, please take care of my sister because, I just love her so much. And Daniel ..." She turned to face him, "You are going to be one kick ass brother to Lauren, thank you. I am so grateful that my sister is becoming a Salvatore today. I am so glad she has you to look out for." Lola raised her glass one last time.

Daniel took her hand and squeezed it firmly when he realized how emotional she had become. When the bride and groom took to the dance floor, Daniel and Lola watched them in silence. For Lola, it was the most beautiful depiction of love, in the entire world, and she was enthusiastically aware of her heart that was all geared up to explode with delight. "So, Dean and I were talking earlier ..." Lola turned to face Daniel, "He's bought a house in Madison, but Lauren has no idea." Daniel was almost whispering when Lola chuckled with delight, convinced that Lauren would be staggered, "Wow!" Lola clapped her hands delicately. "So, they're leaving for the mountains tomorrow. He's hoping to bring her home to the new house. I hope you don't mind, but I offered, I told him that you and I, we'll get their things moved over before they get back?" "Oh, I'd love to!" Lola flung her arms around Daniel.

They spent the night dancing, while Lola spent the remainder of the evening mulling over her conversation with John the night before. It wholly bewildered Lola when she considered all John had discovered, and hoped they would get the appropriate answers to their questions soon. Lola danced with Daniel often. She was deeply indebted to the stars, to be so completely adored by him once more.

When it was time to leave, Lauren and Dean elatedly said their goodbyes, and rushed to a car that was waiting to sweep them off for their intended honeymoon. Lola was sad to see her sister go, but she was convinced that it was exactly where Lauren wanted to be.

Daniel and Lola spent the next two weeks moving Lauren and Dean's belongings into their new home. Lola shopped for curtains and bed linen. Daniel brought in the new furniture that Dean had ordered before the wedding, for their brand-new home. They spent many nights rearranging furniture, hoping it all would be perfect for when Dean and Lauren returned. They would regularly fall asleep on the sofa in their living room, and were overcome with exhaustion by the time the newlyweds returned home. Lola was delighted to share in Lauren's surprise, and was positive that all the work she and Daniel had put into the house, was unquestionably worth it. They left the nursery untouched. Both Daniel and Lola were sure that Lauren would want to decorate it with Dean.

Lauren loved their new home, and she loved the fact that they had an enormous backyard for their child to grow up in.

Alice VL

"Sure, sis, we'll pop over this evening. I can't wait to see the baby's room. See you then!" Lola smiled when she ended her call to Lauren on her way to Salvatore early one morning. "Hey babes, I thought I heard you come in." Daniel kissed her enthusiastically when she walked in. "Ooooh, I missed you." He held her against him for just a moment longer than normal. Lola smiled tenderly before she turned around to place her handbag underneath the counter. "Lauren asked us over this evening, around six?" "Sure. That'll be great, seeing she is nearing her due date." He became quiet when he realized what he was about to say. "Daniel ..." Lola moved closer to him. "We can't not be happy for them. This is one of the most exciting times in their lives, and we just have to move on, and be there for them. We're taking baby steps, but at least, we're taking them. This is just another step forward. It's not their fault. I know it's getting to us a little, and it's just a little harder than we thought it would be, but we promised to let it go, and now we have to."

Lola took his hands. Daniel gazed into her piercing eyes, and even though he conceded to the fact that she was right, he still found it enormously hard to accept. "You're right, I know babes. It just hurts. Not a day goes by that I don't think of him, of the way he looked, of what we almost had. I long for him Lola, and it hurts. I didn't know that it would be so hard, with Lauren being pregnant." He abruptly turned away from her and hurriedly made his way to the workshop, desperate to avoid Lola's response.

Lola sat at her desk, determined to gather and file the documents that Daniel had left for her. She reflected back over the past few months, and smiled graciously when she realized how far they had come. Daniel was attempting with all his might to get them back to where they were before they lost their first child, and although Lola realized that it was a continuous and often overwhelming scuffle, she was certain that her love for Daniel would carry her through any rough terrain. They seemed a little more cautious around one another, but Daniel had never been gentler or more caring towards her. They were slowly re-building their lives together, and continuously reminded themselves of the undying love they had for one another. Daniel would often lay awake at night, thinking of Dean and Lauren. He habitually questioned how it was possible that it was so much less complicated for them. Keeping two people together should by no means be as tiresome as it was for them. He was convinced that they were waging an on-going war with their emotions. The emotional scars were healing gradually, but Daniel continued to feel apprehensive and challenged about the life he was trying to build for him, and for Lola. He knew without a grain of doubt that he intensely loved her, and he knew that she loved him back, but he was sure that the pain of losing Jonathon was inadvertently dragging them down.

Samantha had come into Salvatore on a few occasions after Lola had moved back into their apartment, and took her rightful place at Salvatore again. Even though Daniel insisted that what happened between them was over, and that it meant nothing to him, Lola could hardly tolerate her presence. Daniel was painfully aware of how her charisma tremendously upset Lola, and grew increasingly anxious about her visits until the day she came in uninvited for the last time. Daniel was seated in his office, working out a quotation for a new client when Samantha walked in. "Daniel in?" Daniel heard her voice, and watched her from his office. "No, Samantha, he's not here." "I need to see him." Lola stood up and walked around the counter until she came face to face Samantha. "Sam, please. Daniel and I are trying so hard to put our lives back together. Please, can you just give us a break? I love him, and I just, I love him so much, Sam." Lola was beseeching Samantha to allow them an opportunity at restoring their lives. When Samantha burst out laughing, Daniel made his way down the passage. "I love him too, Lola, and I never had a chance with him because of you!" "Samantha, please. Just stop!" Daniel was suddenly right beside Lola. Samantha glared powerfully at Daniel, "I don't, I just don't get what you see in her! Why her, Daniel? What makes her so damned special?" Lola turned away, having asked herself that same question countless of times before. Daniel grabbed Samantha by her arm, and pulled her towards the big sliding doors. "Don't, just don't. I love her, and I will always, always love her! I never want to see you again! Nothing ever happened between us Samantha, and nothing ever will! I love Lola." Daniel's patience was wearing thin. I've told you that before, and if I ever gave you the wrong impression, I am sorry, but I love Lola. And now, you just have to leave, and don't come back here again, ever." Daniel closed the heavy glass doors behind her, and when he turned around, he noticed that Lola was trembling. He walked up to her and held her protectively against him. "I'm so sorry Lola, but listen to me please, you are who I choose." Daniel whispered softly.

Later that same evening, they were getting ready to leave for a visit with Dean and Lauren when Lola turned to Daniel, "I was thinking, the stuff that you got together for Jonathan, there are so many things that we have just packed away. I was thinking, we should give it to Lauren and Dean." Daniel stared questioningly at her. "I mean, it's just sitting here. We can start over. I don't want to keep these things, Daniel, it just reminds me of him, and I just thought that, they could use it." Daniel bowed his head, agonizingly susceptible to the excruciating lump in his throat that had made its presence known almost at once. "You're right. I'll go get everything together for them."

They cheerfully knocked on the front door of Dean and Lauren's new home. Lola and Daniel had brought all Jonathon's belongings along with them, and contentedly agreed that it should be handed down to Lauren and Dean's child. Lauren discovered early on in her pregnancy that they were preparing for a son and Dean was ecstatic that his first child would be a boy. "Hi!" A heavily pregnant Lauren opened the door to greet them, and Dean followed curtly behind her. "Hey, sissy!" Lola leaned forward to kiss her sister on the cheek. "We've brought you a few things." Lola and Daniel carried the boxes into the living room. "Thanks guys. Come look at Michael's room!" They all followed an animated Lauren, and were astounded to discover how rigidly they had worked to complete the baby's nursery on time.

Lola stood in the doorway and noticed the crib at once. As though in a hypnotic state, Lola walked over to the crib. She stared at it, and couldn't help but admire the handcrafted woodwork. "Wow, sis. This is amazing!" She gently stroked the headboard. "I've seen this somewhere before, I know I have. Where did you get it?" Lola was once again familiar with a detail that she could in no way place. She closed her eyes, and tried to remember where she had seen that crib before. "Actually, you couldn't have. I completely forgot about this." Daniel walked up to her, and gazed at the Salvatore name that was carved into the headboard. "It's an old family crib, passed down from generation to generation. Bo was the last Salvatore to use it, and if I remember correctly, Tallulah Hudson was the only non-Salvatore who slept in it as a baby. I actually completely forgot about it." "No, I know this crib ..." Daniel began telling Lola bits of the history of the crib. He told Lola that it belonged to the first Salvatore grandchild and they both knew that it should undoubtedly, have been Jonathon. Lola listened carefully, and was pleased that Lauren and Dean were handed the crib for Michael.

She was saddened that she and Daniel would never have the same opportunity, but in the innermost part her, she was beyond a doubt, thrilled for her sister. Lola glanced around, and questioned whether she and Daniel would at all, have a nursery of their own someday. Lola and Daniel discussed earlier on that they would welcome a child into their world, yet they never found the right time to consider it. They were both anxious that Lola might struggle with one more pregnancy, and even though Daniel had an inexplicable desire to bring up the topic with Lola on so many nights before, he was not convinced that the time was right for them, and he doubted whether they would ever be.

He understood that Lola was occasionally hostile with all that had happened since her father's funeral, and the loss of their babies. Daniel knew that he himself, would first have to come to terms with losing Jonathan. It felt to Daniel that the longer they lingered, the more time passed them by, and they might never be equipped to open themselves up for another child. He had no intention of placing any unnecessary pressure on Lola, but Daniel was positive that a baby was the one thing missing from their lives.

Daniel watched Lola and Lauren. He could barely mull

over that, that the two sisters had endured in their short lives. Lola placed her hand on Lauren's belly, and was elated when she could feel him kick. "That is such a wonderful feeling, sissy. I used to sit for hours waiting for Jonathan to kick." Lola was oblivious to the fact that Daniel was listening to her. "I know, it's such a privilege, Lola." Lola was the most beautiful girl he had ever laid his eyes on. Watching her brooding with her sister, brought out the broodiness in him. He could barely wait for the day that they would have a child of their own, and he prayed that it would happen sooner, rather than later for them.

Lola turned and glanced over at Daniel. She abruptly discovered that he was staring at her. She smiled, and was a tad bit befuddled by his expression, but seeing him smile back at her, enforced the peace of mind she needed. The look on Daniel's face told a hundred stories, but the most imperative tale she had recognized, was one of love.

When Daniel and Lola arrived back at their apartment after their visit with Dean and Lauren, Lola poured each a cup of coffee, and carried it to their bedroom. Daniel had climbed into bed, and decided against opening up his laptop, as he did almost each night researching options for his projects. Lola placed his coffee on the bedside table, and slid into her side of the bed. Daniel turned to her, smiling sheepishly, "Lola, let's try?" Lola frowned, unsure of what Daniel was asking. "Try for?" "A baby. Let's try. Starting now." Lola grinned from ear to ear, ardently aware of the fact that she had been waiting for months for him to bring up the subject of having another baby. She felt incomplete after losing Jonathan, and the thought of having a child with Daniel was all that was consuming her entire mind. Lola turned him onto his back, and slowly climbed on top of him. "Are you sure, Daniel? I mean, are you sure you want to go there again?" "I can't live without you, Lola, I don't want to. I see my daughter, and I see my son in your eyes. I want this. I want Jonathan. I just want this. I want to get it right, and that's all I can think about." You just have this terrible habit of knocking me up, Daniel Salvatore." Lola let out a faint giggle. "I love knocking you up, third time lucky?" Daniel teased lovingly. Lola looked into the arctic blue eyes that had the power to make her feeble at the knees before she kissed him. First on the mouth, before she slowly made her way down his body.

Daniel could feel each fraction of his body tingle, and when he could no longer resist her, he turned her over, and gazed into her eyes. Lola stared back at him, while each and every element in her body began to quiver.

Lola's Secret

Alice VL

MICHAEL

Lauren and Dean's son, Michael Daniel Salvatore was born in the early hours of December 16th. It was a quick and trouble-free birth for Lauren, but Dean found the entire experience horrifying when he admitted to being deathly afraid by the mere sight of blood. Daniel relentlessly teased Dean about it, but Dean insisted that it was a nightmare for him. Both Lola and Daniel were there to meet their nephew. They were instantly relieved that all went smoothly, and without a glitch for both Lauren and her son.

Lola considered him to be the most beautiful baby boy she had ever seen. She was instantly besotted and smitten with him. His dark brown hair, and eyes virtually bluer than Daniel's, was a clear reflection of both Daniel and Dean. Lola fell in love again that morning, and could barely take her eyes off him, even for just a moment. Daniel held Michael in his arms, admiring the perfect little baby boy who had just entered their world. He unintentionally wondered what their son would have looked like, and sadly realized that he would have turned a year old soon. Daniel felt a twinge of sorrow in his heart, but was equally thrilled at the birth of his nephew. Sarah, John and Bo had driven from Hodgkin's to meet their new grandson and nephew, and were immediately taken by him. John turned to Daniel when they handed baby Michael back to Lauren, "Son, Jonathan will always be our first grandson and grandchild." He gently patted Daniel on his back, is if to say that they too, will never forget him.

Daniel smiled sadly, and glanced over at Lola who was fussing over the baby with Lauren. He never told his parents of what precisely had taken place between him and Lola, and made Dean promise to keep their secret. "This is Dean's moment, pop. We'll get there. Lola and I, we've got to let Jonathan go, dad, we have to. It's eating away at me, and I can't, I just have to let it go." Daniel hurriedly made his way over to Lola. He placed his hand on her shoulder, and winked at her when she turned around to face him.

Lola was naturally maternal with Michael, and it was apparent to Daniel that she had fallen head over heels in love with him. When it was time to leave, Lola discovered that she had to tear herself away from baby Michael, not wanting to leave him just yet. She turned back a few times, before finally allowing Daniel to escort her out. Lola spoke breathlessly to Daniel about Michael. He was over the moon that she was radiant and shimmering once again. He detected an indisputable glow in her eyes, and found her smiling from ear to ear the entire time. Daniel felt like Lola was coming back to him, and for the first time in what felt like forever, he was positive that there was a brilliant chance for them to be just as they once were.

Alice VL

Lauren was discharged from hospital a day later while Lola was waiting for her at their home. Daniel had to wind up a car at Salvatore, and promised to meet her there soon. When Lauren and Dean arrived home, Lola took Michael from her at once. Dean helped Lauren climb into bed, before Lola handed him to her once she had settled in. Lola hastily made her way into the kitchen, and poured them each a cup of tea, overjoyed at having a new man in her life. While watching Lauren with Michael, Lola was convinced that she had undeniably and instantly, become a great mother. She was certain that their childhood, their past, was not without reason or purpose, and that each road they had travelled, had brought them to that precise moment in time, as it should be. "Honey?" Dean glanced over at Lauren, almost whispering, "I want to go and see if I can help Daniel finish off the Ford. Will you be okay for a bit?" Lauren smiled, powerless to take her eyes off Michael, "Sure, Lola's here. I'll be fine." Dean hesitated for a moment, but left shortly afterwards.

Lola sat down at the end of Lauren's bed, scrutinizing her sister who was acquainting herself with her new son. She beamed at the very vision, but was sad that her own parents were not there to observe the immediate connection between them. Lola was distressed to realize how poles apart this moment in time should be for Lauren. "Sis, I've been thinking about mom a lot lately ..." Lola was startled to hear Lauren mention their mother. "What were you thinking, Lauren?" "I was thinking, while looking at Michael, I was just wondering, how is it possible to abandon your child, to hurt your own child?" Lola sighed when she realized that she had not one acceptable answer for Lauren. She presented her with the only honest one she could think of. "I don't know, sis?" Lauren became disenchanted almost at once, "I love this little man so much, Lola. I can't even begin to imagine that he goes through what you went through." The tears began rolling unreservedly down Lauren's cheeks, "I hate her, Lola, and I will never forgive her and dad for what they did to you." Lola felt her own tears brim in her eyes, but was at once relieved that Lauren had realized just how cruel the Storeys truly were. She got up, and gently embraced her sister.

Lauren fell asleep shortly after feeding Michael. Lola took him from her, hoping that her sister was able to indulge in some much-needed rest. She walked out through the living room, and sat down on the front porch on a swing that Dean had set up not too long ago.

Lola gazed down at Michael for what felt like hours, and counted each finger and each toe with pride. She cooed over him, and sang softly to him. Lola was overwhelmed by massive adoration for that little bundle in her arms, and she could scarcely imagine their lives before him.

Daniel and Dean had come home while Lola was blissfully singing to Michael out on the porch, without noticing that they had returned. She was so entirely caught up with Michael, that she did not hear them come in. Daniel and Dean were listening to her singing, and silently made their way to the porch. Dean smiled when he saw her there with Michael, and turned to look in on Lauren, while Daniel stood watching her from a distance. It was an image that Daniel had an urgent need to memorize, and remember for the rest of his life. He noticed once again how glowingly beautiful Lola was when she sang to him, careful not to disturb them. Michael was sleeping serenely in her arms when she got up to lay him down in the Salvatore crib.

She noticed Daniel standing in the hallway, and smiled contently at him. She lifted her index finger to her mouth in an effort to signal to him to remain silent. Daniel followed her into the nursery where Lola gently laid him down. They stood staring at him for a moment, before they turned to one another. Daniel held her against him, before turning away from her, in search of Dean. He stumbled across Dean in the kitchen and sat down on one of the bar stools with his head in his hands. "What's up, bro?" Dean took a seat across from him. When Daniel looked up, Dean noticed that his eyes were red and weary. "You got to take care of them, Dean, of Lauren and Michael. Don't be the man I was." "Hey, where's this coming from?" Daniel just shook his head while ferociously attempting to speak past the bulge in his throat. "I would do anything bro, anything to have what you have. I love Lola so much, but I can't help but feel that I'm letting her down. I've let her down so much. I've pushed her away so many times before. We'd be parents by now if I hadn't been so stubborn. I hurt her, Dean, and I can never take that back." Dean placed his hand on his brother's shoulder when he noticed Lola standing in the doorway. He gave Daniel a gentle squeeze, before he got up to leave. Lola walked up to Daniel, and turned him around to face her. "Daniel, you can never let me down. Where is this coming from? None of that was your fault. We are parents. Just because Jonathan is not here today, doesn't mean that we're not parents. He was real."

She lovingly ran her hand through his hair. Daniel stood up, and took her into his arms while weeping dejectedly. "I made mistakes with you, Lola. I wasted so much time, time we can never get back. I hurt you, over and over again, but, I love you so much. And Jonathan, he'd be here now. I let him down, and I miss him so badly. I held him for only five minutes, but I feel him in my arms every single day. You stood by me even when I pushed you away. You tried for so long, even after everything I put you through. You stuck with me, Lola, even after everything I said to you." She retreated slightly, and looked him sternly in his eyes. "Daniel, it wasn't your fault. I love, love you so much, and maybe, maybe it was the wrong time for us. Maybe we just had to grow a little, and Jonathan knows all this, Daniel. We did some stupid things, but we love each other, and we made it through. The past must stay in the past. We've paid the price Danny, let's not go back there. We've paid the price. You must believe that." Lola was aware of her own tears rolling down her cheeks when Daniel held her tightly against him, "We're going to make this right, Lola. We're going to fix this, and we're going to have our own little family soon, I promise." "But, it's not happening for us, Danny. Maybe I'm being punished for what I did?" "No Lola, you can't think like that. It will happen when it happens. You've got to believe that, all right?" He paused to take in a deep breath, "I love you, and if it never happens, I will still love you. We will find our way around it." "But, I don't want to find my way around it, Daniel. I want this. I want what Lauren and Dean have. I want a family, and I can't bear the thought that it might never happen." "We'll always have Jonathan, Lola, always. We'll always have our little boy, and if we never have another baby, Jonathan is enough. Like you said, he was real, and he made it all real." "No Daniel, we've been trying for months. Now that we both want it, it's not happening? I don't understand?"

A NEW LIFE

Michael was not quite five months old but to Lola, it seemed as though Lauren had been a mother for a great deal longer than that. Dean had returned to work at Salvatore, but Daniel insisted he work mornings only so that he could be home with Lauren and Michael in the afternoons. Salvatore was busier than ever, which forced Daniel to employ two more mechanics, and a designer to assist with the increasing work. Lola and Daniel would stay late most nights while attempting to catch up on the tedious paperwork that evaded them during the day. Just after eight one evening, Daniel walked over to Lola who was printing out the last invoice for the day. "Shall we have supper here?" Lola agreed at once, realizing instantly that she was exhausted. He hurriedly ordered dinner before he took a seat in front of her. "You alright, babes?" He noticed that she had appeared slightly run-down. While switching off her computer, she turned to Daniel. "Just tired. We've been working long hours these days." She dismissed it at once in an attempt to set Daniel's mind at ease.

They promptly ate supper when it had arrived, before heading home directly afterwards. Lola climbed straight into bed, leaving Daniel to switch off the lights and lock up the apartment. When he reached the bedroom, he discovered Lola fast asleep, which utterly surprised him. He stroked her forehead, while considering cutting down on their hours even though it meant that work had to be delayed. After taking a quick shower, he slipped in beside her and held her in his arms. When Daniel awoke the following morning, he was stunned to find Lola still dead to the world. In all the time they had been together, Lola was the first one up, to sit at the window, and wait patiently for the sun to rise. He gently touched her, careful not to frighten her. "Babes?" Lola groggily opened her eyes, and stared at Daniel, "Hey." She let out an exhaustive yawn, incapable of properly opening her eyes. "Are you feeling okay?"

He was unable to shake the feeling of uneasiness when he noticed how pallid she was. "I'm fine, Danny. I'm just so tired." She couldn't understand why it felt to her as though she had no sleep the night before. Daniel quickly made his way to the kitchen to pour her a cup of coffee, but when he returned to their bedroom, Lola was asleep again. He smiled, but worriedly glanced down at her, and decided to allow her a day off to catch up on some much-needed rest. They were working longer hours than before. He suspected that she was nothing more than exhausted. She often rushed over to Lauren to help with Michael, and would then rush back to Salvatore, leaving her very little time to rest. Daniel quietly left for work without waking her, but was wholeheartedly aware of the sudden worry that had made its presence known. When Daniel glanced at his wristwatch, he noticed that it was after eleven. He could not shake the feeling that all was not well with Lola. When he was unable to reach her on her mobile phone, he speedily made his way back to the apartment.

Daniel walked into their bedroom to find Lola as he had left her earlier that morning. He realized at once that it was absolutely out of character for her. He shook her gently, and when she opened her eyes, he discovered that she had grown even paler. "What's the time, Daniel?" "Just after eleven. What's the matter, Lola?" "Eleven? Daniel?" She leaped out of bed, but when she stood up, she at once became light headed, and lost her balance. When Daniel caught her just in time, she giggled softly, "I, I lost my balance. I got up too quickly." "I'm phoning Dr. Stalting." Daniel immediately reached for his phone. "Daniel, I just lost my balance." She was certain that he was overreacting. "I don't care. I want you to see Dr. Stalting. I have never, ever known you to miss a sunrise. Something's wrong." Lola shook her head, and headed for the shower while he called Dr. Stalting. When she returned to the bedroom, she found Daniel sitting on their bed, waiting for her. "Hurry up, you've got half an hour." Lola smiled at him, and promptly slipped on a summer dress before brushing her hair. "My hair's still wet, Daniel." "It will be dry by the time we get there."

When she arrived at Dr. Stalting's consultation rooms, she was at once shown into her office. Daniel followed shortly behind her, dutifully aware that Lola was self-conscious, and convinced that the appointment was needless. "Hello, Lola. It's good to see you again, how have you been?" "Fine thanks, Doc. Just a little tired, but fine, really." She glanced over at Daniel who was visibly concerned. "Daniel, it's good to see you again." "We've been working long hours, and I just want to make sure that it's not taking its toll on her, Doc. So, if you could do whatever you do, that will be great." Daniel took Lola's hand into his. "Is anything worrying you, Lola?" Lola smiled while thinking about Michael. "Not really. I've been helping my sister with her new baby, and we've been really busy at Salvatore. We've just been very busy, but other than that, there is nothing I can think of. I feel fine. I am just tired, but fine." "Won't you get up on the bed over there for a quick examination, please?" Dr. Stalting showed Lola to the bed in the corner of her office.

Lola laid down, and gazed up at the ceiling. She was flatteringly aware of the fact that Daniel worried about her, and even though she completely adored that about him, she was certain there was no need for such drastic measures. Dr. Stalting examined the glands in her neck, and was relieved that they weren't swollen. She examined Lola's breasts, and when she unwittingly cringed, Dr. Stalting frowned. "Sore?" "No, just a little sensitive." Dr. Stalting continued to examine her, but found no further symptoms of anything that could be off-beam with Lola. "Alright, now just a urine sample, and then we are done." She showed Lola to the room adjacent to her office. When Lola returned, she took her seat across from Dr. Stalting again. "So, Doc, anything wrong?" Daniel looked questioningly at Dr. Stalting. "I can't see anything wrong, offhand. Unless she is just exhausted? When is your next period due, Lola?" Lola considered it for a moment, and could in all honestly not recall.

She was overwhelmingly dispersing her time between Lauren and Salvatore, that she hadn't even noticed that she had missed her period. While quickly trying to figure it out, she realized that she was three weeks overdue. "Daniel!" Lola bellowed out unexpectedly. "I'm late. With Lauren and the baby, and Salvatore, I completely lost track of time." Lola turned back to Dr. Stalting. Daniel's eyes grew larger when he realized what Lola was saying. "Give me a second. This will only take a minute." Dr. Stalting abruptly walked out with Lola's urine sample. Daniel grabbed Lola's hand, and realized that she was shuddering slightly. She closed her eyes, and said a swift, but desperate prayer, almost not audacious enough to hope for much. "Lola, this could be it. After months of trying, this could finally be it." "I don't know, Daniel? It doesn't feel like it. It doesn't feel like the other times?" Lola whispered after which they both sat in silence while restlessly anticipating the results.

When Dr. Stalting returned, Lola and Daniel were unnerved at once. Daniel stood up, but Lola chuckled when she noticed that he could not linger for even a second longer. Dr. Stalting smiled at him, and turned to Lola. "It's positive, and you are about twelve weeks along. Congratulations you two!"

Daniel seized Lola into his arms, and turned her around and around, before finally putting her down. He kissed her over and over again, and swabbed at the tears that were liberally rolling from her eyes. "We did it Lola, we did it!" Daniel could not in the slightest contain his enthusiasm. Lola turned back to Dr. Stalting, "Twelve weeks? Wow! I, I lost my first baby at seven weeks, Doc, and then, well, you know about the other one, about Jonathan?" She was overwrought straight away, "From what I understand, you were under a lot of stress the last time. There is no reason it should happen again, Lola. You are much further along, and you are young and healthy. Enjoy it, and don't worry so much. Just eat properly and regularly, and take these vitamins. Everything will be fine. I will see you through this." She reassured Lola before warmly embracing her.   Daniel swept Lola into his arms again and held her rigidly, "I love you, Lola Storey. Everything's going to be alright. We can do this. We're starting again. I can't believe it's happening!" Daniel whispered excitedly in her ear. Lola smiled and kissed him gently before Daniel led her out, and back to his car.

Driving back to Salvatore, Lola could hardly believe that

it was at long last, in the stars for them. She was secretly fearful that she may lose this baby too, but she resolved to put an end to her reservations, and decided that the more she worried over what might happen, the edgier she would become. Lola resolved to do all she could to keep this baby alive, and she wanted in no way, to squander one minute tormenting over her baby's survival.

Daniel was just as profoundly in thought as Lola was, he constantly worried about whether this baby would survive. He could not bear to witness Lola go through all the pain and anguish even one more time, and now that they were having another child, he was terrified almost to death.

When they reached Salvatore, Daniel's first and foremost call was to his parents, before he animatedly called Dean and Lauren. He breathlessly informed them about the new baby, while Lola sniggered quietly. Daniel gazed over at her often, and was delighted that they were finally to become the parents they both yearned to be. He convinced himself that this was their one chance to go back into the past, and mend all that remained broken between them. Lola was powerless to think about much else other than the baby. She wondered desolately about the babies she had lost. Even though it tugged at the very core of her, Lola knew in her heart that this time, all would be different for them. When Daniel ended the call to Dean, Lola walked up to him and gently took his hands, "Daniel, we can do this, right?" Daniel touched her face and smiled persuasively, "Yes, we can, Lola. We can do this. We have to."

Alice VL

REMEMBER THE HUDSONS

Ella Blue Salvatore was born in the early hours of the morning of the 23rd of December, on the exact same day her father, Daniel Salvatore was born. She was perfect. She was beautiful, and she unerringly arrived at the right moment in their lives. Dean and Lauren, along with the rest of the Salvatore family were waiting outside, eagerly anticipating their niece and granddaughter's arrival, and when Lola handed her to Daniel, he introduced her to a family that could no longer contain their enthusiasm. When Daniel brought Ella back to Lola, she smiled proudly at him, "Happy birthday, Danny." "This is by far, the best birthday ever. I love, love, love you."

Ella Blue turned out to be the one element that innocently mended their broken hearts, and repaired all the broken fences between Lola and Daniel. While they lovingly doted on her, the memory of Jonathon became less distressing for them. Lola would often find Daniel rocking Ella Blue for a moment longer after she had fallen asleep, softly whispering to her about her older brother. Lola would notice the sorrow in his eyes, and hastily turn away from them while agonizingly perceptive to the reality that Daniel continued to carry around pestering and nagging guilt in his heart for his son. But, for Lola and Daniel, their days seemed enormously brighter than before, and a smile from Ella Blue would be enough to lighten up Daniel's face, distracting him from all that went wrong in the past. Ella's hair turned entirely fair shortly after her first birthday, but her eyes remained an arctic blue, just as her father's. Michael and Ella were born a little over a year apart, and the two Salvatore brothers were pleased that their children were growing up together. Daniel and Lola spent less time at Salvatore, and when they were at work, they would bring Ella along. Daniel converted a storage area adjoining his office into a nursery, and would contentedly watch her as Lola went about her work.

The New Year approached speedily and unexpectedly, just after Ella turned three-years-old. They had spent their holidays with John and Sarah, and Lola was certain that her life was exactly the way she had wanted it. She had never been happier than at precisely that moment in their lives. The day before they were to start work at Salvatore after the holidays, Lola was once again overcome by a familiar queasiness. She hurriedly dressed Ella before making her way to the kitchen. Daniel had just climbed out of the shower when he snuck up behind her, "Good morning, my Lola." She had just taken two coffee mugs out of the kitchen cabinet when she turned around to kiss him. "I'll get the coffee." "I'll get breakfast." Lola had no sooner broken two eggs in a pan when she became nauseas again. She ran out as expressly as was possible, afraid that she would not quite make it to the bathroom on time. Daniel instantly placed the coffee pot on the counter, and rushed after Lola. When he reached the bathroom, he noticed that she was bending over the basin. "Lola?" He took her hair into his hands, overcome with worry for Lola. She quickly wiped her face down with a wet facecloth before turning to Daniel, "I don't know? The smell of the eggs ..." She had just begun to explain before she turned back to the hand basin. Daniel was at once alarmed and anxiously rubbed her back, "I'm calling Dr. Stalting." "No, Daniel, wait. I'm taking Ella for her shots today. I'll check in with Dr. Stalting while I'm there." Lola was convinced that she was pregnant again, and skipped breakfast entirely, leaving Daniel and Ella to eat together. "Do you want me to come with you?" "No, I'm sure it's nothing. Besides, you should check in at Salvatore before we open tomorrow." Lola promptly kissed him on his cheek, desperate to keep a tight veil over her suspicions.

After Ella Blue was given her shots, Lola was at once reminded of the queasiness she had experienced earlier that morning, "Dr. Stalting?" "Yes?" "I think, I think I might be pregnant again?" Dr. Stalting smiled at the notion, and rose to her feet almost at once, "Oh good. I get to use my new ultrasound equipment. Come, lay on the bed." Lola climbed onto the bed, and nervously laid down. When Dr. Stalting began prepping her for the ultrasound, Lola was sure she could almost hear her heart hammer in her chest. Dr. Stalting took the handheld device, and slowly moved it across Lola's belly. She frowned while moving it around and around, and when Lola noticed her expression, she was panicky immediately, "What's the matter?" Lola's voice had begun to shudder. Dr. Stalting hesitated before she turned her focus back to the monitor. "One minute, Lola." After what felt like an eternity, Dr. Stalting turned to face Lola, and chuckled slightly, "You are pregnant, Lola." "Wow!" Lola was overcome with disbelief. "Before you get up, would you like me to print you out a photograph of your babies?" "Babies?" Lola was instantly bewildered. "Yes, there are two. You're having twins, Lola!" "Twins?" Dr. Stalting broke down with laughter at the staggered expression on Lola's face, "Yes, Lola, twins." When Lola got up, she was entirely flabbergasted by the news that she was having two babies. She glanced over to where Ella had fallen asleep, and was at once delighted that their family was growing. Lola thanked Dr. Stalting, and picked Ella up before leaving her doctor's office, unsure of how to tell Daniel that they were going to parent two more babies, in one single go.

The following day was the morning that Salvatore's doors would open again for the first time after the holidays. Daniel made his way into their bedroom where Lola and Ella were sleeping, and slid in beside Lola before he gently kissed her. "Wake up, Lola." He whispered while lightly caressing her cheek. Lola blurrily opened her eyes, and discovered at once that Ella was lying next to her, still fast asleep. Daniel would often pick her up out of her own bed during the night, and tuck her in next to Lola when he woke up earlier than usual to finalize drawings and designs on his laptop. "Hey." "It's back to work, today." Lola smiled at the thought, thrilled to be back at Salvatore. She slowly sipped her coffee with Daniel, not wanting to wake Ella just yet.

Daniel took her hand after placing his coffee mug down on the pedestal, "Lola, we've talked about this before, but with so many things going on, and with Ella and Salvatore, I was thinking that maybe ..." He paused while gazing over at Ella. "I was thinking that maybe we should get married. Jonathan, it would've been his birthday soon, and I thought that maybe, maybe we could honor him on his birthday. Ella should have her parents legally married." Lola smiled broadly while listening to Daniel stumble over his words. She had dreadfully wanted to become his wife from the moment he had placed the engagement ring on her finger, and she often dreamed of standing beside him, swearing to be only his. Lola wanted to be a fraction of the Salvatore name, just as her daughter and sister were.

Lola in particular, wanted to be Daniel's wife now that they were having two more children. "Wow, Daniel, yes!" She breathlessly placed her arms around his neck. When Daniel turned back to Ella, he knew without an ounce of a doubt that his life was at long last intact. He treasured them both more than anything he could ever envisage, and there was nothing in the world that could be any better than what they had at that very moment.

Walking into Salvatore, Daniel took Ella into the nursery which was now converted into a p ay room for her and for Michael. Dean and Lauren were already at the office when they arrived. Lola hurriedly planted a gigantic kiss on Michael's cheek, unable to resist. She adored her nephew as much as she loved Ella. Lola was thrilled that the two couples turned out to be more than brothers and sisters, but best friends too. Lauren helped with filing and general administrative duties during the day, while Lola focused mainly on Salvatore's book-keeping. The children played together while Daniel and Dean kept a vigilant eye over the two toddlers. "Morning, sissy." Lola was cheerful when she placed her handbag underneath her desk. "Hey!" Dean waved, and followed Daniel to the playroom with Michael on his hip. Lola was endlessly stunned by how closely Michael resembled Daniel, and smiled frequently when she contemplated the many hearts he would rupture someday. Lola gazed at the two brothers when they walked away from them, and was thankful that both she and Lauren had discovered the joy they had brought into their lives. "So, listen sissy …" Lola was almost whispering, "Daniel and I, we've finally decided to get married, and we've been talking about doing it on Jonathan's birthday which is just in time actually." "Wow Lola! It's about time! I think it's so special to do it on Jonathan's birthday. Wait, what do you mean just in time?" "I slipped out to the doctor yesterday. I had to take Ella to get her shots and while I was there, I'm pregnant again, and there's two babies! We struggled so much to have Ella, and now we're having twins!"

Lauren bolted from her seat and animatedly embraced her sister. Lola laughed out loud, knowing that she too, would soon be a Salvatore, just like the rest of them. "What did Daniel say?" "I haven't told him, not yet. I was thinking of telling him tonight, which brings me to my next question. Would you mind taking Ella for a sleepover tonight?" "No, of course not. I love having Ella over. Oh, wow sis! I am so happy for you!" "Just don't say anything yet, I want to surprise Daniel."

They had just taken their places behind their desks, when the enormous sliding doors of Salvatore opened. A tall woman sporting long dark hair walked in, and both Lola and Lauren gasped when they recognized her. Lola promptly turned to Lauren who was slowly getting up from her desk. Lola quickly got up from her seat, and made her way around her desk. "So, this is where the two of you hide out?"

Sally Storey appeared before them in all her glory. Lola was painfully aware of a violent thumping of her heart, sure that it might leap right out of her chest. "Mother?" Lola was horrified by the mere sight of her mother, while not entirely convinced that it was in fact, the woman she had feared the most, standing in front of her. Lola failed to notice that Daniel, who still carried Ella in his arms, had appeared from his office, standing quietly and protectively in the doorway of the reception. "I had to come and see it with my own eyes. Everyone's talking about this, and I must say, I never recognized the Salvatore brothers at the funeral. Imagine my surprise when I found out?" She hastily glanced around her. "So, this is where the two of you are shacking up with the Salvatore brothers. How the hell did you end up with the Salvatore's? How on God's green earth did that happen?" Daniel walked over to Lola, and handed Ella to her. "Hah, the happy family!" Sally hollered when she saw Ella. "Can I help you, Mrs. Storey?"

Daniel was confused by her undesirable presence. "No, but she can." Sally Storey pointed directly to Lola. Daniel abruptly turned to Lauren, "Take Ella to the back and watch her. Stay there, Lauren. Don't come out. You don't come out for anything, understand?" Lauren nodded and quickly took Ella from Lola when Lola once again noticed the fear in her eyes, the identical horror making its way into her own heart. "What do you want, mother?" "Would you just stop calling me mother? I'm not your mother! Can you honestly say that you've never wondered about that?" Lola glanced over at Daniel, totally bemused by what Sally was saying. She quickly turned back to Sally, shocked by her callous statement. "I never wanted you, Tallulah and Lucille. Oh, yes, you two are sisters, if you're wondering?"

She raised her voice when she suddenly began to explain, "Peter promised me that your father's company would make us extraordinarily wealthy, but lo and behold, it turned out that you girls were to go and live with your god-parents, the freaking Salvatore's! So, no money for us. I told Peter I couldn't do it, but he thought he could eventually manipulate the system." She walked up to Lola, "You ungrateful little bitch, Lola!" She began yelling unreservedly at Lola. "I hated you! I despised your parents, and I detested the Salvatore's! And then, only a few months ago, John Salvatore began snooping. And boy, can he go on and on and on." Daniel moved closer to Lola. "You should have died in that car crash with the rest of the Hudson's!"

When she ultimately grasped precisely what it was that Sally was saying, Lola stood back in utter disbelief and unreserved revulsion. Daniel and Lola were entirely gob smacked when it finally sunk in that Lola and Lauren were the Hudson daughters, Tallulah and Lucille, the exact same daughters that John and Sarah had spent countless hours telling them about. Daniel thought about his father and mother who had lost their best friends, and how absolutely diverse life should have been for the two sisters. He was convinced that his parents would have been entirely willing to take care of them, while raising them as their own. Daniel became livid at once, but Lola felt immense relief that they had no blood ties to the Storeys. Lola reflected back on her childhood, and recalled once again how fraught she was to resemble her mother, Sally Storey. She had placed her high upon a pedestal, and scuffled each day while vigorously trying to be more like the woman she thought was her mother. Lola never completely understood why Sally loathed her as profusely as she did, until that day, the day it all became clear to her. "That's why Lauren's DNA doesn't match Peter's? That's why the birth certificates can't be traced?" Lola whispered softly to Daniel. "What do you want from me, mother? Sally? What are you saying, exactly?" Lola turned to face Sally before her tears rolled liberally down her cheeks. Daniel took her hand before Lola pulled away just as expressly as she moved closer to Sally. "I adored you! I treasured my scumbag dad! I wanted to fit in and be like you! I loved you! With all my heart, I loved you, and tried everything to get you to just like me a little bit!" She raised her voice, sensitive to the utter devastation inside of her, "I did everything you asked of me, and it was never enough! I kept to myself, and I took care of Lauren! I tried to be perfect for you! What did I ever do to you?" Lola bowed her head when Sally grew silent. Daniel placed his arm on her shoulder when she swabbed fiercely at her tears. "When he raped me, over and over, when I protested, he beat me. It was okay with you! Was it? Answer me Sally Storey, you will answer me today!" "Yes, it was! Yes, it was!" Sally grabbed Lola by her arm, "You led him on, Lula! Why don't you just admit it? You're just like your mother was!"

Lola could barely believe what she was hearing. Sally was condemning her for seducing the man she thought of as a father. The man she only wanted to love as a parent. Just as the woman from her dreams, Sally had referred to her as 'Lula.' "Led him on? I was eight years old!" Lola unchained herself from Sally's grip. "I watched you, Lola, parading in front of him, sitting on his lap." Lola moved just an inch closer to her before she lifted her arm, and with all her might, slapped her across her face. You could hear a pin drop when the sound echoed through Salvatore. Sally Storey lifted her hand to her cheek, and stared at Lola in silence. Daniel stepped in between them, and heatedly held his finger up to Sally. "You have no right to come in here, and speak to my wife that way! Get out of my shop! Get out, or help me, I have never lifted a hand to a woman before, but I will today!" Daniel was at once enormously proud of Lola. "And rest assured, my family, yes, the Salvatore family will lay criminal and civil charges against you and the entire Storey clan. Whether Peter is dead or not, you will all pay for this." Sally turned to leave, and when she turned around one last time, Lola could witness the unadulterated hatred in her eyes. Lola walked up to her one last time, "You stole me. I. Am. A. Hudson! You deal with that, you miserable bitch!" Lola screeched before Sally stormed out of Salvatore.

Daniel turned back to Lola and held her protectively against him. Lola had stopped crying, and for the first time in her life, she no longer feared Sally Storey. Lauren and Dean had since entered the reception area, carrying Ella and Michael. Lauren handed Ella to Daniel, and placed her arms firmly around her sister. She sobbed into Lola's arms, while Lola gently stroked her locks. "It's over, sissy. We don't belong to them, we never did. You'll never see her or any of them again, I swear. It's really over. We don't belong to them, we are Hudson's. Wow! We are Hudson's." She whispered while sure that Lauren had witnessed the entire uproar. Lauren retreated slightly, "Lola, you hit her!" Lola burst out laughing when she noticed Lauren's shocked expression. "I know, right?" The entire Salvatore erupted into laughter, and for the first time in her life, Lola felt invincible. "Lola, you should have knocked her down!" Dean shouted from behind her. "Next time!" Lola giggle softly.

Daniel held Ella a little tighter, excruciatingly aware of his own heart shattering for the two sisters. He could barely imagine the abhorrence Sally Storey carried around in her heart for them. Daniel could hardly believe that Lola was the girl he fell in love with when he was just a little boy. He could not even begin to consider the hurt they inflicted on Lola, but he was enormously proud of her. She refused to surrender herself to them, instead, she got up each day with the most extraordinary and undeniable force he had ever witnessed before. Daniel finally understood why Lola once said that she never carried around the scars.

She under no circumstances, allowed any of it to trample

her down, and she did not give the Storeys permission to abduct who she was. He implicitly understood for the very first time why it was that the Hudson family commanded such immeasurable reverence. Their might was in their blood, and not one person was powerful enough to eradicate that from them. For the first time, it made complete sense to Daniel why John and Sarah longed for their friends, and why they were so utterly shattered by their unimaginable loss.

It became clear for the very first time, why Daniel was so drawn to Lola from the very start. He realized then that his soul had recognized hers, and he was forever indebted to the stars for placing her back on a path, where she would find her way back to him. The Hudson's were beyond doubt, remarkable people. Daniel was pleased that he was able to share some of their dynamism.

Lola too thought of John and Sarah, and with anxiety and distress in her heart, she glanced up at Daniel, "I saw that picture when your dad showed us that night, that first night, and I felt it Daniel." Lola knew she wasn't imagining all the familiarities that had crept up on her over the years. "I saw me and Lauren in the picture, but I thought, I thought I was just seeing things, you know? I mean, wanting to belong to another family. I just thought that I'd invent anything to belong somewhere else. Your parents, the night before the wedding, your dad, that's what he wanted to talk to me about. He said the thing about the birth certificates and Lauren's DNA, but we weren't sure. I need to speak to your dad. Do you think we should tell him about what just happened?" Daniel smiled desolately at her, "Yes Lola, of course we have to tell them. They have a right to know, and you should have said something to me that night. We have to tell them. This has to end today. My parents deserve to know what happened." Daniel explained without wavering and Dean agreed straight away. "I didn't say anything because I just wanted to be sure, but I never thought, the Hudson's, that we, that would mean I've known you all my life, Daniel." She smiled wretchedly when she touched his face.

Daniel called his parents at once, and told them that there were developments that were important to discuss with them, and it couldn't wait. John was concerned at once, but settled to meet up with them in Hodgkin's that same evening. Daniel and Dean agreed that they would spend the night in Hodgkin's, but Lola and Lauren grew uneasy in anticipation of the Salvatore's reaction.

John and Sarah were waiting restlessly for their children to arrive in Hodgkin's, and when they finally reached the Salvatore home, John was devotedly alert to the fact that Lola's eyes were red and distended. When he inspected Lauren, he became enormously anxious to discover that she too, had been crying. He kissed Lola gently on the cheek, before embracing Lauren. "Hey dad." Daniel made a valiant effort to force a smile. He hugged Sarah tightly and gazed at her with misery in his eyes. "What's wrong, son? You all are scaring us." Sarah was anxious to find out what had shattered the girls so tremendously. "Let's go inside." They reluctantly took their seats around the dining room table, while Bo escorted Michael and Ella into the play room. Daniel clutched Lola's hand in his, before Lauren began crying again. Dean protectively embraced Lauren, and whispered softly into her ear, "It'll be alright." Lola turned to John and Sarah, distressingly aware that Daniel could in no way at all, speak on her behalf. "John, that first night that Lauren and I came to visit, the night we met you, when you were telling us about the Hudson's. You showed me a picture of the Hudson children, remember?" She paused, unsure of how to continue, "I don't know where to start. There's no perfect way to say something like this, so I'm just going to do this the best way I know how. I really need you to listen to what I am saying, and hear what I am asking you. The night before Lauren and Dean got married, the thing with the birth certificates and the DNA, do you remember?"

She silently prayed that they would somehow find recognition in her, and in Lauren. Sarah frowned while John glanced enquiringly at Daniel. "Yes, I remember, what's going on Lola? I'm still trying to figure this whole thing out." John reached for Sarah's hand. "My mother, no, not my mother, Sally Storey came by Salvatore today. She, she told us that we were Tallulah and Lucille Hudson. She told us that Peter had taken us, and that, that everyone believed we were killed in the crash that took my parents and Manoli, but that we survived. She said that they were in line to claim my dad's money, but couldn't because you were our legal guardians, and the only benefactors should all of us die. She also said that out of fear of being prosecuted, they just kept us, and that night you showed us that photograph, I felt like I was looking at myself when I was that age, but I didn't think it could be. And then you told me about Lauren's DNA not matching Peter's, and that our records were linked to deceased records, but they were sealed. I was just so afraid to hope, but I never thought, I never thought the Hudson's. Not once did the thought cross my mind that we are Hudson's."

Lola felt her tears shimmer in her eyes when her voice began to shudder, "What I'm trying to say, or rather ask, is there anything about us, or anything you know that can confirm this?

John, could any of this be true? Could we at all be Hudson's? Is there any way that we are Tallulah and Lucille Hudson?" Lola was desperate for some form of detection and recognition from them.

John stood up and walked over to Lola. He stood staring at Lola in silence when she was at once convinced that she was misguided, that it was all just another elaborate scheme. "Lola, what are you saying here? Are you saying that, actually, we can clear this up right now. I'm waiting for Clark Garrisson to call me." John rubbed his forehead and shook his head. "He was able to unseal the records we spoke about. I spoke to him earlier. I wanted to get it right before you and Daniel got married, but let me give him a call and hear if he has any news yet."

With utter confusion and devastation in his eyes, John walked out to his study, leaving Lola utterly stumped as to what to say next. "Oh, Tallulah, I knew there was something about you. I knew in my heart. I knew when you sat listening to our stories. I knew when Daniel lost his heart to you. I see it when I look at Ella, she is the spitting image of you when you were her age. And you, Lola, you look just like your mother. I just didn't think anybody could be so cruel? I didn't think that it could be you. I wanted to believe it, but it all seemed so unrealistic. I thought, I just thought that my mind was playing utterly cruel tricks on me. I've noticed it so many times, Lola." Sarah took Lola's hand while submitting to her tears which rolled freely down her cheeks. They all sat in silence after that, unsure of what to say next or what to anticipate. Lola and Lauren sat close to one another, and held hands as they did when they were only little girls.

Every so often, Lauren would bury her head in Lola's

shoulders, and Dean and Daniel would stare at the two sisters with dire compassion and empathy. Sarah was at the edge of her seat, and got up often to check on Michael and Ella.

Roughly twenty minutes after John had walked out, he strolled back in, carrying an envelope firmly tugged under his arm, aware that Sarah was doing her utmost to hide her tears. "I just, I just have to breathe. Just give me a minute. Momma, the girls have come home, our girls have come home." John seized Sarah in his arms and wept inconsolably. Lola gasped for air when she realized what John was saying. All she had ever prayed for, every hope she had ever had of belonging to another family, was coming true for them. "Your DNA is a perfect match to that of Tallulah Belle Hudson and you Lauren, you are Lucille Leigh Hudson. There is no doubt at all, in my mind or in anyone else's mind that you are indeed the Hudson girls. Clark found out that an aunt had complained to the authorities' years ago that you girls were taken, but it was shrugged off when she was committed to a mental institution shortly afterwards. He tried to get in touch with her, but she passed away a few years ago. I believe it's the same aunt that left you and Lauren a little money?" He removed his glasses, "I wish, I wish I had known sooner. I wish I listened to my gut. I knew that there was something there, and I should have followed up on that a whole lot sooner. I should have known, it shouldn't have taken four years Lola, Lula."

Lola got up and placed her arms around his neck and sobbed desolately into his chest. When she retreated from him, Daniel held her in his arms and whispered softly, "You were born just for me. I felt you, Lola. Into my soul, I felt you. All this time, I knew there was something. I couldn't let you go, ever, and now I

know why. You were born for me, my soul found yours again."
Sarah had embraced Lauren and Lola before elatedly welcoming
them back as their god-daughters.

After the initial shock had worn off and after none of
them truly knew what to say to each other, they finally spent the
remainder of the evening discussing the Hudson's, and from time
to time, John and Sarah were forced to wipe the tears from their
eyes. They had an enormous mountain of questions for Lola and
Lauren, but John realized at once that there were issues from
their past that they had, to a certain extent, elected to keep
buried there. Daniel was proud of Lola, and again relieved that it
was finally over for the sisters. John reluctantly excused himself
a short while later, "You must excuse me for a bit, I just have a
few things to take care of. Things that have to be put right." John
smiled, overcome with grief, when he made his way back into his
study. Sarah breathlessly spoke of their parents and Manoli to
the girls, and they hung onto every word that Sarah was saying.
Often, Lola and Lauren would dab at their tears and frequently,
they would burst out into laughter. It felt to Lauren and Lola as
though they were unexpectedly living in bewilderment, a life
they had lived once before, but a life they knew so little of.

It was almost midnight, when John made his way back
into the living room, "So girls, I actually have your birth
certificates right here, along with a few other little things that I've
kept throughout the years. I would like you to take it now, it
belongs to you." John handed Lola an envelope. She took the
envelope and nervously opened it, before she burst into tears
when she was faced with their actual birth certificates. She was
overwhelmed by a powerful sense of pride, for being a validated
member of the Hudson family. While retrieving a thicker

document, Lola glowered when she realized what it was. "John?" "That is a transfer deed to replace Salvatore with Salvatore-Hudson as it was, and as it should be. I had our attorneys come in tonight, and draw it up. The courier just delivered it. You and Lauren are 51% shareholders and I hold the other 49%. I will be sure to financially reimburse you for the past sixteen 16 years, you girls will never want for anything again."

Lola glanced over at Lauren who was instantly aware of the displeasure on her face. "John, no. We don't want it. My father trusted you, so keep it as it is, please. We don't want any of that." Lola was insistent. "Lola, I would never have been as successful or have all that I have today, if it wasn't for your father. I am trying to honor him, and trying to make things right with you girls. Your father was a true friend, a brother, and stood by me when everyone else was convinced that I'd fail. He, without question, handed me the money I needed when no-one else would." "You, Sarah, Daniel, Dean, Bo, Ella and Michael, that's what is enough for us, John. Family is enough. We don't want any of it, please, John. I know my dad would agree, and that's what he would want. There's nothing to make right, we have everything we need and so much more."

Lola was pleading ferociously with him, "I know Lauren agrees with me, and we're doing just fine. We don't need any more than what we have. I mean it, please, keep it as it is, or place it in Daniel and Dean's name. I'm begging you John, don't do this." "I am not taking no for an answer, Lola. I've made my decision. Let me reimburse you the profits for the last sixteen years, I sure as hell can afford to. I will keep the name Salvatore-Hudson, and I will establish a trust for the 51% which will be available to you and Lauren anytime you need it. I will have it no other way, Lola, no other way. Believe me my girl, this is what your parents would have wanted. I have to do this, not only for your father, but for me too. I have to do this. I gave your father my word that should anything ever happen to him, that I'd step in and take care of you, just as he would have done for me. Don't take that away from me Lola, I'm begging you to let me do this."

Lola smiled sadly while wiping the tears from her eyes, before she turned to face Daniel. He held her firmly against him and was proud to call himself a Salvatore, proud of his parents, and especially proud of his father. "Oh, there's one more document, Lola. I think it's the most important of the lot." Lola pulled out a single sheet and read it slowly, at once skeptical of her understanding of that one little piece of paper. "That's the title deed to the house next door, the house you fell in love with and often asked about, your parent's home. I've never been able to sell it, and I am so happy we didn't. This is your and Lauren's home now, and we've left everything as it was. I am sure you'll be able to find your many answers there."

Lauren bolted from her seat and excitedly flung her arms around John while Lola sat stock-still, staring in bewilderment at the document. "The house next door, that was our house? You kept our home? That was really our home?" Lola was staggered to learn that the house she had spent so many nights dreaming of, was in fact, their childhood home. Sarah nodded sadly before swabbing at her tears. "Come Lola, let's go over. Mom and dad can watch the kids." Daniel was convinced that Lola was frantic to be there when he recalled how drawn she was to the house with the blue front door. "Lola, its mommy and daddy's house. I want to see. I want to know how things were. I want to go, please, Lola?" Lauren tearfully beseeched her sister. John handed Lola a bunch of keys, "Welcome home, girls. Now go, go get your answers. Go see where it all began and go find your history. Go home."

Lola stood up and held onto John again while sobbing fiercely into his chest. She held him closely, afraid of what she might find when she walked back into her parents' home. Lola stepped back and glanced over at Dariel, "Let's go meet us, the Hudson's." She smiled wretchedly through her tears when finally feeling as though she belonged somewhere and to someone important.

Daniel hesitantly unlocked the front door of the Hudson home, while Lola stood back scrutinizing the house from a distance. She indistinctly began to recall the blue door, and knew impulsively that the balcony at the rear end of the house overlooked the Hodgkin's river.

It took Lola all of five minutes to begin recalling the little details she had forgotten as a child. She turned around swiftly and when she saw the enormous gum tree, Lola ran up to it, certain that she would find her initials carved into the bark somewhere. While walking around the tree at a snail's pace, she took her time, afraid she might miss it. When she found it, it was precisely the way she remembered it. The initials were clearly marked as though they were carved out only yesterday, "DS+TH." "I told you, Lola," She heard Daniel's voice behind her. Lola turned around and flung her arms around his neck. "I remember Daniel! And I remember the four-leaf clover you picked for me! I remember, and when you gave me the pendant, I felt something, there was something!" Lola was laughing and crying all at once, yet she was enormously animated at the same time. "I remember my dad would sit here and read, and your dad would come over with a cigar, and they would sit here for hours. I remember everything! I remember mommy and Aunty Sarah in the kitchen. They would drink wine and laugh a lot, and think our dads didn't know. And, I remember you, Daniel! I remember everything about you! I used to feel so safe around you. You were the love of my life. You are the love of my life. I am the Tallulah chick, holy shit! I can't believe I forgot these things. You've always, it's always only been you, Danny! When I met you in Joe's, there was something there, I just never thought it was from another life or another time, but I felt you. And the crib Daniel, I recognized the crib! There were so many things to tell me, so many things that I forgot. How did I not see these things? She tried telling me. She told me when the time was right, I would know, and that I'd find my answers. I would find our history. She was never just a dream Daniel! I found you again." Lola's heart was bursting with joy. "I came back to you and she knew, and now she's looking after Jonathan." Lola belted out all that she could humanely remember in one breath. When they walked through the front door of the Hudson home, Lauren had begun removing the sheeting that was placed over the furniture. Lola was flabbergasted by how utterly familiar it all seemed. While scrutinizing each item in their home, Lola began to remember all the little things. Lauren was instantly discouraged by not being able to remember as Lola did, "You were so little Lauren, it will come back to you." Lola squeezed her hand. "Come! I want to show you our bedroom!" Lola grabbed Lauren by her arm, and ran up the stairs. She knew intuitively where to go and without faltering, she strolled into what was once their bedroom. "That's where you were supposed to sleep, but you always crawled in with me." Lola pointed to Lauren's bed. Lola turned and walked out to find her parents' bedroom. When she reached the doorway, the mere sight of it took her breath away. It was faithfully unaltered and exactly as Lola remembered it.

Her mother's photographs were displayed precisely as they were all those years ago on the massive bureau directly across from their bed. Lola moved slowly towards it, and casually gazed at each image. They were photographs of the Hudson family, of Lauren, Lola and Manoli when they were still babies. There was a wedding photo of her parents, and one large snapshot of the Salvatore and Hudson family united. Lola swallowed back on her tears, and knew then that there was nothing she would ever want to change. She remembered the trunk at the end of her parent's bed, and she recalled how her mother constantly referred to it as her 'treasure chest.' Lola knelt down in front of it, and while her hands were quivering, she nervously opened it. It took her breath away when she discovered the many treasures it was hiding. Her mother's beautiful ivory and silk wedding gown and her handmade veil was proudly folded and sealed. There was a table cloth her mother had made herself and embroidered the initial "H" onto it.

There were countless of photo albums, just waiting to be opened. Paging quickly through some of them, Lola realized that they had sheltered a lifetime of memories and answers. Scratching further, Lola came across letters, and she promptly realized that they were love notes that her father had written her mother. Lola smiled sadly when she realized how they absolutely adored and cherished one another. She cautiously placed them back where she found them, certain that one day soon, she and Lauren would want to read them. She picked up drawings that her mother had kept that Lola, Lauren and Manoli had made in art class. She was heartbroken that her brother was not there to share all of this with them. Lola wept while holding them in her hands, and was at once sure that they were categorically loved, and wholly treasured.

It was the life that she was sure she had recalled when she was just a little girl. Lola was relieved that she never just imagined any of it. "Mommy!" Lola cried out loud before closing the trunk. She finally had a history, a story to tell, and a sense of belonging and worth.

She knew in her heart, that she belonged to the most imperative people in the entire world. She was immensely proud of herself, and of her name. While seated on her parent's bed that seemed enormously oversized when she was just a little girl, Lola prayed silently that her parents would be proud of her too. She felt a cool breeze around her, and closed her eyes while attempting to embrace the feeling that had washed over her. "Lula, Tallulah Belle." Lola heard a faint, but eerily familiar voice. Glancing around her, she was abruptly mystified, and wondered where the voice was coming from. Lola got up from the bed, and turned to the window. She realized that it was shut, and she questioned at once where the breeze was coming from. "Turn around, Tallulah." Lola instantly turned around, and saw her at once, as clear as daylight. She gasped for air, and suddenly felt as though she could barely more. "Don't be afraid, my girl." Lola wasn't sure that what she was seeing, was in fact real, but at that very moment, it didn't matter to her. The vision before her was that of her mother, Molly Hudson, the woman from her incessant dreams, the woman that she had dreamed of so many nights before, and for the first time in all the years, Molly was showing herself to Lola.

Alice VL

Lola was delighted to see her mother one more time, "Mommy? Is that you? It's been you the whole time. Why didn't you let me see you before? Why didn't you tell me?" Lola's tears rolled unforgivingly down her cheeks. "Don't cry my angel. You had to find us on your own." She gently and tenderly stroked Lola's cheek. "Don't you know that I will never leave you? I'm always here, always with you, and always around Lucy. I will never leave you." "Mommy, I am so lost without you." "You're not lost, my girl. You are doing just fine. I am so proud of you. I am so proud of how you took care of Lucy, and I am so happy that you found us again, your home and the Salvatore's. You are strong, Lola, you survived." Molly paused to take Lola's hands into hers, "I am so sorry, my girl. I am so sorry I left you. You never have to be afraid again, they will take care of you always. I know that man hurt you Lula, and I know what you went through, but I knew you'd get through it. He could never break your spirit, my angel. I was there to make sure. I knew that Daniel would bring you back. He loves you so much my girl, he's always loved you. Bring Ella home, Lula. Bring this house back to life, and make new memories here. This is your home, live here proudly. Never forget how much I love you, and always know that I will forever be by your side. You are a Hudson, Lula, and soon you will become a Salvatore. They are good, good people, trust them. They've got Michael and Ella, but I have Jonathan, and he's beautiful. I will never put him down, my girl. Tell Daniel to forgive himself, Jonathan wants him to. I love you so much my baby girl, those two boys inside of you, they're going to be just fine. They're going to grow up, and become wonderful men someday, just like their father. They will make you so proud." Molly gentle wiped Lola's tears from her eyes. "And Ella, my beautiful granddaughter, teach her about us. Teach her and Michael all there is to know about the Hudson's. I will see you all the time my baby girl, just close your eyes, and think of me. Know how much I love you." Lola closed her eyes, desperate to memorize her mother's voice. "I love you, mommy."

When Lola opened her eyes again, her mother was nowhere to be seen, but Lola was certain that she would linger, she could feel her all around her. She wiped the tears from her eyes and smiled, convinced that which had just taken place was real, even if only to her. Daniel walked in to find her standing there smiling. He was keenly aware of the warm tears on her cheeks, but certain they were tears of joy. "Daniel, she was just here! My mommy was here, and, and she was telling me that Jonathan is there, with her. You must forgive yourself, Daniel. Jonathan wants you to forgive yourself. He's beautiful, and, she loves me, just like in my dreams. I've been dreaming of her all my life! She is the woman from my dreams!"

Lola flung her arms around his neck. Daniel held her snugly against him, unsure of exactly what Lola was saying. "I, I want to live here, Daniel. I want to raise Ella here! I want to raise the boys here! I want to be near your parents, and near my parents! We have a name, Danny. We have a name. Lauren and Dean are happy in Madison, but I want to live here. She wants me to come home, Daniel!" Daniel stared at her and frowned while overcome with confusion, "You want to live next door to my parents?" "Yes, I do! I want Ella and the boys to have what we had when we were children. Please Daniel! I can write here, and you can help your dad in the business. I'll give you my shares of Salvatore-Hudson, and Dean can run Salvatore in Madison. Maybe you can branch out and open one here, there are so many possibilities! I want to come home, Daniel, please. I want to come home. Tallulah Belle Hudson wants to come home, where I belong." Daniel remained silent for a moment, "You keep talking about the boys, what boys?" Lola smiled bashfully when she realized what she had unintentionally said, "I was going to tell you tonight, at home, but then Sally came around, and we came here. I had it all planned and now it's nothing like I wanted to do it." "What are you saying?" "Daniel, do you remember the other day when I took Ella for her shots?" Lola became nervous all of a sudden. "Yeah?" "I went to see Dr. Stalting as well. I missed my period again, and I, I'm pregnant again. We didn't even try!" Daniel took her face into his hands and kissed her passionately. "Daniel, wait!" Lola retreated while he continued to kiss her. He reluctantly recoiled, still grinning from ear to ear. "Wait, that's not all, there's more. And wait for it .." She held up her hand to indicate the number two when Daniel frowned again. "There are two babies?" It suddenly dawned on him that Lola was pregnant with twins. He seized her into his arms and spun her around, clearly overjoyed at the sudden and unexpected revelation. "They're boys, I know they are. I mean, it's still too early to tell, but I know they're boys. My mom said they were boys and they are going to be fine, Daniel! My mom's always been around, she's always been here. And Jonathan is with her!" Lola hurriedly explained when Daniel placed her back on her feet. "So, can we move to Hodgkin's please?" "Yeah, Hodgkin's could use a Salvatore here, let's do it, Lola Storey! I mean Tallulah Hudson, but on one condition only!" "Anything, Daniel, anything! I will do anything you want me to!" "We have to get married first. I am not moving in here or waiting until the babies are born, we're going to do it now, on Jonathan's birthday." "Daniel Salvatore, I will marry you anytime you want. You better believe it! And, I've just seen the perfect dress! And! I have the perfect location in mind!"

Lola and Daniel found Dean and Lauren out on the front porch, seated on a swing that their father had built for them. Lauren smiled disconsolately at Lola, "I remember sitting here with mommy." "Yes, you did, all the time. You used to fall asleep on her lap while she sang to you. You were her baby, and she loved you so much, Lauren." Lola sat down beside her. "Lauren, I was thinking, Daniel and I were talking. How would you feel about it if Daniel and I moved into mom and dad's house?" "Oh Lola, that would be wonderful! Mom and dad would be so happy! You should do it, especially now that, I mean ..." Lauren almost blurted out that it would be perfect with the impending arrival of the twins. Lola burst out laughing, "Daniel knows, I just told him." She gently squeezed Lauren's shoulder. Dean gazed inquisitively at Lauren, "Lola's pregnant again!" Dean embraced Daniel before he embraced Lola. "Wow Lola, you guys should definitely live here!" The excitement was clear and overwhelming in Dean's voice. "I mean, it's still your home too, Lauren." "No sis, it's your house. You raised me and took care of me my entire life. This is your home, and you should have it. Mom and dad would want you to have it. Besides, I love my home in Madison. It's Michael's first home, and I want to raise a lot more babies there!" Lauren embraced Lola affectionately, and for the first time in their lives, they were confident that the secrets of their past could no longer haunt them. The Storeys were an element in bringing them home, but they had returned home as Hudson's.

Alice VL

FULL CIRCLE

The day before Lola and Daniel's wedding arrived almost out of the blue. It was the day that Lola and Lauren had made their way back into the Hudson home for the first time since they had learned their true identities. Daniel and Dean had taken Michael and Ella out for a milkshake, eager for Lola and Lauren to finalize the last of the wedding arrangements.

Sarah had sent in Molly's wedding dress to have it dry cleaned, and Lola was nervous about trying it on for the very first time. When they reached their parent's bedroom, Lola gasped for air when she came face to face with the dress which was proudly and in all its splendor and magnificence, hanging over the closet. Lola and Lauren stood in silence while lost for words by the mere revelation of the dress. Lola instantly questioned whether it would fit her. "Lauren, this was mommy's wedding dress. What if it doesn't fit me? You know there are two babies inside this belly?" Lauren walked up to the dress and gently took it down, "It will fit, try it on." Lola slowly began undressing, all the while praying that the dress would fit her. It was the most graceful and elegant dress Lola had ever laid her eyes on, and she wanted so badly for it to fit.

When Lola turned around for Lauren to button up the dress, Lauren smiled, immediately reassured that it was a perfect fit. Lola turned to face the large mirror in her mother's bedroom, and stood staring at herself in silence. Lauren stood behind Lola, mesmerized by her sister's reflection in the mirror which was almost a manifestation of her mother. "You look beautiful, Lola. Mommy was such a beautiful woman, and now you. You look just like her." Lauren was overwhelmed by Lola's striking resemblance to their mother. Lola was intensely responsive to her tears that were lying shallow in her eyes. She tenderly embraced Lauren before Lauren picked up the veil from the bed, and gently clipped it into Lola's hair. "You are perfect, Lola, you look perfect." Lola had elected not to tell Lauren of the day her mother had appeared to her. She was certain that it would be disconcerting for Lauren to realize that her mother had chosen to talk to Lola instead, of her. "So, sis, where are you guys going on honeymoon?" "We're not going anywhere, Lauren. We rather want to take the time to move in here, you know? Get settled. Daniel wants to look at premises for Salvatore, and I need to get ready for the new babies." "This is so exciting Lola! Dean and I were thinking of trying again. Hopefully Michael will get to have a little brother or sister soon?" "That is wonderful news, Lauren, I can't wait!"

That evening, they were all seated around the dining room table. Ella was sitting on Daniel's lap, and Michael was seated next to John. "So, Lola, I expect you would be sleeping on your own tonight?" Dean remarked matter-of-factly with a broad smile when he thought back to the night before he and Lauren had exchanged their vows. Lola erupted into a fit of laughter, and gazed over at Daniel, only to find him grimacing again. "Not a chance!" Daniel snapped brusquely at Dean. "Oh no, bro, not so fast. What happened to Lola being traditional?" "There's no way, Dean!" "Actually Daniel, Ella and I will be sleeping next door tonight. There's no ways I'm tempting fate." Lola responded nonchalantly through her laughter. "Oh, come on, Lola!" "It's one night Daniel, and then you are a ball and chain man." Lola winked mischievously at him. "Ooooh, do you hear that Ella? Mommy wants to ball and chain me, but little does she know that you, my angel, you have ball and chained me a long time ago!" Daniel whispered in Ella's ear. She stared inquisitively at her father. "Yes!" Ella shouted out while clapping her hands before everyone burst out laughing.

After supper, each said goodnight to the other before Daniel walked Lola and Ella over to the house next door. When they reached the house, Lola glanced around her, "I can't believe we're going to be living here soon." Daniel was at once aware of the indisputable bliss on her face. He smiled when Ella jumped up onto a sofa, "It's nice here, I can't wait to start my life with you, and I cannot wait for these babies to come." Lola was at peace and finally, fulfilled. "Me too, Danny." "Now, you have to go so that Ella and I can get in our beauty sleep." She turned him towards the front door. "Just one kiss, please?" Lola kissed him fervently, and again she could feel him deep into her core. Daniel held her closer and kissed her for just a moment longer. "I don't want to go." Lola gently pushed him away from her, "You're trying to seduce me again, Mr. Salvatore." "Am I succeeding?" Daniel pulled her closer and held her protectively against him. "You will always succeed ..." She kissed him again, and was once again reminded of how effortless it was for Daniel to take her away from it all. Lola was just about to surrender to Daniel, when there was a loud and urgent knock on the front door. Daniel retreated slightly before Lola made her way to the front door, "Thought you were still here. Come, I'm dragging you home!" Dean was fanatically insightful to the fact that Daniel could not tolerate being apart from Lola for even a night. Lola burst out laughing again when Daniel sighed stridently.

He walked up to Ella, and warmly embraced her before he kissed her gently on her forehead, "Goodnight my angel, look after mommy for me." "Goodnight daddy, tomorrow we're getting married!" "Yes, we are! You, me and mommy!" Turning back to Lola, he gently kissed her on her cheek, "See you at the altar, Ella and I will be waiting."

Alice VL

Lola's Secret

Lola glanced over at Ella who had fallen asleep beside her earlier. She gently stroked her cheek, and silently thanked God for trusting her so explicitly, that he blessed her with a daughter. She thought about her own mother again, and could not help but wonder if her mother was there with them. She recalled lying next to her mother in the same bed, and how she would caress her long hair when Lola struggled to fall asleep.

While still deep in thought, she heard a soft patting sound coming from the bedroom window. Lola looked up suddenly, and smiled broadly when she saw Daniel there. She quietly climbed out of bed, and tiptoed over to the window, gently lifting it. "Daniel, what are you doing here? How did you get up here?" "I was lying in bed, and then I remembered the old ladder that your father had out back. Do you remember how many nights I snuck in to visit you? I just wanted to come and tell you that I love you, and please, please meet me at the altar tomorrow. I'll bring Ella, and you bring my boys." Lola took his face in her hands, "You just try and stop me!" "So, I better go. Dean is watching me like a hawk. I love you, and kiss my angel goodnight for me." He cautiously made his way back down the ladder. "I love you too, Romeo!"

Alice VL

John Salvatore wore the exact same suit he wore to the last Hudson wedding many, many years ago. It was the day he had witnessed the coming together of two people that was instantly united as family to him. It was the wedding of his closest friend and the woman that John had known would be perfect for Liam. John recalled the events of that day as though it was yesterday, and silently wished they were there to witness a brand-new union, one that would once again, unite their families.

A joining together that was brought collectively by destiny, a life once forgotten with people once lost. John knew that this day would be one of the most significant days he would ever be a component of, and he knew with appreciation that they had all come full circle. Sarah smiled as John proudly walked down the aisle with his soon to be new daughter-in-law, and the god-daughter he had once known so well, and loved from the moment she was born.

Daniel neglected to inform his parents of the abuse Lola had to endure at the insistence of both Lola and Lauren. It was important to Lola that they not face any more blame, than what they were enduring since discovering who Lola and Lauren were. The wretchedness that John discovered in Lola's eyes a long time ago, so often, was corroboration for John that all was not well with the girls when they were growing up.

Just before reaching the altar, John unexpectedly stopped and turned to Lola, "My girl, nothing makes me happier than to lead you into the arms of my son." John wiped at the tears that were threatening to escape his eyes. "I am so honored to have you and Lauren as a part of my family again. I loved you like my own daughter when you were just a little girl, and we adore you now. I should've found you, Lola, you and Lauren. I let you down. Your father trusted me, and I let him down." John warmly embraced Lola. Glancing over at Sarah, Lola noticed her swabbing away at her own tears and once again, Lola knew that she needed no other family, but the Salvatore's. "Please, don't …" Lola gently placed her hand on his cheek. "Don't do this to yourself, John, we were fine, truly. We found our way back, and maybe my dad or maybe my mom led us here, but we made it back. That's all that matters. We are here now." Lola was desperate for John to absolve himself for failing his friend. John smiled desolately at her, but he was devastatingly aware of the cruelty Lola had suffered.

He felt it into the innermost part of him it from the moment he gazed into her eyes for the very first time, and he felt it again that day. There was more information in the file he kept on Lola and Lauren, but he by no means wanted to admit to her that he was aware of the ill-treatment. "I am so honored to be a part of this family, and I can truly understand why my parents had chosen the Salvatore's as our god- parents. I love you and Sarah, and for the very first time in my life, I have somewhere to call home, John. It wouldn't be home without you or Sarah, our new mom and dad."

Daniel stood unwearyingly, yet anxiously at the altar, watching his bride on his father's arm. He could not at all take his eyes off of her, and while watching her walk step by step, Daniel was suddenly aware of an unyielding lump in his throat again. Ella was standing beside him, clutching his hand, smiling and waiting impatiently for her mother to reach the altar.

Daniel thought back to the day they met, and when his

heart began to shudder, he realized that providence has a unique way of setting things right at the end. He thought back to the night they met at Joe's, and recalled sensing that they had met before. He realized at once how the little voice inside of him was feverishly nudging him. Daniel was reminded of the day that Sally Storey had entered Salvatore. He was relieved that after that incident, Lola seemed more contented, and for the first time since he had known her, she was in blissful harmony with herself. He had never seen Lola stand up for herself as she did on that day. He smiled proudly when he recalled her words, "I am a Hudson!" He giggled in his sleeve when he revived that enormous clout Lola landed on Sally's cheek.

Sarah wiped her never-ending tears from her eyes when she saw Lola strutting down the aisle with John. For Sarah, Lola was the spitting image of her friend, Molly, and she could not avoid feeling as though she was staring at Molly when she and Liam were married many years ago. Sarah became downhearted once again, but was over the moon to finally be able to make her friend proud. She resolved to be the finest mother to Lauren and Lola, and she was undoubtedly swayed by the fact that Molly Hudson relied on her for that.

While walking down the aisle, Lola's eyes caught Daniel's. She was at once bashful, when she realized he was scrutinizing her from head to toe. She was immensely nervous and her hands were shuddering, but at the same time, there was nowhere else she would rather be. Lola had waited for this day for almost an eternity, and could not at all restrain her animation when she woke up that very morning. She thought back to all that had come about in her short life, and realized that every step she had taken was a journey she would take again in a heartbeat, and without a moment's reservation. Each step brought her closer to home, and closer to her name. Lola knew in her heart, that she would wrestle each and every battle over and over again, if it meant that it would bring her to that very moment.

When they reached the altar, Daniel took Lola's hand and found that she was trembling. He squeezed it tightly, and smiled amorously at her. "I am so glad you came, Lola." Turning to the priest, they knelt down in silence. He began the ceremony by welcoming their guests, but Lola was at once sidetracked. She thought only of Daniel and Ella. She thought of Dean, Lauren and Michael, and Lola thought of Jonathan with great sadness. At the same time, her heart was convulsing with elation, and she hurriedly wiped a lost tear from her cheek. Lola was so entirely lost in thought that she was instantly startled when Daniel stood up, and helped to her feet. She gazed up at him, and realized that the time had come to say their vows.

Daniel was once again sensitive to the recognizable lump in his throat that had suddenly made its presence known once more when he gazed into Lola's eyes. "Tallulah Belle Hudson, wow, I just can't believe it's you." Daniel's voice was shuddering when he grabbed Lola's hands. "Before I met you, I dreamed of you. I dreamed about finding my twin flame, and when I met you, I knew that you were the girl I had been dreaming of. Now, I know that it was because I've known you all my life, and I've loved you since I was just a little boy. I carved our initials in a tree, and swore to wed you when you were only a little girl. You brought out the best, and the worst in me, but you also awakened feelings in me that I never knew existed. You became my reason for existence, and for a while, when we weren't together, I felt I had no purpose. Then Jonathan came along, and he entirely change my life, and that's why we chose today, for Jonathan. I think about him each day, and I love him, Lola, so much. Then there's Ella, and when she came along, I just knew that I couldn't live without you, or without her. She just made everything right for us. She lifted us up out of the ashes, and brought us back, and for that, I thank God for blessing us with such a beautiful angel. I love you so much, and I love what we have. I promise you today, Lola, I will spend each day of my life loving you, and proving to you that it was all worth it." Daniel clogged up when he realized he could barely continue with his vows. He gazed down at Lola, she at once understood when she noticed his tears shimmering in his eyes.

"Daniel Salvatore ..." Lola could hardly say his name, when she realized the moment had become increasingly daunting for Daniel. "I ran away to Sutherland, hoping to just get through the rest of my life. I had no idea that I chose a town where I started my life in, a town that raised me. A life I had lived with a family I had forgotten. I had no idea what I was running to, but it's been such a ride. I never even knew that we grew up together, but when I met you, I fell in love with you far too quickly, but I fell in love for, what seemed like, the very first time. You've made so many things right in my life. You brought me happiness I have never known, and with you, I feel safe, and I feel I belong. You gave Jonathan and Ella to me, and you take care of us. There hasn't been one day that I felt I shouldn't have been a part of our journey together. And how life has turned out for us. It's nothing like I imagined it would be, it is so much better than I could ever dream of. I promise you today, Danny, that I, Tallulah Belle Hudson, will spend the remainder of my lifetime, until forever, loving you with everything I have, and dedicating my life to never, ever forgetting how it all started, where it all began, who I am, or who I will become today."

She quickly wiped at her own tears rolling down her cheeks. Lola glanced over Daniel's shoulder, and almost as though her mind was playing tricks on her, she saw her standing there. Molly Hudson stood looking on in pride at her daughter. Lola was convinced that at that very moment, there was nothing in the world that could alter the happiness that had resurfaced in her life.

Daniel bent down, and kissed her gently He was overwhelmed by the crowning certainty that Lola Hudson Salvatore was beyond doubt, the girl he had dreamed straight back into his life.

Daniel & Lola Salvatore, signing off.

<u>THE END</u>

Alice VL

www.ingramcontent.com/pod-product-compliance
Lightning Source LLC
Chambersburg PA
CBHW020504020726
47493CB00001B/179